Tyndale House Novels by Jerry B. Jenkins

Riven

Midnight Clear (with Dallas Jenkins)

Soon

Silenced

Shadowed

The Last Operative

The Brotherhood

The Left Behind® series (with Tim LaHaye)

Left Behind®	*Desecration*
Tribulation Force	*The Remnant*
Nicolae	*Armageddon*
Soul Harvest	*Glorious Appearing*
Apollyon	*The Rising*
Assassins	*The Regime*
The Indwelling	*The Rapture*
The Mark	*Kingdom Come*

Left Behind Collectors Edition

Rapture's Witness (books 1–3)

Deceiver's Game (books 4–6)

Evil's Edge (books 7–9)

World's End (books 10–12)

For the latest information on Left Behind products,
visit www.leftbehind.com.

For the latest information on Tyndale fiction,
visit www.tyndalefiction.com.

LEFT BEHIND
TRIBULATION FORCE
NICOLAE
SOUL HARVEST
APOLLYON
ASSASSINS
THE INDWELLING
THE MARK
DESECRATION
THE REMNANT
ARMAGEDDON
GLORIOUS APPEARING

4

TIM LaHAYE
JERRY B. JENKINS

TYNDALE HOUSE PUBLISHERS, INC., CAROL STREAM, ILLINOIS

Visit Tyndale's exciting Web site at www.tyndale.com.

Discover the latest about the Left Behind series at www.leftbehind.com.

TYNDALE, Tyndale's quill logo, and *Left Behind* are registered trademarks of Tyndale House Publishers, Inc.

Soul Harvest: The World Takes Sides

Copyright © 1998 by Tim LaHaye and Jerry B. Jenkins. All rights reserved.

Cover photograph copyright © by Kyu Oh/iStockphoto. All rights reserved.

Author photo of Jerry B. Jenkins copyright © 2010 by Jim Whitmer Photography. All rights reserved.

Author photo of Tim LaHaye copyright © 2004 by Brian MacDonald. All rights reserved.

Left Behind series designed by Erik M. Peterson

Published in association with the literary agency of Alive Communications, Inc. 7680 Goddard Street, Suite 200, Colorado Springs, CO 80920, www.alivecommunications.com.

Scripture taken from the New King James Version.® Copyright © 1982 by Thomas Nelson, Inc. Used by permission. All rights reserved.

Library of Congress Cataloging-in-Publication Data

LaHaye, Tim F.
   Soul harvest / Tim LaHaye, Jerry B. Jenkins.
      p.   cm.
   ISBN 978-0-8423-2915-6 (hardcover)
   ISBN 978-0-8423-2925-5 (softcover)
   I. Jenkins, Jerry B.   II. Title.
   PS3562.A315S68   1998
813'.54—dc21   98-20929

Repackage first published in 2010 under ISBN 978-1-4143-3493-6.

Printed in the United States of America

17   16   15   14   13   12   11
 7   6   5   4   3   2   1

To our brand-new brothers and sisters

PROLOGUE

From Nicolae

BUCK'S HEART SANK as he saw the steeple of New Hope Village Church. It had to be less than six hundred yards away, but the earth was still churning. Things were still crashing. Huge trees fell and dragged power lines into the street. The closer he got to the church, the emptier he felt in his heart. That steeple was the only thing standing. Its base rested at ground level. The lights of the Range Rover illuminated pews, sitting incongruously in neat rows, some of them unscathed. The rest of the sanctuary, the high-arched beams, the stained-glass windows, all gone. The administration building, the classrooms, the offices were flattened to the ground in a pile of bricks and glass and mortar.

One car was visible in a crater in what used to be the parking lot. The bottom of the car was flat on the ground, all four tires blown, axles broken. Two bare human legs protruded from under the car. Buck stopped the Range Rover a hundred feet from that mess in the parking lot. His door would not open. He loosened his seat belt and climbed out the passenger side. And suddenly the earthquake stopped. The sun reappeared. It was a bright, sunshiny Monday morning in Mount Prospect, Illinois. Buck felt every bone in his body. He staggered over the uneven ground toward that little flattened car. When he was close enough, he saw that the crushed body was missing a shoe. The one that remained, however, confirmed his fear. Loretta had been crushed by her own car.

Buck stumbled and fell facedown in the dirt, something gashing his cheek. He ignored it and crawled to the car. He braced himself and pushed with all his might, trying to roll the vehicle off the body. It would not budge. Everything in him screamed against leaving Loretta there. But where would he take the body if he could free it? Sobbing now, he crawled through the debris, looking for any entrance to the underground shelter. . . . Finally he found the vent shaft. He cupped his hands over it and shouted down into it, "Tsion! Tsion! Are you there?" He turned and put his ear to the shaft, feeling cool air rush from the shelter.

"I am here, Buck! . . . How is Loretta?"

"Gone!"

"Was it the great earthquake?"

"It was!"

"Can you get to me?"

"I will get to you if it's the last thing I do, Tsion! I need you to help me look for Chloe!"

"I am OK for now, Buck! I will wait for you!"

Buck turned to look in the direction of the safe house. People staggered in ragged clothes, bleeding. Some dropped and seemed to die in front of his eyes. He didn't know how long it would take him to get to Chloe. He was sure he would not want to see what he found there, but he would not stop until he did. If there was one chance in a million of getting to her, of saving her, he would do it.

‡

The sun had reappeared over New Babylon. Rayford urged Mac McCullum to keep going toward Baghdad. Everywhere Rayford, Mac, and Carpathia looked was destruction. Craters from meteors. Fires burning. Buildings flattened. Roads wasted.

When Baghdad Airport came into sight, Rayford hung his head and wept. Jumbo jets were twisted, some sticking out of great cavities in the ground. The terminal was flattened. The tower was down. Bodies strewn everywhere.

Rayford signaled Mac to set the chopper down. But as he surveyed the area, Rayford knew. The only prayer for Amanda or for Hattie was that their planes were still in the air when this occurred.

When the blades stopped whirring, Carpathia turned to the other two. "Do either of you have a working phone?"

Rayford was so disgusted he reached past Carpathia and pushed open the door. He slipped out from behind Carpathia's seat and jumped to the ground. Then he reached in, loosened Carpathia's belt, grabbed him by the lapels, and yanked him out of the chopper. Carpathia landed on his seat on the uneven ground. He jumped up quickly, as if ready to fight. Rayford pushed him back up against the helicopter.

"Captain Steele, I understand you are upset, but—"

"Nicolae," Rayford said, his words rushing through clenched teeth, "you can explain this away any way you want, but let me be the first to tell you: You have just seen the wrath of the Lamb!"

Carpathia shrugged. Rayford gave him a last shove against the helicopter and stumbled away. He set his face toward the airport terminal, a quarter mile away. He prayed this would be the last time he had to search for the body of a loved one in the rubble.

"When He opened the seventh seal, there was silence in heaven for about half an hour. And I saw the seven angels who stand before God, and to them were given seven trumpets. Then another angel, having a golden censer, came and stood at the altar. He was given much incense, that he should offer it with the prayers of all the saints upon the golden altar which was before the throne. And the smoke of the incense, with the prayers of the saints, ascended before God from the angel's hand. Then the angel took the censer, filled it with fire from the altar, and threw it to the earth. And there were noises, thunderings, lightnings, and an earthquake.

"So the seven angels who had the seven trumpets prepared themselves to sound."

REVELATION 8:6

CHAPTER 1

RAYFORD STEELE WORE the uniform of the enemy of his soul, and he hated himself for it. He strode through Iraqi sand toward Baghdad Airport in his dress blues and was struck by the incongruity of it all.

From across the parched plain he heard the wails and screams of hundreds he wouldn't begin to be able to help. Any prayer of finding his wife alive depended on how quickly he could get to her. But there was no quick here. Only sand. And what about Chloe and Buck in the States? And Tsion?

Desperate, frantic, mad with frustration, he ripped off his natty waistcoat with its yellow braid, heavy epaulettes, and arm patches that identified a senior officer of the Global Community. Rayford did not take the time to unfasten the solid-gold buttons but sent them popping across the desert floor. He let the tailored jacket slide from his shoulders and clutched the collar in his fists. Three, four, five times he raised the garment over his head and slammed it to the ground. Dust billowed and sand kicked up over his patent leather shoes.

Rayford considered abandoning all vestiges of his connection to Nicolae Carpathia's regime, but his attention was drawn again to the luxuriously appointed arm patches. He tore at them, intending to rip them free, as if busting himself from his own rank in the service of the Antichrist. But the craftsmanship allowed not even a fingernail between the stitches, and Rayford slammed the coat to the ground one more time. He stepped and booted it like an extra point, finally aware of what had made it heavier. His phone was in the pocket.

As he knelt to retrieve his coat, Rayford's maddening logic returned—the practicality that made him who he was. Having no idea what he might find in the ruins of his condominium, he couldn't treat as dispensable what might constitute his only remaining set of clothes.

Rayford jammed his arms into the sleeves like a little boy made to wear a jacket on a warm day. He hadn't bothered to shake the grit from it, so as he plunged on toward the skeletal remains of the airport, Rayford's lanky frame was less impressive than usual. He could have been the survivor of a crash, a pilot who'd lost his cap and seen the buttons stripped from his uniform.

Rayford could not remember a chill before sundown in all the months he'd lived in Iraq. Yet something about the earthquake had changed not only the topography, but also the temperature. Rayford had been used to damp shirts and a sticky film on his skin. But now wind, that rare, mysterious draft, chilled him as he speed-dialed Mac McCullum and put the phone to his ear.

At that instant he heard the chug and whir of Mac's chopper behind him. He wondered where they were going.

"Mac here," came McCullum's gravely voice.

Rayford whirled and watched the copter eclipse the descending sun. "I can't believe this thing works," Rayford said. He had slammed it to the ground and kicked it, but he also assumed the earthquake would have taken out nearby cell towers.

"Soon as I get out of range, it won't, Ray," Mac said. "Everything's down for as far as I can see. These units act like walkie-talkies when we're close. When you need a cellular boost, you won't find it."

"So any chance of calling the States—"

"Is out of the question," Mac said. "Ray, Potentate Carpathia wants to speak to you, but first—"

"I don't want to talk to him, and you can tell him that."

"But before I give you to him," Mac continued, "I need to remind you that our meeting, yours and mine, is still on for tonight. Right?"

Rayford slowed and stared at the ground, running a hand through his hair. "What? What are you talking about?"

"All right then, very good," Mac said. "We're still meeting tonight then. Now the potentate—"

"I understand you want to talk to me later, Mac, but don't put Carpathia on or I swear I'll—"

"Stand by for the potentate."

Rayford switched the phone to his right hand, ready to smash it on the ground, but he restrained himself. When avenues of communication reopened, he wanted to be able to check on his loved ones.

"Captain Steele," came the emotionless tone of Nicolae Carpathia.

"I'm here," Rayford said, allowing his disgust to come through. He assumed God would forgive anything he said to the Antichrist, but he swallowed what he really wanted to say.

"Though we both know how I *could* respond to your egregious disrespect and insubordination," Carpathia said, "I choose to forgive you."

Rayford continued walking, clenching his teeth to keep from screaming at the man.

"I can tell you are at a loss for how to express your gratitude," Carpathia continued. "Now listen to me. I have a safe place and provisions where my international ambassadors and staff will join me. You and I both know we need each other, so I suggest—"

"You don't need me," Rayford said. "And I don't need your forgiveness. You have a perfectly capable pilot right next to you, so let *me* suggest that you forget me."

"Just be ready when he lands," Carpathia said, the first hint of frustration in his voice.

"The only place I would accept a ride to is the airport," Rayford said. "And I'm almost there. Don't have Mac set down any closer to this mess."

"Captain Steele," Carpathia began again, condescendingly, "I admire your irrational belief that you can somehow find your wife, but we both know that is not going to happen."

Rayford said nothing. He feared Carpathia was right, but he would never give him the satisfaction of admitting it. And he would certainly never quit looking until he proved to himself Amanda had not survived.

"Come with us, Captain Steele. Just reboard, and I will treat your outburst as if it never—"

"I'm not going anywhere until I've found my wife! Let me talk to Mac."

"Officer McCullum is busy. I will pass along a message."

"Mac could fly that thing with no hands. Now let me talk to him."

"If there is no message, then, Captain Steele—"

"All right, you win. Just tell Mac—"

"Now is no time to neglect protocol, Captain Steele. A pardoned subordinate is behooved to address his superior—"

"All right, *Potentate* Carpathia, just tell Mac to come for me if I don't find a way back by 2200 hours."

"And should you find a way back, the shelter is three and a half clicks northeast of the original headquarters. You will need the following password: 'Operation Wrath.'"

"What?" Carpathia knew this was coming?

"You heard me, Captain Steele."

Cameron "Buck" Williams stepped gingerly through the rubble near the ventilation shaft where he had heard the clear, healthy voice of Rabbi Tsion Ben-Judah, trapped in the underground shelter. Tsion assured him he was unhurt, just scared and claustrophobic. That place was small enough without the church imploding above it. With no way out unless someone tunneled to him, the rabbi, Buck knew, would soon feel like a caged animal.

Had Tsion been in immediate danger, Buck would have dug with his bare hands to free him. But Buck felt like a doctor in triage, having to determine who most urgently needed his help. Assuring Tsion he would return, he headed toward the safe house to find his wife.

To get through the trash that had been the only church home he ever knew, Buck had to again crawl past the remains of the beloved Loretta. What a friend she had been, first to the late Bruce Barnes and then to the rest of the Tribulation Force. The Force had begun with four: Rayford, Chloe, Bruce, and Buck. Amanda was added. Bruce was lost. Tsion was added.

Was it possible now that they had been reduced to just Buck and Tsion? Buck didn't want to think about it. He found his watch gunked up with mud, asphalt, and a tiny shard of windshield. He wiped the crystal across his pant leg and felt the crusty mixture tear his trousers and bite into his knee. It was nine o'clock in the morning in Mt. Prospect, and Buck heard an air raid siren, a tornado warning siren, emergency vehicle sirens—one close, two farther away. Shouts. Screams. Sobbing. Engines.

Could he live without Chloe? Buck had been given a second chance; he was here for a purpose. He wanted the love of his life by his side, and he prayed—selfishly, he realized—that she had not already preceded him to heaven.

In his peripheral vision, Buck noticed the swelling of his own left cheek. He had felt neither pain nor blood and had assumed the wound was minor. Now he wondered. He reached in his breast pocket for his mirror-lensed sunglasses. One lens was in pieces. In the reflection of the other he saw a scarecrow, hair wild, eyes white with fear, mouth open and sucking air. The wound was not bleeding, yet it appeared deep. There would be no time for treatment.

Buck emptied his shirt pocket but kept the frames—a gift from Chloe. He studied the ground as he moved back to the Range Rover, picking his way through glass, nails, and bricks like an old man, assuring himself solid purchase.

Buck passed Loretta's car and what was left of her, determined not to look. Suddenly the earth moved, and he stumbled. Loretta's car, which he had been unable to budge moments before, rocked and disappeared. The ground had given way under the parking lot. Buck stretched out on his stomach and peeked over the edge of a new crevice. The mangled car rested atop a water main twenty feet beneath the earth. The blown tires pointed up like the feet of bloated roadkill. Curled in a frail ball atop the wreckage was the Raggedy Ann–like body of Loretta, a tribulation saint. There would be more shifting of the earth. Reaching Loretta's body would be impossible. If he was also to find Chloe dead, Buck wished God had let him plunge under the earth with Loretta's car.

Buck rose slowly, suddenly aware of what the roller-coaster ride through the earthquake had done to his joints and muscles. He surveyed the damage to his vehicle. Though it had rolled and been hit from all sides, it appeared remarkably roadworthy. The driver's-side door was jammed, the windshield in gummy pieces throughout the interior, and the rear seat had broken away from the floor on one side. One tire had been slashed to the steel belts but looked strong and held air.

Where were Buck's phone and laptop? He had set them on the front seat. He hoped against hope neither had flown out in the mayhem. Buck opened the passenger door and peered onto the floor of the front seat. Nothing. He looked under the rear seats, all the way to the back. In a corner, open and with one screen hinge cracked, was his laptop.

Buck found his phone in a door well. He didn't expect to be able to get through to anyone, with all the damage to cell towers (and everything else above ground). He switched it on, and it went through a self-test and showed zero range. Still, he had to try. He dialed Loretta's home. He didn't even get a malfunction message from the phone company. The same happened when he dialed the church, then Tsion's shelter. As if playing a cruel joke, the phone made noises as if trying to get through. Then, nothing.

Buck's landmarks were gone. He was grateful the Range Rover had a built-in compass. Even the church seemed twisted from its normal perspective on the corner. Poles and lines and traffic lights were down, buildings flattened, trees uprooted, fences strewn about.

Buck made sure the Range Rover was in four-wheel drive. He could barely travel twenty feet before having to punch the car over some rise. He kept his eyes peeled to avoid anything that might further damage the Rover—it might have to last him through the end of the Tribulation. The best he could figure, that was still more than five years away.

As Buck rolled over chunks of asphalt and concrete where the street once lay, he glanced again at the vestiges of New Hope Village Church. Half the building was underground. But that one section of pews, which had once faced west, now faced north and glistened in the sun. The entire sanctuary floor appeared to have turned ninety degrees.

As he passed the church, he stopped and stared. A shaft of light appeared between each pair of pews in the ten-pew section except in one spot. There something blocked Buck's view. He threw the Rover into reverse and carefully backed up. On the floor in front of one of those pews were the bottoms of a pair of tennis shoes, toes pointing up. Buck wanted, above all, to get to Loretta's and search for Chloe, but he could not leave someone lying in the debris. Was it possible someone had survived?

He set the brake and scrambled over the passenger seat and out the door, recklessly trotting through stuff that could slice through his shoes. He wanted to be practical, but there was no time for that. Buck lost his footing ten feet from those tennis shoes and pitched face forward. He took the brunt of the fall on his palms and chest.

He pulled himself up and knelt next to the tennis shoes, which were attached to a body. Thin legs in dark blue jeans led to narrow hips. From the waist up, the small body was hidden under the pew. The right hand was tucked underneath, the left lay open and limp. Buck found no pulse, but he noticed the hand was broad and bony, the third finger bearing a man's wedding band. Buck slipped it off, assuming a surviving wife might want it.

Buck grabbed the belt buckle and dragged the body from under the bench. When the head slid into view, Buck turned away. He had recognized Donny Moore's blond coloring only from his eyebrows. The rest of his hair, even his sideburns, was encrusted with blood.

Buck didn't know what to do in the face of the dead and dying at a time like this. Where would anyone begin disposing of millions of corpses all over the world? Buck gently pushed the body back under the pew but was stopped by an obstruction. He reached underneath and found Donny's beat-up, hard-sided briefcase. Buck tried the latches, but combination locks had been set. He lugged the briefcase back to the Range Rover and tried again to find his bearings. He was a scant four blocks from Loretta's, but could he even find the street?

Rayford was encouraged to see movement in the distance at Baghdad Airport. He saw more wreckage and carnage on the ground than people scurrying about, but at least not all had been lost.

A small, dark figure with a strange gait appeared on the horizon. Rayford watched, fascinated, as the image materialized into a stocky, middle-aged Asian in a business suit. The man walked directly toward Rayford, who waited expectantly, wondering if he could help. But as the man drew near, Rayford realized he was not aware of his surroundings. He wore a wing-tipped dress shoe on one foot with only a sock sliding down the ankle of the other. His suit coat was buttoned, but his tie hung outside it. His left hand dripped blood. His hair was mussed, yet his glasses appeared to have been untouched by whatever he had endured.

"Are you all right?" Rayford asked. The man ignored him. "Can I help you?"

The man limped past, mumbling in his own tongue. Rayford turned to call him back, and the man became a silhouette in the orange sun. There was nothing in that direction but the Tigris River. "Wait!" Rayford called after him. "Come back! Let me help you!"

The man ignored him, and Rayford dialed Mac again. "Let me talk to Carpathia," he said.

"Sure," Mac said. "We're set on that meeting tonight, right?"

"Right, now let me talk to him."

"I mean our personal meeting, right?"

"Yes! I don't know what you want, but yes, I get the point. Now I need to talk to Carpathia."

"OK, sorry. Here he is."

"Change your mind, Captain Steele?" Carpathia said.

"Hardly. Listen, do you know Asian languages?"

"Some. Why?"

"What does this mean?" he asked, repeating what the man had said.

"That is easy," Carpathia said. "It means, 'You cannot help me. Leave me alone.'"

"Bring Mac back around, would you? This man is going to die of exposure."

"I thought you were looking for your wife."

"I can't leave a man to wander to his death."

"Millions are dead and dying. You cannot save all of them."

"So you're going to let this man die?"

"I do not see him, Captain Steele. If you think you can save him, be my guest. I do not mean to be cold, but I have the whole world at heart just now."

Rayford slapped his phone shut and hurried back to the lurching, mumbling man. As he drew near, Rayford was horrified to see why his gait was so strange and why he trailed a river of blood. He had been impaled by a gleaming white chunk of metal, apparently some piece of a fuselage. Why he was still alive, how he survived or climbed out, Rayford couldn't imagine. The shard was embedded from his hip to the back of his head. It had to have missed vital organs by centimeters.

Rayford touched the man's shoulder, causing him to wrench away. He sat heavily, and with a huge sigh toppled slowly in the sand and breathed his last. Rayford checked for a pulse, not surprised to find none. Overcome, he turned his back and knelt in the dirt. Sobs wracked his body.

Rayford raised his hands to the sky. "Why, God? Why do I have to see this? Why send someone across my path I can't even help? Spare Chloe and Buck! Please keep Amanda alive for me! I know I don't deserve anything, but I can't go on without her!"

Usually Buck drove two blocks south and two east from the church to Loretta's. But now there were no more blocks. No sidewalks, no streets, no intersections. For as far as Buck could see, every house in every neighborhood had been leveled. Could it have been this bad all over the world? Tsion taught that a quarter of the world's population would fall victim to the wrath of the Lamb. But Buck would be surprised if even a quarter of the population of Mt. Prospect was still alive.

He lined up the Range Rover on a southeastern course. A few degrees above the horizon the day was as beautiful as any Buck could remember. The sky, where not interrupted by smoke and dust, was baby blue. No clouds. Bright sun.

Geysers shot skyward where fire hydrants had ruptured. A woman crawled out from the wreckage of her home, a bloody stump at her shoulder where her arm had been. She screamed at Buck, "Kill me! Kill me!"

He shouted, "No!" and leaped from the Rover as she bent and grabbed a chunk of glass from a broken window and dragged it across her neck. Buck continued to yell as he sprinted to her. He only hoped she was too weak to do anything but superficial damage to her neck, and he prayed she would miss her carotid artery.

He was within a few feet of her when she stared, startled. The glass broke and tinkled to the ground. She stepped back and tripped, her head smacking loudly on a chunk of concrete. Immediately the blood stopped pumping from her exposed arteries. Her eyes were lifeless as Buck forced her jaw open and covered her mouth with his. Buck blew air into her throat, making her chest rise and her blood trickle, but it was futile.

Buck looked around, wondering whether to try to cover her. Across the way an elderly man stood at the edge of a crater and seemed to will himself to tumble into it. Buck could take no more. Was God preparing him for the likelihood that Chloe had not survived?

He wearily climbed back into the Range Rover, deciding

he absolutely could not stop and help anyone else who did not appear to really want it. Everywhere he looked he saw devastation, fire, water, and blood.

Against his better judgment, Rayford left the dead man in the desert sand. What would he do when he saw others in various states of demise? How could Carpathia ignore this? Had he not a shred of humanity? Mac would have stayed and helped.

Rayford despaired of seeing Amanda alive again, and though he would search with all that was in him, he already wished he had arranged an earlier rendezvous with Mac. He'd seen awful things in his life, but the carnage at this airport was going to top them all. A shelter, even the Antichrist's, sounded better than this.

CHAPTER 2

BUCK HAD COVERED disasters, but as a journalist he had not felt guilty about ignoring the dying. Normally, by the time he arrived on a scene, medical personnel were usually in place. There was nothing he could do but stay out of the way. He had taken pride in not forcing his way into situations that would make things more difficult for emergency workers.

But now it was just him. Sounds of sirens told him others were at work somewhere, but surely there were too few rescuers to go around. He could work twenty-four hours finding barely breathing survivors, but he would not make a dent in the magnitude of this disaster. Someone else might ignore Chloe to get to his own loved one. Those who had somehow escaped with their lives could hope only that they had their own hero, fighting the odds to get to them.

Buck had never believed in extrasensory perception or telepathy, even before he had become a believer in Christ. Yet now he felt such a deep longing for Chloe, such a desperate grief at even the prospect of losing her, that he felt as if his love oozed from every pore. How could she not know he was thinking of her, praying for her, trying to get to her at all cost?

Having kept his eyes straight ahead as despairing, wounded people waved or screamed out to him, Buck bounced to a dusty stop. A couple of blocks east of the main drag was some semblance of recognizable geography. Nothing looked like it had before, but ribbons of road, gouged up by the churning earth, lay sideways in roughly the same configuration they had before. The pavement of Loretta's street now stood vertically, blocking the view of what was left of the homes. Buck scrambled from his car and climbed atop the asphalt wall. He found the upturned street about four feet thick with a bed of gravel and sand on its other side. He reached up and over and dug his fingers into the soft part, hanging there and staring at Loretta's block.

Four stately homes had stood in that section, Loretta's the second from the right. The entire block looked like some child's box of toys that had been shaken and tossed to the ground. The home directly in front of Buck, larger even than Loretta's, had been knocked back off its foundation, flipped onto its front, and collapsed. The roof had toppled off upside down in one piece, apparently when the house hit the ground. Buck could see the rafters, as he would have had he been in the attic. All four walls of the house lay flat, flooring strewn about. In two places, Buck saw lifeless hands at the ends of stiff arms poking through the debris.

A towering tree, more than four feet in diameter, had been uprooted and had crashed into the basement. Two feet of water lay on the cement floor, and the water level was slowly rising. Strangely, what appeared to be a guest room in the northeast corner of the cellar looked unmolested, neat and tidy. It would soon be under water.

Buck forced himself to look at the next house, Loretta's. He and Chloe had not lived there long, but he knew it well. The house, now barely recognizable, seemed to have been lifted off the ground and slammed down in place, causing the roof to split in two and settle over the giant box of sticks. The roofline, all the way around, was now about four feet off the ground. Three massive trees in the front yard had fallen toward the street, angled toward each other, branches intertwined, as if three swordsmen had touched their blades together.

Between the two destroyed houses stood a small metal shed that, while pitched at an angle, had nonsensically escaped serious damage. How could an earthquake shake, rattle, and roll a pair of five-bedroom, two-story homes into oblivion and leave untouched a tiny utility shed? Buck could only surmise that the structure was so flexible it did not snap when the earth rolled beneath it.

Loretta's home had shrunk flat where it sat, leaving her backyard empty and bare. All this, Buck realized, had happened in seconds.

A fire truck with makeshift bullhorns on the back rolled slowly into view behind Buck. As he hung on that vertical stretch of pavement, he heard: "Stay out of your homes! Do not return to your homes! If you need help, get to an open area where we can find you!"

A half-dozen police officers and firefighters rode the giant ladder truck. A uniformed cop leaned out the window. "You all right there, buddy?"

"I'm all right!" Buck hollered.

"That your vehicle?"

"Yes!"

"We could sure use it in the relief effort!"

"I've got people I'm trying to dig out!" Buck said.

The cop nodded. "Don't be trying to get into any of these homes!"

Buck let go and slid to the ground. He walked toward the fire truck as it slowed to a stop. "I heard the announcement, but what are you guys talking about?"

"We're worried about looters. But we're also worried about danger. These places are hardly stable."

"Obviously!" Buck said. "But looters? You are the only healthy people I've seen. There's nothing of value left, and where would somebody take anything if they found it?"

"We're just doing what we're told, sir. Don't try to go in any of the homes, OK?"

"Of course I will! I'm gonna be digging through that house to find out if somebody I know and love is still alive."

"Trust me, pal, you're not going to find survivors on this street. Stay out of there."

"Are you gonna arrest me? Do you have a jail still standing?"

The cop turned to the fireman driving. Buck wanted an answer. Apparently, the cop was more levelheaded than he was, because they slowly rolled away. Buck scaled the wall of pavement and slid down the other side, covering his entire front with mud. He tried wiping it off, but it stuck between his fingers. He slapped at his pants to get the bulk of it off his hands, then hurried between the fallen trees to the front of the fractured house.

It seemed to Rayford that the closer he got to the Baghdad airport, the less he could see. Great fissures had swallowed every inch of runway in all directions, pushing mounds of dirt and sand several feet into the air, blocking a view of the terminal. As Rayford made his way through, he could barely breathe. Two jumbo jets—one a 747 and the other a DC-10, apparently fully loaded and in line for takeoff on an east-west runway—appeared to have been in tandem before the earthquake slammed them together and ripped them apart. The result was piles of lifeless bodies. He couldn't imagine the force of a collision that would kill so many without a fire.

From a massive ditch on the far side of the terminal, at least a quarter mile from where Rayford stood, a line of survivors clawed their way to the surface from another swallowed aircraft. Black smoke billowed from deep in the earth, and Rayford knew if he was close enough he could hear the screams of survivors not strong enough to climb out. Of those who emerged, some ran from the scene, while most, like the Asian, staggered trancelike through the desert.

The terminal itself, formerly a structure of steel and wood and glass, had not only been knocked flat, but it had also been shaken as a prospector would sift sand through a screen. The pieces were spread so widely that none of the piles stood higher than two feet. Hundreds of bodies lay in various states of repose. Rayford felt as if he were in hell.

He knew what he was looking for. Amanda's scheduled flight had been on a Pan-Continental 747, the airline and equipment he used to fly. It would not have surprised him if she were on one of the very aircraft he had once piloted. It would have been scheduled to land south to north on the big runway.

If the earthquake occurred with the plane in the air, the pilot would have tried to stay airborne until it was over, then looked for a flat patch of ground to put down. If it occurred at any time after landing, the plane could be anywhere on that strip, which was now fully underground and covered with sand. It was a huge, long runway, but surely if a plane was buried there, Rayford ought to be able to sight it before the sun went down.

Might it be facing the other direction on one of the auxiliary runways, having already begun taxiing back to the terminal? He could only hope it was obvious and pray there was something he could do in the event that Amanda had somehow miraculously survived. The best-case scenario, short of the pilot having had enough foresight to have landed somewhere safely, would have been if the plane had landed and either stopped or was traveling very slowly when the earthquake hit. If it had somehow been fortunate enough to be in the middle of the airstrip when the runway slipped from the surface, there was a chance it would still be upright and intact. If it was covered with sand, who knew how long the air supply would last?

It seemed to Rayford there were at least ten people dead for every one alive near the terminal. Those who had escaped had to have been outside when the quake hit. It didn't appear anyone inside the terminal had survived. Those few Global Community uniformed officers who patrolled the area with their high-powered weapons looked as shell-shocked as anyone. Occasionally one shot Rayford a double take as he moved past, but they backed off and didn't even ask to see identification when they noticed his uniform. With hanging threads where the buttons should have been, he knew he looked like just another lucky survivor from the crew of some ill-fated plane.

To get to the runway in question, Rayford had to cross paths with a zombied and bleeding queue of fortunates who staggered out of a crater. He was grateful none of them pleaded for help. Most appeared not to even see him, following one another as if trusting that someone somewhere near the front of the line had an idea where he might find help. From deep in the hole, Rayford heard the wailing and moaning he knew he would never be able to forget. If there was anything he could do, he would have done it.

Finally he reached the near end of the long runway. There, directly in the middle, lay the sand-blown but easily recognizable humpbacked fuselage of a 747.

There might have been an hour's worth of sunlight left, but it was fading. As he hurried along the edge of the canyon the sinking runway had gorged out of the sand, Rayford shook his head and squinted, shading his eyes as he tried to make sense of what he saw. As he came to within a hundred feet of the back of the monstrous plane, it became clear what had happened. The plane had been near mid-runway when the pavement simply dropped at least fifty feet beneath it. The weight of that pavement pulled the sand in toward the plane, which now rested on both wingtips, its body hanging precariously over the chasm.

Someone had had the presence of mind to get the doors open and the inflatable evacuation chutes deployed, but even the ends of those chutes hung several feet in the air over the collapsed runway.

Had the walls of sand at the sides of the plane been any farther apart, no way could the wings have supported the weight of the cabin. The fuselage squeaked and groaned as the weight of the plane threatened to send it plummeting.

The plane might be able to drop another ten feet without seriously injuring anyone, and hundreds could be saved, Rayford believed, if only it could settle gradually.

He prayed desperately that Amanda was safe, that she had been buckled in, that the plane had stopped before the runway gave way. The closer he got, the more obvious it was that the plane must have been moving at the time of the cave-in. The wings were buried several feet in the sand. That may have kept the craft from dropping, but it also would have provided a killing jolt for anyone not fastened in.

Rayford's heart sank when he drew close enough to see that this was not a Pan-Con 747 at all but a British Airways jet. He was struck with such conflicting emotions that he could barely sort them out. What kind of a cold, selfish person is so obsessed with the survival of his own wife that he would be disappointed that hundreds of people might have been saved on this plane? He had to face the ugly truth about himself that he cared mostly for Amanda. Where was her Pan-Con flight?

He spun and scanned the horizon. What a cauldron of death! There was nowhere else to look for the Pan-Con jet. Until he knew for sure, he would not accept that Amanda was gone. With no other recourse and the inability to call Mac for an earlier pickup, he turned his attention back to the British Airways plane. At one of the open doors a flight attendant, staring ghostlike from the cabin, helplessly surveyed their precarious position. Rayford cupped his hands and called out to her, "I am a pilot! I have some ideas!"

"Are we on fire?" she screamed.

"No! And you should be very low on fuel! You don't seem to be in danger!"

"This is very unstable!" she shouted. "Should I move everyone to the back so we don't go nose down?"

"You won't go nose down anyway! Your wings are stuck in the sand! Get everyone toward the middle and see if you can exit onto the wings without breaking up!"

"Can we be sure of that?"

"No! But you can't wait for heavy equipment to tunnel down there and scaffold up to you! The earthquake was world-wide, and it's unlikely anyone will get to you for days!"

"These people want out of here now! How sure are you that this will work?"

"Not very! But you have no choice! An aftershock could drop the plane all the way!"

As far as Buck knew, Chloe had been alone at Loretta's. His only hope of finding her was to guess where she might have been in the house when it collapsed. Their bedroom in the southwest corner upstairs was now at ground level—a mass of brick, siding, drywall, glass, framing, trim, floor, studs, wiring, and furniture—covered by half of the split roof.

Chloe kept her computer in the basement, now buried under the two other floors on that same side of the house. Or she might have been in the kitchen, at the front of the house but also on that same side. That left Buck with no options. He had to get rid of a major section of that roof and start digging. If he didn't find her in the bedroom or the basement, his last hope was the kitchen.

He had no boots, no gloves, no work clothes, no goggles, no helmet. All he had were the filthy, flimsy clothes on his back, normal shoes, and his bare hands. It was too late to worry about tetanus. He leaped onto the shifting roof. He edged up the steep incline, trying to see where it might be weak or could fall apart. It felt solid, though unsteady. He slid to the ground and pushed up under the eaves. No way could he do this by himself. Might there be an ax or chain saw in the metal shed?

He couldn't get it open at first. The door was jammed. It seemed such a frail thing, but having shifted in the earthquake, the shed had bent upon itself and was unwilling to budge. Buck lowered his shoulder and rammed it like a football player. It groaned in protest but snapped back into position. He karate kicked it six times, then lowered his shoulder and barreled into it again. Finally he backed up twenty feet and raced toward it, but his slick shoes slipped in the grass and sent him sprawling. In a rage he trotted back farther, started slower, and gradually picked up speed. This time he smashed into the side of the shed so hard that he tore it from its moorings. It flipped over the tools inside, and he went with it, riding it to the ground before bouncing off. A jagged edge of the roof caught his rib cage as he hurtled down, and flesh gave way. He grabbed his side and felt a trickle, but unless he severed an artery, he wouldn't slow down.

He dragged shovels and axes to the house and propped long-handled garden implements under the eaves. When Buck leaned against them, the edge of the roof lifted and something snapped beneath the few remaining shingles. He attacked that with a shovel, imagining how ridiculous he looked and what his father might say if he saw him using the wrong tool for the wrong job.

But what else could he do? Time was of the essence. He was fighting all odds anyway. Yet stranger things had happened. People had stayed alive under rubble for days. But if water was getting into the foundation of the house next door, what about this one? What if Chloe was trapped in the basement? He prayed that if she had to die, it had already happened quickly and painlessly. He did not want her life to ebb slowly away in a horrifying drowning. He also feared electrocution when water met open electric lines.

With a chunk of the roof gone, Buck shoveled debris away until he hit bigger pieces that had to be removed by hand. He was in decent shape, but this was beyond his routine. His muscles burned as he tossed aside heavy hunks of wall and flooring. He seemed to make little progress, huffing and puffing and sweating.

Buck twisted conduit out of the way and tossed aside ceiling plaster. He finally reached the bed frame, which had been snapped like kindling. He pushed in to where Chloe often sat at a small desk. It took him another half hour to dig through there, calling her name every so often. When he stopped to catch his breath he fought to listen for the faintest noise. Would he be able to hear a moan, a cry, a sigh? If she made the smallest sound, he would find her.

Buck began to despair. This was going too slowly. He hit huge chunks of floor too heavy to move. The distance between the floorboards of the upstairs bedroom and the concrete floor of the basement was simply not that great. Anyone caught between there had surely been smashed flat. But he could not quit. If he couldn't get through this stuff by himself, he would get Tsion to help him.

Buck dragged the tools out to the front and tossed them over the pavement wall. Getting over from this side was a lot harder than from the other because the mud was slippery. He looked up one way and down the other and couldn't see the end of where the road had been flipped vertical. He dug his feet into the mud and finally got to where he could reach the asphalt on the other side at the top. He pulled himself up and slid over, landing painfully on his elbow. He tossed the tools into the back of the Rover and slid his muddy body behind the wheel.

The sun was dropping in Iraq as several survivors of other crashes joined Rayford to watch the plight of the British Air 747. He stood helpless, hoping. The last thing he wanted was to be responsible for injury or death to anyone. But he was certain that exiting onto the wings was their only hope. He prayed they could then climb the steep banks of sand.

Rayford was encouraged at first when he saw the first passengers crawl onto the wings. Apparently the flight attendant had rallied the people and gotten them to work together. Rayford's encouragement soon turned to alarm when he saw how much motion they generated and how it strained the fragile support. The plane was going to break up. Then what would happen to the fuselage? If one end or the other tipped too quickly, dozens could be killed. Those not strapped in would be hurtled to one end of the plane or the other, landing atop each other.

Rayford wanted to shout, to plead with the people inside to spread out. They needed to go about this with more precision and care. But it was too late, and they would never hear him. The noise inside the plane had to be deafening. The two on the right wing leaped into the sand.

The left wing gave way first but was not totally sheared off. The fuselage rotated left, and it was clear passengers inside fell that way too. The rear of the plane was going down first. Rayford could only hope the right wing would give way in time to even it out. At the last instant, that happened. But though the plane landed nearly perfectly flat on its tires, it had dropped much too far. People had to have been horribly bounced against each other and the plane. When the front tire collapsed, the nose of the plane drove so hard into the pavement that it shook more sand avalanches loose from the sides, which quickly filled the gorge. Rayford stuffed his phone in his pants pocket and tossed his jacket aside. He and others dug with their hands and began burrowing to the plane to allow air and escape passages. Sweat soaked through his clothes. The shine of his shoes would never return, but when might he ever again need dress shoes anyway?

When he and his compatriots finally reached the plane, they met passengers digging their way out. Rescuers behind Rayford cleared the area when they heard helicopter blades. Rayford assumed, as everyone probably did, that it was a relief chopper. Then he remembered. If it was Mac, it must be ten already. Was it because he cared, Rayford wondered, or was he more concerned with their meeting?

Rayford phoned Mac from deep in the gorge and told him he wanted to be sure no one had been killed on board the 747. Mac told him he'd be waiting on the other side of the terminal.

A few minutes later, relieved that all had survived, Rayford climbed back to the surface. He could not, however, find his jacket. That was just as well. He assumed Carpathia would soon fire him anyway.

Rayford picked his way through the flattened terminal and around the back. Mac's helicopter idled a hundred yards away. In the darkness, Rayford assumed a clear path to the small craft and began hurrying. Amanda was not here, and this was a place of death. He wanted out of Iraq altogether, but for now he wanted away from Baghdad. He might have to endure Carpathia's shelter, whatever that was, but as soon as he was able he would put distance between himself and Nicolae.

Rayford picked up speed, still in shape in his early forties.

But suddenly he somersaulted into what? Bodies! He had tripped over one and landed atop others. Rayford stood and rubbed a painful knee, fearing he had desecrated these people. He slowed and walked to the chopper.

"Let's go, Mac!" he said as he climbed aboard.

"I don't need to be told *that* twice," Mac said, throttling up. "I need to talk to you in a bad way."

It was afternoon in the Central Standard Time zone when Buck pulled within sight of the wreckage of the church. He was coming out the passenger door when an aftershock rumbled through. It lifted the truck and propelled Buck into the dirt on his rear. He turned to watch the remains of the church sift, shift, and toss about. The pews that had escaped the ravages of the quake now cracked and flipped. Buck could only imagine what had happened to poor Donny Moore's body. Perhaps God himself had handled the burial.

Buck worried about Tsion. What might have broken loose and fallen in his underground shelter? Buck scrambled to the ventilation shaft, which had provided Tsion's only source of air. "Tsion! Are you all right?"

He heard a faint, breathy voice. "Thank God you have returned, Cameron! I was lying here with my nose next to the vent when I heard the rumble and something clattering its way toward me. I rolled out of the way just in time. There are pieces of brick down here. Was it an aftershock?"

"Yes!"

"Forgive me, Cameron, but I have been brave long enough. Get me out of here!"

It took Buck more than an hour of grueling digging to reach the entrance to the underground shelter. As soon as he began the tricky procedure to unlock and open the door, Tsion began pushing it from the inside. Together they forced it open against the weight of cinder blocks and other trash. Tsion squinted against the light and drank in the air. He embraced Buck tightly and asked, "What about Chloe?"

"I need your help."

"Let us go. Any word from the others?"

"It could be days before communication opens to the Middle East. Amanda should be there with Rayford by now, but I have no idea about either of them."

"One thing you can be sure of," Tsion said in his thick Israeli accent, "is that if Rayford was near Nicolae, he is likely safe. The Scriptures are clear that the Antichrist will not meet his demise until a little over a year from now."

"I wouldn't mind having a hand in that," Buck said.

"God will take care of that. But it is not the due time. Repulsive as it must be for Captain Steele to be in proximity to such evil, at least he should be safe."

In the air, Mac McCullum radioed back to the safe shelter and told the radio operator, "We're involved in a rescue here, so we're gonna be another hour or two. Over."

"Roger that. I'll inform the potentate. Over."

Rayford wondered what could be so important that Mac would risk lying to Nicolae Carpathia?

Once Rayford's headset was in place, Mac said, "What the blazes is going on? What is Carpathia up to? What's all this about the 'wrath of the Lamb,' and what in the world was I lookin' at earlier when I thought I was lookin' at the moon? I've seen a lot of natural disasters, and I've seen some strange atmospheric phenomena, but I swear on my mother's eyes I've never seen anything make a full moon look like it's turned to blood. Why would an earthquake do that?"

Man, Rayford thought, *this guy is ripe.* But Rayford was also puzzled. "I'll tell you what I think, Mac, but first tell me why you think I would know."

"I can tell, that's all. I wouldn't dare cross Carpathia in a million years, even though I can tell he's up to no good. You don't seem to be intimidated by him at all. I about lost my lunch when I saw that red moon, and you acted like you knew it would be there."

Rayford nodded but didn't expound. "I have a question for you, Mac. You knew why I went to the Baghdad airport. Why didn't you ask me what I found out about my wife or Hattie Durham?"

"None of my business, that's all," Mac said.

"Don't give me that. Unless Carpathia knows more than I do, he would have wanted to know about Hattie's whereabouts as soon as either of us knew anything."

"No, Rayford, it's like this. See, I just knew—I mean,

everybody knows—that it wasn't likely either your wife or Miss Durham would have survived a crash at that airport."

"Mac! You saw yourself that hundreds of people were going to get off that 747. Sure, nine out of ten people died in that place, but lots survived, too. Now if you want answers from me, you'd better start giving me some."

Mac nodded toward a clearing he had illuminated with a spotlight. "We'll talk down there."

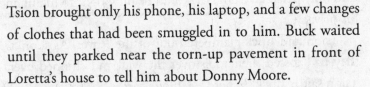

Tsion brought only his phone, his laptop, and a few changes of clothes that had been smuggled in to him. Buck waited until they parked near the torn-up pavement in front of Loretta's house to tell him about Donny Moore.

"That is a tragedy," Tsion said. "And he was—?"

"The one I told you about. The computer whiz who put together our laptops. One of those quiet geniuses. He had gone to this church for years and was still embarrassed that he had this astronomical IQ and yet had been spiritually blind. He said he simply missed the essence of the gospel that whole time. He said he couldn't blame it on the staff or the teaching or anything or anyone but himself. His wife had hardly ever come with him in those days because she didn't see the point. They lost a baby in the Rapture. And once Donny became a believer, his wife soon followed. They became quite devout."

Tsion shook his head. "How sad to die this way. But now they are reunited with their child."

"What do you think I ought to do about the briefcase?" Buck asked.

"Do about it?"

"Donny must have something very important in there. I saw him with it constantly. But I don't know the combinations. Should I leave it alone?"

Tsion seemed in deep thought. Finally he said, "At a time like this you must decide if there is something in there that might further the cause of Christ. The young man would want you to have access to it. Should you break into it and find only personal things, it would be only right to maintain his privacy."

Tsion and Buck clambered out of the Rover. As soon as they had tossed their tools over the wall and climbed over, Tsion said, "Buck! Where is Chloe's car?"

CHAPTER 3

RAYFORD COULD NOT SWEAR to the credibility of Mac McCullum. All he knew was that the freckled, twice-divorced man had just turned fifty and had never had kids. He was a careful and able aviator, facile with various types of aircraft, having flown both militarily and commercially.

Mac had proved a friendly, interested listener, earthy in expression. They had not known each other long enough for Rayford to expect him to be more forthcoming. Though he seemed a bright and engaging guy, their limited relationship had involved only surface cordiality. Mac knew Rayford was a believer; Rayford hid that from no one. But Mac had never shown the slightest interest in the matter. Until now.

Paramount in Rayford's mind was what not to say. Mac had finally expressed frustration over Carpathia, going so far as to allow that he was "up to no good." But what if Mac was a subversive, working for Carpathia as more than a pilot? What a way to entrap Rayford. Dare he both share his faith with Mac *and* reveal all that he and the Tribulation Force knew about Carpathia? And what of the bugging device built into the Condor 216? Even if Mac expressed an interest in Christ, Rayford would keep that volatile secret until he was sure Mac was not a fake.

Mac turned off everything on the chopper except auxiliary power that kept the control panel lights and radio on. All Rayford could see across the expanse of inky desert was moon and stars. If he hadn't known better, he might have been persuaded that the little craft was drifting along on an aircraft carrier in the middle of the ocean.

"Mac," Rayford said, "tell me about the shelter. What does it look like? And how did Carpathia know he needed it?"

"I don't know," Mac said. "Maybe it was a security blanket in case one or more of his ambassadors turned on him again. It's deep, it's concrete, and it'll protect him from radiation. And I'll tell you one more thing: It's plenty big enough for the 216."

Rayford was dumbfounded. "The 216? I left that at the end of the long runway in New Babylon."

"And I was assigned to move it early this morning."

"Move it where?"

"Didn't you ask me just the other day about that new utility road Carpathia had built?"

"That single-lane thing that seemed to lead only to the fence at the edge of the airstrip?"

"Yeah. Well, now there's a gate in the fence where that road ends."

"So you open the gate," Rayford said, "and you go where, across desert sand, right?"

"That's what it looks like," Mac said. "But a huge expanse of that sand has been treated with something. Wouldn't you think a craft as big as the 216 would sink in the sand if it ever got that far?"

"You're telling me you taxied the 216 down that little utility road to a gate in the fence? How big must that gate be?"

"Only big enough for the fuselage. The wings are higher than the fence."

"So you ferried the Condor off the airstrip and across the sand to where?"

"Three and a half clicks northeast of headquarters, just like Carpathia said."

"So this shelter isn't in a populated area."

"Nope. I doubt anyone's ever seen it without Carpathia's knowledge. It's huge, Ray. And it must have taken ages to build. I could have fit two aircraft that size in there and only half filled the space. It's about thirty feet below ground with plenty of supplies, plumbing, lodging, cooking areas, you name it."

"How does something underground withstand the shifting of the earth?"

"Part genius, part luck, I guess," Mac said. "The whole

thing floats, suspended on some sort of a membrane filled with hydraulic fluid and sitting on a platform of springs that serve as mammoth shock absorbers."

"So the rest of New Babylon is in ruins, but the Condor and Carpathia's little hideout, or I should say big hideout, escaped damage?"

"That's where the ingenious part comes in, Ray. The place was rocked pretty good, but the technology delivered. The one eventuality they couldn't escape, even though they predicted it, was that the main entrance, the huge opening that allowed the plane to easily slip in there, was completely covered over with rock and sand by the quake. They were able to shelter a couple of other smaller openings on the other side to maintain passage, and Carpathia already has earthmovers reopening the original entrance. They're working on it right now."

"So, what, he's looking to go somewhere? Can't stand the heat?"

"No, not at all. He's expecting company."

"His kings are on their way?"

"He calls them ambassadors. He and Fortunato have big plans."

Rayford shook his head. "Fortunato! I saw him in Carpathia's office when the earthquake started. How'd he survive?"

"I was as surprised as you, Ray. Unless I missed him, I didn't see him come out that door on the roof. I figured the only people with a prayer of surviving the collapse of that place were the few who were on the roof when the thing went down. That's more than a sixty-foot drop with concrete crashing all around you, so even that's a long shot. But I've heard stranger. I read about a guy in Korea who was on top of a hotel that collapsed, and he said he felt like he was surfing on a concrete slab until he hit the ground and rolled and wound up with only a broken arm."

"So what's the story? How did Fortunato get out?"

"You're not going to believe it."

"I'd believe anything at this point."

"Here's the story the way I saw it. I take Carpathia back to the shelter, and I put her down near the entrance where I had parked the Condor. It was totally covered over, like I say, so Carpathia directs me around to the side where there's a smaller opening. We go in and find a big staff of people working, almost as if nothing's happened. I mean, there's people cooking, cleaning, setting up, all that."

"Carpathia's secretary?"

Mac shook his head. "I guess she was killed in the building collapse, along with most of the other headquarters staff. But he's got her and all the rest of 'em replaced already."

"Unbelievable. And Fortunato?"

"He wasn't there either. Somebody tells Carpathia there were no survivors at headquarters, and I swear, Ray, it looked to me like Carpathia paled. It was the first time I've ever seen him rattled, except when he pretends to go into a rage about something. I think those are always planned."

"Me too. So what about Leon?"

"Carpathia recovers real quick and says, 'We'll just see

about that.' He says he'll be right back, and I ask him can I take him somewhere. He says no and leaves. When was the last time you saw him go anywhere by himself?"

"Never."

"Bingo. He's gone about half an hour, and the next thing you know he's back and he's got Fortunato with him. Fortunato was covered with dust from his head to his feet, and his suit was a mess. But his shirt was tucked in and his coat buttoned up, tie straightened and everything. There wasn't a scratch on him."

"What was his story?"

"It gave me chills, Ray. A bunch of people gathered around, I'd say about a hundred. Fortunato, real emotional, calls for order. Then he claims he went crying and screaming down in the rubble along with everybody else. He said halfway down he was wondering if it was possible to get lucky enough to be wedged in somewhere where he could breathe and stay alive until rescuers might find him. He said he felt himself free-falling and smacking into huge chunks of building; then something caught his feet and flipped him so he was going straight down, headfirst. When he hit, he said, it felt and sounded like he'd cracked his head open. Then it was like the whole weight of the building came down on him. He felt his bones breaking and his lungs bursting and everything went black. He said it was like somebody pulled the plug on his life. He believes he died."

"And yet there he is, wearing a dusty suit and not a scratch on him?"

"I saw him with my own eyes, Ray. He claims he was lying there dead, not conscious of anything, no out-of-body experience or anything like that. Just black nothingness, like the deepest sleep a person could ever have. He says he woke up, came back from the dead, when he heard his name called. At first he thought he was dreaming, he says. He thought he was a little boy again and his mother was softly calling his name, trying to rouse him. But then, he says, he heard Nicolae's loud call, 'Leonardo, come forth!'"

"What?"

"I'm tellin' you, Ray, it gave me the willies. I was never that religious, but I know that story from the Bible, and it sure sounded like Nicolae was pretending to be Jesus or something."

"You think the story's a lie?" Rayford asked. "You know, the Bible also says it's appointed unto man once to die. No second chances."

"I didn't know that, and I didn't know what to think when he told that story. Carpathia bringing somebody back from the dead? You know, at first I loved Carpathia and couldn't wait to work for him. There were times I thought he *was* a godly man, maybe some kind of deity himself. But it didn't add up. Him making me take off from the top of that building while people were hanging onto the struts and screaming for their lives. Him putting you down because you wanted to help that crash survivor in the desert. What kind of a god-man is that?"

"He's no god-man," Rayford said. "He's an anti-god-man."

"You think he's the Antichrist, like some say?"

So there it was. Mac had put the question to him. Rayford knew he had been reckless. Had he now sealed his own fate? Had he revealed himself completely to one of Carpathia's own henchmen, or was Mac sincere? How could he ever know for sure?

Buck spun in a circle. Where *was* Chloe's car? She always parked it in the driveway in front of the garage that contained Loretta's junk. Loretta's own car was usually in the other stall. It wouldn't have made sense for Chloe to move her car into Loretta's stall just because Loretta had driven to the church. "It could have been tossed anywhere, Tsion," Buck said.

"Yes, my friend, but not so far away that we could not see it."

"It could have been swallowed up."

"We should look, Cameron. If her car is here, we can assume she is here."

Buck moved up and down the street, looking between wrecked houses and into great holes in the earth. Nothing resembling Chloe's car turned up anywhere. When he met Tsion back at what used to be Loretta's garage, the rabbi was trembling. Though only in his middle forties, Tsion suddenly looked old to Buck. He moved with a shaky gait and stumbled, dropping to his knees.

"Tsion, are you all right?"

"Have you ever seen anything like it?" Tsion said, his voice just above a whisper. "I have seen devastation and waste, but this is overwhelming. Such widespread death and destruction . . ."

Buck put his hand on the man's shoulder and felt sobs wrack his body. "Tsion, we must not allow the enormity of all this to penetrate our minds. I have to somehow keep it separated from myself. I know it's not a dream. I know exactly what we're going through, but I can't dwell on it. I'm not equipped. If I allow it to overwhelm me, I'll be good to no one. We need each other. Let's be strong." Buck realized his own voice was weak as he pleaded with Tsion to be strong.

"Yes," Tsion said tearfully, trying to collect himself. "The glory of the Lord must be our rear guard. We will rejoice in the Lord always, and he will lift us up."

With that, Tsion rose and grabbed a shovel. Before Buck could catch up, Tsion began digging at the base of the garage.

The helicopter's radio crackled to life, giving Rayford time to search himself, to think and silently pray that God would keep him from saying something stupid. He still didn't know whether Amanda was dead or alive. He didn't know whether Chloe, or Buck, or Tsion were still on earth or in heaven. Finding them, reuniting with them was his top priority. Was he now risking everything?

The dispatcher at the shelter requested Mac's ten-twenty.

Mac glanced ruefully at Rayford. "Better make it sound like we're in the air," he said, cranking the engines. The noise was deafening. "Still workin' rescue at Baghdad," he said. "Be at least another hour."

"Roger that."

Mac shut the chopper down. "Bought us some time," he said.

Rayford covered his eyes briefly. "God," he prayed silently, "all I can do is trust you and follow my instincts. I believe this man is sincere. If he's not, keep me from saying anything I shouldn't. If he is sincere, I don't want to keep from telling him what he needs to know. You've been so overt, so clear with Buck and Tsion. Couldn't you give me a sign? Anything that would assure me I'm doing the right thing?"

Rayford looked uncertainly into Mac's eyes, dimly illuminated by the glow from the control panel. For the moment, God seemed silent. He had not made a habit of speaking directly to Rayford, though Rayford had enjoyed his share of answers to prayer. There was no turning back now. While he sensed no divine green light, neither did he sense a red or even a yellow. Knowing the outcome could be a result of his own foolishness, he realized he had nothing to lose.

"Mac, I'm gonna tell you my whole story and everything I feel about what's happened, about Nicolae, and about what is to come. But before I do, I need you to tell me what Carpathia knows, if you know, about whether Hattie or Amanda were really expected in Baghdad tonight."

Mac sighed and looked away, and Rayford's heart

fell. Clearly he was about to hear something he'd rather not hear.

"Well, Ray, the truth is Carpathia knows Hattie is still in the States. She got as far as Boston, but his sources tell him she boarded a nonstop to Denver before the earthquake hit."

"To Denver? I thought that's where she had come from."

"It was. That's where her family is. Nobody knows why she went back."

Rayford's voice caught in his throat. "And Amanda?"

"Carpathia's people tell him she was on a Pan-Con heavy out of Boston that should have been on the ground in Baghdad before the quake hit. It had lost a little time over the Atlantic for some reason, but the last he knew, it was in Iraqi airspace."

Rayford dropped his head and fought for composure. "So, it's underground somewhere," he said. "Why wouldn't I have seen it at the airport?"

"I don't know," Mac said. "Maybe it was completely swallowed by the desert. But all the other planes monitored by Baghdad tower have been accounted for, so that doesn't seem likely."

"There's still hope then," Rayford said. "Maybe that pilot was far enough behind schedule that he was still in the air and just stayed there until everything stopped moving and he could find a spot to put down."

"Maybe," Mac said, but Rayford detected flatness in his voice. Clearly, Mac was dubious.

"I won't stop looking until I know." Mac nodded, and

Rayford sensed something more. "Mac, what are you not telling me?" Mac looked down and shook his head. "Listen to me, Mac. I've already hinted what I think of Carpathia. That's a huge risk for me. I don't know where your true loyalties lie, and I'm about to tell you more than I should tell anyone that I wouldn't trust with my life. If you know something about Amanda that I need to know, you've got to tell me."

Mac drew a hesitant breath. "You really don't want to know. Trust me, you don't want to know."

"Is she dead?"

"Probably," he said. "I honestly don't know that, and I don't think Carpathia does either. But this is worse than that, Rayford. This is worse than her being dead."

Getting into the garage at the wreckage of Loretta's home seemed impossible even for two grown men. It had been attached to the house and somehow appeared the least damaged. There was no basement under the garage area, thus not far for its cement slab and foundation to go. When the roof had fallen in, the sectioned doors had been so heavily compressed that their panels had overlapped by several inches. One door was angled at least two feet off track, pointing to the right. The other was off track about half that much and pointed in the other direction. There was no budging them. All Buck and Tsion could do was start hacking through them. In their normal state, the wood doors might easily have been cracked through, but now they sat with a huge section of roof and eaves jamming them awkwardly down to concrete, which rested two feet below the surface.

To Buck, every whack at the wood with his ax felt as if he were crashing steel against steel. With both hands at the bottom of the handle and swinging with all his might, the best he could do was chip tiny pieces with each blow. This was a quality door, made only more solid by the crush of nature.

Buck was exhausted. Only nervous energy and grief held in check kept him going. With every swing of the ax, his desire grew to find Chloe. He knew the odds were against him, but he believed he could face her loss if he knew anything for sure. He went from hoping and praying that he would find her alive to that he would simply find her in a state that proved she died relatively painlessly. It wouldn't be long, he feared, before he would be praying that he find her regardless.

Tsion Ben-Judah was in good shape for his age. Up until he had gone into hiding, he had worked out every day. He had told Buck that though he had never been an athlete, he knew that the health of his scholar's mind depended also on the health of his body. Tsion was keeping up his end of the task, whaling away at the door in various spots, testing for any weakness that would allow him to drive through it more quickly. He was panting and sweating, yet still he tried to talk while he worked.

"Cameron, you do not expect to find Chloe's car in here anyway, do you?"

"No."

"And if you do not, from that you will conclude that she somehow escaped?"

"That's my hope."

"So this is a process of elimination?"

"That's right."

"As soon as we have established that her car is not here, Cameron, let us try to salvage whatever we can from the house."

"Like what?"

"Foodstuffs. Your clothes. Did you say you had already cleared your bedroom area?"

"Yes, but I didn't see the closet or its contents. It can't be far."

"And the chest of drawers? Surely you have clothes in there."

"Good idea," Buck said.

Between the two axes and their resounding *thwack*s against the garage door, Buck heard something else. He stopped swinging and held up a hand to stop Tsion. The older man leaned on his ax to catch his breath, and Buck recognized the *thump-thump-thump* of helicopter blades. It grew so loud and close that Buck assumed it was two or three choppers. But when he caught sight of the craft, he was astounded to see it was just one, big as a bus. The only other he'd seen like it was in the Holy Land during an air attack years before.

But this one, setting down just a hundred or so yards away, resembled those old gray-and-black Israeli transport choppers only in size. This was sparkling white and appeared to have just come off the assembly line. It carried the huge insignia of the Global Community.

"Do you believe this?" Buck asked.

"What do you make of it?" Tsion said.

"No idea. I just hope they're not looking for you."

"Frankly, Cameron, I think I have become a very low priority to the GC all of a sudden, don't you?"

"We'll find out soon enough. Come on."

They dropped their axes and crept back to the upturned pavement that had served as Loretta's street not that many hours before. Through a gouge in that fortress they saw the GC copter settle next to a toppled utility pole. A high-tension wire snapped and crackled on the ground while at least a dozen GC emergency workers piled out of the aircraft. The leader communicated on a walkie-talkie, and within seconds power was cut to the area and the sparking line fell dead. The leader directed a wire cutter to snip the other lines that led to the power pole.

Two uniformed officers carried a large circular metal framework from the helicopter, and technicians quickly jury-rigged a connection that fastened it to one end of the now bare pole. Meanwhile, others used a massive earth drill to dig a new hole for the pole. A water tank and fast-setting concrete mixer dumped a solution in the hole, and a portable pulley was anchored on four sides by two officers putting their entire weight on its metal feet at each corner. The rest maneuvered the quickly refashioned pole into position. It was drawn up to a forty-five degree angle, and three officers bent low to slide its bottom end into the hole. The pulley tightened and straightened the pole, which dropped fast and deep, sending the excess concrete solution shooting up the sides of the pole.

Within seconds, everything was reloaded into the helicopter and the GC team lifted off. In fewer than five minutes, a utility pole that had borne both electrical power and telephone lines had been transformed.

Buck turned to Tsion. "Do you realize what we just saw?"

"Unbelievable," Tsion said. "It is now a cell tower, is it not?"

"It is. It's lower than it should be, but it will do the trick. Somebody believes that keeping the cell areas functioning is more important than electricity or telephone wires."

Buck pulled his phone from his pocket. It showed full power and full range, at least in the shadow of that new tower. "I wonder," he said, "how long it will be before enough towers are up to allow us to call anywhere again."

Tsion had started back toward the garage. Buck caught up with him. "It cannot be long," Tsion said. "Carpathia must have crews like this working around the clock all over the world."

❧

"We better get heading back soon," Mac said.

"Oh sure," Rayford said. "I'm going to let you take me

back to Carpathia and his safe shelter before you tell me something about my own wife that I'll hate worse than knowing she's dead?"

"Ray, please don't make me say any more. I said too much already. I can't corroborate any of this stuff, and I don't trust Carpathia."

"Just tell me," Rayford said.

"But if you respond the way I would, you won't want to talk about what I want to talk about."

Rayford had nearly forgotten. And Mac was right. The prospect of bad news about his wife had made him obsess over it to the exclusion of anything else important enough to talk about.

"Mac, I give you my word I'll answer any question you have and talk about anything you want. But you must tell me anything you know about Amanda."

Mac still seemed reluctant. "Well, for one thing, I do know that that Pan-Con heavy would not have had enough fuel to go looking for somewhere else to land. If the quake happened before they touched down and it became obvious to the pilot he couldn't land at Baghdad, he wouldn't have had a whole lot farther to go."

"So that's good news, Mac. Since I didn't find the plane at Baghdad, it has to be somewhere relatively close by. I'll keep looking. Meanwhile, tell me what you know."

"All right, Ray. I don't guess we're at any point in history where it makes sense to play games. If this doesn't convince you I'm not one of Carpathia's spies, nothing will. If it gets back that I quoted him to you, I'm a dead man. So regardless of what you think of this or how you react to it or what you might want to say to him about it, you can't ever let on. Understand?"

"Yes, yes! Now what?"

Mac took a breath but, maddeningly, said nothing. Rayford was about to explode. "I gotta get out of this cockpit," Mac said finally, unbuckling himself. "Go on, Ray. Get out. Don't make me climb over you."

Mac was out of his seat and standing between his and Rayford's, bent low to keep from knocking his head on the ceiling of the Plexiglas bubble. Rayford unstrapped himself and popped the door open, jumping down into the sand. He was through begging. He simply determined he would not let Mac back in that chopper until he told him whatever it was he needed to know.

Mac stood there, hands thrust deep into his pants pockets. Light from the full moon highlighted the reddish-blond hair, the craggy features, and the freckles on his weathered face. He looked like a man on his way to the gallows.

Mac suddenly stepped forward and put both palms on the side of the chopper. His head hung low. Finally, he raised it and turned to face Rayford. "All right, here it is. Don't forget you made me tell you. . . . Carpathia talks about Amanda like he knows her."

Rayford grimaced and held his hands out, palms up. He shrugged. "He does know her. So what?"

"No! I mean he talks about her as if he *really* knows her."

"What's that supposed to mean? An affair? I know better than that."

"No, Ray! I'm saying he talks about her as if he's known her since before she knew you."

Rayford nearly dropped in the sand. "You're not saying—"

"I'm telling you that behind closed doors, Carpathia makes comments about Amanda. She's a team player, he says. She's in the right place. She plays her role well. That kind of stuff. What am I supposed to make of that?"

Rayford could not speak. He didn't believe it. No, of course not. But the very idea. The gall of that man to make such an implication about the character of a woman Rayford knew so well.

"I hardly know your wife, Ray. I have no idea if it's possible. I'm just telling you what—"

"It's not possible," Rayford finally managed. "I know you don't know her, but I do."

"I didn't expect you to believe it, Ray. I'm not even saying it makes me suspicious."

"You don't have to be suspicious. The man is a liar. He works for the father of lies. He would say anything about anybody to further his own agenda. I don't know why he needs to besmirch her reputation, but—"

"Ray, I told you I'm not saying I think he's right or

anything. But you have to admit he's getting information from somewhere."

"Don't even suggest—"

"I'm not suggesting anything. I'm just saying—"

"Mac, I can't say I've known Amanda long in the larger scheme of things. I can't say she bore me children like my first wife did. I can't say we've been together twenty years like I was with Irene. I *can* say, though, that we are not just husband and wife. We are brother and sister in Christ. If I had shared Irene's faith, she and I would have been true soul mates too, but that was my fault. Amanda and I met after we had both become believers, and so we shared an almost instantaneous bond. It is a bond no one could break. That woman is no more a liar or a betrayer or a subversive or a turncoat than anyone. No one could be that good. No one could share my bed and hold my gaze and pledge her love and loyalty to me that earnestly and be a liar without my suspecting. No way."

"That's good enough for me, Cap," Mac said.

Rayford was furious with Carpathia. If he had not pledged to maintain Mac's confidentiality, it would have been difficult to stop himself from jumping on the radio right then and demanding to talk directly to Nicolae. He wondered how he would face the man. What would he say or do when he saw him later?

"Why should I expect any different from a man like him?" Rayford said.

"Good question," Mac said. "Now we'd better get back, don't you think?"

Rayford wanted to tell Mac he was still willing to talk about the questions he had raised, but he really didn't feel like talking anymore. If Mac raised it again, Rayford would follow through. But if Mac let him off the hook, he'd be grateful to wait for a better time.

"Mac," he said as they strapped themselves into the chopper, "since we're supposed to be on a rescue mission anyway, would you mind doing a twenty-five-mile circle search?"

"It'd sure be a lot easier during daylight," Mac said. "You want me to bring you back tomorrow?"

"Yeah, but let's do a cursory look right now anyway. If that plane went down anywhere near Baghdad, the only hope of finding survivors is to find them quick."

Rayford saw sympathy on Mac's face.

"I know," Rayford said. "I'm dreaming. But I can't run back to Carpathia and take advantage of shelter and supplies if I don't exhaust every effort to find Amanda."

"I was just wondering," Mac said. "If there *was* anything to Carpathia's claims—"

"There's not, Mac, and I mean it. Now get off of that."

"I'm just saying, if there is, do you think there might be a chance that he would have had her on another plane? Kept her safe somehow?"

"Oh, I get it!" Rayford said. "The upside of my wife working for the enemy is that she might still be alive?"

"I wasn't looking at it that way," Mac said.

"What's the point then?"

"No point. We don't have to talk about it anymore."

"We sure don't."

But as Mac took the chopper in wider and wider concentric circles from the Baghdad terminal, all Rayford saw on the ground was shifting and sinking sand. Now he wanted to find Amanda, not just for himself, but also to prove that she was who he knew her to be.

By the time they gave up the search and Mac promised the dispatcher they were finally on their way in, a sliver of doubt had crept into Rayford's mind. He felt guilty for entertaining it at all, but he could not shake it. He feared the damage that sliver could do to his love and reverence for this woman who had completed his life, and he was determined to eradicate it from his mind.

His problem was that despite how romantic she had made him, and how emotional he had waxed since his conversion (and his exposure to more tragedy than anyone should ever endure), he still possessed the practical, analytical, scientific mind that made him the airman he was. He hated that he couldn't simply dismiss a doubt because it didn't fit what he felt in his heart. He would have to exonerate Amanda by somehow proving her loyalty and the genuineness of her faith—with her help if she was alive, and without it if she was dead.

It was midafternoon when Buck and Tsion finally ripped a big enough hole in one of the garage doors to allow Tsion to crawl through.

Tsion's voice was so hoarse and faint that Buck had to turn his ear toward the opening. "Cameron, Chloe's car is here. I can get the door open just far enough to put the inside light on. It is empty except for her phone and computer."

"I'll meet you at the back of the house!" Buck shouted. "Hurry, Tsion! If her car's still here, she's still here!"

Buck scooped up as many of the tools as he could carry and raced to the back. This was the evidence he had hoped and prayed for. If Chloe was buried in that rubble, and there was one chance in a million she was still alive, he would not rest.

Buck attacked the wreckage with all his might, having to remind himself to breathe. Tsion appeared and picked up a shovel and an ax. "Should I start in at some other location?" he asked.

"No! We have to work together if we have any hope!"

CHAPTER 4

"SO WHAT HAPPENED to the dusty clothes?" Rayford whispered as he and Mac were escorted into the auxiliary entrance of Carpathia's huge underground shelter. Far across the structure, past the Condor 216 and amongst many subordinates and assistants, Fortunato looked chipper in a fresh suit.

"Nicolae's got him cleaned up already," Mac muttered.

Rayford had eaten nothing for more than twelve hours but had not thought about hunger until now. The milling crowd of surprisingly upbeat Carpathia lackeys had been through a buffet line and sat balancing plates and cups on their knees.

Suddenly ravenous, Rayford noticed ham, chicken, and

beef, as well as all sorts of Middle Eastern delicacies. Fortunato greeted him with a smile and a handshake. Rayford did not smile and barely gripped the man's hand.

"Potentate Carpathia would like us to join him in his office in a few moments. But please, eat first."

"Don't mind if I do," Rayford said. Though an employee, he felt as if he was eating in the enemy's camp. Yet it would be foolish to go hungry just to make a point. He needed strength.

As he and Mac made their way around the buffet, Mac whispered, "Maybe we shouldn't look too buddy-buddy."

"Yeah," Rayford said. "Carpathia knows where I stand, but I assume he sees you as a loyalist."

"I'm not, but there's no future for those who admit that."

"Like me?" Rayford said.

"A future for you? Not a long one. But what can I say? He likes you. Maybe he feels secure knowing you don't hide anything from him."

Rayford ate even as he ladled choices onto his plate. *It might be the enemy's food,* he thought, *but it does the job.*

He felt well fed and suddenly logy when he and Mac were ushered into Carpathia's office. Mac's presence surprised Rayford. He had never before been in on a meeting with Carpathia.

As was often true during times of international crisis and terror, it seemed Nicolae could barely contain a grin. He too had changed into fresh clothes and appeared well rested. Rayford knew he himself looked terrible.

"Please," Carpathia said expansively, "Captain Steele and Officer McCullum. Sit."

"I prefer to stand, if you don't mind," Rayford said.

"There is no need. You look weary, and we have important items on the agenda."

Rayford reluctantly settled into a chair. He did not understand these people. Here was a beautifully decorated office that rivaled Carpathia's main digs, now in a pile less than half a mile away. How was it this man was prepared for every eventuality?

Leon Fortunato stood at a corner of Carpathia's desk. Carpathia sat on the front edge, staring down at Rayford, who decided to beat him to the punch. "Sir, my wife. I—"

"Captain Steele, I have some bad news for you."

"Oh, no." Rayford's mind immediately went on the defensive. It didn't feel as if Amanda was dead, and so she wasn't. He didn't care what this liar said—the same man who dared call her his compatriot. If Carpathia said Amanda was dead, Rayford didn't know if he could keep Mac's confidence and refrain from attacking him and making him retract the slander.

"Your wife, God rest her soul, was—"

Rayford gripped the chair so tight he thought his fingertips might burst. He clenched his teeth. The Antichrist himself bestowing a God-rest-her-soul on his wife? Rayford trembled with rage. He prayed desperately that if it was true, if he had lost Amanda, that God would use him in the death of Nicolae Carpathia. That was not to come until three and a half years into the Tribulation, and the Bible foretold that Antichrist would then be resurrected and indwelt by Satan anyway. Still, Rayford pleaded with God for the privilege of killing this man. What satisfaction, what revenge he might exact from it, he did not know. It was all he could do to keep from executing the deed right then.

"As you know, she was aboard a Pan-Continental 747 flight from Boston to Baghdad today. The earthquake hit moments before the plane was to touch down. The best our sources can tell is that the pilot apparently saw the chaos, realized he could not land near the airport, pulled up, and turned the plane around."

Rayford knew what was coming, if the story was true. The pilot would not have had power to regain altitude if he both pulled up and turned around that quickly.

"Pan-Con officials tell me," Carpathia continued, "that the plane was simply not airworthy at that speed. Eyewitnesses say it cleared the banks of the Tigris, hit first nearly halfway across the river, flipped tail up, then plunged out of sight."

Rayford's whole body pulsed with every heartbeat. He lowered his chin to his chest and fought for composure. He looked up at Carpathia, wanting details, but could not open his mouth, let alone utter a sound.

"The current is swift there, Captain Steele. But Pan-Con tells me a plane like that would drop like a stone. Nothing has surfaced downriver. No bodies have been discovered. It will be days before we get equipment for a salvage operation. I am sorry."

Rayford no more believed Carpathia was sorry than that Amanda was dead. He believed even less that she had ever acted in concert with Nicolae Carpathia.

Buck worked like a madman, his fingers nicked and blistered. Chloe had to be in there somewhere. He didn't want to talk. He just wanted to dig. But Tsion enjoyed hashing things over. "I do not understand, Cameron," he said, "why Chloe's car would have been in the garage where Loretta's car usually sits."

"I don't know," Buck said dismissively. "But it's there, and that means she's here somewhere."

"Perhaps the earthquake plunged the car right into the garage," Tsion suggested.

"Unlikely," Buck said. "I don't really care. I'm still kicking myself for not noticing her car missing when I got here."

"What would you have surmised?"

"That she had driven away! Escaped."

"Is that not still possible?"

Buck straightened up and pressed his knuckles into his back, trying to stretch sore muscles. "She wouldn't have gotten anywhere on foot. This thing hit so suddenly. There was no warning."

"Oh, but there was."

Buck stared at the rabbi. "You were underground, Tsion. How would you know?"

"I heard rumblings, a couple of minutes before the shaking began."

Buck had been in his Range Rover. He had seen roadkill, dogs barking and running, and other animals not usually seen in the daytime. Before the sky turned black he had noticed not a leaf moving, yet stoplights and traffic signs swayed. That was when he knew the earthquake was coming. There had been at least a brief warning. Was it possible Chloe had had an inkling? What would she have done? Where would she have gone?

Buck went back to digging. "What did you say was in her car, Tsion?"

"Just her computer and her phone."

Buck stopped digging. "Could she be in the garage?"

"I am afraid not, Cameron. I looked carefully. If she was there when it all came down," Tsion said, "you would not want to find her anyway."

I might not like it, Buck thought, *but I have to know.*

Rayford's body went rigid when Carpathia touched his shoulder. He envisioned leaping from the chair and choking the life out of Carpathia. He sat seething, eyes closed, feeling as if he were about to explode.

"I can sympathize with your grief," Nicolae said. "Perhaps you can understand my own feeling of loss over the many lives this calamity has cost. It was worldwide, every continent suffering severe damage. The only region spared was Israel."

Rayford wrenched away from Carpathia's touch and regained his voice. "And you don't believe this was the wrath of the Lamb?"

"Rayford, Rayford," Carpathia said. "Surely you do not lay at the feet of some Supreme Being an act so spiteful and capricious and deadly as this."

Rayford shook his head. What had he been thinking? Was he actually trying to persuade the Antichrist he was wrong?

Carpathia moved behind his desk to a high-backed leather chair. "Let me tell you what I am going to tell the rest of the staff, so you can skip the meeting and find your quarters and get some rest."

"I don't mind hearing it along with the rest."

"Magnanimous, Captain Steele. However, there are as well things I need to say only to you. I hesitate to raise this while your loss is so fresh, but you do understand that I could have you imprisoned."

"I'm sure you could," Rayford said.

"But I choose not to do that."

Should he feel grateful or disappointed? A stretch in prison didn't sound bad. If he knew his daughter and son-in-law and Tsion were all right, he could endure that.

Carpathia continued, "I understand you better than you know. We will put behind us our encounter, and you will continue to serve me in the manner you have up to now."

"And if I resign?"

"That is not an option. You will come through this nobly,

as you have other crises. Otherwise, I will charge you with insubordination and have you imprisoned."

"That's putting the encounter behind us? You *want* someone working for you who would rather not?"

"In time I will win you over," Carpathia said. "You are aware that your living quarters were destroyed?"

"I can't say I'm surprised."

"Teams will try to salvage anything of use. Meanwhile, we have uniforms and necessities for you. You will find your quarters adequate, though not luxurious. Top priority for my administration is to rebuild New Babylon. It will become the new capital of the world. All banking, commerce, religion, and government will start and end right here. The greatest rebuilding challenge in the rest of the world is in communications. We have already begun rebuilding an international network that—"

"Communications is more important than people? More than cleaning up areas that might otherwise become diseased? Clearing away bodies? Reuniting families?"

"In due time, Captain Steele. Such efforts depend on communications too. Fortunately, the timing of my most ambitious project could not have been more propitious. The Global Community recently secured sole ownership of all international satellite and cellular communications companies. We will have in place in a few months the first truly global communications network. It is cellular, and it is solar powered. I call it Cellular-Solar. Once the cell towers have been re-erected and satellites are maneuvered to geosynchronous orbit, anyone will be able to communicate with anyone else anywhere at any time."

Carpathia appeared to have lost the ability to hide his glee. If this technology worked, it solidified Carpathia's grip on the earth. His takeover was complete. He owned and controlled everything and everybody.

"As soon as you are up to it, you and Officer McCullum are to fly my ambassadors here. A handful of major airports around the world are operational, but with the use of smaller aircraft, we should be able to get my key men to where you can collect them in the Condor 216 and deliver them to me."

Rayford could not concentrate. "I have a couple of requests," he said.

"I love when you ask," Carpathia said.

"I would like information about my family."

"I will put someone on that right away. And?"

"I need a day or two to be trained by Mac in helicopters. I may be called upon to ferry someone from somewhere only a chopper can go."

"Whatever you need, Captain, you know that."

Rayford glanced at Mac, who looked puzzled. He shouldn't have been surprised. Unless Mac was a closet Carpathia sympathizer, they had serious things to discuss. They wouldn't be able to do that inside, where every room was likely wiretapped. Rayford wanted Mac for the kingdom. He would be a wonderful addition to the Tribulation Force, especially as long as they kept his true loyalties from Carpathia.

"I am weak from hunger, Cameron," Tsion said. They had dug halfway through the rubble, Buck despairing more with every shovelful. There was plenty of evidence Chloe lived in this place, but none that she was still there, dead or alive.

"I can dig to the basement within the hour, Tsion. Start on the kitchen. You might find food there. I'm hungry too."

Even with Tsion just around the side of the house, Buck felt overwhelmed with loneliness. His eyes stung with tears as he dug and grabbed and lifted and tossed in what was a likely futile effort to find his wife.

Early in the evening Buck climbed wearily out of the basement at the back corner. He dragged his shovel to the front, willing to help Tsion, but hoping the rabbi had found something to eat.

Tsion lifted a split and crushed secretary desk and flung it at Buck's feet. "Oh, Cameron! I did not see you there."

"Trying to get to the refrigerator?"

"Exactly. The power has been out for hours, but there must be something edible still in there."

Two large beams were lodged in front of the refrigerator door. As Buck tried to help move them, his foot caught the edge of the broken desk, and papers and phone books flopped out onto the ground. One was the membership directory at New Hope Village Church. *That might come in handy,* he thought. He rolled it up and stuck it in his pants pocket.

A few minutes later Buck and Tsion sat back against the

refrigerator, munching. That took the edge off his hunger, but Buck felt he could sleep for a week. The last thing he wanted was to finish digging. He dreaded evidence that Chloe had died. He was grateful Tsion finally didn't need to converse. Buck needed to think. Where would they spend the night? What would they eat tomorrow? But for now, Buck wanted to just sit, eat, and let memories of Chloe wash over him.

How he loved her! Was it possible he had known her less than two years? She had seemed much older than twenty when they had met, and she had the bearing of someone ten or fifteen years older now. She had been a gift from God, more precious than anything he had ever received except salvation. What would his life have been worth following the Rapture, had it not been for Chloe? He would have been grateful and would have enjoyed that deep satisfaction of knowing he was right with God, but he would have also been lonely and alone.

Even now, Buck was grateful for his father-in-law and Amanda. Grateful for his friendship with Chaim Rosenzwieg. Grateful for his friendship with Tsion. He and Tsion would have to work on Chaim. The old Israeli was still enamored of Carpathia. That had to change. Chaim needed Christ. So did Ken Ritz, the pilot Buck had used so many times. He would have to check on Ken, make sure he was all right, see if he had planes that still flew. He pushed his food aside and hung his head, nearly asleep.

"I need to go back to Israel," Tsion said.

"Hm?" Buck mumbled.

"I need to go back to my homeland."

Buck raised his head and stared at Tsion. "We're homeless," he said. "We can barely drive to the next block. We don't know we'll survive tomorrow. You are a hunted criminal in Israel. You think they'll forget about you, now that they have earthquake relief to do?"

"On the contrary. But I have to assume the bulk of the 144,000 witnesses, of whom I am one, must come from Israel. Not all of them will. Many will come from tribes all over the globe. But the greatest source of Jews is Israel. These will be zealous as Paul but new to the faith and untrained. I feel a call to meet them and greet them and teach them. They must be mobilized and sent out. They are already empowered."

"Let's assume I get you to Israel. How do I keep you alive?"

"What, you think *you* kept me alive on our flight across the Sinai?"

"I helped."

"You helped? You amuse me, Cameron. In many ways, yes, I owe you my life. But you were as much in the way as I was. That was God's work, and we both know it."

Buck stood. "Fair enough. Still, taking you back to where you are a fugitive seems lunacy."

He helped Tsion stand. "Send word ahead that I was killed in the earthquake," the rabbi said. "Then I can go in disguise under one of those phony names you come up with."

"Not without plastic surgery you won't," Buck said. "You're a recognizable guy, even in Israel where everybody your age looks like you."

The sunlight softened and faded as they finished picking through the kitchen. Tsion found plastic bags and wrapped food he would store in the car. Buck wrenched a few clothes out of the mess that had been his and Chloe's bedroom while Tsion collected Chloe's computer and phone from the garage.

Neither had the strength to climb over the pavement barrier, so they took the long way around. When they reached the Range Rover, both had to get in the passenger side.

"And so what do you think now?" Tsion said. "If Chloe were alive somewhere in there, she would have heard us and called out to us, would she not?"

Buck nodded miserably. "I'm trying to resign myself to the fact that she's at the bottom. I was wrong, that's all. She wasn't in the bedroom or the kitchen or the basement. Maybe she ran to another part of the house. It would take heavy equipment to pull all the trash out of that place and find her. I can't imagine leaving her there, but neither can I think about more digging tonight."

Buck drove toward the church. "Should we stay in the shelter tonight?"

"I worry it is unstable," Tsion said. "Another shift and it could come down on us."

Buck drove on. He was a mile south of the church when he came to a neighborhood twisted and shaken but not broken. Many structures were damaged, but most still stood. A filling station, illuminated by butane torches, serviced a small line of cars.

"We're not the only civilians who survived," Tsion said.

Buck pulled into line. The man running the station had a shotgun propped up against the pumps. He shouted over a gasoline generator, "Cash only! Twenty-gallon limit! When it's gone, it's gone."

Buck topped off his tank and said, "I'll give you a thousand cash for—"

"The generator, yeah, I know. Take a number. I could get ten thousand for it by tomorrow."

"Know where I could get another one?"

"I don't know anything," the man said wearily. "My house is gone. I'll be sleeping here tonight."

"Need some company?"

"Not especially. If you get desperate, come back. I wouldn't turn you away."

Buck couldn't blame him. Where would you start and end taking in strangers at a time like this?

"Cameron," Tsion began when Buck got back in the car, "I have been thinking. Do we know whether the computer technician's wife knows about her husband?"

Buck shook his head. "I met his wife only one time. I don't remember her name. Wait a minute." He dug into his pocket and pulled out the church directory. "Here it is," he said. "Sandy. Let me call her." He punched in the numbers, and while he was not surprised the call did not go through, he was encouraged to get as far as a recorded message that all circuits were busy. That was progress, at least.

"Where do they live?" Tsion said. "It's not likely standing, but we could check."

Buck read the street address. "I don't know where that is." He saw a squad car ahead, lights flashing. "Let's ask him." The cop was leaning against his car, having a cigarette. "You on duty?" Buck asked.

"Takin' a break," the cop said. "I've seen more in one day than I cared to see in a lifetime, if you know what I mean." Buck showed him the address. "I don't know what I'll tell you as far as landmarks, but, ah, just follow me."

"You sure?"

"There's nothin' more I can do for anybody tonight. In fact, I didn't do anybody any good today. Follow me, and I'll point out the street you want. Then I'm gone."

A few minutes later Buck flashed his lights in thanks and pulled in front of a duplex. Tsion opened the passenger door, but Buck put a hand on his arm.

"Let me see Chloe's phone."

Tsion crawled back and fished it from a pile he had wrapped in a blanket. Buck flipped it open and found it had been left on. He rummaged in the glove box and produced a cigarette lighter adapter that fit the phone and made it come to life. He touched a button that brought up the last dialed number. He sighed. It was his own.

Tsion nodded, and they got out. Buck pulled a flashlight from his emergency toolbox. The left side of the duplex had broken windows all around and a foundational brick wall that had crumbled and left the front of the place sagging. Buck got into position where he could shine his light through the windows.

"Empty," he said. "No furniture."

"Look," Tsion said. A For Rent sign lay in the grass.

Buck looked again at the directory. "Donny and Sandy lived on the other side."

The place looked remarkably intact. The drapes were open. Buck gripped the wrought iron railing on the steps and leaned over to flash his light into the living room. It looked lived-in. Buck tried the front door and found it unlocked. As he and Tsion tiptoed through the house, it became obvious something was amiss in the tiny breakfast nook at the back. Buck gaped, and Tsion turned away and bent at the waist.

Sandy Moore had been at the table with her newspaper and coffee when a huge oak tree crashed through the roof with such force that it flattened her and the heavy wood table. The dead girl's finger was still curled around the cup handle, and her cheek rested on the Tempo section of the *Chicago Tribune.* Had not the rest of her body been compressed to inches, she might have appeared to be dozing.

"She and her husband must have died within seconds of each other," Tsion said quietly. "Miles apart."

Buck nodded in the faint light. "We should bury this girl."

"We will never get her out from under that tree," Tsion said.

"We have to try."

In the alley Buck found planks, which they forced under the tree as levers, but a trunk with enough mass to destroy roof, wall, window, woman, and table would not be budged.

"We need heavy equipment," Tsion said.

"What's the use?" Buck said. "No one will ever be able to bury all of the dead."

"I confess I am thinking less of respect for her body than for the possibility that we have found a place to live." Buck shot him a double take. "What?" Tsion said. "Is it not ideal? There's actually a bit of pavement out front. This room, open to the elements, can be easily closed off. I don't know how long it would take to get power, but—"

"Say no more," Buck said. "We have no other prospects."

Buck threaded the Rover between the duplex and the burned-out shell of whatever had been next door. He parked out of sight in the back, and he and Tsion unloaded the car. Coming through the back door Buck noticed they might be able to extricate Mrs. Moore's body from underneath. Branches were lodged against a huge cabinet in the corner. That would keep the tree from dropping further if they could somehow cut under the floor.

"I am so tired I can barely stand, Cameron," Tsion said as they descended narrow stairs to the cellar.

"I'm about to collapse myself," Buck said. He shined his light toward the underside of the first floor and saw that Sandy's elbow had been driven through and hung exposed. They found mostly discarded computer parts until they came upon Donny's stash of tools. *A hammer, chisels, a crowbar, and a handsaw should do it,* Buck thought. He dragged a stepladder under the spot, and Tsion held it as Buck wrapped his legs around the top step to brace himself. Then began the arduous task of driving the crowbar up through the floorboards with a hammer. His arms ached, but he stayed at it until he had punched out a few holes large enough to get the saw wedged in. He and Tsion traded off sawing the hardwood, which seemed to take forever with the dull blade.

They were careful not to touch Sandy Moore's body with the saw. Buck was struck that the shape of the cut looked like the pine boxes in which cowboys were buried in the old west. When they had sawn to about her waist, the weight of her upper body made the boards beneath her give way, and she slowly dropped into Buck's arms. He gasped and held his breath, fighting to keep his balance. His shirt was covered with her sticky blood, and she felt light and fragile as a child.

Tsion guided him down. All Buck could think of as he carried her broken body out the back door was that this was what he had expected to do with Chloe at Loretta's. He lay her body gently in the dewy grass, and he and Tsion quickly dug a shallow grave. The work was easy because the quake had loosened the topsoil. Before they lowered her into the hole, Buck pulled Donny's wedding ring from deep in his pocket. He put it in her palm and closed her fingers around it. They covered her with the dirt. Tsion knelt, and Buck followed suit.

Tsion had not known Donny or his wife. He pronounced no eulogy. He merely quoted an old hymn, which made Buck cry so loudly he knew he could be heard down the block. But no one was around, and he could not stop the sobs.

> *"I will love Thee in life, I will love Thee in death,*
> *And praise Thee as long as Thou lendest me breath;*
> *And say, when the death-dew lies cold on my brow;*
> *If ever I loved Thee, my Jesus, 'tis now."*

Buck and Tsion found two tiny bedrooms upstairs, one with a double bed, the other with a single. "Take the bigger bed," Tsion insisted. "I pray Chloe will join you soon." Buck took him up on it.

Buck went into the bathroom and shed his mud- and blood-caked clothes. With only his flashlight for illumination, he hand dipped enough water out of the toilet tank for a sponge bath. He found a big towel to dry off with, then collapsed onto Donny and Sandy Moore's bed.

Buck slept the sleep of the mourning, praying he would never have to wake up.

Half a world away, Rayford Steele was awakened by a phone call from his first officer. It was nine o'clock Tuesday morning in New Babylon, and he had to face another day whether he wanted to or not. At the very least, he hoped he would get a chance to tell Mac about God.

CHAPTER 5

RAYFORD ATE with the stragglers at a bountiful breakfast. Across the way, dozens of aides hunched over maps and charts and crowded phone and radio banks. He ate lethargically, Mac next to him drumming his fingers and bouncing a foot. Carpathia sat with Fortunato and other senior staffers at a table not far from his office. Now he pressed a cell phone to his ear and talked earnestly in a corner, his back to the room.

Rayford eyed him with disinterest. He wondered about himself now, about his resolve. If it was true Amanda had gone down with the 747, Chloe and Buck and Tsion were all he cared about. Could he be the only Tribulation Force member left standing?

Rayford could muster not a whit of interest in whom Carpathia might be talking to or what about. If a gadget allowed him to listen in, he wouldn't even flip the switch. He had prayed before he ate, a prayer ambivalent about sustenance provided by the Antichrist. Still, he had eaten. And it was good that he had. His spirits began to lift. No way could he cogently share his faith with Mac if he stayed in a funk.

Mac's fidgeting made him nervous. "Eager to get flying?" Rayford said.

"Eager to get talking. But not here. Too many ears. But are you up for this, Rayford? With what you're going through?"

Mac seemed as ready to hear about God as anyone he had ever talked to. Why did it happen this way? When he had been most eager to share, he had tried to get through to his old senior pilot, Earl Halliday, who had had no interest and was now dead. He had tried without success to reach Hattie Durham, and now he could only pray there was still time for her. Here was Mac, in essence begging him for the truth, and Rayford would rather be back in bed.

He crossed his legs and folded his arms. He would will himself to move today. In the corner Carpathia wheeled around and stared at him, the phone still at his ear. Nicolae waved enthusiastically, then seemed to think better of showing such enthusiasm to a man who had just lost his wife. His face grew somber and his wave stiffened. Rayford did not respond, though he held Carpathia's gaze. Nicolae beckoned with a finger.

"Oh, no," Mac said. "Let's go, let's go."

But they couldn't walk out on Nicolae Carpathia.

Rayford was in a testy mood. He didn't want to talk to Carpathia; Carpathia wanted to talk to him. He could come Rayford's way. *What have I become?* Rayford wondered. He was playing games with the potentate of the world. Petty. Silly. Immature. *But I don't care.*

Carpathia snapped his phone shut and slipped it into his pocket. He waved at Rayford, who pretended not to notice and turned his back. Rayford leaned toward Mac. "So, what are you going to teach me today?"

"Don't look now, but Carpathia wants you."

"He knows where I am."

"Ray! He could still toss you in jail."

"I wish he would. So anyway, what *are* you going to teach me today?"

"Teach you! You've flown whirlybirds."

"A long time ago," Rayford said. "More than twenty years."

"Chopper jockeying is like riding a bike," Mac said. "You'll be as good as me in an hour."

Mac looked over Rayford's shoulder, stood, and thrust out his hand. "Potentate Carpathia, sir!"

"Excuse Captain Steele and me for a moment, would you, Officer McCullum?"

"I'll meet you in the hangar," Rayford said.

Carpathia slid McCullum's chair close to Rayford's and sat. He unbuttoned his suit coat and leaned forward, forearms on his knees. Rayford still had legs crossed and arms folded.

Carpathia spoke earnestly. "Rayford, I hope you do not mind my calling you by your first name, but I know you are in pain."

Rayford tasted bile. "Lord, please," he prayed silently, "keep my mouth shut." It only made sense that the embodiment of evil himself was the slimiest of liars. To imply that Amanda had been his plant, a mole in the Tribulation Force for the Global Community, and then to feign sorrow over her death? A lethal wound to the head was too good for him. Rayford imagined torturing the man who led the forces of evil against the God of the universe.

"I wish you had been here earlier, Rayford. Well, actually I am glad you were able to get the rest you needed. But those of us here for the first breakfast were treated to Leon Fortunato's account of last night."

"Mac said something about it."

"Yes, Officer McCullum has heard it twice. You should ask him to share it with you again. Better yet, schedule some time with Mr. Fortunato."

It was all Rayford could do to feign civility. "I'm aware of Leon's devotion to you."

"As am I. However, even I was moved and flattered at how his view has been elevated."

Rayford knew the story but couldn't resist baiting Carpathia. "It doesn't surprise me that Leon is grateful for your rescuing him."

Carpathia sat back and looked amused. "McCullum has heard the story twice, and that is his assessment? Have you not heard? I did not rescue Mr. Fortunato at all! I did not even save his life! According to *his* testimony, I brought him back from the dead."

"Indeed."

"I do not claim this for myself, Rayford. I am telling you only what Mr. Fortunato says."

"You were there. What's *your* account?"

"Well, when I heard that my most trusted aide and personal confidant had been lost in the ruins of our head-quarters, something came over me. I simply refused to believe it. I willed it to be untrue. Every fiber of my being told me to simply go, by myself, to the site and bring him back."

"Too bad you didn't take witnesses."

"You do not believe me?"

"It's quite a tale."

"You must talk with Mr. Fortunato."

"I'm really not interested."

"Rayford, that fifty-foot pile of bricks, mortar, and debris had been a two-hundred-foot tall building. Leon Fortunato had been with me on the top floor when that building gave way. Despite the earthquake precautions designed into it, everyone in there should have been killed. And they were. You know there were no survivors."

"So you're saying it's Leon's contention, and yours, that even he was killed in the fall."

"I called him out of the middle of that wreckage. No one could have survived that."

"And yet he did."

"He did not. He was dead. He had to be."

"And how did you extricate him?"

"I commanded him to come forth, and he did."

Rayford leaned forward. "That had to make you believe the story of Lazarus. Too bad it's from a book of fairy tales, huh?"

"Now, Rayford, I have been most tolerant and have never disparaged your beliefs. Neither have I hidden that I believe you are, at best, misguided. But, yes, it gave me pause that this incident mirrored an account I believe was allegorical."

"Is it true you used the same words Jesus used with Lazarus?"

"So Mr. Fortunato says. I was unaware of precisely what I said. I left here with full confidence that I would come back with him, and my resolve never wavered, not even when I saw that mountain of ruins and knew that rescuers had found no one alive."

Rayford wanted to vomit. "So now you're some sort of deity?"

"That is not for me to say, though clearly, raising a dead man is a divine act. Mr. Fortunato believes I could be the Messiah."

Rayford raised his eyebrows. "If I were you, I'd be quick to deny that, unless I knew it to be true."

Carpathia softened. "It does not seem the time for me to make such a claim, but I am not so sure it is untrue."

Rayford squinted. "You think you might be the Messiah."

"Let me just say, especially after what happened last night, I have not ruled out the possibility."

Rayford thrust his hands in his pockets and looked away.

"Come now, Rayford. Do not assume I do not see the irony. I am not blind. I know a faction out there, including many of your so-called tribulation saints, labels me an antichrist, or even *the* Antichrist. I would delight in proving the opposite."

Rayford leaned forward, pulled his hands from his pockets, and entwined his fingers. "Let me get this straight. There's a possibility you are the Messiah, but you don't know for sure?"

Carpathia nodded solemnly.

"That makes no sense," Rayford said.

"Matters of faith are mysteries," Carpathia intoned. "I urge you to spend time with Mr. Fortunato. See what you think after that."

Rayford made no promises. He looked toward the exit.

"I know you need to go, Captain Steele. I just wanted to share with you the tremendous progress already made in my rebuilding initiative. As early as tomorrow we expect to be able to communicate with half the world. At that time I will address anyone who can listen." He pulled a sheet from his coat pocket. "Meanwhile, I would like you and Mr. McCullum to load whatever equipment you need onto the 216 and chart a course to bring these international ambassadors to join those who are already here."

Rayford scanned the list. It appeared he would fly more than twenty thousand miles. "Where are you on rebuilding runways?"

"Global Community forces are working around the clock in every country. Cellular-Solar will network the entire world within weeks. Virtually anyone not on that project is rebuilding airstrips, roads, and centers of commerce."

"I have my assignment," Rayford said flatly.

"I would like to know your itinerary as soon as it is set. Did you notice the name on the back?"

Rayford turned the sheet over. "Pontifex Maximus Peter Mathews, Enigma Babylon One World Faith. So we bring him, too?"

"Though he is in Rome, pick him up first. I would like him on the plane when each of the other ambassadors boards."

Rayford shrugged. He wasn't sure why God had put him in this position, but until he felt led to leave it, he would hang in.

"One more thing," Carpathia said. "Mr. Fortunato will go with you and serve as host."

Rayford shrugged again. "Now may I ask you something?" Carpathia nodded, standing. "Could you let me know when the dredging operation commences?"

"The what?"

"When they pull the Pan-Con 747 out of the Tigris," Rayford said evenly.

"Oh, yes, that. Now, Rayford, I have been advised it would be futile."

"There's a chance you won't do it?"

"Most likely we will not. The airline informed us who was

aboard, and we know there are no survivors. We are already at a loss for what to do with the bodies of so many victims of this disaster. I have been advised to consider the aircraft a sacred burial vault."

Rayford felt his face flush, and he slumped. "You're not going to prove to me my wife is dead, are you?"

"Oh, Rayford, is there any doubt?"

"As a matter of fact, there is. It doesn't feel like she's dead, if you know what I—well, of course you don't know what I mean."

"I know it is difficult for loved ones to let go unless they see the body. But you are an intelligent man. Time heals—"

"I want that plane dredged up. I want to know whether my wife is dead or alive."

Carpathia stepped behind Rayford and placed a hand on each shoulder. Rayford closed his eyes, wishing he could melt away. Carpathia spoke soothingly. "Next you will be asking me to resurrect her."

Rayford spoke through clenched teeth. "If you are who you think you are, you ought to be able to pull that off for one of your most trusted employees."

Buck had fallen asleep atop the bedspread. Now, well after midnight, he couldn't imagine he had slept more than two hours. Sitting up, gathering the covers around him, he didn't want to move. But what had awakened him? Had he seen lights flicker in the hallway?

It had to have been a dream. Surely electricity would not be reconnected in Mount Prospect for days, maybe weeks. Buck held his breath. Now he *did* hear something from the other room, the low, whispering cadence of Tsion Ben-Judah. Had something awakened him too? Tsion was praying in his own tongue. Buck wished he understood Hebrew. The prayer grew fainter, and Buck lay back down and rolled onto his side. As he lost consciousness he reminded himself that in the morning he needed one last look around Loretta's neighborhood—one more desperate attempt to find Chloe.

Rayford found Mac in the cockpit of the idle helicopter. He was reading.

"Finally let you go, did he?" Mac said. Rayford always ignored obvious questions. He just shook his head. "I don't know how he does it," Mac said.

"What's that?"

Mac rattled his magazine. "The latest *Modern Avionics.* Where would Carpathia get this? And how would he know to stock it in the shelter?"

"Who knows?" Rayford said. "Maybe he's the god he thinks he is."

"I told you about Leon's diatribe last night."

"Carpathia told me again."

"What, that he agrees with Leon about his own divinity?"

"He's not going that far yet," Rayford said. "But he will. The Bible says he will."

"Whoa!" Mac said. "You're gonna have to start from the beginning."

"Fair enough," Rayford said, unfolding Carpathia's passenger list. "First let me show you this. After my training, I want you to plot our course to these countries. First we pick up Mathews in Rome. Then let's go to the States and pick up all the other ambassadors on the way back."

Mac studied the sheet. "Should be easy. Take me a half hour or so to plot it. Are there spots to land in all these places?"

"We'll get close enough. We'll put the chopper and a fixed-wing in the cargo hold, just in case."

"So when do we get to talk?"

"Our training session should take until about five, don't you think?"

"Nah! I told you, you'll be up to speed in no time."

"We'll need to break for a late lunch somewhere," Rayford said. "And then we'll still have several hours to train, right?"

"You're not following me, Ray. You don't need a whole day playing with this toy. You know what you're doing, and these things fly themselves."

Rayford leaned close. "Who's not following whom?" he said. "You and I are away from the shelter today, training until 1700 hours. Is that understood?"

Mac smiled sheepishly. "Oh. You learn the whirlybird by late lunch at around one, and we're still on leave until five."

"You catch on quick."

Rayford took notes as Mac walked him through every button, every switch, every key. With the blades at top speed, Mac feathered the controls until the bird lifted off. He went through a series of maneuvers, turning this way and that, dipping and climbing. "It'll come back to you quick, Ray."

"Let me ask you something first, Mac. You were stationed in this area, weren't you?"

"For many years," Mac said, slowly flying south.

"You know people, then."

"Locals, you mean? Yeah. I couldn't tell you if any of them survived the earthquake. What are you looking for?"

"Scuba equipment."

Mac glanced at Rayford, who did not return his gaze. "There's a new one for the middle of the desert. Where do you want to go diving? In the Tigris?" Mac grinned, but Rayford shot him a serious look and he paled. "Oh, sure, forgive me, Rayford. Man, you don't really want to do that, do you?"

"I've never wanted anything more, Mac. Now do you know somebody or not?"

"Let 'em dredge the thing, Ray."

"Carpathia says they're gonna leave it alone."

Mac shook his head. "I don't know, Ray. You ever scuba dive in a river?"

"I'm a good diver. But no, never in a river."

"Well, I have, and it's not the same, believe me. The current isn't much calmer at the bottom than the top. You'll spend half your time keeping from getting sucked down-stream. You could wind up three hundred miles southeast in the Persian Gulf."

Rayford was not amused. "What's the story, Mac? You got a source for me?"

"Yeah, I know a guy. He was always able to get anything I wanted from just about anywhere. I've never seen scuba stuff around here, but if it's available and he's still alive, he can get it."

"Who and where?"

"He's a national. He runs the tower at the airstrip down at Al Basrah. That's northwest of Abadan where the Tigris becomes the Shatt al Arab. I wouldn't begin to try to pro-nounce his real name. To all of his, ahem, clients, he goes by Al B. I call him Albie."

"What's his arrangement?"

"He takes all the risks. Charges you double retail, no questions asked. You get caught with contraband stuff, he's never heard of you."

"Try to reach him for me?"

"Just say the word."

"That's what I'm saying, Mac."

"Quite a risk."

"Being honest with you is a risk, Mac."

"How do you know you can trust me?"

"I don't. I have no choice."

"Thanks a lot."

"You'd feel the same way if the shoe was on the other foot."

"True enough," Mac said. "Only time will prove I'm not a rat."

"Yeah," Rayford said, feeling as reckless as he had ever been. "If you're not a friend, there's nothing I can do about it now."

"Uh-huh, but would a fink make a dangerous dive with you?"

Rayford stared at him. "I couldn't let you do that."

"You can't stop me. If my guy can get a suit and a tank for you, he can get them for me, too."

"Why would you do that?"

"Well, not just to prove myself. I'd like to keep you around awhile. You deserve to know if your wife's in the drink. But that dive's gonna be dangerous enough for two, let alone solo."

"I'll have to think about that."

"For once, quit thinking so much. I'm goin' with you and that's that. I gotta figure some way to keep you alive long enough to tell me what the devil has been going on since the disappearances."

"Put her down," Rayford said, "and I'll tell you."

"Right here? Right now?"

"Right now."

Mac had flown a few miles to where Rayford could see the city of Al Hillah. He banked left and headed for the desert, landing in the middle of nowhere. He shut the engine down quickly to avoid sand damage. Still, Rayford saw grains on the back of his hands and tasted them on his lips.

"Let me get behind the controls," Rayford said, unstrapping himself.

"Not on your life," Mac said. "Next you're gonna try startin' her up and liftin' off. I know you can do it and it's not that dangerous, but Lord knows nobody else around here can explain things to me. Now out with it, let's go."

Rayford hopped out and landed in the sand. Mac followed. They strolled half an hour in the sun, Rayford sweating through his clothes. Finally Rayford led the way back to the helicopter, where they leaned against the struts on the shade side.

He told Mac his life story, starting with the kind of family he was raised in—decent, hardworking, but uneducated people. He had shown a proclivity for math and science and was fascinated by aviation. He did well in school, but his father could not afford to send him to college. A high school counselor told him he should be able to get scholarships, but that he needed something extra on his résumé.

"Like what?" Rayford had asked her.

"Extracurricular activities, student government, things like that."

"What about flying solo before I graduate?"

"Now *that* would be impressive," she admitted.

"I've done it."

That helped him earn a college education that led to military training and commercial flying. All the while, he said, "I was a pretty good guy. Good citizen—you know the drill. Drank a little, chased a little. Never anything illegal. Never saw myself as a rascal. Patriotic, the whole bit. I was even a churchgoer."

He told Mac he had been smitten with Irene from the beginning. "She was a little too goody-goody for me," he admitted, "but she was pretty and loving and selfless. She amazed me. I asked, she accepted, and though it turned out she was a lot more into church than I was, I wasn't about to let her go."

Rayford told of how he broke his promise to be a regular churchgoer. They'd had fights and Irene had shed tears, but he sensed she had resigned herself to the fact that "at least in this one area, I was a creep who couldn't be trusted. I was faithful, a good provider, respected in the community. I thought she was living with the rest of it. Anyway, she left me alone about it. She couldn't have been happy about it, but I told myself she didn't care. I sure didn't.

"When we had Chloe, I turned over a new leaf. I believed I was a new man. Seeing her born convinced me of miracles, forced me to acknowledge God, and made me want to be the best father and husband in history. I made no promises. I just started going back to church with Irene."

Rayford explained how he realized that "church wasn't that bad. Some of the same people we saw at the country club we saw at church. We showed up, gave our money, sang the songs, closed our eyes during the prayers, and listened to the homilies. Every once in a while a sermon or part of one offended me. But I let it slide. Nobody was checking up on me. The same things offended most of our friends. We called it getting our toes stepped on, but it never happened twice in a row."

Rayford said he had never stopped to think about heaven or hell. "They didn't talk much about that. Well, never about hell. Any mention of heaven was that everybody winds up there eventually. I didn't want to be embarrassed in heaven by having done too many bad things. I compared myself with other guys and figured if they were going to make it, I was too.

"The thing is, Mac, I was happy. I know people say they feel some void in their lives, but I didn't. To me, this was life. Funny thing was, Irene talked about feeling empty. I argued with her. Sometimes a lot. I reminded her I was back in church and she hadn't even had to badger me about it. What more did she want?"

What Irene wanted, Rayford said, was something more. Something deeper. She had friends who talked about a personal relationship with God, and it intrigued her. "Scared *me* to death," Rayford said. "I repeated the phrase so she could hear how wacky it sounded, 'personal relationship with God'? She said, of all things, 'Yes. Through his Son, Jesus Christ.'" Rayford shook his head. "Well, I mean, you can imagine how that went down with me."

Mac nodded. "I know what I would have thought."

Rayford said, "I had just enough religion to make me feel all right. Saying words like *God* or *Jesus Christ* out loud, in front of people? That was for pastors and priests and theologians. I resonated with people who said religion was private.

Anybody who tried to convince you of something from the Bible or 'shared his faith' with you, well, those guys were right-wingers or zealots or fundamentalists or something. I stayed as far away from them as I could."

"I know what you mean," Mac said. "There was always somebody around trying to 'win souls for Jesus.'"

Rayford nodded. "Well, fast forward a whole bunch of years. Now we've got Rayford Junior. I had the same feeling when he was born as I had with Chloe. And I admit I had always wanted a son. I figured God must be pretty pleased with me to bless me that way. And let me tell you something I've told precious few other people, Mac. I was almost unfaithful to Irene while she was pregnant with Raymie. I was drunk, it was at a company Christmas party, and it was stupid. I felt so guilty, not because of God I don't think, but because of Irene. She didn't deserve that. But she never suspected, and that made it worse. I knew she loved me. I convinced myself I was the scum of the earth and I made all kinds of bargains with God. Somewhere I had this idea he might punish me. I told him if I could just put this behind me and never do it again, would he please not let our unborn baby die. If anything had been wrong with our baby, I don't know what I would have done."

But the baby had been perfect, Rayford explained. He soon got a promotion and a raise, they moved to a beautiful home in the suburbs, he kept going to church, and he was soon satisfied with his life again.

"But . . ."

"But?" Mac said. "What happened then?"

"Irene switched churches on me," Rayford said. "You getting hungry?"

"I'm sorry?"

"Are you hungry? It's coming up on one o'clock."

"That's the storyteller you are? Leave me hanging so you can eat? You ran that all together like Irene's changing churches should make me hungry."

"Point me to a place to eat," Rayford said. "I'll get us there."

"You'd better."

CHAPTER 6

RAYFORD SPENT TWENTY MINUTES scaring the life out of himself and Mac. The skill of piloting a chopper may never leave, but with the advance of technology, this took some getting used to. He remembered bulky, sluggish, heavy copters. This one darted like a dragonfly. The control was as responsive as a joystick, and he found himself overcompensating. He banked one way—too hard and too fast—then the other, straightening himself quickly but then rolling the other way.

"I'm about to barf!" Mac shouted.

"Not in my chopper, you're not!" Rayford said.

He put the helicopter down four times, the second time much too hard. "That won't happen again," he promised. As he took off for the last time, he said, "I've got it now. This should be easy to keep straight and steady."

"It is for me," Mac said. "You want to go all the way to Albie's?"

"You mean put down at an airport, in front of people?"

"A baptism of fire." Mac plotted their bearings. "Keep her set right there, and we could snooze till we see the tower at Al Basrah. Line her up, let her go, and tell me about Irene's new church."

Rayford spent the trip finishing his story. He told how Irene's frustration with finding nothing deep or meaty or personal at their church gave him an excuse to start going only sporadically himself. When she called him on it, he reminded her that she wasn't happy there either. "When I pretty much stopped going altogether, she started church shopping. She met a couple of women she really liked at a church she didn't care so much for, but they invited her to a women's Bible study. That's where she heard something about God she had never known was in the Bible. She found out where the speaker went to church, started going there, and eventually dragged me along."

"What was it she heard?"

"I'm getting to it."

"Don't stall."

Rayford checked his instruments to make sure the engines were still operating in the green arcs.

"I mean don't stall your story," Mac said.

"Well, I didn't understand the new message myself,"

Rayford said. "In fact, I never really got it until after she was gone. The church was different all right. It made me uncomfortable. When people didn't see me around, they had to figure I was working. When I did show up, people asked me about work, and I just kept smiling and telling them how wonderful life was. But even when I *was* home I went only about half the time. My daughter, Chloe, was a teenager by then, and she picked up on that. If Dad didn't have to go, she didn't have to go."

"Irene, however, really loved the new church. She made me nervous when she started talking about sin and salvation and forgiveness and the blood of Christ and winning souls. She said she had received Christ and been born again. She was pushing me, but I would have none of that. It sounded weird. Like a cult. The people seemed all right, but I was sure I was going to get pushed into knocking on doors and handing out literature or something. I found more reasons to not be in church.

"One day Irene was going off about how Pastor Billings was preaching on the end times and the return of Christ. He called it the Rapture. She said something like, 'Wouldn't it be great to not die but to meet Jesus in the air?' I came back with something like, 'Yeah, that would kill me.' I offended her. She told me I shouldn't be so flippant if I didn't know where I was going. That made me mad. I told her I was glad she was sure. I told her I figured she'd fly to heaven and I'd go straight to hell. She didn't like that a bit."

"I can imagine," Mac said.

"The whole issue of church became so volatile that we just avoided it. Eventually I started to get those old stirrings again, and I had my eye on my senior flight attendant."

"Uh-oh," Mac said.

"Tell me about it. We had a few drinks, shared a few meals, but it never went past that. Not that I didn't want it to. One night I decided to ask her out when we got to London. Then I thought, hey, I'll ask her in advance. I'm way out over the Atlantic in the middle of the night with a fully loaded seven-four-seven, so I put it on auto pilot and go looking for her."

Rayford paused, disgusted with himself even now for how low he had sunk.

Mac looked at him. "Yeah?"

"Everybody remembers where they were when the disappearances happened."

"You're not saying . . ." Mac said.

"I was looking for a date when all those people disappeared."

"Man!"

Rayford snorted. "She wanted to know what was going on. Were we gonna die? I told her I was pretty sure we weren't going to die, but that I had no more idea than she did what had happened. The truth was, I knew. Irene had been right. Christ had come to rapture his church, and we had all been left behind."

There was a lot more to Rayford's story, of course, but he just wanted that to sink in. Mac sat staring straight ahead.

He would turn, take a breath, and then turn back and watch the scenery as they continued toward Al Basrah.

Mac checked his clipboard and stared at the dials. "We're close enough," he said. "I'm gonna see what I can find out." He set the frequency and depressed the mike button. "Golf Charlie Niner Niner to Al Basrah tower. Do you read?"

Static.

"Al Basrah tower, this is Golf Charlie Niner Niner. I'm switching to channel eleven, over." Mac made the switch and repeated the call.

"Al Basrah tower," came the reply. "Go ahead, Niner Niner."

"Albie around?"

"Stand by, niner."

Mac turned to Rayford. "Here's hoping," he said.

"Golf Charlie, this is Albie, over."

"Albie, you old son of a gun! Mac here! You're OK then?"

"Not totally, my friend. We just raised our temporary tower. Lost two hangars. I'm on crutches. Please, not to be bringing a fixed-wing plane. Not for two, three days."

"We're in a bird," Mac said.

"Welcome then," Albie said. "We need help. We need company."

"We can't stay long, Albie. Our ETA is thirty minutes."

"Roger that, Mac. We watch for you."

Rayford saw Mac bite his lip. "That's a relief," he whispered, his voice shaky. He monitored the controls, stashed his clipboard, and turned to Rayford. "Back to your story."

Rayford was intrigued that Mac cared so much for his friend. Had Rayford had a friend like that before he was a believer? Had he ever cared about another man enough to become emotional over his well-being?

Rayford looked at the devastation below. Tents had been erected where homes had disappeared in the quake. Bodies dotted the landscape, and expeditions of cheap trailers came to cart them off. Here and there bands of people with shovels and pickaxes worked on a paved road. If they saw what Rayford could see, they would know that even if they spent days on their tiny stretch of twisted pavement, the road for miles ahead would take months to fix, even with heavy equipment.

Rayford told Mac how he had landed at O'Hare after the disappearances, walked to the terminal, saw the devastating reports from around the world, lost his copilot to suicide, paid heavily for a ride home, and had his worst fears confirmed. "Irene and Raymie were gone. Chloe, a skeptic like me, was trying to get home from Stanford. It was my fault. She followed my example. And we had both been left behind."

Rayford remembered as if it were yesterday. He didn't mind telling the story because it came to a good end, but he hated this part. Not just the horror, not just the loneliness, but the blame. If Chloe had never come to Christ, he wasn't sure he could have forgiven himself.

He wondered about Mac. He would tell Mac what was going on, exactly who Nicolae Carpathia was, the whole package. He would tell him of the prophecies in Revelation, walk him through the judgments that had already come, show him how they had been foretold and could not be disputed. But if Mac was phony, if Mac worked for Carpathia, he would have already been brainwashed. He could fake this emotion, this interest. He could even insist he wanted to make a dangerous scuba dive with Rayford, just to stay on his good side.

But Rayford was already beyond the point of no return. Again he prayed silently that God might give him a sign whether Mac was sincere. If he wasn't, he was one of the better actors Rayford had seen. It was hard to trust anyone anymore.

When they finally came in sight of the airfield at Al Basrah, Mac coached Ray to a gentle, if lengthy, touchdown. As Ray shut down the engine, Mac said, "That's him. Coming down the ladder."

They scrambled out of the chopper as a tiny, dark-faced, long-nosed, turbaned man in bare feet gingerly made his way down from a tower that looked more like a guard station at a prison. He had tossed his crutches down, and when he reached the ground, he hopped to them and deftly used them to rush to Mac. They embraced.

"What happened to you?" Mac asked.

"I was in the mess hall," Albie said. "When the rumbles began, I knew immediately what it was. Foolishly, I raced for the tower. No one was there. We were not expecting traffic for a couple of hours. What I would do up there, I had no idea. The tower began falling before I even reached it. I was able to elude it, but a fuel truck was thrown into my path. I saw it at the last instant and tried to leap over the cab, which lay on its side. I almost reached the other side but twisted my ankle on the tire and scraped my shin on the lug nuts. But that is not the worst of it. I have broken bones in my foot. But there are no supplies to set it, and I am low on the priority list. It will grow strong. Allah will bless me."

Mac introduced Rayford. "I want to hear your stories," Albie said. "Where were you when it hit? Everything. I want to know everything. But first, if you have time, we could use help."

Heavy machinery was already grading a huge area, preparing it for asphalt. "Your boss, the potentate himself, has expressed pleasure at our cooperation. We are trying to get underway as soon as possible to help the global peacekeeping effort. What a tragedy to have thrown in our way after all he has accomplished."

Rayford said nothing.

Mac said, "Albie, we might be able to help later, but we need to eat."

"The mess hall is gone," Albie said. "As for your favorite place in town, I have not heard. Shall we check?"

"Do you have a vehicle?"

"That old pickup," Albie said. They followed as he crutched his way to it. "Clutching will be difficult," he said. "Do you mind?"

Mac slid behind the wheel. Albie sat in the middle, knees spread to keep from blocking the gearshift. The pickup rattled and lurched over unpaved roads until it arrived at the outskirts of the city. Rayford was sickened by the smell. He still found it hard to accept that this was part of God's ultimate plan. Did this many people have to suffer to make some eternal point? He took comfort in that this was not God's desired result. Rayford believed God was true to his word, that he had given people enough chances that he could now justify allowing this to get their attention.

Wailing men and women carried bodies over their shoulders or pushed them in wheelbarrows through the crowded streets. It seemed every other block had been left in pieces by the earthquake. Mac's favorite eatery was missing a concrete block wall, but the management had draped something over it and was open for business. One of few eating establishments still open, it was wall to wall with customers who ate while standing. Mac and Rayford shouldered their way in, drawing angry stares until the townspeople saw Albie. Then they made room, as much as they could, still pressed shoulder to shoulder.

Rayford had little faith in the sanitation of this food, but still he was grateful for it. After two bites of a rolled-up pastry stuffed with ground lamb and seasonings, he whispered to Mac, "I can see and I can smell and yet somehow, even here, hunger is the best seasoning."

On the way back, Mac pulled to the side of a dusty field and turned off the engine. "I wanted to know you were all right, Albie," he said. "But this is also a business mission."

"Splendid," Albie said. "How can I help?"

"Scuba gear," Mac said.

Albie furrowed his brow and pursed his lips. "Scuba," he said simply. "You need everything? Wet suit, mask, snorkel, tanks, fins?"

"All that, yes."

"Weights? Ballast? Lights?"

"I suppose."

"Cash?"

"Of course."

"I'll have to check," Albie said. "I have a source. I have not heard from him since the disaster. If the stuff is to be had, I can get it. Let's leave it this way: If you do not hear from me, return in one month and it will be here."

"I can't wait that long," Rayford said quickly.

"I cannot guarantee any sooner. Even that long seems very fast to me at a time like this." Rayford couldn't argue with that. "I thought this was for you, Mac," Albie added.

"We need two sets."

"Are you going to make a career of diving?"

"Hardly," Mac said. "Why? You think we should rent instead?"

"Could we?" Rayford said.

Albie and Mac looked at Rayford and burst into laughter. "No rental on the black market," Albie said.

Rayford had to grin at his own naiveté, but laughing seemed a distant pleasure.

Back at the airport Rayford and Mac each manned a shovel while a dump truck brought in a gravel base for the runway.

Before they knew it, several hours had passed. They sent someone for Albie.

"Can you get a message to New Babylon?" Mac said.

"It will require a relay, but both Qar and Wasit have been on the air since this morning, so yes, is possible."

Mac wrote the instructions, asking that a dispatch go to Global Community radio base informing them that Steele and McCullum were engaged in a cooperative volunteer airport rebuilding project and would return by nightfall.

It was nearly nine-thirty Tuesday morning, Central Standard Time, when Buck was jolted awake. The day was bright and sunny, yet he had slept soundly since that brief dream in the middle of the night. A constant sound had played at the edges of his consciousness. But for how long? As his eyes grew accustomed to the light, he realized the noise had been with him for some time.

It seemed to come from the backyard, from beyond the Range Rover. He padded to the window and opened it, pressing his cheek against the screen and looking as far that way as he could. Maybe it was emergency workers, and he and Tsion would have power sooner than they thought.

What was that smell? Had a catering truck pulled up for the workmen? He threw on some clothes. The light was on in the hallway. Had it not been a dream after all? He skipped down the stairs in his bare feet. "Tsion! We have power! What's happening?"

Tsion came from the kitchen with a skillet full of food and began scooping it onto a plate at the table. "Sit down, sit down, my friend. Are you not proud of me?"

"You found food!"

"I did more than that, Buck! I discovered a generator, and a big one!"

Buck bowed his head and said a brief prayer. "Did you eat, Tsion?"

"Yes, go ahead. I could not wait. I could not sleep in the middle of the night, so I tiptoed in and took your flashlight. I did not rouse you, did I?"

"No," Buck said, his mouth full. "But later I thought I dreamed I saw lights in the hallway."

"It was not a dream, Buck! I lugged that generator out of the cellar and into the backyard myself. It took me forever to fill it with gas and clean the spark plug and get it fired up. But as soon as I hooked it to the cable in the basement, lights came on, the refrigerator came on, everything started happening. I am sorry to have disturbed you. I tiptoed into my bedroom and knelt by my bed, just praising the Lord for our good fortune."

"I heard you."

"Forgive me."

"It was like music," Buck said. "And this food is like nectar."

"You need sustenance. You are going back to Loretta's. I will stay here and see if I can get on the Internet. If I cannot, I have much studying to do and messages to write so they will be ready to go to the faithful when I can get hooked up. Before you leave, however, you will help me get into Donny's briefcase, no?"

"You've decided that's OK, then?"

"Under other circumstances, no. But we have so few tools for survival now, Cameron. We must take advantage of anything that might be there."

Fortunately, Donny's well remained intact, and somehow, under a steaming shower a few minutes later, Buck's spirits were raised. What was it about creature comforts that made the day look brighter, despite the crisis? Buck knew he was in denial. Whenever he felt his realistic, practical, journalist side take over, he fought it. He wanted to think Chloe had somehow escaped death, but her car was still at the house. On the other hand, he hadn't found her body. Tons of debris still covered the place, and he had not been able to dig through much of it. Was he up to displacing every piece of trash from the foundation to prove to himself she was or wasn't there? He was willing. He simply hoped there was a better way.

On his way out of the house, Buck was intrigued that Tsion had not waited for him to get Donny's briefcase from the Rover. The rabbi had it on the table. He wore a shy, impish look. They were about to break into someone's personal belongings, and both had convinced themselves it was what Donny would have wanted. They were also prepared to close it back up and discard it if what they found was personal.

"There are all kinds of tools in the basement," Tsion said.

"I could use some care and do this in such a way that it would not threaten the integrity of the structure."

"What!?" Buck said. "Threaten the integrity of the structure? You mean not hurt this cheap briefcase? How 'bout I just save you the time and effort?"

Buck turned the five-inch-deep plastic briefcase vertically and held it between his knees as he sat in a kitchen chair. He angled both knees left and drove the heel of his hand into the case, forcing it to fall between his ankles and land on one corner. That caused the latches to separate and the case to spring out of shape and fly open. His legs kept it from opening wide and spilling. With a feeling of accomplishment, he plopped it on the table and spun it around so Tsion could open it.

"This is what this young man has been lugging with him everywhere he goes?" Tsion said.

Buck leaned over to peek in. There, in neatly stacked rows, were dozens of small spiral notebooks, each not quite as large as a stenographer's notebook. They were labeled on the front with dates in block hand printing. Tsion grabbed a few and Buck took more. He fanned them in his hands and noticed that each contained approximately two months' worth of entries.

"This may be his personal diary," Buck said.

"Yes," Tsion said. "If so, we must not violate his confidence."

They looked at each other. Buck wondered which of them was going to look, to determine whether these were private notes that should be discarded or technical notes that might be of assistance to the Tribulation Force. Tsion raised his eyebrows and nodded to Buck. Buck opened one notebook to the middle. It read: "Talked to Bruce B. about underground necessities. He still seems reluctant about suggesting location. I don't need to know. I outlined specifications, electric, water, phone, ventilation, etc."

"That is not personal," Tsion said. "Let me study these today and see if there is anything we can use. I am amazed how he stacked them. I do not believe he could have fit another one in, and he used every bit of space."

"What's this?" Buck said, leafing to the back. "Look at these. He hand drew these schematics."

"That is my shelter!" Tsion exalted. "That is where I have been staying. So, *he* designed it."

"But it looks like Bruce never told him where he was building it."

Tsion pointed to a passage on the next page: "Putting a duplicate shelter in my backyard has proven more labor intensive than I expected. Sandy is getting a kick out of it. Bagging the dirt and storing it in her van takes her mind off our loss. She enjoys the clandestine nature of it. We take turns dumping it in various locations. Today we loaded so much that the back tires looked as if they might explode. It was the first time I had seen her smile in months."

Buck and Tsion looked at each other. "Is it possible?" Tsion said. "A shelter in his backyard?"

"How did we miss it?" Buck said. "We were digging out there last night."

They moved to the back door and gazed out on the lawn. A fence between Donny's home and the rubble next door had been ripped up and moved by the quake. "Maybe I parked over the entrance," Buck said.

He backed the Rover out of the way. "I see nothing here," Tsion said. "But the journal indicates this was more than a dream. They were moving dirt."

"I'll find some metal rods today," Buck said. "We can poke them through the grass and see if we can find this thing."

"Yes, you go. Finish up at Loretta's. I have much work today on the computer."

⁂

The sun was setting in Iraq. "We'd better head back," Rayford said, breathing hard.

"What are they gonna do?" Mac said. "Fire us?"

"As long as he's got you around, Mac, he could follow through on his threat to put me in jail."

"That would be just like him, to think one man can fly that Condor halfway around the world and back. By the way, you ever wonder why he calls that thing the 216? The number on his office was 216 too, even though it was on the top floor of an eighteen-story building."

"Never thought about it," Rayford said. "I can't see a reason to care. Maybe he's got a fetish for that number."

As he and Mac trudged back toward the new tower with shovels over their shoulders, Albie hurried to them on his crutches. "I can't thank you enough for your help, gentlemen. You are true friends of Allah and Iraq. True friends of the Global Community."

"The Global Community might not appreciate hearing you honor Allah," Rayford said. "You are a loyalist, and yet you have not joined Enigma Babylon Faith?"

"On my mother's grave, I should never mock Allah with such blasphemy."

So, Rayford thought, Christians and Jews are not the only holdouts against the new Pope Peter.

Albie led them back to where they turned in their shovels. He spoke in hushed tones. "I am happy to inform you that I have already made some initial inquiries. I should have no trouble procuring your equipment."

"All of it?" Mac said.

"All of it."

"How much?" Mac said.

"I have taken the liberty of writing that down," Albie said.

He pulled a scrap of paper from his pocket and leaned on his crutches as he opened it in the fading light.

"Ho! Man!" Rayford said. "That's four times what I would pay for two scuba outfits."

Albie stuffed the paper back into his pocket. "It is exactly double retail. Not a penny more. If you do not want the merchandise, tell me now."

"That does look high," Mac said. "But you have never done me wrong. We will trust you."

"Need a deposit?" Rayford said, hoping to assuage the man's feelings.

"No," he said, eyes darting to Mac but not at Rayford. "You trust me, I'll trust you."

Rayford nodded.

Albie thrust out his bony hand and gripped Rayford's fiercely. "I will see you in thirty days then, unless you hear from me otherwise."

Mac took the controls for the flight back. "Got enough energy to finish your story, Ray?"

Buck stopped at the ruins of New Hope Village Church on his way to Loretta's and strolled past the crater where the old woman's car rested twenty feet below. Her body was there too, but he could not bring himself to look. If animals had gotten to her, he didn't want to know. He also avoided the spot where he had found Donny Moore. More movement of the earth had further entombed him.

He carefully climbed to where the underground shelter lay. Clearly, more debris had shifted. He slipped and nearly fell down the concrete stairs that led to the door. He wondered if anything salvageable could be dragged out. He could always come back. Buck headed for the Range Rover and brushed his fingers across his still swollen cheek. Why was it flesh wounds looked worse and felt more tender the second day?

Traffic dotted the area today. Any front-end loader, bull-dozer, or dragline that had not sunk out of sight appeared to have been called into service. Buck couldn't park where he had the day before. Road crews rammed the uptwisted pavement in front of Loretta's house. Dump trucks were loaded with the huge chunks. Where they would take it and what they would do with it, Buck had no idea. All he knew was that there was nothing else for anyone to do but start rebuilding. He couldn't imagine this area ever looking like its old self again, but he knew it wouldn't be long before it was rebuilt.

Buck drove over a small pile of trash and parked next to one of the felled trees in Loretta's front yard. Workers ignored him as he slowly circled the house, wondering whether to continue picking through what was left of it.

A man with a clipboard studied the residue of the house next door. He shot pictures and took notes.

"Didn't think insurance would cover an act of God like this," Buck said.

"It wouldn't," the man said. "I'm not with an insurance company." He turned so Buck could see the ID tag clipped to his collar. It read, "Sunny Kuntz, Senior Field Supervisor, Global Community Relief."

Buck nodded. "What happens next?"

"We fax pictures and stats to headquarters. They send money. We rebuild."

"GC headquarters is still standing?"

"Nope. They're rebuilding too. Whoever's left there is in an underground shelter with pretty sophisticated technology."

"You can communicate with New Babylon?"

"Since this morning."

"My father-in-law works over there. You think I could get through?"

"You ought to be able to." Kuntz glanced at his watch. "It's not 9:00 p.m. there yet. I talked to somebody there about four hours ago. I wanted them to know we found at least one survivor from this area."

"You did? Who?"

"I'm not at liberty to share that information, Mr. —"

"Oh, sorry." Buck reached for his own ID, identifying himself as also a GC employee.

"Ah, press," Kuntz said. He peeled up two pages from his clipboard. "Name's Cavenaugh. Helen. Age seventy."

"She lived here?"

"That's right. Said she ran to the basement when she felt the place rattling. Never heard of an earthquake in this area before, so she thought it was a tornado. She was just flat lucky. Last place you want to be in an earthquake is where everything can fall on you."

"She survived though, huh?"

Kuntz pointed to the foundation about twenty feet east of Loretta's house. "See those two openings, one up here and the other in back?" Buck nodded. "That's one long room in the basement. First she ran to the front. When the whole house shifted and the glass blew in from that window, she ran to the other end. The glass was already out of that window, so she just planted herself in the corner and waited it out. If she had stayed up front, she'd have never made it. Wound up in the only corner of the house where she wouldn't have been killed."

"She told you this?"

"Yep."

"She didn't say whether she saw anybody next door, did she?"

"Matter of fact, she did."

Buck nearly lost his breath. "What'd she say?"

"Just that she saw a young woman running out of the house. Just before the window gave way on this end, the woman jumped in her car, but when the road started rising on her, she drove into the garage."

Buck trembled, desperate to stay calm until he got the whole story. "Then what?"

"Mrs. Cavenaugh said she had to move to the back because of that window, and when that house started to give way, she thought she saw the woman come out the side door of the garage and run through the backyard."

Buck lost all objectivity. "Sir, that was my wife. Any more details?"

"None I can remember."

"Where is this Mrs. Cavenaugh?"

"In a shelter about six miles due east. A furniture store somehow suffered very little damage. There's probably two hundred survivors in there, the least injured. It's more of a holding station than a hospital."

"Tell me exactly where this place is. I need to talk to her."

"OK, Mr. Williams, but I need to caution you not to get your hopes up about your wife."

"What are you talking about? I didn't have my hopes up until I found out she ran from this. My hopes were nowhere when I tried to dig through the mess. Don't tell me to not get my hopes up now."

"I'm sorry. I'm just trying to be realistic. I worked disaster relief for more than fifteen years before joining the GC task force. This is the worst I've ever seen, and I need to ask you if you've seen the escape route your wife might have taken, if Mrs. Cavenaugh was right and she ran through that backyard."

Buck followed Kuntz to the back. Kuntz swept the horizon with his arm. "Where would you go?" he asked. "Where would anybody go?"

Buck nodded somberly. He got the message. As far as he could see was nothing but piles, crevices, craters, fallen trees, and downed utility poles. There had certainly been no place to run.

CHAPTER 7

"So," MAC SAID, "your daughter was your real reason for finding out what happened to your wife and son."

"Right."

"Did you wonder about your motive?"

"You mean guilt? Maybe partly. But I *was* guilty, Mac. I had let down my daughter. I wasn't going to let that happen again."

"You couldn't force her to believe."

"No. And for a while I thought she wouldn't. She was tough, analytical, the way I had been."

"Well, Ray, we flyboys are all alike. We get off the ground because of aerodynamics. No magic, no miracles, nothing you can't see, feel, or hear."

"That was me all the way."

"So what happened? What made the difference?"

The sun dipped below the horizon, and from the helicopter Rayford and Mac saw the yellow ball flatten and melt in the distance. Rayford was into his story, earnestly trying to persuade Mac of the truth. He was suddenly warm. Though the Iraqi desert cooled quickly after sundown, he had to shed his jacket.

"No closets here, Ray. I just lay mine behind the seat."

Once situated, Rayford continued. "Ironically, everything that convinced me of the truth I should have known in time to go with Irene when Christ came back. I had gone to church for years, and I had even heard the terms *Virgin Birth* and *atonement* and all that. But I never stopped to figure what they meant. I understood that one of the legends said Jesus was born to a woman who had never been with a man. I couldn't have told you whether I believed that or even thought it was important. It seemed like just a religious story and, I thought, explained why a lot of people thought sex was dirty."

Rayford told Mac of finding Irene's Bible, digging out the phone number of the church she loved so much, reaching Bruce Barnes, and seeing Pastor Billings's DVD prepared for those left behind.

"He had this whole thing figured out?" Mac said.

"Oh, yes. Just about anybody who was raptured knew it was coming. They didn't know when, but they looked forward to it. That DVD really did it for me, Mac."

"I'd like a look at that."

"I might be able to track down a copy for you, if the church is still standing."

Buck got directions to the makeshift shelter from Kuntz and hurried to the Range Rover. He tried calling Tsion and was frustrated to get a busy signal. But that was encouraging, too. It wasn't the normal buzz of a malfunctioning phone. It sounded like a true busy signal, as if Tsion's phone was engaged. Buck dialed Rayford's private number. If this worked, through cell technology and solar power, they should have been able to connect with each other anywhere on Earth.

The problem was, Rayford was not on Earth. The roar of the engine, the *thwock-thwock-thwock* of the blades, and the static in his headset made a cacophony of chaos. He and Mac heard the phone at the same time. Mac slapped his pocket and yanked out his phone. "Not mine," he said.

Rayford turned to fish his out of his folded jacket, but by the time he whipped off his headphones, flipped open the phone, and pressed it to his ear, he heard only that empty echo of an open connection. He couldn't imagine cell towers close enough to relay a signal. He had to have gotten that ring off a satellite. He turned in his seat, angling the phone to try to pick up a stronger signal.

"Hello? Rayford Steele here. Can you hear me? If you can, call me back! I'm in the air and can hear nothing. If you're family, call me within twenty seconds to make this phone ring again right away, even if we can't communicate. Otherwise, call me in about—" He looked to Mac.

"Ninety minutes."

"Ninety minutes from now. We should be on the ground and reachable. Hello?"

Nothing.

Buck had heard Rayford's phone ringing. Then nothing but static. At least he had not gotten an unanswered ring. Another busy signal would have been encouraging. But what was this? A click, static, nothing understandable. He slapped his phone shut.

Buck knew the furniture store. It was on the way to the Edens Expressway. The drive normally took no more than ten minutes, but the terrain had changed. He had to drive miles out of the way to go around mountains of destruction. His landmarks were gone or flat. His favorite restaurant was identifiable only by its massive neon sign on the ground. About forty feet away, the roof peeked from a hole that swallowed the rest of the place. Rescue crews filed in and out of the hole, but they weren't hurrying. Apparently anyone they brought out of there was in a bag.

Buck dialed the Chicago bureau office of *Global Community*

Weekly. No answer. He called headquarters in New York City. What had been a lavish area covering three floors of a skyscraper had been rebuilt in an abandoned warehouse following the bombing of New York. That attack had cost Buck the life of every friend he had ever made at the magazine.

After several rings, a harried voice answered. "We're closed. Unless this is an emergency, please let us leave the lines open."

"Buck Williams from Chicago," he said.

"Yes, Mr. Williams. You've gotten the word then?"

"I'm sorry?"

"You've not been in touch with anyone in the Chicago office?"

"Our phones just came back up. I got no answer."

"You won't. The building is gone. Almost every staff member is confirmed dead."

"Oh no."

"I'm sorry. A secretary and an intern survived and checked on the staff. They never reached you?"

"I was not reachable."

"It's a relief you're OK. You *are* OK?"

"I'm looking for my wife, but I'm all right, yes."

"The two survivors are cooperating with the *Tribune* and have a Web page already. Punch in any name, and whatever is known is flashed: dead, alive, being treated, or no known whereabouts. I'm the only one on the phones here. We've been decimated, Mr. Williams. You know we're printed on, what, ten or twelve different presses around the world—"

"Fourteen."

"Yes, well, as far as we know, one in Tennessee still has some printing capability and one in southeast Asia. Who knows how long it will be before we can go back to press?"

"How about the North American staff?"

"I'm online right now," she said. "We're about 50 percent confirmed dead and 40 percent unaccounted for. It's over, isn't it?"

"For the *Weekly*, you mean?"

"What else would I mean?"

"Mankind, I thought you were saying."

"It's pretty much over for mankind, too, wouldn't you say, Mr. Williams?"

"It looks bleak," Buck said. "But it's far from over. Maybe we can talk about that sometime." Buck heard phones ringing in the background.

"Maybe," she said. "I've got to get these."

After more than forty minutes of driving, Buck had to stop for a procession of emergency vehicles. A grader built a dirt mound over a fissure in a road that had otherwise escaped damage. No one could drive through until that mound was leveled off. Buck grabbed his laptop and plugged it into the cigarette lighter. He searched the Web for the *Global Community Weekly* information page. It was not working. He called up the *Tribune* page. He ran a people search and found the listing the secretary had told him about. A warning stipulated that no one could vouch for the authenticity of the information, given that many reports of the dead could not be corroborated for days.

Buck entered Chloe's name and was not surprised to find her in the "no known whereabouts" category. He found himself, Loretta, and even Donny Moore and his wife in the same category. He updated each entry, but he chose not to include his private phone number. Anyone needing that already had it. He entered Tsion's name. No one seemed to know where he was either.

Buck tapped in "Rayford Steele, Captain, Global Community Senior Administration." He held his breath until he saw: "Confirmed alive; Global Community temporary headquarters, New Babylon, Iraq."

Buck let his head fall back and breathed a quivering sigh. "Thank you, God," he whispered.

He straightened and checked the rearview mirror. Several cars were behind him, and he was fourth in line. It would be several more minutes. He entered "Amanda White Steele."

The computer ground on for a while and then noted with an asterisk, "Check domestic airlines, Pan-Continental, international."

He entered that. "Subject confirmed on Boston to New Babylon nonstop, reported crashed and submerged in Tigris River, no survivors."

Poor Rayford! Buck thought. Buck had never gotten to know Amanda as well as he'd wanted to, but he knew her to be a sweet person and a true gift to Rayford. Now he wanted all the more to reach his father-in-law.

Buck checked on Chaim Rosenzweig, who was confirmed alive and en route from Israel to New Babylon. *Good,* he thought. He listed his own father and brother, and they came up unaccounted for. No news, he decided, was good news for now.

He entered Hattie Durham's name. The name was not recognized. Hattie can't be her real name. What is Hattie short for? Hilda? Hildegard? What else starts with an H? Harriet? That sounds as old as Hattie. It worked.

He was again directed to the airlines, this time for a domestic flight. He found Hattie confirmed on a nonstop flight from Boston to Denver. "No report of arrival."

So, Buck thought, *if Amanda made her flight, she's gone. If Hattie made her flight, she* could *be gone. If Mrs. Cavenaugh was right, and she saw Chloe run from Loretta's house, Chloe might still be alive.*

Buck could not get his mind around the possibility that Chloe could be dead. He wouldn't allow himself to consider it until he had no other alternatives.

"I have to admit, Mac, a lot of it was just plain logic," Rayford said. "Pastor Billings had been raptured. But he'd made that DVD first, and on it he talked about everything that had just happened, what we were going through, and what we were probably thinking about. He had me pegged. He knew I'd be scared, he knew I'd be grieving, he knew I'd be desperate and searching. And he showed from the Bible the prophecies that told of this. He reminded me I'd probably heard about it somewhere along the line. He even told of things to watch out for. Best of all, he answered my biggest question: Did I still have a chance?

"I didn't know a lot of people had questions about that very thing. Was the Rapture the end? If you missed out because you didn't believe, were you lost forever? I had never thought about it, but supposedly lots of preachers believed you couldn't become a believer after the Rapture. They used that to scare people into making their decisions in advance. I wish I'd heard that before because I might have believed."

Mac looked sharply at Rayford. "No you wouldn't. If you were going to believe before, you would have believed your wife."

"Probably. But I sure couldn't argue now. What other explanation was there? I was ready. I wanted to tell God that if there was one more chance, if the Rapture had been his last attempt to get my attention, it had worked."

"So then, what? You had to do something? Say something? Talk to a pastor, what?"

"On the DVD, Billings walked through what he called the Bible's plan of salvation. That was a strange term to me. I'd heard it at some time or another, but not in our first church. And at New Hope I wasn't listening. I was sure listening now."

"So, what's the plan?"

"It's simple and straightforward, Mac." Rayford outlined from memory the basics about man's sin separating him from God and God's desire to welcome him back. "Everybody's a sinner," Rayford said. "I wasn't open to that before. But with everything my wife said coming true, I saw myself for what I was. There were worse people. A lot of people would say I was better than most, but next to God I felt worthless."

"That's one thing I don't have any problem with, Ray. You won't find me claiming to be anything but a scoundrel."

"And yet, see? Most people think you're a nice guy."

"I'm OK, I guess. But I know the real me."

"Pastor Billings pointed out that the Bible says, 'There is none righteous, no, not one' and that 'all we like sheep have gone astray,' and that 'all our righteousnesses are like filthy rags.' It didn't make me feel better to know I wasn't unique. I was just grateful there was some plan to reconnect me with God. When he explained how a holy God had to punish sin but didn't want any of the people he created to die, I finally started to see it. Jesus, the Son of God, the only man who ever lived without sin, died for everybody's sin. All we had to do was believe that, repent of our sins, receive the gift of salvation. We would be forgiven and what Billings referred to as 'reconciled' to God."

"So if I believe that, I'm in?" Mac said.

"You also have to believe that God raised Jesus from the dead. That provided the victory over sin and death, and it also proved Jesus was divine."

"I believe all that, Ray, so is that it? Am I in?"

Rayford's blood ran cold. What was troubling him? Whatever made him sure Amanda was alive was also making him wonder whether Mac was sincere. This was too easy. Mac had seen the turmoil of almost two years of the Tribulation already. But was that enough to persuade him?

He seemed sincere. But Rayford didn't really know him, didn't know his background. Mac could be a loyalist, a Carpathia plant. Rayford had already exposed himself to mortal danger if Mac was merely entrapping him. Silently he prayed again, "God, how will I know for sure?"

"Bruce Barnes, my first pastor, encouraged us to memorize Scripture. I don't know if I'll find my Bible again, but I remember lots of passages. One of the first I learned was Romans 10:9-10. It says, 'If you confess with your mouth the Lord Jesus and believe in your heart that God has raised Him from the dead, you will be saved. For with the heart one believes unto righteousness, and with the mouth confession is made unto salvation.'"

Mac stared ahead, as if concentrating on flying. He was suddenly less animated. He spoke more deliberately. Rayford didn't know what to make of it. "What does it mean to confess with your mouth?" Mac said.

"Just what it sounds like. You've got to say it. You've got to tell somebody. In fact, you're supposed to tell lots of people."

"You think Nicolae Carpathia is the Antichrist. Is there anything in the Bible about telling him?"

Rayford shook his head. "Not that I know of. Not too many people have to make that choice. Carpathia knows where I stand because he has ears everywhere. He knows my son-in-law is a believer, but Buck never told him. He thought it best to keep that to himself so he could be more effective." Rayford was either persuading Mac or burying himself, he wasn't sure which.

Mac was silent several minutes. Finally he sighed. "So how does it work? How did you know when you'd done whatever it was God wanted you to do?"

"Pastor Billings walked the viewers of that DVD through a prayer. We were to tell God we knew we were sinners and that we needed his forgiveness. We were to tell him we believed Jesus died for our sins and God raised him from the dead. Then we were to accept his gift of salvation and thank him for it."

"Seems too easy."

"Believe me, it might have been easier if I had done it before. But this isn't what I call easy."

For another long stretch, Mac said nothing. Every time that happened, Rayford felt gloomier. Was he handing himself to the enemy? "Mac, this is something you can do on your own, or I could pray with you, or—"

"No. This is definitely something a person should do on his own. *You* were alone, weren't you?"

"I was," Rayford said.

Mac seemed nervous. Distracted. He didn't look at Rayford. Rayford didn't want to push, and yet he hadn't decided yet whether Mac was a live prospect or just playing him. If the former was true, he didn't want to let Mac off the hook by being too polite.

"So what do you think, Mac? What are you gonna do about this?"

Rayford's heart sank when Mac not only did not respond, but also looked the other way. Rayford wished he was clairvoyant. He would have liked to know whether he had come on too strong or had exposed Mac for the phony he was.

Mac took a deep breath and held it. Finally he exhaled and shook his head. "Ray, I appreciate your telling me this. It's quite a story. Very impressive. I'm moved. I can see why you believe, and no doubt it works for you."

So that was it, Rayford thought. *Mac was going to blow it off by using the glad-it-works-for-you routine.*

"But it's personal and private, isn't it?" Mac continued. "I want to be careful not to pretend or rush into it in an emotional moment."

"I understand," Rayford said, desperately wishing he knew Mac's heart.

"So you won't take it personally if I sleep on this?"

"Not at all," Rayford said. "I hope there's no aftershock or attack that might get you killed before you are assured of heaven, but—"

"I have to think God knows how close I am and wouldn't allow that."

"I don't claim to know the mind of God," Rayford said. "Just let me say I wouldn't push my luck."

"Are you pressuring me?"

"Sorry. You're right. No one can be badgered into it."

Rayford feared he had offended Mac. That or Mac's attitude was a stalling technique. On the other hand, if Mac *was* a subversive, he wouldn't be above faking a salvation experience to ingratiate himself to Rayford. He wondered when he would ever be sure of Mac's credibility.

When Buck finally reached the furniture store, he found jerry-built construction. No semblance of streets or roads existed, so emergency vehicles staked out their spots with no thought to conserving space or leaving paths open to the doors. Global Community peacekeeping emergency forces traipsed in and out with supplies as well as new patients.

Buck got in only because of the security clearance level on his Global Community identification tag. He asked for Mrs. Cavenaugh and was pointed to a row of a dozen wood-and-canvas cots lining a wall in one corner. They were so close no one could walk between them.

Buck smelled freshly cut wood and was surprised to see new two-by-fours nailed together for railings throughout. The rear of the building had sunk about three feet, causing the concrete floor to split in the middle. When he got to the crack, he had to hang on to the two-by-fours because the pitch was so steep. Wood blocks anchored to the floor kept the cots from sliding. Emergency personnel took tiny steps, shoulders back, to keep from tumbling forward.

Each cot had a strip of paper stapled to the foot end, with either a hand-printed or computer-generated name. When Buck walked through, most of the conscious patients rolled up on their elbows, as if to see if he was their loved one. They reclined again when they didn't recognize him.

The paper on the third cot from the wall read "Cavenaugh, Helen."

She was asleep. Men were on either side of her. One, who appeared homeless, sat with his back to the wall. He seemed to protect a paper bag full of clothes. He eyed Buck warily and pulled out a department store catalog, which he pretended to read with great interest.

On Helen Cavenaugh's other side was a thin young man who appeared in his early twenties. His eyes darted and he ran his hands through his hair. "I need a smoke," he said. "You got any cigarettes?"

Buck shook his head. The man rolled onto his side, pulled his knees up to his chest, and lay rocking. Buck would not have been surprised to find the man's thumb in his mouth.

Time was of the essence, but who knew what trauma Mrs. Cavenaugh was sleeping off? She had very nearly been killed, and she had no doubt seen the remains of her house when she was carted away. Buck grabbed a plastic chair and sat at the foot of her cot. He wouldn't wake her, but he would talk to her at the first sign of consciousness.

Rayford wondered when he had become such a pessimist. And why hadn't it affected his bedrock belief that his wife was still alive? He didn't believe Carpathia's implication that she had been working for the Global Community. Or was that, too, just a story from Mac?

Since he had become a believer, Rayford had begun to look on the brighter side, in spite of the chaos. But now, a deep, dark sense of foreboding came over him as Mac landed, still silent. They secured the helicopter and completed post-flight procedures. Before they passed security to enter the shelter, Mac said, "This is all complicated too, Captain, because you are my boss."

That had not seemed to affect anything else that day. They had flown more as buddies than as boss and subordinate. Rayford would have no trouble maintaining decorum, but it sounded as if Mac might.

Rayford wanted to leave their conversation concrete, but he didn't want to give Mac an ultimatum or tell him to report back. "I'll see you tomorrow," he said.

Mac nodded, but as they headed for their own quarters, a uniformed orderly approached. "Captain Steele and Officer McCullum? You are requested in the central command area." He handed each a card.

Rayford read silently, "My office, ASAP. Leonardo Fortunato." Since when had Leon begun using his entire first name?

"Wonder what Leon wants at this time of the night?"

Mac peeked at Rayford's card. "Leon? I've got a meeting with Carpathia." He showed Rayford his card.

Was that really a surprise to Mac, or was this all one big setup? He and Mac had not gotten into why Rayford and the rest of the Tribulation Force believed Carpathia fit the bill of the Antichrist. Still, Mac had enough information on Rayford to bury him. And, apparently, he had the right audience.

Buck was fidgety. Mrs. Cavenaugh looked healthy, but she lay so still he was hardly able to detect the rise and fall of her chest. He was tempted to cross his legs and kick her cot in the process, but who knew how an old woman would respond to that? It might push her over the edge. Antsy, Buck dialed Tsion. He finally got through, and Buck gushed that he had reason to believe Chloe was alive.

"Wonderful, Cameron! I am doing well here, too. I have been able to get on the Net, and I have more reason than ever to get back to Israel."

"We'll have to talk about that," Buck said. "I still think it's too dangerous, and I don't know how we would get you there."

"Cameron, there is news all over the Internet that one of Carpathia's top priorities is rebuilding transportation networks."

Buck spoke louder than he needed to, hoping to rouse Mrs. Cavenaugh. "I'll be back as soon as I can, and I plan to have Chloe with me."

"I will pray," Tsion said.

Buck hit the speed dial for Rayford's phone.

Rayford was amazed that Leon's office was only slightly smaller and every bit as exquisitely appointed as Nicolae's.

Everything in the shelter was state-of-the-art, but the opulence began and ended in those two offices.

Fortunato had a glow. He shook Rayford's hand, bowed at the waist, motioned to a chair, then sat behind his desk. Rayford had always found him curious, a dark, swarthy man, short and stocky with black hair and dark eyes. He didn't unbutton his suit jacket when he sat, so it bowed comically at the chest, spoiling whatever formality he was trying to engender.

"Captain Steele," Fortunato began, but before he could say anything, Rayford's phone chirped. Fortunato raised a hand and let it fall, as if he couldn't believe Rayford would take a call at a time like this.

"Excuse me, Leon, but this could be family."

"You can't take calls in here," Leon said.

"Well, I'm going to," Rayford said. "I have no information about my daughter and son-in-law."

"I mean you're technically not able to receive phone calls in here," Leon said. All Rayford heard was static. "We're way underground and surrounded by concrete. Think, man."

Rayford knew the trunk lines from the center led to solar panels and satellite dishes on the surface. Of course his cell phone would not work here. Still, he was hopeful. Few people knew his number, and the ones who did he cared about most in the world.

"You have my full attention, Leon."

"Not willingly, I surmise." Rayford shrugged. "I have more than one reason for asking to see you," Leon said. Rayford wondered when these people slept. "We have information on your family, at least part of it."

"You do?" Rayford said, leaning forward. "What? Who? My daughter?"

"No, I'm sorry. Your daughter is unaccounted for. However, your son-in-law has been spotted in a Chicago suburb."

"Unharmed?"

"To the best of our knowledge."

"And what is the state of communications between here and there?"

Fortunato smiled condescendingly. "I believe those lines are open," he said, "but of course not from down here, unless you use our equipment."

Chalk one up for Fortunato, Rayford thought. "I'd like to call him as soon as possible to check on my daughter."

"Of course. Just a few more items. Salvage teams are working around the clock in the compound where you lived. In the unlikely event they are able to find anything of value, you should submit a detailed inventory. Anything of value not preidentified will be confiscated."

"That makes no sense," Rayford said.

"Nevertheless . . . ," Fortunato said dismissively.

"Anything else?" Rayford said, as if he wanted to leave.

"Yes," Fortunato said slowly. Rayford had the idea Fortunato was stalling to make him squirm before calling Buck. "One of His Excellency's most trusted international advisers has arrived from Israel. I'm sure you know of Dr. Chaim Rosenzweig."

"Of course," Rayford said. "But *His Excellency*? At first I thought you were referring to Mathews."

"Captain Steele, I have been meaning to talk to you about protocol. You inappropriately refer to me by my first name. Sometimes you even refer to the potentate by his first name. We are aware that you do not sympathize with the beliefs of Pontifex Maximus Peter; however, it is most disrespectful for you to refer to him by only his last name."

"And yet you are using a title that has for generations been limited to religious leaders and royalty for Carpath—uh, Nicolae Carpath—, Potentate Carpathia."

"Yes, and I believe the time has come to refer to him in that manner. The potentate has contributed more to world unity than anyone who ever lived. He is beloved by citizens of every kingdom. And now that he has demonstrated supernatural power, *Excellency* is hardly too lofty a title."

"Demonstrated these powers to whom?"

"He has asked me to share with you my own story."

"I have heard the story."

"From me?"

"From others."

"Then I won't bore you with the details, Captain Steele. Let me just say that regardless of the differences you and I have had, because of my experience I am eager to reconcile. When a man is literally brought back from death, his perspectives change. You will feel a new sense of respect from me, whether you deserve it or not. And it will be genuine."

"I can't wait. Now what was it about Rosen—?"

"Now, Captain Steele! That was sarcastic, and I was being sincere. And there you go again. It's *Dr.* Rosenzweig to you. The man is one of the leading botanists in history."

"OK, fine, Leon. I mean, Dr. Fortunato—"

"I am not a doctor! You should refer to me as Commander Fortunato."

"I'm not sure I'm going to be able to do that," Rayford said with a sigh. "When did you get that title?"

"Truth be known, my title has recently changed to Supreme Commander. It was bestowed upon me by His Excellency."

"This is all getting a little crazy," Rayford said. "Wasn't it more fun when you and I were just Rayford and Leon?"

Fortunato grimaced. "Apparently you are unable to take anything seriously."

"Well, I'm serious about whatever it is you have to tell me about Rosenzweig. Um, *Dr.* Rosenzweig."

CHAPTER 8

WHILE HE WAITED for Mrs. Cavenaugh, Buck thought about heading to the Range Rover so he could look up Ken Ritz's number on his computer. If Ken could get him and Tsion to Israel, he was taking Chloe. He never wanted her out of his sight again.

He was about to step out when Mrs. Cavenaugh finally stirred. He didn't want to startle her. He just watched her. When her eyes opened, he smiled. She looked puzzled, then sat up and pointed at him.

"You were gone, young man. Weren't you?"

"Gone?"

"You and your wife. You lived with Loretta, didn't you?"

"Yes, ma'am."

"But you weren't there yesterday morning."

"No."

"And your wife. I saw her! Is she all right?"

"That's what I want to talk about, Mrs. Cavenaugh. Are you up to it?"

"Oh, I'm all right! I just have nowhere to stay. I got the dickens scared out of me, and I don't care to see the remains of my house, but I'm all right."

"Want to take a walk?"

"There's nothing I'd like more, but I'm not going anywhere with a man unless I know his name."

Buck apologized and introduced himself.

"I knew that," she said. "I never met you, but I saw you around and Loretta told me about you. I met your wife. Corky?"

"Chloe."

"Of course! I should remember because I liked that name so much. Well, come on, help me up."

Thumbsucker hadn't budged except to keep rocking. Homeless looked wary and held his bag tighter. Buck considered yanking one of their cots so he could get in and help Mrs. Cavenaugh off of hers. But he didn't want a scene. He just stood at the end of her cot and reached for her. As she stepped off the end of the flimsy thing, the other end went straight up. Buck saw it coming at him over her head. He blocked it with his hand and it slammed back down with such a thunderous resound that Homeless cried out and Thumbsucker jumped two feet. He split the canvas cot when he came back down. It slowly separated, and he dropped out of sight. Homeless lowered his face into his sack, and Buck couldn't tell if he was laughing or crying. Thumbsucker reappeared looking as if he thought Buck might have done that on purpose. Mrs. Cavenaugh, who missed it all, slipped her hand through Buck's elbow, and they walked to where they could talk with more privacy.

"I already told this to one young man with disaster relief or some such, but anyway I thought all the racket was a tornado. Who ever heard of an earthquake in the Midwest? You hear about a little rattling and shaking downstate once in a while, but an honest to goodness earthquake that knocks over buildings and kills people? I thought I was smart, but I was a fool. I ran to the basement. Of course, *ran* is relative. It just means I didn't go a step at a time, as usual. I went down those stairs like a little girl. The only pain now is in my knees.

"I went to the window to see if there was a funnel. It was bright and sunny, but the noise was getting louder and the house banged all around me, so I still figured I knew what it was. That's when I saw your wife."

"Where, exactly?"

"That window is too high for me to see out. All I could see was the sky and the trees. They were really moving. My late husband kept a stepladder down there. I climbed just high enough so I could see the ground. That's when your wife, Chloe, came running out. She was carrying something. Whatever it was was more important than putting something on her feet. She was barefoot."

"And she ran where?"

"To your car. It's stupid, but I hollered at her. She was holding her stuff in one arm and trying to unlock the car with the other, and I was yelling, 'You don't want to be outside, girl!' I was hoping she'd put that stuff down and get in the car quick enough to outrun the funnel, but she wasn't even looking up. She finally got it open and started the car, and that's when everything broke loose. I swear one of my basement walls actually moved. I've never seen anything like that in my life. That car started to move, and the biggest tree in Loretta's yard tore itself right from the ground, roots and all. It took half Loretta's yard with it and sounded like a bomb dropping in the street, right in front of her car.

"She backed up, and the tree on the other side of Loretta's yard started to give way. I was still yellin' at that girl like she could hear me inside the car. I was sure that second tree would land right on her. She jerked left, and the whole road twisted up right in front of her. If she had pulled onto that pavement a split second earlier, that street flipping up would have tipped her over. She must have been scared to death, one tree lying in front of her, one threatening to fall on her, and the street sticking straight up. She whipped around that first tree and raced right up the driveway into the garage. I was cheering for her. I hoped she'd have enough sense to get to the basement. I couldn't believe a tornado could do that much damage without me seeing it. When I heard everything crash to the floor like the whole house was coming apart—well, of course, it was—I finally got it into my thick head that this wasn't a tornado. When the other two trees in Loretta's yard came down, that window blew out, so I climbed down and ran to the other end of the basement.

"When my front room furniture crashed into where I'd just been, I stepped over the sump pump and pulled myself up on the concrete cutout to the window. I don't know what I was thinking. I was just hoping Chloe was where she could hear me. I screamed bloody murder out that window. She came out the side door white as a sheet, still barefooted and now empty-handed, and she went runnin' to the back as fast as she could go. That was the last I saw of her. The rest of my house fell in, and somehow the pipes deflected everything a little and left me a tiny space to wait until somebody found me."

"I'm glad you're all right."

"It was pretty exciting. I hope you find Chloe."

"Do you remember what she was wearing?"

"Sure. That off-white dress, a shift."

"Thank you, Mrs. Cavenaugh."

The old woman stared into the distance and shook her head slowly.

Chloe's still alive, Buck thought.

"The first thing Dr. Rosenzweig asked about was your well-being, Captain Steele."

"I hardly know the man, Supreme Commander Fortunato," Rayford said, carefully enunciating.

"*Commander* is sufficient, Captain."

"You can call me Ray."

Now Fortunato was angry. "I could call you *Private*," he said.

"Oh, good one, Commander."

"You're not going to bait me, Captain. As I told you, I'm a new man."

"Brand-new," Rayford said, "if you really were dead yesterday and alive today."

"The truth is, Dr. Rosenzweig next asked after your son-in-law, daughter, and Tsion Ben-Judah."

Rayford froze. Rosenzweig couldn't have been that stupid. On the other hand, Buck always said Rosenzweig was enamored of Carpathia. He didn't know Carpathia was as much an enemy of Ben-Judah as the State of Israel was. Rayford maintained eye contact with the glaring Fortunato, who seemed to know he had Rayford on the ropes. Rayford prayed silently.

"I brought him up-to-date and told him your daughter was unaccounted for," Leon said. He let that hang in the air. Rayford did not respond. "And what did you wish us to tell him of Tsion Ben-Judah?"

"What did *I* wish?" Rayford said. "I have no knowledge of his whereabouts."

"Then why did Dr. Rosenzweig ask about him in the same breath with your daughter and son-in-law?"

"Why don't you ask him?"

"Because I'm asking you, Captain! You think we weren't

aware that Cameron Williams aided and abetted his escape from the State of Israel?"

"Do you believe everything you hear?"

"We know that to be fact," Fortunato said.

"Then why do you need my input?"

"We want to know where Tsion Ben-Judah is. It is important to Dr. Rosenzweig that His Excellency come to Dr. Ben-Judah's aid."

Rayford had listened in when that request was brought to Carpathia. Nicolae had laughed it off, suggesting his people make it appear he tried to help while actually informing Ben-Judah's enemies where they could find him.

"If I knew the whereabouts of Tsion Ben-Judah," Rayford said, "I would not tell you. I would ask him if he wanted you to know."

Fortunato stood. Apparently the meeting was over. He walked Rayford to the door. "Captain Steele, your disloyalty has no future. I say again, you will find me most conciliatory. I would consider it a favor if you would not intimate to Dr. Rosenzweig that His Excellency is as eager to know the whereabouts of Dr. Ben-Judah as he is."

"Why would I do you a favor?"

Fortunato spread his hands and shook his head. "I rest my case," he said. "Nicolae, er, the poten—His Excellency has more patience than I. You would not be my pilot."

"That's correct, Supreme Commander. I will, however, be piloting this week when you pick up the rest of the Global Community boys."

"I assume you're referring to the other world leaders."

"And Peter Mathews."

"Pontifex Maximus, yes. But he's not actually GC."

"He has a lot of power," Rayford said.

"Yes, but more popular than diplomatic. He has no political authority."

"Whatever you say."

Buck walked Mrs. Cavenaugh back to her bunk, but before helping her settle, he approached the woman in charge of that area. "Does she have to be between these wackos?"

"You can put her in any open cot," the woman said. "Just make sure her name sticker goes with her."

Buck guided Mrs. Cavenaugh to a cot near other people her age. On his way out he approached the supervisor again. "What is anyone doing about missing persons?"

"Ask Ernie," she said, pointing to a small, middle-aged man plotting something on a map on the wall. "He's with GC, and he's in charge of the transfer of patients between shelters."

Ernie proved formal and distracted. "Missing persons?" he repeated, not looking at Buck but still working on his map. "First off, most of them are going to wind up dead. There are so many, we don't know where to start."

Buck pulled a photo of Chloe from his wallet. "Start here," he said.

He finally had Ernie's attention. He studied the picture,

turning it toward the battery-powered lights. "Wow," he said. "Your daughter?"

"She's twenty-two. To be her dad I'd have to be at least forty."

"So?"

"I'm thirty-two," he said, astounded at his vanity at a time like this. "This is my wife, and I was told she escaped from our house before the quake leveled it."

"Show me," Ernie said, turning toward his map. Buck pointed to Loretta's block. "Hmm. Not good. This was a worldwide quake, but GC has pinpointed several epicenters. That part of Mt. Prospect was close to the epicenter for northern Illinois."

"So it's worse here?"

"It's not much better anywhere else, but this is pretty much the worst of it in this state." Ernie pointed to a mile stretch from behind Loretta's block in direct line with where they were. "Major devastation. She would not have been able to get through there."

"Where might she have gone?"

"Can't help you there. Tell you what I can do, though. I can blow her picture up and fax it to the other shelters. That's about it."

"I'd be grateful."

Ernie did the clerical work himself. Buck was impressed at how sharp the enlarged copy was. "We only got this machine working about an hour ago," Ernie said. "Obviously, it's cellular. You hear about the potentate's communications company?"

"No," Buck said, sighing. "But it wouldn't surprise me to know he's cornered the market."

"That's fair," Ernie said. "It's called Cellular-Solar, and the whole world will be linked again before you know it. GC headquarters calls it Cell-Sol for short."

Ernie wrote on the enlargement, "Missing Person: Chloe Irene Steele Williams. Age 22. 5'7", 125. Blonde hair. Green eyes. No distinguishing marks or characteristics." He added his name and phone number.Adobe Garamond Pro

"Tell me where I can reach you, Mr. Williams. You know not to get your hopes up."

"Too late, Ernie," Buck said, jotting his number. He thanked him again and turned to leave, then returned. "You say they call the potentate's communications network Cell-Sol?"

"Yeah. Short for—"

"Cellular-Solar, yeah." Buck left, shaking his head.

As he climbed into the Range Rover, he felt helpless. But he couldn't shake the feeling that Chloe was out there somewhere. He decided to drive back to Loretta's another way. No sense being out without looking for her. Always.

It was late, and Rayford was tired. Carpathia's office door was shut, but light streamed beneath the door. He assumed Mac was still there. Curious as he was, Rayford wasn't confident Mac would honestly debrief him. For all he knew, Mac was spilling his guts about everything Rayford had said that day.

His top priority before sleep was to try to get through to Buck. At the communications command post he was told he had to have permission from a superior to use a secure outside line. Rayford was surprised. "Look up my level of clearance," he said.

"Sorry, sir. Those are my orders."

"How long will you be here?" Rayford asked.

"Another twenty minutes, sir."

Rayford was tempted to interrupt Carpathia's meeting with Mac. He knew Nicolae would give him permission to use the phone, and by barging in, he would show he was not afraid of His Excellency the Potentate meeting with his own subordinate. But he thought better of it when he saw Fortunato had turned the light off in his office and was locking his door.

Rayford walked briskly to him. Without a trace of sarcasm, he said, "Commander Fortunato, sir, a request."

"Certainly, Captain Steele."

"I need permission from a superior to use an outside line."

"And you're calling—?"

"My son-in-law in the States."

Fortunato backed up against the wall, spread his feet, and crossed his arms. "This is interesting, Captain Steele. Let me ask you, would the Leonardo Fortunato of last week have acceded to this request?"

"I don't know. Probably not."

"Would my permitting it, despite how cavalierly you treated me this evening, prove to you I have changed?"

"Well, it would show me something."

"Feel free to use the phone, Captain. Take all the time you need, and best wishes on finding everything OK at home."

"Thank you," Rayford said.

Buck prayed for Chloe as he drove, imagining Chloe had found her way to safety and simply needed to hear from him. He called to give Tsion an update but didn't stay on the phone long. Tsion seemed down, distracted. Something was on his mind, but Buck didn't want to pursue it while trying to keep the phone open.

Buck flipped open his laptop and looked up Ken Ritz's number. A minute later Ritz's voice mail said, "I'm either flyin', eatin', sleepin', or on the other line. Leave a message."

"Ken, Buck Williams. The two of us you flew out of Israel might need a return trip soon. Call me."

Rayford couldn't believe Buck's phone was busy. He slammed the phone down and waited a few minutes before redialing. *Busy again!* Rayford smacked his hand on the table.

The young communications supervisor said, "We've got a gadget that will keep dialing that number and leave a message."

"I can tell him to call me here, and you'll wake me?"

"Unfortunately, no, sir. But you could ask that he call you at 0700 hours, when we open."

Buck wondered about Ritz's voice mail. How would anyone know if he had been killed in the earthquake? He lived alone, and that system would just take calls until it filled.

Buck was about half an hour from Donny and Sandy Moore's house when his phone rang. "God, let it be Ernie," he pleaded.

"This is Buck."

"Buck, this is a recorded message from Rayford. I'm sorry I couldn't reach you. Please call me at the following number at seven o'clock in the morning my time. That's going to be 10:00 p.m., if you're in the Central Standard Time zone. Praying Chloe's all right. You and our friend, too, of course. I want to hear everything. I'm still looking for Amanda. I feel in my soul she's still alive. Call me."

Buck looked at his watch. Why couldn't he call Rayford right then? Buck was tempted to call Ernie, but he didn't want to bug him. He wended his way back to Tsion. As soon as he came into the house, Buck knew something was wrong. Tsion would not look him in the eye.

Buck said, "I didn't find any rods to poke in the backyard. Did you find the shelter?"

"Yes," Tsion said flatly. "It is a duplicate of where I lived at the church. You want to see it?"

"What's wrong, Tsion?"

"We need to talk. Did you want to see the shelter?"

"That can wait. I just want to know how you get to it."

"You will not believe how close we were last night when we were doing our unpleasant business. The door that appears to lead to a storage area actually opens into a larger door. Through that door is the shelter. Let us pray we never have to use it."

"Here's thanking God it's there if we *do* need it," Buck said. "Now, what's up? We've been through too much for you to keep anything from me."

"I am not keeping it from you for my sake," Tsion said. "I would not want to hear if I were you."

Buck slumped in a chair. "Tsion! Tell me you didn't get word about Chloe!"

"No, no. I am sorry, Cameron. It is not that. I am still praying for the best there. It is just that for all the treasures in Donny's briefcase, the journals also led me where I wish I had not gone."

Tsion sat too, and he looked as bad as he had when his family had been massacred. Buck laid a hand on the rabbi's forearm. "Tsion, what is it?"

Tsion stood and looked out the window over the sink, then turned to face Buck. With his hands deep in his pockets, he moved to the doors that separated the kitchen from the breakfast nook. Buck hoped he wouldn't open them. He didn't need to be reminded of cutting Sandy Moore's body from under the tree. Tsion opened the door and walked to the edge of the cutout.

Buck was struck by the weirdness of where he was and what he was looking at. How had it come to this? He had been Ivy League educated, New York headquartered, at the top of his profession. Now here he sat in a tiny duplex in a Chicago suburb, having moved into the home of a dead couple he barely knew. In less than two years he had seen millions disappear from all over the globe, become a believer in Christ, met and worked for the Antichrist, fallen in love and married, befriended a great biblical scholar, and survived an earthquake.

Tsion slid the door shut and trudged back. He sat wearily, elbows on the table, his troubled face in his hands. Finally, he spoke. "It should come as no surprise, Cameron, that Donny Moore was a genius. I was intrigued by his journals. I have not had time to get through all of them, but after discovering his shelter, I went in to see it. Impressive. I spent a couple of hours putting the finishing touches on one of Bruce Barnes's studies that was quite ingenious. I added some linguistics that I humbly believe added some insight, and then I tried to connect to the Internet. You will be happy to know I was successful."

"You kept your own e-mail address invisible, I hope."

"You have taught me well. I posted the teaching on a central bulletin board. My hope and prayer is that many of the 144,000 witnesses will see it and benefit from it and respond to it. I'll check tomorrow. Much bad teaching is going out on the Net, Cameron. I am jealous that believers not be swayed."

Buck nodded.

"But I digress," Tsion said. "Finished with my work,

I went back to Donny's journals and started from the beginning. I am only about a quarter of the way through. I want to finish, but I am heartsick."

"Why?"

"First let me say that Donny was a true believer. He wrote eloquently of his remorse over missing his first chance to receive Christ. He told of the loss of their baby and how his wife eventually also found God. It is a very sad, poignant account of how they found some joy in anticipation of being reunited with their child. Praise the Lord that has now been realized." Tsion's voice began to quaver. "But, Cameron, I came upon some information I wish I had not discovered. Maybe I should have known it was to be avoided. Donny taught Bruce to encrypt personal messages to make anything he wished inaccessible without his own password. As you recall, no one knew that password. Not Loretta; not even Donny."

"That's right," Buck said. "I asked him."

"Donny must have been protecting Bruce's privacy when he told you that."

"Donny knew Bruce's password? We could have used that. There was a whole gigabyte or so of information we were never able to access off Bruce's computer."

"It was not that Donny knew the password," Tsion said, "but he developed his own code-breaking software. He loaded it onto all the computers he sold you. As you know, during my time in the shelter, I downloaded to my computer— which has astounding storage capacity—everything that had been on Bruce's. We also had those thousands and thousands of pages of printouts, helpful for when my eyes grew tired of peering at the screen. However, it simply seemed to make sense to also make an electronic backup for that material."

"You weren't the only one who did that," Buck said. "I think that stuff is on Chloe's computer and maybe Amanda's."

"We did not, however, leave anything out. Even encrypted files were copied because we didn't want to slow the process by being selective. But we never had access to those."

Buck stared at the ceiling. "Until now, right? That's what you're telling me?"

"Sadly, yes," Tsion said.

Buck stood. "If you're about to tell me something that will affect my esteem for Bruce and his memory, be careful. He is the man who led me to Christ and who helped me grow and—"

"Put your mind at ease, Cameron. My esteem for Pastor Barnes was only elevated by what I found. I found the encryption-solving files on my own computer. I applied these to Bruce's files, and within a few minutes, everything encrypted glowed from my screen.

"The files were not locked. I confess I took a peek and noticed many that were merely personal. Mostly memories of his wife and family. He wrote of his remorse over losing them, not being with them, that sort of thing. I felt guilty and did not read everything there. It must have been my old nature that attracted me to other private files.

"Cameron, I confess this excited me to no end. I believed

I had found more riches from his personal study, but what I found I thought better to not risk printing. It is on my computer in my bedroom. Painful as it will be, you must see it."

Nothing would have kept Buck from it. But he mounted the stairs with the same reluctance he had felt digging through the rubble at Loretta's. Tsion followed Buck into the bedroom and sat on the edge of the high, squeaky bed. A plastic folding chair sat in front of the dresser, on which Tsion's laptop rested. The screen saver bore the message "I Know That My Redeemer Liveth."

Buck sat and brushed the touchpad with his finger. The date of the file indicated it had been in Bruce's computer since two weeks after he had officiated the double wedding of Buck and Chloe and Rayford and Amanda.

Buck spoke into the computer's microphone. "Open document."

The screen read:

Personal prayer journal. 6:35 a.m.: My question this morning, Father, is what would you have me do with this information? I don't know it to be true, but I cannot ignore it. I feel heavily my responsibility as shepherd and mentor to the Tribulation Force. If an interloper has compromised us, I must confront the issue.

Is it possible? Could it be true? I don't claim special powers of discernment; however, I loved this woman and trusted her and believed in her from the day I met her. I thought her perfect for Rayford, and she seemed so spiritually attuned.

Buck stood, his seat hitting the back of the chair and knocking it to the floor. He bent over the laptop, palms on the dresser. *Not Amanda!* he thought. *Please! What damage might she have done?*

Bruce's journal continued: "They are planning a visit soon. Buck and Chloe will come from New York and Rayford and Amanda from Washington. I will be returning from an international trip. I will have to get Rayford alone and show him what has come to me. In the meantime, I feel impotent, given their proximity to NC. Lord, I need wisdom."

Buck's heart raced and he panted. "So where's the file in question?" he said. "What did he receive and from whom?"

"It's attached to the previous day's journal entry," Tsion said.

"Whatever it is, I'm not going to believe it."

"I feel the same, Cameron. I feel it deep in my heart. And yet, here we are, despairing."

Buck said, "Previous entry. Open document."

That day's entry: "God, I feel like David when you refused to respond to him. He pleaded with you not to turn away from him. That is my plea today. I feel so desolate. What am I to make of this?"

"Open attached," Buck said.

The message had been sent from Europe. It was to Bruce,

but his last name had been misspelled *Barns*. The sender was "an interested friend."

"Scroll down," Buck said, sick to his stomach. As the computer responded, the phone rang in his pocket.

CHAPTER 9

HE FLIPPED HIS PHONE OPEN. "This is Buck."

"I'm trying to reach Cameron Williams of *Global Weekly Magazine.*"

"Speaking."

"Lieutenant Ernest Kivisto here. Met you earlier today."

"Yes, Ernie! What have you got?"

"First off, headquarters is looking for you."

"Headquarters?"

"The big man. Or at least somebody close to him. I thought I'd widen the search for your wife, so I faxed that sheet to surrounding states. You never know. If she was hurt or got evacuated, she could be anywhere. Anyway, somebody recognized the name. Then a guy named Kuntz said he'd seen you earlier too. Somehow your whereabouts gets into the database and we get word headquarters is looking for you."

"Thanks. I'll check in."

"I know you don't report to me, and I have no jurisdiction, but since I'm the last one who saw you, I'm gonna have to answer for it if you don't check in."

"I said I would check in."

"I'm not naggin' ya or anything. I'm just saying—"

Buck was tired of military types covering their own tails. But this was a man he wanted to get back to him as soon as possible if Chloe turned up. "Ernie, I appreciate all you're doing for me, and you may rest assured that I will not only check in with headquarters, but I will also mention that I got the word from you. You want to spell that last name for me?"

Kivisto did. "Now for the good news, sir. One of the Cell-Sol guys got the fax in his truck. He wasn't happy about me broadcasting it everywhere. He said I shouldn't be tying up the whole GC network for a missing person's bulletin. Anyway, he said they saw a young woman who might fit that description being lifted into one of those Ambu-Vans late yesterday."

"Where?"

"I'm not sure exactly where, but for sure it was between that block you pointed out to me and where I am now."

"That's a pretty big area, Ernie. Can we narrow that at all?"

"Sorry, I wish I could."

"Can I talk to this guy?"

"I doubt it. He said something about having been awake since the earthquake. I think he's bedding down in one of the shelters."

"I didn't see any Ambu-Vans at your shelter."

"We're taking in only the ambulatory."

"This woman wasn't?"

"Apparently not. If she had serious ailments, she would have been taken to, just a minute here . . . Kenosha. A couple of hotels right next to each other just inside the city limits have been turned into hospitals."

Ernie gave Buck the number for the medical center in Kenosha. Buck thanked him and asked, "In case I have trouble getting through, what are the odds I can drive to Kenosha?"

"Got a four-wheel drive?"

"Yeah."

"You're gonna need it. I-94 lost every overpass between here and Madison. There's a couple places you can get on, but then before you get to the next overpass you have to go through single-lane roads, little towns, or just open fields and hope for the best. Thousands are trying it. It's a mess."

"I don't have a helicopter, so I have no choice."

"Call first. No sense trying a trip like that for nothing."

Buck couldn't help feeling as if Chloe were within reach. It bothered him that she might be hurt, but at least she was alive. What would she think about Amanda?

Buck scrolled back down through Bruce's journal entry

and found the e-mail Bruce had received. The message, from the "interested friend" read: "Suspect the root beer lady. Investigate her maiden name and beware the eyes and ears of New Babylon. Special forces are only as strong as their weakest links. Insurrection begins in the home. Battles are lost in the field, but wars are lost from within."

Buck turned to face Tsion. "What did you deduce from that?"

"Someone was warning Bruce about somebody within the Tribulation Force. We have only two women. The one with a maiden name Bruce might not know would have been Amanda. I still do not know why he or she referred to her as the root beer lady."

"Her initials."

"A. W.," Tsion said, as if to himself as he righted Buck's chair. "I do not follow."

"A&W is an old brand of root beer in this country," Buck said. "How is she supposed to be the ears and eyes of, what, Carpathia? Is that what we're supposed to get out of New Babylon?"

"It is all in the maiden name," Tsion said. "I was going to look it up, but you will see Bruce has already done the work. Amanda's maiden name was Recus, which meant nothing to Bruce and stalled him for a while."

"It means nothing to me either," Buck said.

"Bruce dug deeper. Apparently, Amanda's mother's maiden name, before she married Recus, was Fortunato."

Buck blanched and dropped into the chair again.

"Bruce must have had the same reaction," Tsion said. "He writes in there, 'Please God, don't let it be true.' What is the significance of that name?"

Buck sighed. "Nicolae Carpathia's right-hand man, a total sycophant, is named Leonardo Fortunato."

Buck turned back to Tsion's computer. "Close files. Re-encrypt. Open search engine. Find *Chicago Tribune*. Open name search. Ken or Kenneth Ritz, Illinois, U.S.A."

"Our pilot!" Tsion said. "You are going to get me home after all!"

"I only want to see if the guy's still alive, just in case."

Ritz was listed "among patients in stable condition, Arthur Young Memorial Hospital, Palatine, Illinois."

"How come all the good news is about someone else?"

Buck dialed the number Ernie had given him for Kenosha. It was busy. Again and again for fifteen minutes. "We can keep trying while we're on the road."

"The road?" Tsion said.

"In a manner of speaking," Buck said. He looked at his watch. It was after seven in the evening, Tuesday.

Two hours later, he and Tsion were still in Illinois. The Rover bounced slowly along with hundreds of other cars snaking their way north. Just as many were coming the other way, fifty to a hundred feet from where I-94 once propelled cars at eighty-plus miles an hour in both directions.

While Buck looked for alternate routes or some way to pass poky vehicles, Tsion manned the phone. They powered it from the cigarette lighter to save the battery, and every minute or so Tsion hit the redial button. Either the phone in Kenosha was hopelessly overloaded or it was not working.

For the second day in a row, his first officer, Mac McCullum, awakened Rayford. A tick past 6:30 Wednesday morning in New Babylon, Rayford heard soft but insistent knocking. He sat up, tangled in sheet and blankets. "Gimme a minute," he slurred, realizing this might be news of his call from Buck. He opened the door, saw it was Mac, and collapsed back into bed. "I'm not ready to wake up yet. What's up?"

Mac flipped the light on, making Rayford hide his face in the pillow. "I did it, Cap. I did it!"

"Did what?" Rayford said, his voice muffled.

"I prayed. I did it."

Rayford turned over, covering his left eye and peeking at Mac through a slit in his right. "Really?"

"I'm a believer, man. Can you believe it?"

Keeping his eyes shielded, Rayford reached with his free hand to shake Mac's. Mac sat on the edge of Rayford's bed. "Man, this feels great!" he said. "Just a while ago I woke up and decided to quit thinking about it and do it."

Rayford sat up with his back to Mac and rubbed his eyes. He ran his hands through his hair and felt his bangs brush his eyebrows. Few people ever saw him that way.

What was he to make of this? He hadn't even debriefed

Mac on his meeting with Carpathia from the night before. How he wished it were true. What if it was all a big act, a plot to reel him in and incapacitate him? Surely that had to be Carpathia's long-range plan—to take at least one member of the opposition out of action.

All he could do until he knew for sure was to take this at face value. If Mac could fake a conversion and the emotion that went along with it, Rayford could fake being thrilled. His eyes finally adjusted to the light, and he turned to face Mac. The usually dapper first officer was wearing his uniform as usual. Rayford had never seen him casual. But what was that? "Did you shower this morning, Mac?"

"Always. What do you mean?"

"You've got a smudge on your forehead."

Mac swiped with his fingers just below the hairline.

"Still there," Rayford said. "Looks like what Catholics used to get on Ash Wednesday."

Mac stood and moved to the mirror attached to Rayford's wall. He leaned close, turning this way and that. "What the heck are you talking about, Ray? I don't see a thing."

"Maybe it was a shadow," Rayford said.

"I've got freckles, you know."

When Mac turned around, Rayford saw it again, plain as day. He felt foolish, making such a big deal of it, but he knew Mac was fastidious about his appearance. "You don't see that?" Rayford said, standing, grabbing Mac by the shoulders, and turning him back to face the mirror.

Mac looked again and shook his head.

Rayford pushed him closer and leaned in so their faces were side by side. "Right there!" he said, pointing at the mirror. Mac still had a blank stare. Rayford turned Mac's face toward him, put a finger directly on his forehead, and turned him back toward the mirror. "Right there. That charcoal-looking smudge about the size of a thumbprint."

Mac's shoulders slumped and he shook his head. "Either you're seeing things, or I'm blind," he said.

"Wait just a doggone minute," Rayford said slowly. Chills ran up his spine. "Let me look at that again."

Mac looked uncomfortable with Rayford staring at him, their noses inches apart. "What are you looking for?"

"Shh!"

Rayford held Mac by the shoulders. "Mac?" he said solemnly. "You know those 3-D images that look like a complicated pattern until you stare at it—"

"Yeah, and you can make out some sort of a picture."

"Yes! There it is! I can see it!"

"What?!"

"It's a cross! Oh, my word! It's a cross, Mac!"

Mac wrenched away and looked in the mirror again. He leaned to within inches of the glass and held his hair back from his forehead. "Why can't I see it?"

Rayford leaned into the mirror and held his own hair away from his forehead. "Wait! Do I have one too? Nope, I don't see one."

Mac paled. "You do!" he said. "Let me look at that."

Rayford could barely breathe as Mac stared. "Unbelievable!"

Mac said. "It *is* a cross. I can see yours and you can see mine, but we can't see our own."

Buck's neck and shoulders were stiff and sore. "I don't suppose you've driven a vehicle like this one, Tsion," he said.

"No, brother, but I am willing."

"No, I'm all right." He glanced at his watch. "Less than a half hour before I'm supposed to call Rayford."

The caravan to nowhere finally crossed into Wisconsin, and the traffic weaved west of the expressway. Thousands began to blaze new trails. Thirty to thirty-five miles an hour was top speed, but there were always nuts in all-terrain vehicles who took advantage of the fact that there were no rules anymore. When Buck got inside the city limits of Kenosha, he asked a member of the Global Community Peacekeeping Force for directions.

"You're gonna go east about five miles," the young woman said. "And it's not gonna look like a hospital. It's two—"

"Hotels, yeah, I heard."

Traffic into Kenosha was lighter than that heading north, but that soon changed too. Buck could not get within a mile of the hospital. GC forces detoured vehicles until it became obvious that anyone getting to those hotels had to do it on foot. Buck parked the Range Rover, and they set off toward the east.

By the time their destination came into view, it was time to call Rayford.

"Mac," Rayford said, fighting tears, "I can hardly believe this. I prayed for a sign, and God answered. I needed a sign. How can I know who to trust these days?"

"I wondered," Mac said. "I was hungry for God and knew you had what I needed, but I was afraid you would be suspicious."

"I was, but I had already said way too much if you were working against me for Carpathia."

Mac was gazing into the mirror and Rayford was dressing when he heard a brief knock and the door flew open. A young assistant from the communications center said, "Excuse me, sirs, but whichever one of you is Captain Steele has a phone call."

"Be right there," Rayford said. "By the way, have I got a smudge on my forehead right here?"

The young man looked. "No sir. Don't think so."

Rayford caught Mac's eye. Then he tucked in his undershirt and slid off down the hall in his stocking feet. Somebody like Fortunato—or worse, Carpathia—could court-martial him for appearing in front of subordinates half dressed. He knew he couldn't be in the employ of the Antichrist much longer anyway.

Buck stood silently in the Wisconsin wasteland with the phone pressed to his ear. When Rayford finally came on, he said quickly, "Buck, just answer yes or no. Are you there?"

"Yes."

"This is not a secure phone, so tell me how everyone is without using names, please."

"I'm fine," Buck said. "Mentor is safe and OK. She escaped, we believe. Close to reconnecting now."

"Others?"

"Secretary is gone. Computer techie and wife are gone."

"That hurts."

"I know. You?"

"They tell me Amanda went down with a Pan-Con flight into the Tigris," Rayford said.

"She's listed on the manifest, if you can believe what's on the Internet, but you're not buying it?"

"Not until I see her with my own eyes."

"I understand. Boy, it's good to hear your voice."

"Yours too. Your own family?"

"Unaccounted for, but that's true of most everyone."

"How are the buildings?"

"Both gone."

"You have accommodations?" Rayford asked.

"I'm fine. Keeping a low profile."

They agreed to e-mail each other and disconnected. Buck turned to Tsion. "She couldn't be a double-crosser. He's too perceptive, too aware."

"He could have been blinded by love," Tsion said. Buck looked sharply at him. "Cameron, I no more want to believe this than you do. But it appears Bruce strongly suspected."

Buck shook his head. "You'd better stay out here in the shadows, Tsion."

"Why? I'm the least of anyone's worries here, now."

"Maybe, but GC communications makes this a small world. They know I'm bound to show up sooner or later if Chloe is here. If they're still looking for you and Verna Zee broke our agreement and ratted on me to Carpathia, they might expect to find you with me."

"You have a creative mind, Buck. Paranoid too."

"Maybe. But let's not take chances. If I'm being followed when I come out, hopefully with Chloe, keep your distance. I'll pick you up about two hundred yards west of where I'm parked."

Buck walked into chaos. Not only was the place a madhouse of equipment and patients and officials competing to prove who had authority, but there was also a lot of yelling. Things had to happen fast, and no one had time for cordiality.

It took Buck a long time to get the attention of a woman at the front desk. She appeared to be doing the work of reception and admittance and also a bit of triage. After getting out of the way of two stretchers, each bearing a bloody body Buck bet was dead, he pushed up to the counter. "Excuse me, ma'am, I'm looking for this woman." He held up a copy of the fax Ernie had broadcast.

"If she looks like that, she wouldn't be here," the woman barked. "Does she have a name?"

"The name's on the picture," Buck said. "You need me to read it to you?"

"What I don't need is your sarcasm, pal. As a matter of fact, I *do* need you to read it to me."

Buck did.

"I don't recognize the name, but I've processed hundreds today."

"How many without names?"

"About a quarter. We found most of these people in or under their homes, so we cross-checked addresses. Anybody away from home mostly carried ID."

"Let's say she was away from home but had no ID, and she's not in a position to tell you who she is?"

"Then your guess is as good as mine. We don't have a special ward for unidentifieds."

"Mind if I look around?"

"What are you gonna do, check every patient?"

"If I have to."

"Not unless you're a GC employee and—"

"I am," Buck said, flashing his ID.

"—make sure you stay out of the way."

Buck traipsed through the first hotel, pausing at any bed that had a patient with no name card. He ignored several huge bodies and didn't waste time on people with gray or white hair. If anyone looked small or thin or feminine enough to be Chloe, he took a good look.

He was on his way to the second hotel when a tall black man backed out of a room, locking the door. Buck nodded and kept moving, but the man apparently noticed his fax. "Looking for someone?"

"My wife." Buck held up the page.

"Haven't seen her, but you might want to check in here."

"More patients?"

"This is our morgue, sir. You don't have to if you don't want to, but I've got the key."

Buck pursed his lips. "Guess I'd better."

Buck stepped behind the man as he unlocked the door. When he pushed, however, the door stuck a bit and Buck bumped into him. Buck apologized, and the man turned and said, "No prob—"

He stopped and stared at Buck's face. "Are you all right, sir? I'm a doctor."

"Oh, the cheek's all right. I just fell. It looks OK, doesn't it?"

The doctor cocked his head to look more closely. "Oh, that looks superficial. I thought I noticed a bruise on your forehead, just under the hairline."

"Nope. Didn't get banged there, far as I know."

"Bumps there can cause subcutaneous bleeding. It's not dangerous, but you could look like a raccoon in a day or two. Mind if I take a peek?"

Buck shrugged. "I'm in kind of a hurry. But go ahead."

The doctor grabbed a fresh pair of rubber gloves from a box in his pocket and pulled them on.

"Oh, please don't make a big production of it," Buck said. "I don't have any diseases or anything."

"That may be," the doctor said, pushing Buck's hair out of the way. "I can't claim the same for all the bodies I deal with." They were in a huge room, nearly every foot of the floor covered with sheeted corpses.

"You *do* have a mark there," the doctor said. He pushed on it and around it. "No pain?"

"No."

"You know," Buck said, "you've got something on your forehead too. Looks like a smudge."

The doctor swiped his forehead with his sleeve. "May have picked up some newsprint."

The doctor showed Buck how to pull back the shroud at the head of each body. He would have a clear view of the face and could simply let the material drop again. "Ignore this row. It's all men."

Buck jumped when the first body proved that of an elderly woman with bared teeth, eyes open and scared.

"I'm sorry, sir," the doctor said. "I have not manipulated the bodies. Some appear asleep. Others look like that. Sorry to startle you."

Buck grew more cautious and breathed a prayer of desperation before each unveiling. He was horrified at the parade of death but grateful each time he did not find Chloe. When he finished, Buck thanked the doctor and headed for the door. The doctor looked at him curiously and apologetically reached for Buck's "smudge" once more, rubbing it lightly with his thumb, as if he could wash it away. He shrugged. "Sorry."

Buck opened the door. "Yours is still there too, Doc."

In the first room of the other hotel, Buck saw two

middle-aged women who looked as if they'd been through a war. On his way out he caught a glimpse of himself in a mirror. He held his hair away from his forehead. He saw nothing.

Buck waited so long for an elevator that he almost gave up and took the stairs. But when a car finally had room for him, he stood there with the picture of Chloe dangling from his fingers. A heavyset, older doctor stepped on at the third floor and stared. Buck raised the picture to eye level. "May I?" the doctor asked, reaching for it. "She belong to you?"

"My wife."

"I saw her."

Buck felt a lump in his throat. "Where is she?"

"Don't you mean *how* is she?"

"Is she all right?"

"When last I saw her, she was alive. Step off on four so we can talk."

Buck tried to withhold his excitement. She was alive, that was all that mattered. He followed the doctor off the elevator, and the big man motioned him to a corner. "I advised she needed surgery, but we're not operating here. If they followed my advice, they scheduled her for Milwaukee or Madison or Minneapolis."

"What was wrong with her?"

"At first I thought she had been run over. Her right side was pretty banged up from her ankle to her head. She had what appeared to be chunks of asphalt embedded into that side of her body, and she had broken bones and possibly a fractured skull, totally on that side. But for her to be run over on asphalt, she would have had to have damage on her other side. And there was nothing there but a slight abrasion on her hip."

"Is she going to live?"

"I don't know. We couldn't do X-rays or MRIs here. I have no idea about the extent of damage to bones or to internal organs. I did, however, finally come to some hypothesis of what might have happened to her. I believe she was struck by a section of roofing. It probably knocked her to the ground, causing that abrasion. She was brought here by Ambu-Van. I understand she was unconscious, and they had no idea how long she'd been lying there."

"Did she regain consciousness?"

"Yes, but she was unable to communicate."

"She couldn't speak?"

"No. And she did not squeeze my hand or blink or nod or shake her head."

"You're sure she's not here?"

"I'd be disappointed if she was still here, sir. We're sending all the acute cases to one of the three *M*s, as I told you."

"Who would know where she was sent?"

The doctor pointed down the hall. "Ask that man right there for the disposition of Mother Doe."

"Thanks so much," Buck said. He hurried down the hall, then stopped and turned around. "*Mother* Doe?"

"We have been through the alphabet several times with all the unidentified Does. By the time your wife arrived, we were into descriptive terms."

"But she's not."

"Not what?"

"A mother."

"Well, if she and the baby survive this, she *will* be, in about seven months."

The doctor strode away; Buck nearly fainted.

Rayford and Mac sat at breakfast that morning planning the lengthy tour in the Condor 216 that would commence Friday. "So, what did His Excellency want last night?"

"His Excellency?"

"Haven't you been informed that that's what we're to call him from now on?"

"Oh brother!"

"I got that straight from Leon, or should I say 'Supreme Commander Leonardo Fortunato.'"

"That's his new moniker?" Rayford nodded. Mac shook his head. "These guys get more like Keystone Kops all the time. All Carpathia wanted to know was how long I thought you'd be staying with him. I told him I thought that was up to him and he said no, that he sensed you were getting restless. I told him he ought to let up on you over that little incident near the airport, and he said he already had. He said he could have really come down hard on you for that, and he hoped you'd stay with him longer since he hadn't."

"Who knows?" Rayford said. "Anything else?"

"He wanted to know if I knew your son-in-law. I told him I knew who he was but that I had never met him."

"Why do you think he asked that?"

"I don't know. He was trying to get in good with me for some reason. Maybe he's gonna be checking up on you. He told me he thought it strange that he'd gotten an intelligence report that Mr. Williams, as he likes to call him, had survived but not checked in. He told me Mr. Williams was publisher of *Global Community Weekly*, as if I wouldn't know that."

"Buck called this morning. I'm sure they have that logged, probably even recorded. If they wanted to talk to him so bad, why didn't they break in and do it then?"

"Maybe they're trying to let him hang himself. How long do you think Carpathia will trust a believer in a position like that?"

"That honeymoon is already over. You have to do what you have to do, Mac, but if I were you, I wouldn't be quick to declare myself as a new believer. Obviously, nobody but fellow believers can see these marks."

"Yeah, but what about that verse about confessing with your mouth?"

"I have no idea. Do the rules still stand at a time like this? Are you supposed to confess your faith to the Antichrist? I just don't know."

"Well, I already confessed it to you. I don't know whether that counts, but meanwhile, you're right. I'll be more help to you this way. What they don't know won't hurt them, and it can only help us."

With a lump in his throat, Buck prayed silently as he approached the doctor at the other end of the hall. "Lord, keep her alive. I don't care where she is, as long as you take care of her and our baby."

A moment later he was saying, "Minneapolis! That's got to be over three hundred miles from here."

"I drove it last week in six hours," the doctor said. "But I understand the foothills that make that western edge of Wisconsin so beautiful around Tomah were turned into mini mountains in the quake."

CHAPTER 10

RAYFORD AND MAC were on their way to board the Condor 216 and confirm she was flightworthy. Rayford threw an arm around Mac's shoulder and drew him close. "There's also something I need to show you on board," he whispered. "Installed just for me by an old friend no longer with us."

Rayford heard footsteps behind him. It was a uniformed young woman with a message. It read, "Captain Steele: Please meet briefly with Dr. Chaim Rosenzweig of Israel and me in my office immediately. I shall not keep you long. Signed, Supreme Commander Leonardo Fortunato."

"Thank you, Officer," Rayford said. "Tell them I'm on my way." He turned back to Mac and shrugged.

"Any chance I can drive to Minnesota?" Buck said.

"Sure, but it'll take you forever," the doctor said.

"What would be the chance of my catching a ride with one of the Medivac planes?"

"Out of the question."

Buck showed him his ID. "I work for the Global Community."

"Doesn't just about everybody?"

"How do I find out if she made it up there?"

"We'd know if she didn't. She's there."

"And if she took a turn for the worse, or if she, you know . . ."

"We're informed of that, too, sir. It'll be on the computer so everyone is up-to-date."

Buck ran down four flights of stairs and emerged at the far end of the second hotel. He looked across the parking lot and saw Ben-Judah where he had left him. Two uniformed GC officers were talking with him. Buck held his breath. Somehow, the conversation did not look like a confrontation. It appeared friendly banter.

Tsion turned and began walking away, turning again after a few steps to proffer a shy wave. They both waved, and he kept walking. Buck wondered where he was going. Would he go straight to the Range Rover or to the prearranged meeting spot?

Buck stayed in the shadows as Ben-Judah steadily made

his way past the front of the hotels and into a rocky area gouged by the earthquake. When he was nearly out of sight, the GC men began following. Buck sighed. He prayed Tsion would have the wisdom to not lead them to the Range Rover. *Just go to the spot, friend,* he thought, *and stay a couple of hundred yards ahead of these yokels.*

Buck did a couple of jumping jacks to loosen up and get the blood pumping. He jogged around the back of the second hotel, continued around the back of the first hotel, and emerged into the parking lot. He made a wide arc fifty yards to the left of the GC pair and maintained a leisurely pace as he jogged into the night. If the GC men noticed him, they didn't let on. They concentrated on the smaller, older man. Buck hoped that if Tsion noticed him, he wouldn't call out or follow.

It had been a long time since Buck had jogged more than a mile, especially scared to death. He huffed and puffed as he reached the area where he had left the Range Rover. A new section of cars had parked beyond his, so he had to search to find it.

Tsion plodded along, making his own trail over a difficult course. The GC men were still 100 to 150 yards behind him. Buck guessed Tsion knew he was being followed. He was not heading for the Rover but toward their spot. When Buck started the engine and turned on the headlights, Tsion touched a hand to his nose and increased his tempo. Buck raced over the open spaces, bouncing and banging but on pace to intersect with Tsion. The rabbi began trotting, and the GC men now sprinted. Buck was doing about thirty miles an hour, much too fast for the uneven ground. As he flopped in the seat, corralled only by his seat belt, he leaned over and lifted the handle on the passenger door. When he slid to a stop in front of Tsion, the door flew open, Tsion grabbed the inside handle, and Buck floored the accelerator. The door swung back and smacked Tsion in the rear, sending him across the seat and nearly into Buck's lap. Tsion laughed hysterically.

Buck looked at him, bemused, and jerked the wheel left. He put such distance between himself and the GC men that they would not have been able to see even the color of the vehicle, let alone the license number.

"What is so funny?" he asked Tsion, who cackled through his tears.

"I am Joe Baker," Tsion said in a ridiculously labored American accent. "I run a bakery shop and bake the rolls for you, because I am Joe Baker!" He laughed and laughed, covering his face and letting the tears come.

"Have you lost your mind?" Buck asked. "What is this about?"

"Those officers!" Tsion said, pointing over his shoulder. "Those brilliant, highly trained bloodhounds!" He laughed so hard he could hardly breathe.

Buck had to laugh himself. He had wondered if he would ever smile again.

Tsion kept one hand over his eyes and raised the other as if to inform Buck that if he could just calm himself he would be able to tell the story. Finally, he managed. "They greeted me in a friendly way. I was wary. I camouflaged my Hebrew accent and did not say much, hoping they would get bored and walk away. But they continued to study me in the dim light. Finally they asked who I was." He began to giggle again and had to collect himself. "That is when I told them. I said, 'My name is Joe Baker, and I am a baker. I have a bakery.'"

"You didn't!" Buck roared.

"They asked me where was I from, and I asked them to guess. One said Lithuania, and so I pointed at him and smiled and said, 'Yes! Yes, I am Joe the Baker from Lithuania!'"

"You're crazy!"

"Yes," he said. "But am I not a good soldier?"

"You are."

"They asked me if I had papers. I told them I had them at the bakery. I had just come out for a stroll to see the damage. My bakery survived, you know."

"I had heard that," Buck said.

"I told them to come by sometime for free donuts. They said they just might do that and asked where Joe's Bakery was located. I told them to head west to the only establishment on Route 50 still standing. I said God must like donuts, and they laughed. When I left, I waved at them, but soon enough they began to follow. I knew you would know where to look for me if I was not where I was supposed to be. But I worried that if you stayed in the hotels much longer, they would overtake me. God was watching over us, as usual."

"You are acquainted with Dr. Rosenzweig, I'm sure," Fortunato said.

"I am indeed, Commander," Rayford said, shaking Chaim's hand.

Rosenzweig was his usual enthusiastic self, an elflike septuagenarian with broad features, a deeply lined face, and wisps of curly white hair independent of his control.

"Captain Steele!" he said, "It is such an honor to see you again. I came to ask after your son-in-law, Cameron."

"I spoke with him this morning, and he's fine." Rayford looked directly into Rosenzweig's eyes, hoping to communicate the importance of confidentiality. "*Everyone* is fine, Doctor," he said.

"And Dr. Ben-Judah?" Rosenzweig said.

Rayford felt Fortunato's eyes all over him. "Doctor Ben-Judah?" he said.

"Surely you know him. An old protégé of mine. Cameron helped him escape zealots in Israel, with the help of Poten—, I mean Excellency Carpathia."

Leon appeared pleased that Rosenzweig had used the proper title. He said, "You know how much His Excellency thinks of you, Doctor. We promised to do all we could."

"And so where did Cameron take him?" Rosenzweig asked. "And why has he not reported to the Global Community?"

Rayford fought for composure. "If what you say is true, Dr. Rosenzweig, it was done independent of my involvement.

I followed the news of the rabbi's misfortune and escape, but I was here."

"Surely your own son-in-law would tell you—"

"As I say, Doctor, I have no firsthand knowledge of the operation. I was unaware the Global Community was involved."

"So he didn't bring Tsion back to the States?"

"I am unaware of the rabbi's whereabouts. My son-in-law is in the States, but whether he is with Dr. Ben-Judah, I could not say."

Rosenzweig slumped and crossed his arms. "Oh, this is awful! I had so hoped to learn that he is safe. The Global Community could offer tremendous assistance in protecting him. Cameron was not sure of Excellency Carpathia's concern for Tsion, but surely he proved himself by helping to find Tsion and get him out of the country!"

What had Fortunato and Carpathia fed Dr. Rosenzweig?

Fortunato spoke up. "As I told you, Doctor, we provided manpower and equipment that escorted Mr. Williams and Rabbi Ben-Judah as far as the Israeli-Egyptian border. Past that, they fled, apparently by plane, out of Al Arish on the Mediterranean. Naturally we hoped to be brought up to speed, if for no other reason than that we expected some modicum of gratitude. If Mr. Williams feels Dr. Ben-Judah is safe, wherever he has hidden him, that's fine with us. We simply want to be of assistance until you feel it is no longer necessary."

Rosenzweig leaned forward and gestured broadly. "That

is the point! I hate to leave it in Cameron's hands. He is a busy man, important to the Global Community. I know that when His Excellency pledges support, he follows through. And with the personal story you just told me, Commander Fortunato, well, there is clearly much, much more to my young friend Nicolae—pardon the familiar reference—than meets the eye!"

It was after midnight in the Midwest. Buck had brought Tsion up to speed on Chloe. Now he was on the phone to the Arthur Young Memorial Hospital in Palatine. "I understand that," Buck said. "Tell him it's his old friend, Buck."

"Sir, the patient is stable but sleeping. I will not be telling him anything tonight."

"It's urgent that I talk to him."

"You've said that, sir. Please try again tomorrow."

"Just listen—"

Click.

Buck hardly noticed road construction ahead. He skidded to a stop. A traffic director approached. "Sorry, sir, but I'm gonna hold you here for a minute. We're filling in a fissure."

Buck put the Rover in park and rested his head against the back of the seat. "So, what do you think, Joe the Baker? Should we let Ritz test his wings to Minneapolis before we let him take us back to Israel?"

Tsion smiled at the mention of Joe the Baker, but he suddenly sobered.

"What is it?" Buck said.

"Just a minute," Tsion said.

Up ahead a bulldozer turned, its lights shining through the Range Rover. "I did not notice you had injured your forehead, too," Tsion said.

Buck sat up quickly and looked in the rearview mirror. "I don't see anything. You're the second person tonight who said he saw something on my forehead." He spread his hair. "Now where? What?"

"Look at me," Tsion said. He pointed to Buck's forehead.

Buck said, "Well, look at yourself! There's something on yours, too."

Tsion pulled down the visor mirror. "Nothing," he muttered. "Now you are teasing me."

"All right," Buck said, frustrated. "Let me look again. OK, yours is still there. Is mine still there?"

Tsion nodded.

"Yours looks like some kind of a 3-D thing. What does mine look like?"

"The same. Like a shadow or a bruise, or a, what do you call it? A relief?"

"Yes," Buck said. "Hey! This is like one of those puzzles that looks like a bunch of sticks until you sort of reverse it in your mind and see the background as the foreground and vice versa. That's a cross on your forehead."

Tsion seemed to stare desperately at Buck. Suddenly he said, "Yes! Cameron! We have the seal, visible to only other believers."

"What are you talking about?"

"The seventh chapter of Revelation tells of 'the servants of our God' being sealed on their foreheads. That has to be what this is!"

Buck didn't notice the flagman waving him through. The man approached the car. "What's up with you two? Let's go!"

Buck and Tsion looked at each other, grinning stupidly. They laughed, and Buck drove on. Suddenly, he slammed on the brakes.

"What?" Tsion said.

"I met another believer back there!"

"Where?"

"At the hospital! A black doctor in charge of the morgue had the same sign. He saw mine and I saw his, but neither of us knew what we were looking at. I've got to call him."

Tsion dug out the number. "He will be most encouraged, Cameron."

"If I can get through. I may have to drive back and find him."

"No! What if those GC men figured out who I was? Even if they think I am Joe the Baker, they are going to want to know why I ran away."

"It's ringing!"

"GC Hospital, Kenosha."

"Hello, yes. I need the doctor in charge of the morgue."

"He has his own cell phone, sir. Here's that number."

Buck wrote it down and punched it in.

"Morgue. This is Floyd Charles."

"Doctor Charles! Are you the one who let me into the morgue to look for my wife tonight?"

"Yes, any luck?"

"Yes, I think I know where she is, but—"

"Wonderful. I'm happy for—"

"But that's not why I'm calling. Remember that mark on my forehead?"

"Yes," Doctor Charles said slowly.

"That's the sign of the sealed servants of God! You have one too, so I know you're a believer. Right?"

"Praise God!" the doctor said. "I am, but I don't think I have the mark."

"We can't see our own! Only others'."

"Wow! Oh, hey, listen! Your wife isn't Mother Doe, is she?"

Buck recoiled. "Yes, why?"

"Then I know who you are, too. And so do they. You're driving to Minneapolis. That gives them time to get your wife out of there."

"Why do they want to do that?"

"Because you've got something or somebody they want. . . . Are you still there, sir?"

"I'm here. Listen, brother to brother, tell me what you know. When will they move her and where would they take her?"

"I don't know. But I heard something about flying some-one out of Glenview Naval Air Station—you know, the old shut-down base that—"

"I know."

"Late tomorrow."

"Are you sure?"

"That's what I heard."

"Let me give you my private number, Doctor. If you hear any more, please let me know. And if you ever, and I mean ever, need anything, you let me know."

"Thank you, Mr. Doe."

Rayford showed Mac McCullum the bugging device that con-nected the pilot's headphone to the cabin. McCullum whistled through his teeth. "Ray, when they discover this and put you away for the rest of your life, I'm gonna deny any knowledge."

"It's a deal. But in case anything happens to me before they find out, you know where it is."

"No I don't," Mac said, smiling.

"Invent something to get us outside. I need to talk to Buck on my own phone."

"I could use some help with the skyhooks on that chop-per," Mac said.

"With the what?"

"The skyhooks. The ones I attach to the sky that let me pull the helicopter off the ground and work underneath it."

"Oh, *those* skyhooks! Yes, let's check on those."

It was well after midnight when Buck and Tsion dragged themselves into the house. "I don't know what I'm going to run into in Minneapolis," Buck said, "but I have to go there in better shape than I'm in right now. Pray that Ken Ritz is up to this. I don't know if I should even hope for that."

"We don't hope," Tsion said. "We pray."

"Then pray for this: One, that Ritz is healthy enough. Two, that he's got a plane that works. Three, that it's at an airport he can take off from."

Buck was at the top of the stairs when his phone rang. "Rayford!"

Rayford quickly filled Buck in on the fiasco with Rosenzweig.

"I love that old buzzard," Buck said, "but he sure is naive. I told him and told him not to trust Carpathia. He loves the guy."

"He more than loves him, Buck. He believes he's divine."

"Oh, no."

Rayford and Buck debriefed each other on everything that had happened that day. "I can't wait to meet Mac," Buck said.

"If you're in as much trouble as it appears, Buck, you may never meet him."

"Well, maybe not this side of heaven."

Rayford brought up Amanda. "Would you believe Carpathia tried to make Mac think she was working for him?"

Buck didn't know what to say. "Working for Carpathia?" he said lamely.

"Think of it! I know her like I know myself, and I'll tell you something else. I'm convinced she's alive. I'm praying you can get to Chloe before the GC does. You pray I find Amanda."

"She wasn't on the plane that went down?"

"That's all I can believe," Rayford said. "If she was on it, she's gone. But I'm gonna check that out too."

"How?"

"I'll tell you later. I don't want to know where Tsion is, but just tell me, you're not taking him to Minnesota, are you? If something goes wrong, there's no way you want to be forced to trade him for Chloe."

"Of course not. He thinks he's going, but he'll understand. I don't think anybody knows where we are, and there is that shelter I told you about."

"Perfect."

Wednesday morning Buck had to talk Tsion out of coming with him even to Palatine. The rabbi understood the danger of going to Minnesota, but he insisted he could help Buck get Ken Ritz out of the hospital. "If you need a distraction, I could be Joe the Baker again."

"Much as I would enjoy seeing that, Tsion, we just don't know who's onto us. I don't even know whether anyone ever found out it was Ken who flew me to Israel and you and me back. Who knows whether they've got that hospital staked out? Ken might not even be there. It could all be a setup."

"Cameron! Don't we have enough real worries without you inventing more?"

Tsion reluctantly stayed. Buck urged him to prepare the shelter in the event things went haywire in Minneapolis and Global Community forces began to track him in earnest. Tsion would be broadcasting his teachings and encouragement to the 144,000 witnesses and any other clandestine believers all over the world via the Internet. That would irritate Carpathia, not to mention Peter Mathews, and no one knew whether they were engaged in tracing such messages.

The normally short jaunt from Mt. Prospect to Palatine was now an arduous two-hour journey. Arthur Young Memorial Hospital had somehow escaped serious damage, though with only a few exceptions, the rest of Palatine had been wasted. It looked nearly as bad as Mt. Prospect. Buck parked near fallen trees about fifty yards from the entrance. Seeing nothing suspicious, he walked straight in. The hospital was full and busy, and with auxiliary power and the fact that the place was not just a retrofitted hotel like the ones the night before, it seemed to run much more efficiently.

"I'm here to see Ken Ritz," he said.

"And you are?" a candy striper said.

Buck hesitated. "Herb Katz," he said, using an alias Ken Ritz would recognize.

"May I see some identification?"

"No, you may not."

"I'm sorry?"

"My identification was lost with my house in Mt. Prospect, which is now earthquake residue, OK?"

"Mt. Prospect? I lost a sister and brother-in-law there. I understand it was the hardest hit."

"Palatine doesn't look much better."

"We're short-staffed, but several of us were lucky, knock on wood."

"So, how 'bout it? Can I see Ken?"

"I'll try. But my supervisor is tougher than me. She hasn't let anyone in without ID. But I'll tell her your situation."

The girl left the desk and poked her head through a door behind her. Buck was tempted to just head into the main hospital and find Ritz, especially when he overheard the conversation.

"Absolutely not. You know the rules."

"But he lost his home and his ID and—"

"If you can't tell him no, I'll have to."

The candy striper turned and shrugged apologetically. She sat as her supervisor, a striking, dark-haired woman in her late twenties, stepped into view. Buck saw the mark on her forehead and smiled, wondering if she was aware of it yet. She smiled shyly, quickly growing serious when the girl turned to look. "Who was it you wanted to see, sir?"

"Ken Ritz."

"Tiffany, please show this gentleman to Ken Ritz's room." She held Buck's gaze, then turned and went back into her office.

Tiffany shook her head. "She's always had a thing for blonds." She walked Buck to the ward.

"I have to make sure the patient wants visitors," she said.

Buck waited in the hall as Tiffany knocked and entered Ken's room. "Mr. Ritz, are you up to a visitor?"

"Not really," came the gravelly but weak voice Buck recognized. "Who is it?"

"A Herb Katz."

"Herb Katz, Herb Katz." Ritz seemed to turn the name over in his mind. "Herb Katz! Send him in, and shut the door."

When they were alone, Ken winced as he sat up. He thrust out an entubed hand and shook Buck's weakly. "Herb Katz, how in the world are ya?"

"That's what I was gonna ask you. You look terrible."

"Thanks for nothing. I got hurt in the stupidest possible way, but please tell me you've got a job for me. I need to get out of this place and get busy. I'm going stir-crazy. I wanted to call you, but I lost all my phone numbers. Nobody knows how to get ahold of you."

"I've got a couple of jobs for you, Ken, but are you up to them?"

"I'll be good as new by tomorrow," he said. "I just got banged on the head with one of my own little fixed-wingers."

"What?"

"The danged earthquake hit while I was in the air. I circled and circled waitin' for the thing to stop, almost crashed when the sun went out, and finally put down over here at Palwaukee. I didn't see the crater. In fact, I don't think it was there until after I hit the ground. Anyway, I was almost stopped, just rolling a couple miles an hour, and the plane fell right down into that thing. Worst of it is I was OK, but the plane wasn't anchored like I thought it was. I jumped out, worrying about fuel and everything and wanting to see how my other aircraft were and how everybody else was, so I hopped up top and ran down the wing to jump out of the hole.

"Just before I took my last step, my weight flipped that little Piper right over and the other wing conked me on the back of the head. I was hanging there on the edge of the hole, trying to get all the way up, and I knew I'd been sliced pretty deep. I reach back there with one hand and feel this big flap of scalp hanging down, and then I start getting dizzy. I lost my grip and slid down underneath that plane. I was scared I was gonna make it fall on me again, so I just stayed put till somebody pulled me out. Dang near bled to death."

"You look a little pale."

"Aren't you full of encouragement today."

"Sorry."

"You want to see it?"

"See it?"

"My wound!"

"Sure, I guess."

Ritz turned so Buck could see the back of his head. Buck grimaced. It was as ugly an injury as he had seen. The huge flap that had been stitched into place had been shaved, along with an extra one-inch border around the area.

"No brain damage, they tell me, so I still got no excuse for bein' crazy."

Buck filled him in on his dilemma and that he needed to get to Minneapolis before the GC did something stupid with Chloe. "I'm gonna need you to recommend somebody, Ken. I can't wait till tomorrow."

"The heck I'll recommend somebody else," Ken said. He unhooked the IV and yanked the tape off.

"Slow down, Ken. I can't let you do this. You've got to get a clean bill of health before—"

"Forget me, will ya? I may have to go slow, but we both know if there's no brain trauma, there's little danger I'm gonna hurt myself worse. I'll be a little uncomfortable, that's all. Now come on, help me get dressed and get out of here."

"I appreciate this, but really—"

"Williams, if you don't let me do this, I'm gonna hate you for the rest of my life."

"I sure wouldn't want to be responsible for that."

There was no way to sneak out. Buck put his arm around Ken and tucked his hand in Ken's armpit. They moved as quickly as possible, but a male nurse came running. "Whoa! He's not allowed out of bed! Help! Someone! Get his doctor!"

"This ain't prison," Ken called out. "I signed in, and I'm checkin' out!"

They were headed through the lobby when a doctor hurried toward them. The girl at the desk summoned her supervisor. Buck pleaded with his eyes. The supervisor glared at him but stepped directly in front of the doctor, and he stumbled trying to avoid her. "I'll handle this," she said.

The doctor left with a suspicious look, and the candy striper was sent to the pharmacy to get Ken's prescriptions. The supervisor whispered, "Being a believer doesn't guarantee you're not stupid. I'm making this happen, but it had better be necessary."

Buck nodded his thanks.

Once in the Rover, Ken sat still, gently cradling his head in his fingers. "You OK?" Buck asked.

Ritz nodded. "Run me by Palwaukee. I got a bag of stuff they're keepin' for me. And we've got to get to Waukegan."

"Waukegan?"

"Yeah. My Learjet got blown around over there, but it's OK. Only problem is, the hangars are gone. Their fuel tanks are fine, they tell me. One problem, though."

"I'll bite."

"Runways."

"What about 'em?"

"Apparently they don't exist anymore."

Buck was cruising as quickly as he could manage. One advantage of no roads was that he could drive from one place to another as the crow flies. "Can you take off in a Learjet without pavement beneath you?"

"Never had to worry about it before. We'll find out though, won't we?"

"Ritz, you're crazier than I am."

"That'll be the day. Every time I'm with you I'm sure you're gonna get me killed." Ritz fell silent for a moment.

Then, "Speakin' of getting killed, you know I wasn't just calling you because I needed work."

"No?"

"I read your article. That 'wrath of the Lamb' thing in your magazine."

"What did you think?"

"Wrong question. It isn't what I thought when I read it, which frankly wasn't much. I mean, I've always been impressed with your writing."

"I didn't know that."

"So sue me, I didn't want you to get the big head. Anyway, I didn't like any of the theories you came up with. And no, I didn't believe we were going to suffer the wrath of the Lamb. But what you ought to be asking is what do I think about it now?"

"All right. Shoot."

"Well, a guy would have to be a fool to think the first worldwide earthquake in the history of mankind was a coincidence, after you predicted it in your article."

"Hey, I didn't predict it. I was totally objective."

"I know. But you and I talked about this stuff before, so I knew where you were comin' from. You made it look like all those Bible scholar guys were just giving more opinions to stack up against the space aliens and the conspiracy nuts. Then, wham, bang, my head's split open, and all of a sudden the only guy I know crazier than me is the one that had the thing figured out."

"So you wanted to get hold of me. Here I am."

"Good. 'Cause I figure if what the globe just went through *was* the wrath of the Lamb, I better make friends with that Lamb."

Buck always thought Ritz was too smart to miss all the signs. "I can help you there," he said.

"I kind of thought you might."

It was close to noon by the time Buck came out of the ditch where Green Bay Road used to be and drove slowly over the flattened fence and around the crumpled landing lights at the Waukegan Airport. The runways had not just sunk or twisted. They lay in huge chunks from end to end.

There, in one of the few open spaces, was Ken Ritz's Learjet, apparently none the worse for wear.

Ritz moved slowly, but he was able to gingerly taxi the thing between hazards to the fuel pump. "She'll take us to Minneapolis and back more than once with a full tank," he said.

"The question is how fast?" Buck said.

"Less than an hour."

Buck looked at his watch. "Where are you gonna take off from?"

"It's sloped, but from the cockpit I saw one patch across Wadsworth on the golf course that looks like our best bet."

"How are you gonna get across the road and through those thickets?"

"Oh, we'll do it. But it's gonna take longer than flying to Minneapolis. You're gonna be doing most of the work. I'll steer the jet, and you'll clear the way. It's not gonna be easy."

"I'll hack my way to Minneapolis if I have to," Buck said.

CHAPTER 11

RAYFORD WAS LEARNING joy in the midst of sorrow. His heart told him Amanda was alive. His mind told him she was dead. As for her betrayal of him, of the Tribulation Force, and ultimately of God himself, neither Rayford's head nor heart accepted that.

Yet with his conflicting emotions and turmoil of spirit, Rayford was as grateful for Mac's conversion as he had been for his own, for Chloe's, and for Buck's. And the timing of God's choosing to put his mark on his own! Rayford would be eager to get Tsion Ben-Judah's input on that.

It was late Wednesday evening in New Babylon. Rayford and Mac had been working side by side all day. Rayford had told him the whole story of the Tribulation Force and each of their accounts of their own conversions. Mac seemed especially intrigued that God had provided them a pastor/ teacher/mentor from the beginning in Bruce Barnes. And then, following Bruce's death, God sent a new spiritual leader with even more biblical expertise.

"God has proven personal to us, Mac," Rayford said. "He doesn't always answer our prayers the way we think he will, but we've learned he knows best. And we have to be careful not to think that everything we feel deeply is necessarily true."

"I don't follow," Mac said.

"For instance, I can't shake the feeling that Amanda is still alive. But I can't swear that is from God." Rayford hesitated, suddenly overcome. "I want to be sure that if it turns out I'm wrong, I don't hold it against God."

Mac nodded. "I can't imagine holding anything against God, but I see what you mean."

Rayford was thrilled by Mac's hunger to learn. Rayford showed him where to search on the Internet for Tsion's teachings, his sermons, his commentaries on Bruce Barnes's messages, and especially his end-times chart that plotted where he believed the church was in the sequence of the seven-year tribulation.

Mac was fascinated by evidence that pointed to Nicolae Carpathia as the Antichrist. "But this wrath of the Lamb and the moon turning to blood, man, if nothing else convinced me, that sure did."

Once their route plans were finished, Rayford e-mailed Buck his itinerary. After picking up Peter Mathews in Rome, he and Mac were to fly him and Leon to Dallas to pick up a former Texas senator. He was the newly installed ambassador to the Global Community from the United States of North America. "You have to wonder, Mac, whether this guy ever dreamed when he got into politics that he would one day be one of the ten kings foretold of in the Bible."

A little more than half the Dallas/Ft. Worth airport was still operational, and the rest was quickly being rebuilt. To Rayford, reconstruction around the world already clipped along at a staggering pace. It was as if Carpathia had been a student of prophecy, and though he insisted that events were not as they seemed, he seemed to have been prepared to begin rebuilding immediately.

Rayford knew Carpathia was mortal. Still, he wondered if the man ever slept. He saw Nicolae around the compound at all hours, always in suit and tie, shoes polished, face shaved, hair trimmed. He was amazing. Despite the hours he kept, he was short-tempered only when it served his purpose. Normally he was gregarious, smiling, confident. When appropriate, he feigned grief and empathy. Handsome and charming, it was easy to see how he could deceive so many.

Earlier that evening, Carpathia had broadcast a live global television and radio address. He told the masses: "Brothers and sisters in the Global Community, I address you from New Babylon. Like you, I lost many loved ones, dear friends, and loyal associates in the tragedy. Please accept my deepest and most sincere sympathy for your losses on behalf of the administration of the Global Community.

"No one could have predicted this random act of nature, the worst in history to strike the globe. We were in the final stages of our rebuilding effort following the war against a resistant minority. Now, as I trust you are able to witness wherever you are, rebuilding has already begun again.

"New Babylon will, within a very short time, become the most magnificent city the world has ever known. Your new international capitol will be the center of banking and commerce, the headquarters for all Global Community governing agencies, and eventually the new Holy City, where Enigma Babylon One World Faith will relocate.

"It will be my joy to welcome you to this beautiful place. Give us a few months to finish, and then plan your pilgrimage. Every citizen should make it his or her life's goal to experience this new utopia and see the prototype for every city."

With a couple of hundred other GC employees, Rayford and Mac had watched on a television high in the corner of the mess hall. Nicolae, in a small studio down the hall, played a virtual reality disk that took the viewer through the new city, gleaming as if already completed. It was dizzying and impressive.

Carpathia pointed out every high-tech, state-of-the-art convenience known to man, each blended into the beautiful new metropolis. Mac whispered, "With those gold spires, it looks like old Sunday school pictures of heaven."

Rayford nodded. "Both Bruce and Tsion say Antichrist just counterfeits what God does."

Carpathia finished with a stirring pep talk. "Because you are survivors, I have unwavering confidence in your drive and determination and commitment to work together, to never give up, to stand shoulder to shoulder and rebuild our world.

"I am humbled to serve you and pledge that I will give my all for as long as you allow me the privilege. Now let me just add that I am aware that, due to speculative reporting in one of our own Global Community publications, many have been confused by recent events. While it may appear that the global earthquake coincided with the so-called wrath of the Lamb, let me clarify. Those who believe this disaster was God's doing are also those who believe that the disappearances nearly two years ago were people being swept away to heaven.

"Of course, every citizen of the Global Community is free to believe as he or she wants and to exercise that faith in any way that does not infringe upon the same freedom for others. The point of Enigma Babylon One World Faith is religious freedom and tolerance.

"For that reason, I am loath to criticize the beliefs of others. However, I plead for common sense. I do not begrudge anyone the right to believe in a personal god. However, I do not understand how a god they describe as just and loving would capriciously decide who is or is not worthy of heaven and effect that decision in what they refer to as 'the twinkling of an eye.'

"Has this same loving god come back two years later to rub it in? He expresses his anger to those unfortunates he left behind by laying waste their world and killing off a huge percentage of them?" Carpathia smiled condescendingly. "I humbly ask devout believers in such a Supreme Being to forgive me if I have mischaracterized your god. But any thinking citizen realizes that this picture simply does not add up.

"So, my brothers and sisters, do not blame God for what we are enduring. See it simply as one of life's crucibles, a test of our spirit and will, an opportunity to look within ourselves and draw on that deep wellspring of goodness we were born with. Let us work together to make our world a global phoenix, rising from the ashes of tragedy to become the greatest society ever known. I bid you good-bye and goodwill until next I speak with you."

When the Global Community employees in the mess hall leaped to their feet, cheering and clapping, Rayford and Mac stood only to keep from appearing conspicuous. Rayford noticed Mac staring off to the left.

"What?" Rayford said.

"Just a minute," Mac said. Rayford was about to leave when everyone sat back down, still glued to the TV. "I noticed someone else slow to stand," Mac whispered. "A young guy. Works in communications, I think."

Everyone had sat back down because a message on the screen read, "Please stand by for Supreme Commander Leonardo Fortunato."

Fortunato did not cut as impressive a figure as Carpathia, but he had a dynamic television visage. He came across friendly and approachable, humble yet direct, seeming to look the viewer in the eye. He told the story of his death in the earthquake and subsequent resurrection by Nicolae. "My only regret," he added, "was that there were no witnesses. But I know what I experienced and believe with all my heart that this gift our Supreme Potentate possesses will be used in public in the future. A man bestowed with this power is worthy of a new title. I am suggesting that he hereafter be referred to as His Excellency Nicolae Carpathia. I have already instituted this policy within the Global Community government and urge all citizens who respect and love our leader to follow suit.

"As you may know, His Excellency would never require or even request such a title. Though reluctantly thrust into leadership, he has expressed a willingness to give his life for his fellow citizens. Though he will never insist upon appropriate deference, I urge it on your part.

"I have not consulted His Excellency on what I am about to tell you, and I only hope he accepts it in the spirit in which I offer it and is not embarrassed. Most of you could not know that he is going through intense personal pain."

"I do not believe where this is going," Rayford muttered.

"Our leader and his fiancée, the love of his life, joyfully anticipate the birth of their child within the next several months. But the soon-to-be Mrs. Carpathia is currently unaccounted for. She was about to return from the United States of North America after a visit to her family when the earthquake made international travel impossible. If anyone knows the whereabouts of Miss Hattie Durham, please forward that information to your local Global Community representative as soon as possible. Thank you."

Mac made a beeline to the young man he had been watching. Rayford headed back toward the Condor 216 and was near the steps when Mac caught up with him. "Rayford, that kid had the mark on his forehead. When I said I knew he was a believer, he turned white. I showed him my mark, told him about you and me, and he almost cried. His name is David Hassid. He's a Jew from Eastern Europe who joined GC because he was impressed with Carpathia. He's been surfing the Net for six months, and get this, he considers Tsion Ben-Judah his spiritual mentor."

"When did he become a believer?"

"Just a few weeks ago, but he's not ready to make it known. He was convinced he was the only one here. He says Tsion put something on the Net called the 'Romans Road' to salvation. I guess all the verses come from Romans. Anyway, he wants to meet you. He can't believe you know Ben-Judah personally."

"Shoot, I can probably get the kid an autograph."

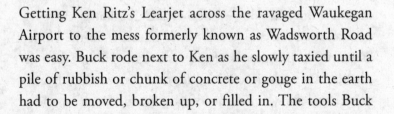

Getting Ken Ritz's Learjet across the ravaged Waukegan Airport to the mess formerly known as Wadsworth Road was easy. Buck rode next to Ken as he slowly taxied until a pile of rubbish or chunk of concrete or gouge in the earth had to be moved, broken up, or filled in. The tools Buck had found were not intended for what he was doing, but his aching muscles and calloused hands told him he was making progress.

The tricky part was getting across Wadsworth Road to the golf course. First there was the ditch. "It's not the best thing to do to a Lear," Ken said, "but I think I can roll in there and up and out. It's going to take just the right momentum, and I have to stop within a few feet."

The pavement had been bowed at least eight feet, so steep that a car would not have the right angle to get over it. "Where do we go from there?" Buck asked.

"Every action has a reaction, right?" Ritz said cryptically. "Where there's a bow, there's gotta be a dip somewhere. How far east do we have to go till we can cross?"

Buck jogged about two hundred yards before seeing a huge split in the pavement. If Ritz could get the plane that far, keeping his left wing from touching the bowed pavement and his right wheel from the ditch, he could turn left across the road. After guiding Ken in and out of the ditch on that side, Buck would have to clear a fence and shrubbery that blocked the golf course.

Ritz negotiated the first ditch easily, but being careful to stop before the upcropping of pavement, he rolled back down. At the nadir of the ditch, he couldn't back out and had a trickier time going forward. He finally made it but jumped out to find he had bent the front landing gear. "Shouldn't affect anything, but I wouldn't want to land on it too many times," he said.

Buck was not reassured. He walked ahead as Ritz taxied east down the shoulder. Ken kept an eye on the left wing, keeping it inches from the bulge of the road, while Buck watched the right tire and made sure it didn't slip into the ditch.

Once across the road, it was down into and up out of the other ditch, Ken jamming the brakes again to miss the fence. He began helping Buck move stuff out of the way, but when they started yanking shrubbery, he had to sit down. "Save your strength," Buck said. "I can do this."

Ritz looked at his watch. "You'd better hurry. What time did you want to be in Minneapolis?"

"Not much after three. My source says GC guys are coming from Glenview late this afternoon."

When Rayford and Mac finished in the Condor, Rayford said, "Let me leave first. You and I shouldn't constantly be seen together. You need credibility with the brass."

Rayford was tired but eager to get the long trip behind him and get back for his scuba expedition. He prayed his hunch would be right and he would not find Amanda in that submerged plane. Then he would demand to know what Carpathia had done with her. As long as she was alive and he could get to her, he didn't worry about the ridiculous claims of her being a plant.

An officer greeted Rayford as he got to his quarters. "His Excellency would like to see you, sir."

Rayford thanked him and masked his disgust. He had enjoyed a day without Carpathia. His disappointment was doubled when he discovered Fortunato in Carpathia's office as well. They apparently didn't feel the need for their usual smarmy cordiality. Neither rose to greet him or shake his hand. Carpathia pointed to a chair and referred to a copy of Rayford's itinerary.

"I see you have scheduled a twenty-four-hour layover in North America."

"We need the downtime for the plane and the pilots."

"Will you be seeing your daughter and son-in-law?"

"Why?"

"I am not implying your personal time is my business," Carpathia said. "But I need a favor."

"I'm listening."

"It is the same matter we discussed before the earthquake."

"Hattie."

"Yes."

"You know where she is, then?" Rayford said.

"No, but I assume you do."

"How would I, if you don't?"

Carpathia stood. "Is it time for the gloves to come off, Captain Steele? Do you really think I could run the international government and not have eyes and ears everywhere? I have sources you could not even imagine. You do not think I know that the last time you and Miss Durham flew to North America, you were on the same flight?"

"I have not seen her since, sir."

"But she interacted with your people. Who knows what they might have filled her head with? She was supposed to have come back much earlier. You had your assignment. Whatever she was doing over there, she missed her original flight, and we know she was then traveling with your wife."

"That was my understanding too."

"She did not board that plane, Captain Steele. If she had, as you know, she would no longer be a problem."

"She's a problem again?" Carpathia did not respond. Rayford continued. "I saw your broadcast. I was under the impression you were despairing over your fiancée."

"I did not say that."

"I did," Fortunato said. "I was on my own there."

"Oh," Rayford said. "That's right. His Excellency had no idea you were going to confer divinity upon him and then overstate his turmoil over the missing fiancée."

"Do not be naive, Captain Steele," Carpathia said. "All I want to know is that you will have the talk with Miss Durham."

"The talk in which I tell her she can keep the ring, live in New Babylon, and then, what was it about the baby?"

"I'm going to assume she's already made the right decision there, and you may assure her that I will cover all expenses."

"For the child throughout its life?"

"That is not the decision I was referring to," Carpathia said.

"Just so I'm clear, then, you will pay for the murder of the child?"

"Do not be maudlin, Rayford. It is a safe, simple procedure. Just pass along my message. She will understand."

"Believe it or not, I don't know where she is. But if I do pass along your message, I can't guarantee she'll make the choice you want. What if she chooses to bear the child?"

Carpathia shook his head. "I must end this relationship, but it will not go over well if there is a child."

"I understand," Rayford said.

"We agree then."

"I didn't say that. I said I understood."

"You will talk to her then?"

"I have no idea of her whereabouts or well-being."

"Could she have been lost in the earthquake?" Carpathia said, his eyes brightening.

"Wouldn't that be the best solution?" Rayford suggested with disgust.

"Actually, yes," Carpathia said. "But my contacts believe she is hiding."

"And you think I know where."

"She is not the only person in exile with whom you have a connection, Captain Steele. Such leverage is keeping you out of prison."

Rayford was amused. Carpathia had overestimated him. If Rayford had thought harboring Hattie and Tsion would give him the upper hand, he might have done it on purpose. But Hattie was on her own. And Tsion was Buck's doing.

Nonetheless, he left Carpathia's office that night with a temporary advantage, according to the enemy himself.

Buck was sweaty and exhausted when he finally strapped himself in next to Ken Ritz. The plane sat at the south end of the golf course, which itself had been snapped and rolled by the earthquake. Before them lay a long stretch of rolling, grassy turf. "We really ought to walk that and see if it's as solid as it looks," Ken said. "But we don't have time."

Against his better judgment, Buck did not protest. Still, Ken sat there staring. "I don't like it," he said finally. "It looks long enough, and we'll know right away if it's solid. The question is, can I gain enough speed to get airborne?"

"Can you abort if you don't?"

"I can try."

Ken Ritz trying was better than anyone else promising. Buck said, "Let's do it."

Ritz throttled up and gradually increased the speed. Buck felt his pulse race as they roller-coastered the hills of the fairway, engines screaming. Ken hit the flat stretch and throttled up all the way. The force pressed Buck to his seat, but as he braced for liftoff, Ritz throttled back.

Ritz shook his head. "We've got to be at top speed by the flats. I was only at about three-quarters." He turned around and took the plane back. "Just have to start faster," he said. "It's like popping the clutch. If you spin, you don't accelerate fast. If you feather it for the right purchase, you've got a chance."

The rolling start was slow again, but this time Ken throttled up as quickly as possible. They nearly left the ground as they skimmed dips and skipped mounds. They reached the flat area at what seemed twice the speed as before. Ken shouted over the din, "Now we're talkin', baby!"

The Learjet took off like a shot, and Ken maneuvered it so it felt as if they were going straight up. Buck was plastered against the back of his seat, unable to move. He could barely catch his breath, but when he did he let out a yelp and Ritz laughed. "If I don't die of this headache, I'm gonna get you to the church on time!"

Buck's phone was chirping. He had to will his hand to pull it out, so strong were the g-forces. "This is Buck!" he hollered.

It was Tsion. "You are still on the plane?" he said.

"Just took off. But we're going to make good time."

Buck told Tsion about Ken's injury and getting him out of the hospital.

"He is amazing," Tsion said. "Listen, Cameron, I just received an e-mail from Rayford. He and his copilot have discovered that one of the Jewish witnesses works right there at the shelter. A young man. I will be e-mailing him personally. I have just put out onto a central bulletin board the result of several days of study and writing. Check it when you get a chance. I call it 'The Coming Soul Harvest,' and it concerns the 144,000 witnesses, their winning many millions to Christ, the visible seal, and what we can expect in the way of judgments over the next year or so."

"What *can* we expect?"

"Read it on the Net when you get back. And please talk to Ken about getting us to Israel."

"That seems impossible now," Buck said. "Didn't Rayford tell you Carpathia's people are claiming to have helped you escape so they can be reunited with you?"

"Cameron! God will not let anything happen to me for a while. I feel a huge responsibility to the rest of the witnesses. Get me to Israel and leave my safety in the Lord's hands!"

"You have more faith than I do, Tsion," Buck said.

"Then start working on yours, my brother!"

"Pray for Chloe!" Buck said.

"Constantly," Tsion said. "For all of you."

Less than an hour later, Ritz radioed Minneapolis for landing instructions and asked to be put through to a rental car agency. With the shortage of staff and vehicles, prices had been doubled. However, cars were available, and he was given directions to the Global Community hospital.

Buck had no idea what he might encounter there. He couldn't imagine easy access or the ability to get Chloe out. GC officials weren't expected to take custody of her until late that afternoon, but surely she was already under guard. He wished he had some clue to her health. Was it wise to move her? Should he kidnap her even if he could?

"Ken, if you're up to it, I might use you and your crazy head wound as a distraction. They might be looking for me, hopefully not this soon, but I don't think anyone's ever put you together with us anyway."

"I hope you're serious, Buck," Ken said, "because I love to act. Plus, you're one of the good guys. Somebody's watching out for you and your friends."

Just outside Minneapolis, Ritz was informed that air traffic was heavier than expected and he would be in a landing pattern for another ten minutes. "Roger that," he said. "I do have a bit of an emergency here. It's not life or death, but one passenger on this plane has a serious head wound."

"Roger, Lear. We'll see if we can move you up a couple of slots. Let us know if your situation changes."

"Pretty crafty," Buck said.

When Ritz was finally cleared to bring in the Learjet, he banked and swooped over the terminal, apparently the target of major quake damage. Rebuilding had begun, but the entire operation, from ticket counters to rental car agencies, was now housed in mobile units. Buck was stunned at the amount of activity at an airport where only two runways functioned.

The harried ground control manager apologized for having nowhere to hangar the Learjet. He accepted Ken's pledge that he would not leave the plane longer than twenty-four hours. "I hope not," Buck whispered.

Ritz taxied near one of the old runways where heavy equipment was moving massive amounts of earth. He parked the Lear in line with everything from single engine Piper Cubs to Boeing 727s. They couldn't have stopped farther from the car rental agencies and still been on airport property.

Ken, wincing, gasping, and moving slowly, urged Buck to hurry ahead, but Buck was afraid Ken might collapse.

"Don't go into your wounded old coot act yet," Buck teased. "At least wait until we get to the hospital."

"If you know me," Ritz said, "you know this is no act."

"I don't believe this," Buck said, when they finally reached the car rental area and found themselves at the end of a long line. "Looks like they're sending people to the other side of the parking lot for cars."

Ken, several inches taller than Buck, stood on tiptoes and peered into the distance. "You're right," he said. "And you may have to get the car and come get me. I'm not up to walking any more now."

As they neared the head of the line, Buck told Ritz to rent the car on his credit card and Buck would reimburse him. "I don't want my name all over the state, in case the GC thinks to check around."

Ritz slapped his card on the counter. A young woman studied it. "We're down to subcompacts. Will that be acceptable?"

"What if I say no, honey?" he said.

She made a face. "That's all we have."

"Then what difference does it make whether it's acceptable?"

"You want it then?"

"I don't have any choice. Just how subcompact is this rig?"

She slid a glossy card across the counter and pointed to the smallest car pictured. "My word," Ritz said, "there's barely room in there for me, let alone my son here."

Buck fought a smile. The young woman, already

clearly weary of Ritz and his banter, began filling out the paperwork.

"That thing even have a backseat?"

"Not really. There's a little space behind the seats, though. You put your luggage there."

Ritz looked at Buck, and Buck knew what he was thinking. The two of them were going to get to know each other better than they cared to in that car. Adding a grown woman in fragile condition took more imagination than Buck possessed.

"Do you have a color preference?" the girl asked.

"I get to choose?" Ritz said. "You've got only one model left, but it comes in different colors?"

"Usually," she said. "We're down to just the red ones now."

"But I get to choose?"

"If you choose red."

"OK, then. Give me a second. You know what I think I'd like? You got any red ones?"

"Yes."

"I'll take a red one. Wait a minute. Son, red OK with you?"

Buck just closed his eyes and shook his head. As soon as he had the keys he ran for the car. He tossed his and Ritz's bags behind the seats, pushed both seats back as far as they would go, jammed himself behind the wheel, and raced back to the exit road where Ritz waited. Buck had been gone only a few minutes, but apparently standing there had become too much for Ken. He sat with his knees pulled up, hands clasped in front of him.

Ritz struggled to his feet and appeared woozy, covering his eyes. Buck whipped open his door, but Ken said, "Stay there. I'm all right."

He squeezed himself in, knees pushing against the dashboard and his head pressing against the roof. He chuckled. "Buddy boy, I have to duck to see out."

"There's not much to see," Buck said. "Try to relax."

Ritz snorted. "You must've never been hit in the back of the head with an airplane."

"Can't say I have," Buck said, pulling onto the shoulder and passing several cars.

"Relaxing isn't the point. Surviving is. Why did you let me out of that hospital anyway? I needed another day or two of shut-eye."

"Don't put that on me. I tried to talk you out of leaving."

"I know. Just help me find my dope, would ya? Where's my bag?"

The Twin Cities' expressways were in relatively decent shape, compared to the Chicago area. By snaking between lane closures and detours, Buck moved at a steady pace. With his eyes on the road and one hand on the wheel, he reached behind Ken and grabbed his big leather bag. He strained, pulling it over the back of Ken's seat, and in the process dragged it hard across the back of Ken's head, causing him to screech.

"Oh, Ken! I'm so sorry! Are you all right?"

Ken sat with the bag in his lap. Tears streamed, and he grimaced so hard his teeth showed. "If I thought you did that on purpose," he rasped, "I'd kill you."

CHAPTER **12**

RAYFORD STEELE enjoyed a hunger for the Word of God from the day he had received Christ. He found, however, that as the world slowly began to get back to speed following the disappearances, he became busier than ever. It became increasingly difficult to spend the time he wanted to in the Bible.

His first pastor, the late Bruce Barnes, had impressed upon the Tribulation Force how important it was that they "search the Scriptures daily." Rayford tried to get himself in that groove, but for weeks he was frustrated. He tried getting up earlier but found himself involved in so many late night discussions and activities that it wasn't practical. He tried reading his Bible during breaks on his flights, but that caused tension between him and his various copilots and first officers.

Finally he hit upon a solution. No matter where he was in the world, regardless of what he had done during the day or evening, sometime he would be going to bed. Regardless of the location or situation, before he turned out the light, he would get his daily Bible study in.

Bruce had at first been skeptical, urging him to give God the first few minutes of the day rather than the last. "You have to get up in the morning too," Bruce had said. "Wouldn't you rather give God your freshest and most energetic moments?"

Rayford saw the wisdom of that, but when it didn't seem to work, he went back to his own plan. Yes, he had at times fallen asleep while reading or praying, but usually he was able to stay alert, and God always showed him something.

Since losing his Bible in the earthquake, Rayford had been frustrated. Now, in the wee hours, he wanted to get online, download a Bible, and see if Tsion Ben-Judah had posted anything. Rayford was grateful he had kept his laptop in his flight bag. If only he had kept his Bible there, he would still have that too.

In his undershirt, trousers, and socks, Rayford lugged his laptop to the communications center, found a hot spot, and sat where he could see his own door down the hall.

As information began appearing on his screen, he was distracted by footsteps. He lowered the screen and stared down the hall. A young, dark-haired man stopped at Rayford's door and knocked quietly. When there was no answer, he tried the knob. Rayford wondered if someone had been assigned to rob him or look for clues to the whereabouts of Hattie Durham or Tsion Ben-Judah.

The young man knocked again, his shoulders slumped, and he turned away. Then it hit Rayford. Could it be Hassid? He gave a loud "Psst!"

The young man stopped and looked toward the sound. Rayford was in the dark, so he raised his computer screen. The young man paused, clearly wondering if the figure at the computer was whom he wanted to see. Rayford imagined his concocting a story in case he encountered a superior officer.

Rayford signaled him, and the young man approached. His nameplate read David Hassid.

"May I see your mark?" Hassid whispered. Rayford put his face near the screen and pulled his hair back. "Like the young Americans say, that is so cool."

Rayford said, "You were looking for me?"

"I just wanted to meet you," Hassid said. "By the way, I work here in communications." Rayford nodded. "Though we don't have phones in our rooms, we do have wireless."

"I don't. I looked."

"They are covered with stainless steel plates."

"I did see that," Rayford said.

"So you don't need to risk getting caught out here, Captain Steele."

"That's good to know. It wouldn't surprise me if they could tell where I've been on the Web through here."

"They could. They can trace it through the lines in your room, too, but what will they find?"

"I'm just trying to find out what my friend, Tsion Ben-Judah, is saying these days."

"I could tell you by heart," Hassid said. "He is my spiritual father."

"Mine too."

"He led you to Christ?"

"Well, no," Rayford admitted. "That was his predecessor. But I still see the rabbi as my pastor and mentor."

"Let me write down for you the address of the central bulletin board where I found his message for today. It's a long one, but it's so good. He and a brother of his discovered their marks yesterday too. It's so exciting. Do you know that I am probably one of the 144,000 witnesses?"

"Well, that would be right, wouldn't it?" Rayford said.

"I can't wait to find out my assignment. I feel so new to this, so ignorant of the truth. I know the gospel, but it seems I need to know so much more if I'm going to be a bold evangelist, preaching like the apostle Paul."

"We're all new at this, David, if you think about it."

"But I'm newer than most. Wait till you see all the messages on the bulletin board. Thousands and thousands of believers have already responded. I don't know how Dr. Ben-Judah will have time to read them all. They're pleading with him to come to their countries and to teach them and train them face-to-face. I would give everything I owned for that privilege."

"You know, of course, that Dr. Ben-Judah is a fugitive."

"Yes, but he believes he is one of the 144,000 as well. He's teaching that we are sealed, at least for a time, and that the forces of evil cannot come against us."

"Really?"

"Yes. That protection is not for everyone who has the mark, apparently. But it is for the converted Jewish evangelists."

"In other words, I could be in danger, but you couldn't, at least for a while."

"That seems to be what he's teaching. I'll be eager to hear your response."

"I can't wait to plug in."

Rayford unplugged his machine and the two strolled down the corridor, whispering. Rayford discovered Hassid was just twenty-two years old, a college graduate who had aspired to military service in Poland. "But I was so enamored of Carpathia, I immediately applied for service to the Global Community. It wasn't long before I discovered the truth on the Internet. Now I am enlisted behind enemy lines, but I didn't plan it that way."

Rayford advised the young man that he was wise in not declaring himself until the time was right. "It will be dangerous enough for you to be a believer, but you'll be of greater help to the cause right now if you remain silent about it, as Officer McCullum is doing."

At Rayford's door, Hassid gripped his hand fiercely and

squeezed hard. "It is so good to know I am not alone," he said. "Did you want to see my mark?"

Rayford smiled. "Sure."

Still shaking Rayford's hand, Hassid reached with his free hand and pulled his hair out of the way.

"Sure enough," Rayford said. "Welcome to the family."

Buck found parking at the hospital similar to what it had been at the airport. The original pavement had sunk, and a turn-around had been scraped from the dirt at the front. But people had created their own parking places, and the only spot Buck could find was several hundred yards from the entrance. He dropped Ken off in front with his bag and told him to wait.

"If you promise not to smack me in the head again," Ken said. "Man, gettin' out of this car is like being born."

Buck parked in a haphazard line of other vehicles and grabbed a few toiletries from his own bag. As he headed toward the hospital, he tucked in his shirt, brushed himself down, combed his hair, and applied a few sprays of deodorant. When he got near the entrance he saw Ken on the ground, using his bag as a pillow. He wondered if pressing him into service had been a good idea. A few people stared at him. Ken appeared comatose. *Oh no!* Buck thought.

He knelt by Ken. "Are you all right?" he whispered. "Let me get you up."

Ken spoke without opening his eyes. "Oh, man! Buck, I did something royally stupid."

"What?"

"'Member when you got me my medicine?" Ken's words were slurred. "I popped 'em in my mouth without water, right?"

"I offered to get you something to drink."

"That's not the point. I was s'posed to take one from one bottle and three from the other, every four hours. I missed my last dose, so I took two of one and six of the other."

"Yeah?"

"But I mixed up the bottles."

"What are they?"

Ritz shrugged and his breathing became deep and regular.

"Don't fall asleep on me, Ken. I've got to get you inside."

Buck pawed through Ken's bag and found the bottles. The larger recommended dose was for local pain. The smaller appeared to be a combination of morphine, Demerol, and Prozac. "You took six of *these*?"

"Mm-hmm."

"Come on, Ken. Get up. Right now."

"Oh, Buck. Let me sleep."

"No way. Right now, we have to go."

Buck didn't think Ken was in danger or had to have his stomach pumped, but if he didn't get him inside, he'd be a dead weight and worthless. Worse, he would probably be hauled away.

Buck lifted one of Ken's hands and stuck his own head

under Ken's arm. When he tried to straighten, Ken was no help and too heavy. "Come on, man. You've got to help me."

Ken just mumbled.

Buck held Ken's head gently and pulled the bag out from under him. "Let's go, let's go!"

"You mm-hmm."

Buck feared Ken's head was the only place still sensitive, and that might be dulled soon too. Rather than risk contaminating the wound, Buck looked for inflammation other than at the opening. Below where Ken had been gouged the hairline was fiery red. Buck spread his feet and braced himself, then pressed directly on the spot. Ritz leaped to his feet as if he'd been shot from a gun. He swung at Buck, who ducked, wrapped one arm around Ken's back, scooped up the bag with the other, and marched him to the entrance.

Ken looked and sounded like the deliriously injured man that he was. People moved out of the way.

Inside the hospital, things were worse. It was all Buck could do to hold Ken up. The lines at the front desk were five deep. Buck dragged Ken to the waiting area, where every chair was filled and several people were standing. Buck looked for someone who might give up his seat, and finally a stocky middle-aged woman stood. Buck thanked her and lowered Ken into the chair. Ken curled sideways, lifted his knees, drew his hands to his cheek, and rested on the shoulder of an old man next to him. The man caught sight of the wound, recoiled, then apparently resigned himself to serving as Ken's pillow.

Buck stuffed Ken's bag under his chair, apologized to the

old man, and promised to be back as soon as he could. When he tried to move to the front at the receptionist's desk, people in two lines rebuffed him. He called out, "I'm sorry, but I have an emergency here!"

"We all do!" one shouted back.

He stood in line for several minutes, worrying more about Chloe than Ken. Ken would sleep this off. The only problem was, Buck was still stuck. Unless . . .

Buck stepped out of line and hurried into a public washroom. He washed his face, watered down and slicked back his hair, and made sure his clothes were as neat as possible. He pulled his identification card from his pocket and clipped it to his shirt, turning it around so his picture and name were hidden.

He popped the remaining lens out of his broken sunglasses, but the frames looked so phony that he pulled them up into his hair. He looked in the mirror and affected a grim expression, telling himself, "You are a doctor. A no-nonsense, big ego, all-action doctor."

He burst from the bathroom as if he knew where he was going. He needed a pigeon. The first two doctors he passed looked too old and mature for his ruse. But here came a thin, young doctor looking wide-eyed and out of place. Buck stepped in front of him.

"Doctor, did I not tell you to check on that trauma in emergency two?"

The young physician was speechless.

"Well?" Buck demanded.

"No! No, Doctor. That must have been someone else."

"All right, then! Listen! I need a stethoscope—a sterile one this time!—a large, freshly laundered smock, and the chart on Mother Doe. You got that?"

The intern closed his eyes and repeated, "Stethoscope, smock, chart."

Buck continued barking. "Sterile, big, Mother Doe."

"Right away, Doctor."

"I'll be at the elevators."

"Yes, sir."

The intern turned and walked away. Buck called after him, "Sometime today, Doctor!" The intern ran.

Now Buck had to find the elevators. He slipped back into the reception area to find Ken still snoozing in the same position, the old man next to him looking as intimidated as ever. He asked a Hispanic woman if she knew where the elevators were. She pointed down the hall. As he hurried that way, he saw his intern behind the counter, hassling the receptionists. "Just do it!" he was saying.

A few minutes later the young doctor rushed to him with everything he had asked for. He held the smock open and Buck hastily slipped into it, draped the stethoscope around his neck, and grabbed the chart.

"Thank you, Doctor. Where are you from?"

"Right here!" the intern said. "This hospital."

"Oh, well then, good. Very good. I'm from . . ." Buck hesitated a second. "Young Memorial. Thanks for your help."

The intern looked puzzled, as if trying to think where Young Memorial was. "Any time," he said.

Buck left the elevators and hurried to the washroom. He locked himself in a stall and flipped open Chloe's chart. The photographs made him burst into tears. Buck set the clipboard on the floor and doubled over. "God," he prayed silently, "how could you have let this happen?"

He clenched his teeth and shuddered, willing himself to calm down. He didn't want to be heard. After about a minute, he opened the chart again. Staring at him from the photographs was the almost unrecognizable face of his young wife. Had she looked that swollen when she was brought to Kenosha, no doctor would have recognized her from Buck's picture.

As the doctor in Kenosha had told him, the right side of her body had apparently been slammed full force by a section of roofing. Her normally smooth, pale skin was now blotched red and yellow and invaded by pitch, tar, and bits of shingling. Worse, her right foot looked as if someone had tried to fold it. A bone protruded from her shin. Bruising began on the outside of her knee and ran to the kneecap, which looked severely damaged. From the position of her body, it appeared her right hip had been knocked out of joint. Bruises and bumps in her midsection evidenced broken ribs. Her elbow had been laid open, and her right shoulder appeared dislocated. Her right collarbone pressed against the skin. The right side of her face appeared flatter, and there was damage to her jaw, teeth, cheekbone, and eye. Her face was so misshapen that Buck could hardly bear to look. The eye was swollen huge and shut. The only abrasion on her left side was a raspberry near her hip, so the doctor had probably correctly deduced that she had been knocked off her feet by a blow to her right side.

Buck determined he would not recoil when he saw her in person. Of course, he wanted her to survive. But was that best for her? Could she communicate? Would she recognize him? He flipped through the rest of the chart, trying to interpret the notations. It appeared she had escaped injury to her internal organs. She suffered several fractures, including three in her foot, one in her ankle, her kneecap, her elbow, and two ribs. She had dislocated both hip and shoulder. She had also sustained fractures of the jaw, cheekbone, and cranium.

Buck scanned the rest quickly, looking for a key word. There it was. Fetal heartbeat detected. *Oh, God! Save them both!*

Buck didn't know medicine, but her vital signs looked good for someone who had suffered such a trauma. Though she had not regained consciousness at the time of the report, her pulse, respiration, blood pressure, and even brain waves were normal.

Buck looked at his watch. The GC contingent should arrive soon. He needed time to think and to collect himself. He would be no good to Chloe if he went off half-cocked. He memorized as much of the chart as he could, noted that she was in room 335A, and tucked the clipboard under his arm. He left the restroom with rubbery knees, but he affected a purposeful stride once he was in the corridor. While he pondered his options, he moved back into the reception area. The old man was gone. Ken Ritz no longer leaned on anyone, but his gigantic frame was curled in a fetal position like an overgrown child, the healthy part of his head resting on the back of the chair. He looked as if he could sleep for a week.

Buck took the elevator to the third floor to get the lay of the land. As the doors opened, however, something struck him. He whipped open the chart. "335A." She was in a double room. What if he was the doctor for the other patient? Even if he wasn't on a security list, they'd have to let him in, wouldn't they? He might have to bluster, but he would get in.

Two uniformed GC guards stood on either side of the 335 doorway. One was a young man, the other a slightly older woman. Two strips of white adhesive tape were attached to the door, both written on in black marker. The top said, "A: Mother Doe, No Visitors." The other read, "B: A. Ashton."

Buck was weak with longing to check on Chloe. With the clock working against him, he wanted to get in there before GC officials did. He passed the room, and at the end of the hall turned and walked directly back to 335.

Rayford had not been prepared for what he found on the Internet. Tsion had outdone himself. As David Hassid had said, thousands upon thousands had already responded. Many put messages on the bulletin board identifying themselves as members of the 144,000. Rayford scrolled through the messages for more than an hour, still not coming to the end. Hundreds testified that they had received Christ after reading Tsion's message and the verses from Romans that showed their need of God.

It was late, and Rayford was bleary-eyed. He had intended to spend not more than an hour on the Net, but he had spent that and more merely working through Tsion's message. "The Coming Soul Harvest" was a fascinating study of biblical prophecy. Tsion made himself so understandable and personable that it did not surprise Rayford that thousands considered themselves his protégés, though they had never met him. From the looks of the bulletin board, however, that would have to change. They clamored for him to come where they could meet him and sit under his tutelage.

Tsion responded to the requests by telling his own story, how as a biblical scholar he had been commissioned by the State of Israel to study the claims of the coming Messiah. He explained that by the time of the rapture of the church, he had come to the conclusion that Jesus of Nazareth fulfilled every qualification of the Messiah prophesied in the Old Testament. But he did not receive Christ as his own savior until the Rapture convinced him.

He kept his belief to himself until he was asked to go on international television to reveal the results of his lengthy study. He was astounded that the Jews still refused to believe that Jesus was who the Bible claimed he was. Tsion revealed his finding at the very end of the program, causing tremendous outcry, especially among the orthodox. His wife and two teenage children were later slaughtered, and he barely escaped. He told his Internet audience he was now in hiding but that he would "continue to teach and to proclaim that Jesus Christ is the only name under heaven given among men through whom one can be saved."

Rayford forced himself to stay awake, poring over Tsion's teachings. A meter on his screen showed the number of responses as they were added to the central bulletin board. He believed the meter was malfunctioning. It raced so fast he could not even see the individual numerals. He sampled a few of the responses. Not only were many converted Jews claiming to be among the 144,000 witnesses, but Jews and Gentiles were also trusting Christ. Thousands more encouraged each other to petition the Global Community for protection and asylum for this great scholar.

Rayford felt a tingle behind his knees that shot to his head. One bit of leverage with Nicolae Carpathia was the court of public opinion. It wasn't beyond him to have Tsion Ben-Judah assassinated or "accidentally" killed and make it appear other forces were at work. But with thousands all over the globe appealing to Nicolae on Tsion's behalf, he would be forced to prove he could deliver. Rayford wished there was some way to make him do the right thing by Hattie Durham as well.

Tsion's main message for the day was based on Revelation 8 and 9. Those chapters supported his contention that the earthquake, the foretold wrath of the Lamb, ushered in the second twenty-one months of the Tribulation.

There are seven years, or eighty-four months, in all. So, my dear friends, you can see that we are now one quarter of the way through. Unfortunately, as bad as things have been, they get progressively worse as we race headlong toward the end, the glorious appearing of Christ.

What is next? In Revelation 8:5 an angel takes a censer, fills it with fire from the altar of God, and throws it to the earth. That results in noise, thunder, lightning, and an earthquake.

That same chapter goes on to say that seven angels with seven trumpets prepared themselves to sound. That is where we are now. Sometime over the next twenty-one months, the first angel will sound, and hail and fire will follow, mingled with blood, thrown down to the earth. This will burn a third of the trees and all the green grass.

Later a second angel will sound the second trumpet, and the Bible says a great mountain burning with fire will be thrown into the sea. This will turn a third of the water to blood, kill a third of the living creatures in the sea, and sink a third of the ships.

The third angel's trumpet sound will result in a great star falling from heaven, burning like a torch. It will somehow fall over a wide area and land in a third of the rivers and springs. This star is even named in Scripture. The book of Revelation calls it

Wormwood. Where it falls, the water becomes bitter and people die from drinking it.

How can a thinking person see all that has happened and not fear what is to come? If there are still unbelievers after the third Trumpet Judgment, the fourth should convince everyone. Anyone who resists the warnings of God at that time will likely have already decided to serve the enemy. The fourth Trumpet Judgment is a striking of the sun, the moon, and the stars so that a third of the sun, a third of the moon, and a third of the stars are darkened. We will never again see sunshine as bright as we have before. The brightest summer day with the sun high in the sky will be only two-thirds as bright as it ever was. How will this be explained away?

In the middle of this, the writer of the Revelation says he looked and heard an angel "flying through the midst of heaven." It was saying with a loud voice, "Woe, woe, woe to the inhabitants of the earth, because of the remaining blasts of the trumpet of the three angels who are about to sound!"

In my next lesson, I will cover those last three Trumpet Judgments of the second twenty-one months of the Tribulation. But, my beloved brothers and sisters in Christ, victory is also coming. Let me remind you with a few choice passages of Scripture that the outcome has already been determined. We win! But we must share the truth and expose the darkness and bring as many as possible to Christ in these last days.

I want to show you why I believe there is a great soul harvest coming. But first, consider these statements and promises:

In the Old Testament book of Joel 2:28-32, God is speaking. He says, "And it shall come to pass afterward that I will pour out My Spirit on all flesh; your sons and your daughters shall prophesy, your old men shall dream dreams, your young men shall see visions. And also on My menservants and on My maidservants I will pour out My Spirit in those days.

"And I will show wonders in the heavens and in the earth: blood and fire and pillars of smoke. The sun shall be turned into darkness, and the moon into blood, before the coming of the great and awesome day of the Lord.

"And it shall come to pass that whoever calls on the name of the Lord shall be saved. For in Mount Zion and in Jerusalem there shall be deliverance, as the Lord has said, among the remnant whom the Lord calls."

Is that not a wonderful and most blessed promise? Revelation 7 indicates that the Trumpet Judgments I just mentioned will not come until the servants of God have been sealed on their foreheads. There will no longer be any question who the true believers are. Those first four angels, to whom it was granted to carry out the first four Trumpet Judgments, were instructed, "Do not harm the earth, the sea, or the trees till we have sealed the servants of our God on their foreheads." Thus it is clear that this sealing comes first. Just within the last several hours, it has become clear to me and to other brothers and sisters in Christ that the seal on the forehead of the true believer is already visible, but apparently only to other believers. This was a thrilling discovery, and I look forward to hearing from many of you who detect it on each other.

The word *servants*, from the Greek word *doulos*, is the same word the apostles Paul and James used when they referred to themselves as the bond slaves of Jesus Christ. The chief function of a servant of Christ is to communicate the gospel of the grace of God. We will be inspired by the fact that we can understand the book of Revelation, which was given by God, according to the first verse of the first chapter "to show His servants things which must shortly take place." The third verse says, "Blessed is he who reads and those who hear the words of this prophecy, and keep those things which are written in it, for the time is near."

Although we will go through great persecution, we can comfort ourselves that during the Tribulation we look forward to astounding events outlined in

Revelation, the last book in God's revealed plan for man.

Now indulge me for one more verse from Revelation 7, and I will conclude with why I anticipate this great harvest of souls.

Revelation 7:9 quotes John the revelator, "After these things I looked, and behold, a great multitude *which no one could number* [emphasis mine], of all nations, tribes, peoples, and tongues, standing before the throne and before the Lamb, clothed with white robes, with palm branches in their hands. . . ."

These are the tribulation saints. Now follow me carefully. In a later verse, Revelation 9:16, the writer numbers the army of horsemen in a battle at two hundred million. If such a vast army *can* be numbered, what might the Scriptures mean when they refer to the tribulation saints, those who come to Christ during this period, as "a great multitude *which no one could number*" [emphasis mine]?

Do you see why I believe we are justified in trusting God for more than a billion souls during this period? Let us pray for that great harvest. All who name Christ as their Redeemer can have a part in this, the greatest task ever assigned to mankind. I look forward to interacting with you again soon.

With love, in the matchless name of the Lord Jesus Christ, our Savior, Tsion Ben-Judah.

Rayford could barely keep his eyes open, but he was thrilled with Tsion's boundless enthusiasm and insightful teaching. He returned to the bulletin board and blinked. The number at the top of the screen was in the tens of thousands and rising. Rayford wanted to add to the avalanche, but he was exhausted.

Nicolae Carpathia had addressed the globe on radio and television. No doubt the response would be monumental. But would it rival the reaction to this converted rabbi, communicating from exile to a new, growing family?

Buck reminded himself that, for the moment, he was not just a doctor, but also an egomaniac. He strode to room 335 without so much as a nod to the two Global Community guards. As he pushed open the door, they stepped into his path.

"Excuse me!" he said with disgust. "Miss Ashton's alarm rang, so unless you want to be responsible for the death of my patient, you will let me pass."

The guards looked at each other, appearing uncertain. The woman reached for Buck's ID tag. He pushed her hand away and entered the room, locking the door. He hesitated before turning around, prepared to respond if they began banging. They didn't.

Draperies hid both patients. Buck pulled back the first to reveal his wife. He held his breath as his eyes traveled over the sheet from feet to neck. It felt as if his heart was literally breaking. Poor sweet Chloe had no idea what she was getting into when she agreed to marry him. He bit his lip hard. There was no time to emote. He was grateful she seemed to be sleeping peacefully. Her right arm was in a cast from wrist to shoulder. Her left arm lay motionless at her side, an IV needle in the back of her hand.

Buck set the clipboard on the bed and slipped his hand under hers. The baby-soft skin he cherished made him long to gather her in his arms, to soothe her, to take her pain. He bent and brushed her fingers with his lips, his tears falling between them. He jumped when he felt a weak grip and looked at her. She stared at him. "I'm here!" he whispered desperately. He moved to where he could caress her cheek. "Chloe, sweetheart, it's Buck."

He leaned close. Her gaze followed him. He forced himself not to look at her shattered right side. She was his sweet, innocent wife on one side and a monster on the other. He took her hand again.

"Can you hear me? Chloe, squeeze my hand again."

No response.

Buck hurried to the other side and pulled back the drape to peek through to the other bed. A. Ashton was in her late fifties and appeared to be in a coma. Buck returned, grabbed his clipboard, and studied Chloe's face. Her look still followed him. Could she hear? Was she conscious?

He unlocked the door and stepped quickly into the hall. "She's out of danger for the moment," he said, "but we've got a problem. Who told you Miss Ashton was in bed B?"

"Excuse me, doctor," the woman guard said, "but we have nothing to do with the patients. Our responsibility is the door."

"So, you're not responsible for this screwup?"

"Absolutely not," the woman said.

Buck pulled the adhesive strips from the door and reversed them. "Ma'am, can you handle this post yourself while this young man finds me a marker?"

"Certainly, sir. Craig, get him a marker."

CHAPTER 13

BUCK SLIPPED BACK into Chloe's room, desperate to let her know he was there and she was safe.

He could hardly bear to look at her black and purple face with the eye so swollen. He gently took her hand and leaned close. "Chloe, I'm here, and I won't let anything happen to you. But I need your help. Squeeze my hand. Blink. Let me know you're with me."

No response. Buck laid his cheek on her pillow, his lips inches from her ear. "Oh, God," he prayed, "why couldn't you have let this happen to me? Why her? Help me get her out of here, God, please!"

Her hand felt like a feather, and she seemed fragile as a

251

newborn. What a contrast to the strong woman he had loved and come to know. She was not only fearless, but she was also smart. How he wished she was up to being his ally in this.

Chloe's breathing accelerated, and Buck opened his eyes as a tear slid past her ear. He looked her in the face. She blinked furiously, and he wondered if she was trying to communicate. "I'm here," he said over and over. "Chloe, it's Buck."

The GC guard had been gone too long. Buck prayed he was out there waiting with the marker but too intimidated to knock. Otherwise, who knew whom he might bring with him and what might squash any chance Buck had to protect Chloe.

He spoke quickly. "Sweetheart, I don't know if you can hear me, but try to concentrate. I'm switching your name with the woman's in the other bed. Her name is Ashton. And I'm pretending to be your doctor. OK? Can you grasp that?"

Buck waited, hoping. Finally, a flicker.

"I got you those," she whispered.

"What? Chloe, what? It's me, Buck. You got me what?"

She licked her lips and swallowed. "I got you those, and you broke them."

He concluded she was delirious. This was gibberish. He shook his head and smiled at her. "Stick with me, kid, and we'll pull something off."

"Doctor Buck," she rasped, attempting a lopsided smile.

"Yes! Chloe! You know me."

She squinted and blinked slowly now as if staying awake was an effort. "You should take better care of gifts."

"I don't know what you're saying, sweetness, and I'm not sure you do either. But whatever I did, I'm sorry."

For the first time, she turned to face him. "You broke your glasses, Doctor Buck."

Buck reflexively touched the frames on his head. "Yes! Chloe, listen to me. I'm trying to protect you. I switched the names on the door. You're—"

"Ashton," she managed.

"Yes! And your first initial is *A*. What's a good *A* name?"

"Annie," she said. "I'm Annie Ashton."

"Perfect. And who am I?"

She pressed her lips together and started to form a *B*, then changed. "My doctor," she said.

Buck turned to go see if Craig, the guard, had brought the marker. "Doctor," Chloe called out. "Wristbands."

She was thinking! How could he forget that someone could easily check their hospital ID bracelets?

He yanked hers apart, careful not to dislodge the IV. He slipped behind A. Ashton's curtain. She still appeared sound asleep. He carefully removed her bracelet, noticing she did not appear even to be breathing. He put his ear close to her nose but heard and felt nothing. He could find no pulse. He switched the wristbands.

Buck knew this only bought him time. It wouldn't be long before someone discovered that this postmenopausal dead woman was not a pregnant twenty-two-year-old. But for the time being, she was Mother Doe.

When Buck emerged, the guards were talking to an older

doctor. Craig, black marker in hand, was saying, ". . . we weren't sure what to do."

The doctor, tall, bespectacled, and gray, carried three charts. He scowled at Buck.

Buck sneaked a peek at the name sewn on his breast pocket. "Dr. Lloyd!" he exulted, thrusting out his hand.

The doctor reluctantly shook it, "Do I—?"

"Why, I haven't seen you since that, uh, that—"

"The symposium?"

"Right! The one at, um—"

"Bemidji?"

"Yeah, you were brilliant."

The doctor looked flustered, as if trying to remember Buck, yet the praise had not been lost on him. "Well, I—"

"And one of your kids was up to something. What was it?"

"Oh, I may have mentioned my son, who just got his internship."

"Right! How's he doing anyway?"

"Wonderfully. We're very proud of him. Now, Doctor—"

Buck interrupted. "I'll bet you are. Listen," he said, pulling Ken Ritz's pill bottles from his pocket, "I wonder if you could advise me. . . ."

"I'll certainly try."

"Thank you, Doctor Lloyd." He held up the tranquilizer bottle. "I prescribed this to a patient with a severe head wound, and he inadvertently exceeded the dosage. What's the best antidote?"

Dr. Lloyd studied the bottle. "It's not that serious. He'll be very sleepy for a few hours, but it'll wear off. Head trauma, you say?"

"Yes, that's why I'd rather he not sleep."

"Of course. You'll most safely counteract this with an injection of Benzedrine."

"Not being on staff here," Buck said, "I can't get anything from the pharmacy. . . ."

Dr. Lloyd scribbled him a prescription. "If you'll excuse me, Doctor—?"

"Cameron," Buck said before thinking.

"Of course, Dr. Cameron. Great to see you again."

"You too, Dr. Lloyd, and thanks."

Buck accepted the marker from the chagrined Craig and changed the strips on the door from *B* and *A* to *A* and *B*. "I'll be back soon, Craig," he said, slapping the marker into the guard's palm.

Buck hurried off, pretending to know where he was going but scanning directories and following signs as he went. Dr. Lloyd's prescription was like gold at the pharmacy, and he was soon on his way back to the lobby for Ken Ritz. On the way he appropriated a wheelchair.

He found Ken leaning forward, elbows on his knees, chin in his hands, snoring. Grateful for his training taking his turn giving his mother insulin injections, Buck deftly opened the package, raised Ken's sleeve without toppling him, swabbed the area, and pulled the cap off the hypodermic needle with his teeth. As he drove the point into Ken's biceps, the cap popped from his mouth and rattled to the floor. Someone muttered, "Shouldn't he be wearing gloves?"

Buck found the cap, replaced it, and put everything in his pocket. Facing Ken, he thrust his wrists into the big man's armpits and pulled him from the chair. He turned him 45 degrees and lowered him into the wheelchair, having forgotten to set the brake. When Ken hit the chair, it began rolling backwards, and Buck had no leverage to remove his hands. Straddling Ritz's long legs, his face in Ken's chest, Buck stumbled across the waiting room as onlookers dived out of the way. As the chair picked up speed, Buck's only option was to drag his feet. He wound up sprawled across the lanky pilot, who roused briefly and called out, "Charlie Bravo Alpha to base!"

Buck extracted himself, lowered the footrests, and lifted Ritz's knees to set his feet in place. Then they were off to find a gurney. His hope was that Ritz would respond quickly enough to the Benzedrine to be able to help him take Miss Ashton's body, with Mother Doe's wristband, to the morgue. If he could temporarily convince the Global Community delegation that their potential hostage had expired, he could buy time.

As Buck wheeled him toward the elevators, Ken's arms kept flopping out of the chair and acting as brakes on the wheels. Buck would grab them and tuck them back in, only to find himself veering into traffic. Buck finally secured Ken's arms by the time they backed onto an elevator, but Ritz chose that moment to let his chin drop to his chest, exposing his scalp wound to everyone aboard.

When Ritz seemed to begin coming out of his fog, Buck was able to get him out of the chair and onto a gurney he had absconded with. The sudden rise, however, had made Ken dizzy. He flopped onto his back, and his head wound brushed the sheet. "OK!" he hollered like a drunk. "All right!"

He rolled to his side, and Buck covered him to the neck, then wheeled him next to the wall, where he waited for him to fully awaken. Twice, as lots of traffic walked by, Ken spontaneously sat up, looked around, and lay back down.

When he finally came to and was able to sit and then stand without dizziness, he was still disoriented. "Man, that was some good sleep. I could use more of that."

Buck explained that he wanted to find Ken a smock and have him play an orderly, helping Dr. Cameron. Buck went over it several times until Ken convinced him he was awake and understood. "Wait right here," Buck said.

Near a surgical unit he saw a doctor hang a smock on a hook before heading the other way. It looked clean, so Buck took it back to Ken. But Ken was gone.

Buck found him at the elevator. "What are you doing?"

"I've gotta get my bag," Ken said. "We left it outside."

"It's under a chair in the waiting room. We'll get it later. Now put this on." The sleeves were four inches short. Ken looked like the last renter in a costume shop.

Pushing the gurney, they hurried to 335 as fast as Ken could go. The woman guard said, "Doctor, we just got a call from our superiors that a delegation is on its way from the airport, and—"

"I'm sorry, ma'am," Buck said, "but the patient you're guarding has died."

"Died?" she said. "Well, it certainly wasn't our fault. We—"

"No one is saying it's your fault. Now I need to take the body to the morgue. You can tell your delegation or whomever where to find her."

"Then we don't need to stay here, do we?"

"Of course not. Thanks for your service."

As Buck and Ken entered the room, Craig caught sight of Ritz's head. "Man, are you an orderly or a patient?"

Ken whirled around. "Are you discriminating against the handicapped?"

"No, sir, I'm sorry. It's just—"

"Everybody needs a job!" Ken said.

Chloe tried to smile when she saw Ken, whom she had met at Palwaukee after Buck and Tsion's flight from Egypt. Buck looked pointedly at Ritz. "Meet Annie Ashton," he said. "I'm her doctor."

"Dr. Buck," Chloe said quietly. "He broke his glasses."

Ritz smiled. "Sounds like we're on the same medication."

Buck pulled the sheet over the dead woman's head, rolled her bed out, and replaced it with the gurney. He wheeled the bed to the door and asked Ken to stay with Chloe, "just in case."

"In case what?"

"In case those GC guys show up."

"I get to play doctor?"

"In a manner of speaking. If we can convince them the woman they want is in the morgue, we might have time to hide Chloe."

"You don't want to strap her to the top of our rental car?"

Buck pushed the bed down the corridor to the elevators. Getting off were four people, three of them men, dressed in dark business suits. Tags on their jackets identified them as Global Community operatives. One said, "What are we looking for again?"

Another said, "335."

Buck averted his face, not knowing whether his picture had been circulated. As soon as he rolled the bed onto the elevator, a doctor hit the emergency stop button. A half dozen people were in the car with Buck and the body. "I'm sorry, ladies and gentlemen," the doctor said. "Just a moment, please."

He whispered in Buck's ear, "You're not a resident here, are you?"

"No."

"There are strict rules about transporting corpses on other than the service elevators."

"I didn't know."

The doctor turned to the others. "I'm sorry, but you're going to need to take another elevator."

"Gladly," somebody said.

The doctor turned the elevator back on, and everyone else got off. He hit the button for the subbasement. "First time in this hospital?"

"Yes."

"Left and all the way to the end."

At the morgue, Buck thought about leaving the body outside the door and hoping it would be misidentified temporarily as Mother Doe. But he was seen by a man behind the desk who said, "You're not supposed to bring beds in here. We can't be responsible for that. You'll have to take it back with you."

"I'm on a tight schedule."

"That's your problem. We're not answering for a room bed being down here."

Two orderlies lifted the body to a gurney, and the man said, "Papers?"

"I'm sorry?"

"Papers! Death certificate. Doctor's sign-off."

Buck said, "Wristband says Mother Doe. I was told to bring her down here. That's all I know."

"Who's her doctor?"

"I have no idea."

"What room?"

"335."

"We'll look it up. Now get this bed out of here."

Buck hurried back to the elevator, praying the ruse had worked and that the GC contingent was on its way to the morgue to make sure about Mother Doe. He did not cross paths with them, however, on the way back.

He was almost at room 335 when they emerged. He looked the other way and kept walking.

One said, "Where's Charles, anyway?"

The woman said, "We should have waited. He was parking the car. How's he supposed to find us now?"

"He can't be far. When he gets here, we'll get to the bottom of this."

When they were out of sight, Buck pushed the bed back into 335. "It's just me," he said as he passed Chloe's curtain. He found Chloe even paler and now trembling. Ken sat next to the bed, hands resting lightly atop his head.

"Are you cold, hon?" Buck asked. Chloe shook her head. Her discoloration had spread. The ugly streaks caused by bleeding under the skin nearly reached her temple.

"She's a little shook, that's all," Ritz said. "Me too, though I deserve an Oscar."

"Doctor Airplane," Chloe said, and Ritz laughed.

"That's what she said. That's all they could get out of her, except her name."

"Annie Ashton," she whispered.

"Screwed up those guys' heads something awful. They come in complaining, especially the woman, about having no guards assigned like they asked. 'We didn't ask,' Ken said, mimicking her voice. 'It was a directive.'"

Chloe nodded.

Ken continued. "They shuffle past, snagging the end of our drape, talking about how she's in bed B, all proud of themselves because they can read an adhesive strip on the door. I call out, 'Two visitors at a time, please, and I'd appreciate you keeping it down. I have a toxic patient here.' I meant infectious, but it means the same, doesn't it?

"'Course they saw right away there was just an empty gurney over there. One of the guys pokes his head in here and I raise way up on my tiptoes, doctorlike, and say, 'If you don't want typhoid fever, you'd better pull your face outta here.'"

"Typhoid fever?"

"It sounded good to me. And it did the trick."

"That scared them off?"

"Well, almost. He shut the curtain and said from behind it, 'Doctor, may we speak to you in private, please?' I said, 'I can't leave my patient. And I'd have to scrub before I talk to anybody. I'm immune, but I can carry the disease.'"

Buck raised his eyebrows. "They bought this?"

Chloe shook her head, appearing amused.

Ken said, "Hey, I was good. They asked who my patient was. I could have told them Annie Ashton, but I thought it was more realistic if I acted insulted by the question. I said, 'Her name's not as important as her prognosis. Anyway, her name's on the door.' I heard them *tsk-tsk*ing and one said, 'Is she conscious?' I said, 'If you're not a doctor, it's none of your business.' The woman said something about their having a doctor who hadn't caught up to them yet, and I said, 'You can ask me whatever you need to know.'

"One of them says, 'We know what it says on the door, but we were told Mother Doe was in that bed.' I said, 'I'm not going to stand here and argue. My patient is not Mother Doe.'

"One of the guys says, 'You mind if we ask *her* what her name is?' I say, 'As a matter of fact, I do mind. She needs to concentrate on getting better.' The guy says, 'Ma'am, if you can hear me, tell me your name.'

"I nod to Chloe so she'll tell 'em, but I'm stomping toward the curtain like I'm mad. She hesitates, not sure what I'm up to, but finally she says, acting real weak like, 'Annie Ashton.'"

Chloe raised her hand. "Not acting," she said. "Why'd they name me Mother Doe?"

"You don't know?" Buck said, reaching for her hand.

She shook her head.

"Let me finish my story," Ritz said. "I think they're coming back. I whipped that curtain open and stared them down. I don't guess they expected me to be so big. I said, 'There! Satisfied? Now you've upset her and me too.' The woman says, 'Excuse us, Doctor, ah—' and Chloe says, 'Doctor Airplane.' I had to bite my tongue. I said, 'The medication's getting to her,' which it was. I said, 'I'm Doctor Lalaine, but we'd better not shake hands, all things considered.'

"The rest of 'em are all crowded around the door, and the woman peeks through the curtain and says, 'Do you have any idea what happened to Mother Doe?' I tell her, 'One patient from this room was taken to the morgue.'

"She says, 'Oh, really?' in a tone that tells me she doesn't believe that one bit. She says, 'What caused *this* young lady's injuries? Typhoid?' Real sarcastic. I wasn't ready for that one, and while I'm trying to think up a smart, doctory answer, she says, 'I'm going to have our physician examine her.'

"I tell her, 'I don't know how they do it where you're

from, but in this hospital only the attending physician or the patient can ask for a second opinion.' Well, even though she's a good foot shorter than me, she somehow looks down her nose at me. She says, 'We are from the Global Community, here under orders from His Excellency himself. So be prepared to give ground.'

"I say, 'Who the heck is His Excellency?' She says, 'Where have you been, under a rock?' Well, I couldn't tell her that was just about right and that because I had OD'd on tranqs I wasn't too sure where I was now, so I said, 'Servin' mankind, trying to save lives, ma'am.' She huffed out, and a couple minutes later, you walked in. You're up-to-date."

"And they're bringing in a doctor," Buck said. "Terrific. We'd better hide her someplace and see if we can get her lost in the system."

"Answer me," Chloe whispered.

"What?"

"Buck, am I pregnant?"

"Yes."

"Is the baby OK?"

"So far."

"How 'bout me?"

"You're pretty banged up, but you're not in danger."

"Your typhoid fever is almost gone," Ritz said.

Chloe frowned. "Dr. Airplane," she scolded. "Buck, I have to get better fast. What do these people want?"

"It's a long story. Basically, they want to trade you for either Tsion or Hattie or both."

"No," she said, her voice stronger.

"Don't worry," Buck said. "But we'd better get going. We're not going to fool a real doctor for long, despite Joe Thespian here."

"That's Dr. Airplane to you," Ken said.

Buck heard people at the door. He dropped to the floor and crawled under two curtains, squatting in the area already crowded with both bed and gurney.

"Dr. Lalaine," one of the men said, "this is our physician from Kenosha. We would appreciate it if you would let him examine this patient."

"I don't understand," Ritz said.

"Of course you don't," the doctor said, "but I helped treat an unidentified patient yesterday who matched this description. That's why I was invited."

Buck shut his eyes. The voice sounded familiar. If it was the last doctor he had talked to in Kenosha, the one who'd taken pictures of Chloe, all hope was gone. Even if Buck surprised them and came out swinging, there was no way he could get Chloe out of that place.

Ritz said, "I've already told these people who this patient is."

"And we've already proven your story false, Doctor," the woman said. "We asked for Mother Doe in the morgue. It didn't take long to determine that that was the real Ms. Ashton."

Buck heard an envelope being opened, something being pulled out. "Look at these pictures," the woman said. "She may not be a dead ringer, but she's close. I think that's her."

"There's one way to be sure," the doctor said. "My patient had three small scars on her left knee from arthroscopic surgery when she was a teenager, and also an appendectomy scar."

Buck was reeling. Neither was true of Chloe. What was going on?

Buck heard the rustle of blanket, sheet, and gown. "You know, this doesn't really surprise me," the doctor said. "I thought the face was a little too round and the bruising more extensive on this girl."

. "Well," the woman said, "even if this isn't who we're looking for, it isn't Annie Ashton, and she certainly doesn't have typhoid fever."

"Nobody in this hospital has typhoid fever," Ken said. "I say that to keep people's noses out of my patients' business."

"I want this man brought up on charges," the woman said. "Why wouldn't he know the name of his own patient?"

"There are too many patients right now," Ken said. "Anyway, I was told this was Annie Ashton. That's what it says on the door."

"I'll talk to the chief of staff here about Dr. Lalaine," the doctor said. "I suggest the rest of you check admissions again for Mother Doe."

"Doctor?" Chloe said in a tiny voice. "You have something on your forehead."

"I do?" he said.

"I don't see anything," the woman said. "This girl is doped up."

"No, I'm not," Chloe said. "You do have something there, Doctor."

"Well," he said, pleasantly but dismissively, "you're probably going to have something on your forehead too, once you recover."

"Let's get going," one of the men said.

"I'll find you after I've talked to the chief of staff," the doctor said.

The others left. As soon as the door shut, the doctor said, "I know who *she* is. Who are *you*?"

"I'm Dr. —"

"We both know you're no doctor."

"Yes he is," Chloe slurred. "He's Dr. Airplane."

Buck emerged from behind the curtain. "Dr. Charles, meet my pilot, Ken Ritz. Have you ever been an answer to prayer before?"

"It wasn't easy getting assigned to this," Floyd Charles said. "But I thought I might come in handy."

"I don't know how I can ever thank you," Buck said.

"Keep in touch," the doctor said. "I may need you someday. I suggest we transfer your wife out of here. They'll come look more closely when they don't find Mother Doe."

"Can you arrange transportation to the airport and everything we'll need to take care of her?" Buck asked.

"Sure. As soon as I get Dr. Airplane's medical license suspended."

Ken whipped off his smock. "I've had enough of doctorin' anyway," he said. "I'm going back to sky jockeying."

"Will I be able to take care of her at home?" Buck asked.

"She'll be in a lot of pain for a long time and may never feel like she used to, but there's nothing life-threatening here. The baby's fine too, as far as we know."

"I didn't know until today," Chloe said. "I suspected, but I didn't know."

"You almost gave me away with that forehead remark," Dr. Charles said.

"Yeah," Ken said. "What was that all about?"

"I'll tell you both on the plane," Buck said.

Early Thursday morning in New Babylon, Nicolae Carpathia and Leon Fortunato met with Rayford. "We have communicated your itinerary to the dignitaries," Carpathia said. "They have arranged for appropriate accommodations for the Supreme Commander, but you and your first officer should make your own arrangements."

Rayford nodded. This meeting, as with so many, was unnecessary.

"Now on a personal note," Carpathia added, "while I understand your position, it has been decided not to dredge the wreckage of the Pan-Con flight from the Tigris. I am sorry, but it has been confirmed your wife was on board. We should consider that her final resting place, along with the other passengers."

Rayford believed in his gut Carpathia was lying. Amanda was alive, and she was certainly no traitor to the cause of Christ. He and Mac had scuba gear coming, and while he had no idea where Amanda *was*, he would start by proving she was *not* on board that submerged 747.

Two hours before flight time Friday, Mac told Rayford he had replaced the fixed-wing aircraft in the cargo hold. "We're already takin' the chopper," he said. "That little two-engine job is redundant. I replaced it with the Challenger 3."

"Where'd you find that?" The Challenger was about the size of a Learjet but nearly twice as fast. It had been developed during the last six months.

"I thought we lost everything but the chopper, the fixed-wing, and the Condor. But beyond the rise in the middle of the airstrip, I found the Challenger. I had to install a new antenna and a new tail rudder system, but she's good as new."

"I wish I knew how to fly it," Rayford said. "Maybe I could see my family while Fortunato's laying over in Texas."

"They found your daughter?"

"Just got the word. She's banged up, but she's fine. And I'm going to be a grandpa."

"That's great, Ray!" Mac said, patting Rayford on the shoulder. "I'll teach you the Challenger. You'll know how to drive it in no time."

"I've got to finish packing and get an e-mail to Buck," Rayford said.

"You're not sending or receiving through the system here, are you?"

"No. I got a coded e-mail from Buck informing me when my private phone would be ringing. I made sure I was outside at that time."

"We've got to talk to Hassid about how secure the Internet is in here. You and he and I have all been on the Net, keeping track of your friend Tsion. I'm worried that the brass can tell who's been on. Carpathia's got to be furious about Tsion. We could all be in trouble."

"David told me that if we stay with the bulletin boards, we're not traceable."

"He'd like to be going with us, you know," Mac said.

"David? I know. But we need him right where he is."

CHAPTER 14

THE FLIGHT TO WAUKEGAN had been difficult for Chloe. The drive from Waukegan to Wheeling to drop off Ken Ritz, and then on to Mt. Prospect, was worse. She had slept in Buck's arms during virtually the entire flight, but the Range Rover had been torture.

The best Buck could do was let her lie across the backseat, but one of the fasteners connecting the seat to the floor had broken loose during the earthquake, so he had to drive even slower than normal. Still, Chloe seemed to bounce the whole way. Finally Ken knelt, facing the back, and tried to brace the seat with his hands.

When they got to Palwaukee Airport, Buck walked Ken

to the Quonset hut where he had been given a corner to move into. "Always an adventure," Ken said wearily. "One of these days you're gonna get me killed."

"It was stupid to ask you to fly so soon after surgery, Ken, but you were a lifesaver. I'll send you a check."

"You always do. But I also want to know more about where all you guys are, you know, with your beliefs and everything."

"Ken, we've been through this before. It's becoming pretty clear now, wouldn't you say? This whole period of history, this is it. Just a little more than five more years, and it's all over. I can see why people might not have understood what was happening before the Rapture. I was one of them. But it's come to one giant countdown. The whole deal now is which side you're on. You're either serving God or you're serving the Antichrist. You've been a supplier for the good guys. It's time you joined our team."

"I know, Buck. I've never seen anything like how you people take care of each other. It'd be good for me if I could see it all one more time in black and white, you know, like on one sheet of paper, pros and cons. That's how I am. I figure it out, and I make my decision."

"I can get you a Bible."

"I've got a Bible somewhere. Are there like one or two pages that have the whole deal spelled out?"

"Read John. And then Romans. You'll see the stuff we've talked about. We're sinners. We're separated from God. He wants us back. He's provided the way."

Ken looked uncomfortable. Buck knew he was light-headed and in pain. "Have you got a computer?"

"Yeah, and of course an e-mail address."

"Let me have it, and I'll write down a newsgroup for you. The guy you brought back from Egypt with me is the hottest thing on the Internet. Talk about putting everything on one page for you, he does it."

"So once I join up I get the secret mark on my forehead?"

"You sure do."

Buck reclined the front passenger seat and moved Chloe there. But it wasn't flat enough, and she soon retreated again to the back. When Buck finally pulled into the backyard at Donny's, Tsion rushed out to greet Chloe. As soon as he saw her he burst into tears. "Oh, you poor child. Welcome to your new home. You are safe."

Tsion helped Buck remove her from the backseat and opened the door so Buck could carry her inside. Buck headed for the stairs, but Tsion stopped him. "Right here, Cameron. See?" Tsion had brought down his bed for her. "She cannot use the stairs yet."

Buck shook his head. "I suppose next comes the chicken soup."

Tsion smiled and pushed a button on the microwave. "Give me sixty seconds."

But Chloe did not eat. She slept through the night and off and on the next day.

"You need a goal," Tsion told her. "Where would you like to go on your first day out?"

"I want to see the church. And Loretta's house."

"Will not that be—"

"It will be painful. But Buck says if I hadn't run, I never would have survived. I need to see why. And I want to see where Loretta and Donny died."

When she hobbled to the kitchen table and sat by herself, she asked only for her computer. It pained Buck to watch her peck away with one hand. When he tried to help, she rebuffed him. He must have looked hurt.

"Honey, I know you want to help," she said. "You searched for me until you found me, and nobody can ask for more than that. But, please, don't do anything for me unless I ask."

"You never ask."

"I'm not a dependent person, Buck. I don't want to be waited on. This is war, and there aren't enough days left to waste. As soon as I get this hand working, I'm gonna take some of the load off Tsion. He's on the computer day and night."

Buck got his own laptop and wrote to Ken Ritz about the possibility of going to Israel. He couldn't imagine it ever being safe for Tsion there, but Tsion was so determined to go, Buck was afraid there would be no choice. His ulterior motive with Ken, of course, was to see if he had come to a spiritual decision. As he was transmitting the message, Chloe called out from the kitchen.

"Oh, my word! Buck! You've got to see this!"

He hurried to peer over her shoulder. The message on the screen was several days old. It was from Hattie Durham.

Rayford was afraid Leon Fortunato would be bored on the trip to Rome and might pester him and Mac in the cockpit. But every time Rayford clicked on the secret intercom to monitor the cabin, Leon was whistling, humming, singing, talking on the phone, or noisily moving about.

Once Rayford had Mac take over while he found an excuse to wander into the cabin. Leon was arranging the mahogany table where he and Pontifex Maximus Peter Mathews and the ten kings would meet prior to seeing Carpathia.

Leon looked excited enough to burst. "You will remain in the cockpit as soon as our guests join us, will you not?"

"Sure," Rayford said. It was clear Leon needed no company.

Rayford didn't expect any secrets listening in on Leon and Mathews, but he loved the entertainment possibilities. Fortunato was such a Carpathia groupie and Mathews so condescending and independent that the two were like oil and water. Mathews was used to being treated like royalty. Fortunato treated Carpathia like the king of the world that he was but was slow to serve anyone else and often curt with those who served him.

When Mathews boarded in Rome he immediately treated Fortunato as one of his valets. And he already had two. A young man and woman carried his things aboard and stood chatting with him. As Rayford listened in, he was exposed again to Mathews's gall. Every time Fortunato suggested it was time to get under way, Mathews interrupted.

"Could I get a cold drink, Leon?" Mathews said.

There was a long pause. "Certainly," Fortunato said flatly. Then, with sarcasm, "And your staff?"

"Yes, something for them as well."

"Fine, Pontiff Mathews. And then I think we should really be—"

"And something to munch. Thank you, Leon."

After two such encounters, Fortunato's silence was deafening. Finally Leon said, "Pontiff Mathews, I really think it's time—"

"How long are we going to sit here, Leon? What do you say we get this show on the road?"

"We cannot move with unauthorized personnel on the plane."

"Who's not authorized?"

"Your people."

"I introduced you, Leon. These are my personal assistants."

"You were under the impression they were invited?"

"I go nowhere without them."

"I'm going to have to check with His Excellency."

"I'm sorry?"

"I'll have to check with Nicolae Carpathia."

"You said 'His Excellency.'"

"I planned to talk that over with you en route."

"Talk to me now, Leon."

"Pontiff, I would appreciate your addressing me by my title. Is that too much to ask?"

"Titles are what we're talking about. Where does Carpathia get off using *Excellency*?"

"It was not his choice. I—"

"Yes, and I suppose *Potentate* wasn't his choice either. *Secretary-general* just never did it for him, did it?"

"As I said, I want to discuss the new title with you during the trip."

"Then let's get going!"

"I'm not authorized to transport uninvited guests."

"Mr. Fortunato, these are *invited* guests. I invited them."

"My title is not *mister.*"

"Oh, so the Potentate is now His Excellency and you're what, Potentate? No, let me guess. You're Supreme Something-or-Other. Am I right?"

"I need to check this with His Excellency."

"Well, hurry. And tell 'His Excellency' that Pontifex Maximus thinks it's nervy to switch from a royal title—already an overstatement—to a sacred one."

Rayford heard only Fortunato's end of the conversation with Nicolae, of course, but Leon had to eat crow.

"Pontiff," he said finally, "His Excellency has asked me to express his welcome and his assurance that anyone you feel necessary to make your flight comfortable is an honor for him to have on board."

"Really?" Mathews said. "Then I insist on a cabin crew." Fortunato laughed. "I'm serious, Leon—or, I mean, what *is* your title, man?"

"I serve at the rank of Commander."

"Commander? Tell the truth now, Commander, is it actually *Supreme* Commander?" Fortunato did not respond, but Mathews must have detected something in his face. "It is, isn't it? Well, even if it isn't, I insist. If I am to call you Commander, it shall be Supreme Commander. Is that acceptable?"

Fortunato sighed loudly. "The actual title is Supreme Commander, yes. You may call me either."

"Oh, no I may not. Supreme Commander it is. Now, Supreme Commander Fortunato, I am deadly serious about cabin service on a long flight like this, and I'm shocked at your lack of foresight in not providing it."

"We have all the amenities, Pontiff. We felt it more necessary to have a full complement of service personnel when the regional ambassadors begin to join us."

"You were wrong. I wish not to leave the ground until this plane is properly staffed. If you have to check that with His Excellency, feel free."

There was a long silence, and Rayford assumed the two were staring each other down. "You're serious about this?" Fortunato said.

"Serious as an earthquake."

The call button sounded in the cockpit. "Flight deck," Mac said. "Go ahead."

"Gentlemen, I have decided to employ a cabin crew between here and Dallas. I shall be contracting with one of the airlines here. Please communicate with the tower that we could be delayed for as long as two or three hours. Thank you."

"Begging your pardon, sir," Mac said, "but our delay here has already cost us four places in line for takeoff. They're being flexible because of who we are, but—"

"Did you misunderstand something?" Leon said.

"Not at all, sir. Roger that delay."

Hattie's e-mail message read:

Dear CW, I didn't know who else to turn to. Well, actually I did. But I got no response from AS at the private number she gave me. She said she carries her phone all the time, so I'm worried what happened to her.

I need your help. I lied to my former boss and told him my people were from Denver. When I changed my flight from Boston to go west instead of east, I was hoping he would think I was going to see my family. Actually, they live in Santa Monica. I'm in Denver for a whole other reason.

I'm at a reproductive clinic here. Now, don't overreact. Yes, they do abortions, and they're pushing me that direction. In fact, that's mostly what they do. But they do also ask every mother if she's considered her options, and every once in a while a baby is carried to term. Some are put up for adoption; some are raised by the mother. Others are raised by the clinic.

This place also serves as a safe house, and I am here anonymously. I cut my hair short and dyed it black, and I wear colored contact lenses. I'm sure no one recognizes me.

They give us access to these computers a few hours every week. At other times we write things and draw pictures and exercise. They also encourage us to write to friends and loved ones and make amends. Sometimes they urge us to write to the fathers of our children.

I couldn't do that. But I do need to talk to you. I have a private satellite phone. Do you have a number like AS does? I'm scared. I'm confused. Some days abortion seems the easiest solution. But I'm already growing attached to this child. I might be able to give it up, but I don't think I could end its life. I told a counselor I felt guilty about becoming pregnant when I wasn't married. She had never heard anything like that in her life. She said I ought to stop obsessing about right and wrong and start thinking about what was best for me.

I feel more guilty about considering abortion than I do about what you would call immorality. I don't want to make a mistake. And I don't want to keep living like this. I envy you and your close friends. I sure hope you all survived the earthquake. I suppose your dad and your husband believe it was the wrath of the Lamb. Maybe it was. I wouldn't be surprised.

If I don't hear from you, I'm going to assume the worst, so please get back to me if you can. Say hi to everybody. My love to L. Love, H.

"Now, Buck," Chloe said, "I don't mind if you help me. Just reply as fast as you can that I was hurt and away from my e-mail, that I'm going to be fine, and here's my phone number. OK?"

Buck was already typing.

Rayford slipped his laptop out of his flight bag and left the plane. On the way he passed the two bored young people, a red-faced and sweating Leon on the phone, and Mathews. The Supreme Pontiff of Enigma Babylon glanced at Rayford and looked away. *So much for pastoral interest,* Rayford thought. Pilots were just props on this guy's stage.

Rayford sat near a window in the terminal. With his amazing computer, powered by the sun, he could communicate from anywhere. He checked the bulletin board where Tsion kept in touch with his growing church. In just a few days, hundreds of thousands of people had responded to his messages. Open messages to Nicolae Carpathia pleaded for amnesty for Tsion Ben-Judah. One poignantly summarized the consensus: "Surely a lover of peace like yourself, Potentate

Carpathia, who aided in Rabbi Ben-Judah's escape from orthodox zealots in his homeland, has the power to return him safely to Israel, where he can communicate with so many of us who love him. We're counting on you."

Rayford smiled. Many were so new in the faith that they did not know Carpathia's true identity. When, he wondered, might Tsion himself have to blatantly expose Carpathia?

When he checked his mail, Rayford was dumbfounded to learn of the contact from Hattie. He had strangely mixed emotions. He was glad she and her baby were safe, but he so badly wanted a message from Amanda that he found himself jealous. He resented that Chloe had heard from Hattie before he heard from Amanda. "God, forgive me," he prayed silently.

Several hours later, the Condor 216 finally took off from Rome with a full cabin crew, compliments of Alitalia Airlines.

When Rayford wasn't planning the Tigris River dive, he eavesdropped on the cabin.

"Now this is more like it, Supreme Commander Fortunato," Mathews was saying. "Isn't this better than the buffet line you had planned? Admit it."

"Everyone appreciates being served," Fortunato allowed. "Now there are some issues His Excellency has asked me to brief you on."

"Quit calling him that! It drives me nuts. I was going to save this news, but I might as well tell you now. Response to my leadership has been so overwhelming that my staff has planned a weeklong festival next month to celebrate my installation. Though I no longer serve the Catholic church, which has been blended into our much bigger faith, it seemed appropriate to some that my title change as well. I believe it will have more immediate impact and be more easily understood by the masses if I simply go by Peter the Second."

"That sounds like a pope's title," Fortunato said.

"Of course it is. Though some would call my position a papacy, I frankly see it as much larger."

"You prefer Peter the Second over Supreme Pontiff or even Pontifex Maximus?"

"Less is more. It has a ring to it, doesn't it?"

"We'll have to see how His—ah, Potentate Carpathia feels about it."

"What does the Global Community potentate have to do with the One World Faith?"

"Oh, he feels responsible for the idea and for your elevation to this post."

"He needs to remember that democracy wasn't all bad. At least they had separation between church and state."

"Pontiff, you asked what His Excellency has to do with you. I must ask, where would Enigma Babylon be without financing from the Global Community?"

"I could ask the reverse. People need something to believe in. They need faith. They need tolerance. We need to stand together and rid the world of the hatemongers. The vanishings took care of narrow-minded fundamentalists and intolerant zealots. Have you seen what's happening on the Internet? That rabbi who blasphemed his own religion in his own country is now developing a huge following. It falls to me to compete with that. I have a request here—" Rayford heard rustling papers—"for increased financial support from the Global Community."

"His Excellency was afraid of that."

"Bull! I've never known Carpathia to be afraid of anything. He knows we have tremendous expenses. We are living up to our name. We're a one-world faith. We influence every continent for peace and unity and tolerance. Every ambassador ought to be mandated to increase his share of contributions to Enigma Babylon."

"Pontiff, no one has ever faced the fiscal problems His Excellency faces now. The balance of power has shifted to the Middle East. New Babylon is the capital of the world. Everything will be centralized. The rebuilding of that city alone has caused the potentate to propose significant tax increases across the board. But he's also rebuilding the whole world. Global Community forces are at work on every continent, reestablishing communications and transportation and engaging in cleanup, rescue, relief, sanitation, you name it. Every region leader will be asked to call his subjects to sacrifice."

"And you get that dirty work, don't you, Supreme Commander?"

"I do not consider it dirty work, Pontiff. It is my honor to facilitate His Excellency's vision."

"There you go again with that *excellency* business."

"Allow me to tell you a personal story I will share with

each ambassador during this trip. Indulge me, and you'll see that the potentate is a deeply spiritual man with a spark of the divine."

"This I have to hear," Mathews said, chuckling. "Carpathia as clergy. Now there's a picture."

"I pledge that every word is true. It will change forever the way you see our potentate."

Rayford turned off the surveillance switch. "Leon's telling Mathews his Lazarus story," he muttered.

"Oh boy," Mac said.

The Condor was over the Atlantic in the middle of the night, and Rayford was dozing. The intercom roused him. "When convenient, Captain Steele," Fortunato said, "I would appreciate a moment."

"I hate to cater," Rayford told Mac. "But I'd just as soon get it out of the way." He depressed the button. "Is now OK?"

Fortunato met him midplane and beckoned him to the rear, far from where Mathews and his two young charges were sleeping. "His Excellency has asked me to approach you on a delicate matter. It is becoming increasingly embarrassing to not be able to produce Rabbi Tsion Ben-Judah of Israel for his followers."

"Oh?"

"His Excellency knows you to be a man of your word. When you tell us you do not know where Ben-Judah is, we take this at face value. The question then becomes, do you have access to someone who does know where he is?"

"Why?"

"His Excellency is prepared to personally ensure the rabbi's safety. He will make any threat to the safety of Ben-Judah simply not worth the consequences."

"So why not put that word out, and see if Ben-Judah comes to you?"

"Too risky. You may think you know how His Excellency views you. However, as the one who knows him best, I know he trusts you. He admires your integrity."

"And he's convinced I have access to Ben-Judah."

"Let's not play games, Captain Steele. The Global Community is far-reaching now. We know from more sources than just the talkative Dr. Rosenzweig that your son-in-law helped the rabbi escape."

"Rosenzweig is one of Carpathia's greatest admirers, more loyal than Nicolae deserves. Didn't Chaim seek Carpathia's help in the Ben-Judah matter back when Nicolae first became prominent?"

"We did all we could—"

"That is not true. If you expect me to be a man of my word, don't insult my intelligence. If my own son-in-law aided in Ben-Judah's flight from Israel, wouldn't I have an idea whether he had assistance from the Global Community?"

Fortunato did not respond.

Rayford was careful not to reveal anything he had heard solely through the bugging device. He would never forget when Fortunato had passed on Rosenzweig's plea for help for his beleaguered friend. Ben-Judah's family had been massacred and he was in hiding, yet Carpathia had laughed it off and said in so many words that he might turn Ben-Judah over to the zealots.

"Those close to the situation know the truth, Leon. Carpathia's claim to credit for the well-being of Tsion Ben-Judah is bogus. I have no doubt he could protect the rabbi, and he would have been able to then, but he did not."

"You may be right, Captain Steele. I do not have personal knowledge of that situation."

"Leon, you know every detail of everything that goes on."

It appeared Leon enjoyed hearing that. He didn't argue it. "Regardless, it would be counterproductive from a public relations standpoint for us to adjust our position now. We are believed to have helped him escape, and we would lose credibility to admit we had nothing to do with that."

"But since I know," Rayford said, "am I not allowed some skepticism?"

Leon sat back and steepled his fingers. He exhaled. "All right," he said. "His Excellency has authorized me to ask what you require in order to grant him this favor."

"And the favor is?"

"The delivery of Tsion Ben-Judah."

"To?"

"Israel."

What Rayford wanted was his wife's name cleared, but he could not betray Mac's confidence. "So I'm asked my price now, rather than being required to trade my own daughter?"

It didn't seem to surprise Fortunato that Rayford had heard about the fiasco in Minneapolis. "That was a mistake in communications," he said. "You have His Excellency's personal word that he intended that the wife of one of his employees be reunited with her husband and given the best care."

Rayford wanted to laugh aloud or spit in Fortunato's face; he couldn't decide which. "Let me think about it," he said.

"How long do you need? There is pressure on His Excellency to do something about Ben-Judah. We will be in the States tomorrow. Can we not make some arrangement?"

"You want me to ferry him back on the Condor with all the ambassadors?"

"Of course not. But as long as we are going to be in that region, it only makes sense that we take care of it now."

"Assuming Tsion Ben-Judah is there."

"We believe that if we can locate Cameron Williams, we will have located Tsion Ben-Judah."

"Then you know more than I do."

Rayford began to stand, but Fortunato held up a hand. "There is one more thing."

"Let me guess. Are her initials H. D.?"

"Yes. It is important to His Excellency that the relationship be gracefully severed."

"Despite what he said to the world?"

"Actually, I said it. He did not sanction it."

"I don't believe that."

"Believe what you wish. You are aware of the exigencies of public perception. His Excellency is determined not to be embarrassed by Miss Durham. You'll recall they were introduced by your son-in-law."

"Whom I had not even met yet," Rayford said.

"Granted. Her disappearance was a nuisance. It made His Excellency appear incapable of controlling his own household. The earthquake provided a logical explanation for their separation. It is crucial that while out on her own, Miss Durham not do or say anything embarrassing."

"And so you want me to do what? Tell her to behave?"

"Frankly, Captain, you would not be overstating it to inform her that accidents happen. She cannot remain invisible long. If it becomes necessary to eliminate the risk, we have the ability to effect this with expediency, and in a manner that would not reflect on His Excellency but would allow him to gain sympathy."

"May I tell you what I just heard you say, so we're clear?"

"Certainly."

"You want me to tell Hattie Durham to keep her mouth shut or you'll kill her and deny it."

Fortunato appeared stricken. Then he softened and stared at the ceiling. "We are communicating," he said.

"Rest assured that if I make contact with Miss Durham, I will pass along your threat."

"I assume you will remind her that repeating that message would constitute cause."

"Oh, I got it. It's a blanket threat."

"You'll handle both assignments then?"

"You don't see the irony? I'm to pass along a death

threat to Miss Durham yet trust you with protecting Tsion Ben-Judah."

"Right."

"Well, it may be correct, but it's not right."

Rayford trudged to the cockpit, where he was met with Mac's knowing look. "You hear that?"

"I heard," Mac said. "I wish I had recorded it."

"Who would you play it for?"

"Fellow believers."

"You'd be preaching to the choir. In the old days, you could take a DVD like that to the authorities. But these *are* the authorities."

"What's your price gonna be, Ray?"

"What do you mean?"

"Ben-Judah belongs in Israel. And Carpathia has to ensure his safety, doesn't he?"

"You heard Fortunato. They can cause an accident and wind up with sympathy."

"But if he pledges a personal guarantee, Ray, he'll keep Tsion safe."

"Don't forget what Tsion wants to do in Israel. He's not just going to chat with the two witnesses or look up old friends. He'll be training as many of the 144,000 evangelists as can get there. He'll be Nicolae's worst nightmare."

"Like I said, what's your price?"

"What's the difference? You expect the Antichrist to stand by a deal? I wouldn't give a nickel for Hattie Durham's future, whether she toes the line or not. Maybe if I string this out long enough I can learn something from Fortunato about Amanda. I'm telling you, Mac, she's alive somewhere."

"If she's alive, Ray, why no contact? I don't want to offend you, but is it possible she's what they say she is?"

CHAPTER 15

BUCK WAS AWAKENED a little after midnight by the chirping of Chloe's phone downstairs. Though she kept it within arm's length, it kept ringing. Buck sat up, wondering. He decided her medication must have kicked in, so he hurried down.

Only people most crucial to the Tribulation Force knew the members' private sat phone numbers. Every incoming call was potentially momentous. Buck couldn't see the phone in the darkness, and he didn't want to turn on the light. He followed the sound to the ledge above Chloe. He put a knee carefully on the mattress, trying not to wake her, grabbed the phone, and settled in a chair next to her bed.

"Chloe's phone," he whispered.

All he heard was crying. "Hattie?" he tried.

"Buck!" she said.

"Chloe slept through the ring, Hattie. I hate to wake her."

"Please don't," she said through sobs. "I'm sorry to call so late."

"She really wanted to talk to you, Hattie. Is there anything I can do?"

"Oh, Buck!" she said, and lost control again.

"Hattie, I know you don't know where we are, but it's not close enough to help if you're in danger. Do you need me to call someone?"

"No!"

"Don't rush, then. I can wait. I'm not going anywhere."

"Thank you," she managed.

As Buck waited, his eyes grew accustomed to the darkness. For the first time since she had been home, Chloe was not on her left side, keeping weight off the myriad breaks, bruises, strains, sprains, and scrapes of her other side. Every morning she spent half an hour massaging sleeping body parts. He prayed that someday soon she would enjoy a restful night's sleep. Maybe she was doing that now. But could one really enjoy a sleep so deep that a ringing phone a few feet away would not penetrate? He hoped her body would benefit, and her spirit as well. Chloe lay still, flat on her back, her left arm by her side, her mangled right foot pigeon-toed to the left, her casted arm resting on her stomach.

"Bear with me," Hattie managed.

"No rush," Buck said, scratching his head and stretching.

He was struck by Chloe in repose. What a gift of God she was, and how grateful he was that she had survived. Her top sheet and blanket were bunched. She often fell asleep uncovered and curled under blankets later.

Buck pressed the back of his hand to her cheek. She felt cool. Still listening for Hattie, Buck pulled the sheet and blanket up to Chloe's neck, worrying that he might have dragged it across her foot, her most sensitive injury. But she did not move.

"Hattie, are you there?"

"Buck, I got word tonight that I lost my mother and my sisters in the earthquake."

"Oh, Hattie, I'm so sorry."

"It's such a waste," she said. "When L.A. and San Francisco were bombed, Nicolae and I were still close. He warned me they should leave the area and swore me to secrecy. His intelligence people feared a militia attack, and he was right."

Buck said nothing. Rayford had told him he had heard Carpathia himself, through the Condor 216's bugging device, give the order for the bombing of San Francisco and Los Angeles.

"Hattie, where are you calling from?"

"I told you in the e-mail," she said.

"I know, but you're not using their phones, are you?"

"No! That's why I'm calling so late. I had to wait until I could sneak outside."

"And the news about your family. How did that get to you?"

"I had to let the authorities in Santa Monica know where they could reach me. I gave them my private number and the number of the clinic here."

"I'm sorry to say this at such a difficult time for you, Hattie, but that was not a good idea."

"I didn't have a choice. It took a long time to get through to Santa Monica, and when I finally did, my family was unaccounted for. I had to leave numbers. I've been worried sick."

"You've probably led the GC right to you."

"I don't care anymore."

"Don't say that."

"I don't want to go back to Nicolae, but I want him to take responsibility for our child. I have no job, no income, and now no family."

"We care about you and love you, Hattie. Don't forget that."

She broke down again.

"Hattie, have you considered that the news about your family may be untrue?"

"What?"

"I wouldn't put it past the GC. Once they knew where you were, they may have just wanted to give you a reason to stay there. If you think your family is gone, there's no reason for you to go to California."

"But I told Nicolae my family had moved here after the bombings out there."

"It wouldn't have taken him long to discover that was untrue."

"Why would he want me to stay here?"

"Maybe he assumes that the longer you're there, the more likely you are to have an abortion."

"That's true."

"Don't say that."

"I don't see any options, Buck. I can't raise a child in a world like this with my prospects."

"I don't want to make you feel worse, Hattie, but I don't think you're safe there."

"What are you saying?"

Buck wished Chloe would rouse and help him talk to Hattie. He had an idea, but he'd rather consult her first.

"Hattie, I know these people. They would much rather have you out of the picture than deal with you."

"I'm nobody from nowhere. I can't hurt him."

"Something happening to you could engender tremendous sympathy for him. More than anything, he wants attention, and he doesn't care whether that comes as fear, respect, admiration, or pity."

"I'll tell you one thing, I'll have an abortion before I'll let him hurt me or my child."

"You're not making sense. You would kill your child so he can't?"

"You sound like Rayford now."

"We happen to agree on this," Buck said. "Please don't do that. At the very least get somewhere where you're not in danger and can think this through."

"I have nowhere to go!"

"If I came and got you, would you come here with us?"

Silence.

"Chloe needs you. We could use help with her. And she could be good for you during your pregnancy. She's pregnant too."

"Really? Oh, Buck, I couldn't burden you. I'd feel so obliged, so in the way."

"Hey, this was my idea."

"I don't see how it would work."

"Hattie, tell me where you are. I'll come and get you by noon tomorrow."

"You mean noon today?"

Buck looked at the clock. "I guess I do."

"Shouldn't you run this by Chloe?"

"I don't dare bother her. If there's a problem, I'll get back to you. Otherwise, be ready to go."

No response.

"Hattie?"

"I'm still here, Buck. I was just thinking. Remember when we met?"

"Of course. It was a rather momentous day."

"On Rayford's 747 the night of the disappearances."

"The Rapture," Buck said.

"If you say so. Look what we've been through since then."

"I'll call you when we're within an hour of you," Buck said.

"I'll never be able to repay you."

"Who said anything about that?"

Buck put the phone away, straightened Chloe's covers, and knelt to kiss her. She still seemed cold. He went to get her a blanket but stopped midstride. Was she too still? Was she breathing? He rushed back and put his ear to her nose. He couldn't tell. He ran his thumb and forefinger under her jaw to check her pulse. Before he could detect anything, she pulled away. She was alive. He slipped to his knees. "Thank you, God!"

Chloe mumbled something. He took her hand in both of his. "What, sweetie? What do you need?"

She appeared to be trying to open her eyes. "Buck?" she said.

"It's me."

"What's wrong?"

"I just got off the phone with Hattie. Go back to sleep."

"I'm cold."

"I'll get you a blanket."

"I wanted to talk to Hattie. What did she say?"

"I'll tell you tomorrow."

"Mm-hm."

Buck found a coverlet and spread it over her. "OK?" he said.

She did not respond. When he began to tiptoe away, she said something. He turned back. "What, hon?"

"Hattie."

"In the morning," he said.

"Hattie has my bunny."

Buck smiled. "Your bunny?"

"My blanket."

"OK."

"Thanks for my blanket."

Buck wondered if she would remember any of this.

Mac was in the cockpit and Rayford asleep in his quarters when his personal phone rang. It was Buck.

Rayford sat up. "What time is it where you are?"

"If I tell you that, anyone listening will know what time zone I'm in."

"Donny assured us these phones were secure."

"That was last month," Buck said. "These phones are almost obsolete already."

They filled in each other on the latest. "You're right about getting Hattie away from there. After what I told you Leon said, don't you agree she's in danger?"

"No question," Buck said.

"And is Tsion willing to go to Israel?"

"Willing? I have to sit on him to keep him from starting to walk there now. He's going to be suspicious, though, if the big man wants to take credit for getting him there."

"I don't see how he could go otherwise, Buck. His life would be worthless."

"He takes comfort in the prophecies that he and the rest of the 144,000 witnesses are sealed and protected, at least for now. He feels he could walk into the enemy's lair and come out unharmed."

"He's the expert."

"I want to go with him. Being in the same country as the two witnesses at the Wailing Wall would make this soul harvest he's been predicting just explode."

"Buck, have you checked in with headquarters? All I hear from the top is that you're on dangerous ground. You have no secrets anymore."

"Funny you should ask. I just transmitted a long message to the big boss."

"Is it going to do you any good?"

"You seem to have survived by being straightforward, Rayford. I'm doing the same. I told them I've been too busy rescuing friends and burying others to worry about my publication. Besides, 90 percent of the staff is gone and virtually all the production capabilities. I'm proposing continuing the magazine online until Carpathia decides whether to rebuild printing plants and all that."

"Ingenious."

"Yeah, well, the fact is there might be two simultaneous magazines coming out on the Internet at the same time, if you know what I mean."

"There are already dozens."

"I mean there might be two coming out simultaneously, edited by the same guy."

"But only one of them financed and sanctioned by the king of the world?"

"Right. The other wouldn't be funded at all. It would tell the truth. And no one would know where it's coming from."

"I like your mind, Buck. I'm glad you're part of my family."

"It hasn't been dull, I can say that."

"So what should I tell Leon I'll do about Hattie and Tsion?"

"Tell him you'll get the message to the lady. As for Tsion, negotiate whatever you want and we'll get him to Israel inside a month."

"You think there's that kind of patience in the East?"

"It's important to stretch it out. Make it a huge event. Keep control of the timing. That'll drive Tsion crazy too, but it will give us time to rally everyone on the Internet so they can show up."

"Like I said, I like your mind. You ought to be a magazine publisher."

"Before long we'll all be just fugitives."

Buck was right. In the morning Chloe recalled nothing from the night before. "I woke up toasty and knew somebody had brought me a blanket," she said. "It doesn't surprise me it was one of the guys upstairs."

She grabbed her phone and used a cane to get to the table. She punched the buttons with her bloated right hand. "I'm going to call her right now," she said. "I'm going to tell her I can't wait to have some female companionship around here."

Chloe sat with the phone to her ear for several moments.

"No answer?" Buck said. "You'd better hang up, hon. If

she's where she can't talk, she probably turned it off at the first ring. You can try her later, but don't jeopardize her."

A chortle came from Tsion upstairs. "You two are not going to believe this!" he hollered, and Buck heard his footsteps overhead. Chloe closed her phone and looked up expectantly.

"He's so easily entertained," she said. "What a joy! I learn something from him every day."

Buck nodded, and Tsion emerged from the stairs. He sat at the table, eagerness on his face. "I am reading through some of the thousands of messages left for me on the bulletin board. I do not know how many I miss for every few I read. I am guessing I have seen only about ten percent of the total, because the total keeps growing. I feel bad I cannot answer them individually, but you see the impossibility. Anyway, I got an anonymous message this morning from 'One Who Knows.' Of course, I cannot be sure he actually *is* one who knows, but he may be. Who can know? It is an interesting conundrum, is it not? Anonymous correspondence could be phony. Someone could claim to be me and engage in false teaching. I must come up with something that proves my authenticity, no?"

"Tsion!" Chloe said. "What did One Who Knows write that amused you so?"

"Oh, yes. That is why I came down here, right? Forgive me. I printed it out." He looked at the table, then patted his shirt pocket. "Oh," he said, checking his pants pockets. "It is still in my printer. Do not go away."

"Tsion?" Chloe called after him. "I just wanted to tell you I'll be here when you get back."

He looked puzzled. "Oh, well, yes. Of course."

"He's going to be thrilled he's going home," Buck said.

"And you're going with him?"

"Wouldn't miss it," Buck said. "Big story."

"I'm going with you."

"Oh, no you're not!" Buck said, but Tsion was back.

He spread the sheet on the table and read, "'Rabbi, it is only fair to tell you that one person who has been assigned to carefully monitor all your transmissions is the top military adviser for the Global Community. That may not mean much to you, but he is particularly interested in your interpretation of the prophecies about things falling to the earth and causing great damage in the upcoming months. The fact that you take these prophecies literally has him working on nuclear defenses against such catastrophes. Signed, One Who Knows.'"

Tsion looked up, bright-eyed. "It is so funny because it must be true! Carpathia, who continually tries to explain as natural phenomenon anything that supports biblical prophecy, has his senior military adviser planning to, what? Shoot a burning mountain from the sky? This is like a gnat shaking his tiny fist in the elephant's eye. Anyway, is this not a private admission on his part that there may be something to these prophecies?"

Buck wondered if One Who Knows was Rayford's and Mac's new brother inside GC headquarters. "Intriguing," Buck said. "Now are you ready for some good news?"

Tsion put a hand on Chloe's shoulder. "The daily

improvement in this precious little one is good news enough for me. Unless you are talking about Israel."

Chloe said, "I'll forgive that condescending remark, Tsion, because I'm sure no insult was intended."

Tsion looked puzzled.

"Forgive her," Buck said. "She's going through a twenty-two-year-old's bout with political correctness."

Chloe leveled her eyes at Buck. "Excuse me for saying this in front of Tsion, Cameron, but that truly offended me."

"OK," Buck said quickly, "guilty. I'm sorry. But I'm about to tell Tsion he's going to get his wish—"

"Yes!" Tsion exulted.

"And, Chloe, I don't have the energy to fight over whether you're going."

"Then let's not fight. I'm going."

"Oh, no!" Tsion said. "You must not! You are not nearly up to it."

"Tsion! It's not for another month. By then I'll—"

"Another month?" Tsion said. "Why so long? I am ready now. I must go soon. The people are clamoring for it, and I believe God wants me there."

"We're concerned about security, Tsion," Buck said. "A month will also allow us to get as many of the witnesses there as possible from around the world."

"But a month!"

"Works for me," Chloe said. "I'll be walking on my own by then."

Buck shook his head.

Tsion was already in his own world. "You do not need to worry about security, Cameron. God will protect me. He will protect the witnesses. I do not know about other believers. I know they are sealed, but I do not know yet if they are also supernaturally protected during this time of harvest."

"If God can protect you," Chloe said, "he can protect me."

Buck said, "Chloe, you know I have your best interest at heart. I'd love for you to go. I never miss you more than when I'm away from you in Jerusalem."

"Then tell me why I can't go."

"I would never forgive myself if something happened to you. I can't risk it."

"I'm just as vulnerable here, Buck. Every day is a risk. Why are we allowed to risk your life and not mine?"

Buck had no answer. He scrambled for one. "Hattie will be that much closer to her delivery date. She'll need you. And what about our child?"

"I won't even be showing by then, Buck. I'll be three months along. You're going to need me. Who's going to handle logistics? I'll be communicating with thousands of people on the Internet, arranging these meetings. It only makes sense that I show up."

"You haven't answered the Hattie question."

"Hattie's more independent than I am. She would want me to go. She can take care of herself."

Buck was losing, and he knew it. He looked away, unwilling to give in so soon. Yes, he was being protective. "It's just that I so recently nearly lost you."

"Listen to yourself, Buck. I knew enough to get out of that house before it crushed me. You can't blame that flying roof on me."

"We'll see how healthy you are in a few weeks."

"I'll start packing."

"Don't jump to conclusions."

"Don't parent me, Buck. Seriously, I don't have a problem submitting to you because I know how much you love me. I'm willing to obey you even when you're wrong. But don't be unreasonable. And don't be wrong if you don't have to be. You know I'm going to do what you say, and I'll even get over it if you make me miss out on one of the greatest events in history. But don't do it out of some old-fashioned, macho sense of protecting the little woman. I'll take this pity and help for just so long, and then I want back in the game full-time. I thought that was one of the things you liked about me."

It was. Pride kept him from agreeing right then. He'd give it a day or two and then tell her he'd come to a decision. Her eyes were boring into his. It was clear she was eager to win this one. He tried to stare her down and lost. He glanced at Tsion.

"Listen to her," Tsion said.

"You keep out of it," Buck said, smiling. "I don't need to be ganged up on. I thought you were on *my* side. I thought you would agree that this was no place for—"

"For what?" Chloe said. "A girl? The 'little woman'? An injured, pregnant woman? Am I still a member of the Tribulation Force, or have I been demoted to mascot now?"

Buck had interviewed heads of state easier than this.

"You can't defend this one, Buck," she added.

"You want to just pin me while I'm down," Buck said.

"I won't say another word," she said.

Buck chuckled. "That'll be the day."

"If you two chauvinists will excuse me, I want to try Hattie again. We're going to have a telephone meeting of the weak sister club."

Buck flinched. "Hey! You weren't going to say another word."

"Well then get out of here so you don't have to listen."

"I need to call Ritz anyway. When you reach Hattie, be sure and find out what name she was admitted under there."

Buck went to follow Tsion up the stairs, but Chloe called out to him.

"C'mere a minute, big guy." He turned to face her. She beckoned him closer. "C'mon," she said. She lifted her arm, the one with the cast from shoulder to wrist, and hooked him with it behind the neck. She pulled his face to hers and kissed him long and hard. He pulled back and smiled shyly. "You're so easy," she whispered.

"Who loves ya, baby?" he said, heading for the stairs again.

"Hey," she said, "if you see my husband up there, tell him I'm tired of sleeping alone."

Rayford listened through the bugging device as Peter Mathews and Leon Fortunato spent the last hour and a half of the flight arguing over protocol for their arrival in Dallas. Mathews, of course, prevailed on nearly every point.

The regional ambassador, the former U.S. senator from Texas, had arranged for limousines, a red carpet, an official welcome and greeting, and even a marching band. Fortunato spent half an hour on the phone with the ambassador's people, slowly reading the official announcement and presentation of honored guests that was to be read as he and Mathews disembarked. Though Rayford could hear only Fortunato's end of the conversation, it was clear the ambassador's people were barely tolerating this presumption.

After Fortunato and Mathews had showered and changed for the occasion, Leon buzzed the cockpit.

"I would like you gentlemen to assist the ground crew with the exit stairs as soon as we have come to a stop."

"Before postflight checks?" Mac said, giving Rayford a look as if this was one of the dumbest things he had ever heard. Rayford shrugged.

"Yes, before postflight checks," Fortunato said. "Be sure everything is in order, tell the cabin crew to wait until after the welcoming ceremony to deplane, and you two should be last off."

Mac switched off the intercom. "If we're putting off postflight checks, we'll be the last off all right. Wouldn't you think priority would be making sure this rig is airworthy for the return trip?"

"He figures we've got thirty-six hours, we can do it anytime."

"I was trained to check the important stuff while it's hot."

"Me too," Rayford said. "But we'll do what we're told when we're told, and you know why?"

"Tell me, O Supreme Excellent Pilot."

"Because the red carpet ain't for us."

"Doesn't that just break your heart?" Mac said.

Rayford updated ground control as Mac followed the signalman's directions to the tarmac and a small grandstand area where the public, the band, and dignitaries waited. Rayford peered out at the ragtag musicians. "Wonder where they got this bunch?" he said. "And how many they had with them before the quake."

The signalman directed Mac to the edge of the carpet and crossed his coned flashlights to signify a slow stop. "Watch this," Mac said.

"Careful, you rascal," Rayford said.

At the last instant, Mac rolled over the end of the red carpet.

"Did I do that?" he asked.

"You're bad."

Once the stairs were in place, the band was finished, and the dignitaries were situated, the Global Community ambassador stepped to the microphone. "Ladies and gentlemen," he announced with great solemnity, "representing His Excellency, Global Community Potentate Nicolae Carpathia, Supreme Commander Leonardo Fortunato!"

The crowd broke into cheering and applause as Leon waved and made his way down the steps.

"Ladies and gentlemen, the personal attendants from the office of the Supreme Pontiff of Enigma Babylon One World Faith!"

The reaction was subdued as the crowd seemed to wonder if these two young people had names, and if so, why they were not mentioned.

After a pause long enough to make people wonder if anyone else was aboard, Mathews stepped near the door but stayed out of sight. Rayford stood by the cockpit, waiting to start the postflight check when the folderol was over. "I'm waiting," Mathews sing-songed to himself. "I'm not stepping out until I'm announced."

Rayford was tempted to poke his head out and say, "Announce Pete!" He restrained himself. Finally Fortunato trotted back up the steps. He didn't come far enough to see Mathews just beyond the edge of the door. He stopped when he saw Rayford and mouthed, "Is he ready?" Rayford nodded. Leon skipped back down the steps and whispered to the ambassador.

"Ladies and gentlemen, from Enigma Babylon One World Faith, Pontifex Maximus Peter the Second!"

The band struck up, the crowd erupted, and Mathews stepped to the doorway, waiting for several beats and looking humbled at the generous response. He solemnly descended, waving a blessing as he went.

As the welcoming speeches droned, Rayford grabbed his clipboard and settled into the cockpit. Mac said, "Ladies and gentlemen! First officer of the Condor 216, with a lifetime batting average of—"

Rayford smacked him on the shoulder with his clipboard. "Knock it off, you idiot."

"How are you feeling, Ken?" Buck asked over the phone.

"I've been better. There are days that hospital looks pretty good. But I'm a far sight better than I was last time I saw you. I'm supposed to get the stitches out Monday."

"I've got another job for you, if you're up to it."

"I'm always game. Where we goin'?"

"Denver."

"Hmm. The old airport's open there, they tell me. The new one will probably never be open again."

"We pick up an hour going, and I told my client I'd pick her up by noon."

"Another damsel in distress?"

"As a matter of fact, yes. You got wheels?"

"Yep."

"I need you to pick me up on the way this time. Need to leave a vehicle here."

"I'd like to check in on Chloe anyway," Ken said. "How's she doing?"

"Come see for yourself."

"I better get goin' if you're gonna keep your commitment. You never schedule a lot of play time, do ya?"

"Sorry. Hey, Ken, did you check out that Web site I told you about?"

"Yeah. I've spent a good bit of time there."

"Come to any conclusions?"

"I need to talk to you about that."

"We'll have time in the air."

"I appreciate your giving me so much flying time on this trip," Mac said as he and Rayford left the plane.

"I had an ulterior motive. I know the FAA rules are out the window now that Carpathia is a law unto himself, but I still follow the maximum flying hours rules."

"So do I. You going somewhere?"

"As soon as you teach me how to get around in the Challenger. I'd like to drop in on my daughter and surprise her. Buck gave me directions."

"Good for you."

"What are you gonna do, Mac?"

"Hole up here awhile. I got some buddies I might look up a couple hundred miles west. If I can track them down, I'll use the chopper."

Ken Ritz's Suburban came rumbling around the back of the house just before nine.

"Somebody wants to see you when you're halfway conscious," Buck said.

"Find out if he wants to arm wrestle," Chloe said.

"Aren't *you* getting frisky?"

Tsion was on his way down the stairs when Buck met Ken at the back door. Ken wore cowboy boots, blue jeans, a long-sleeve khaki shirt, and a cowboy hat. "I know we're in a hurry," he said, "but where's the patient?"

"Right here, Dr. Airplane," Chloe said. She hobbled to the kitchen door. Ken tipped his hat.

"You can do better than that, cowboy," she said, extending her good arm for a hug. He hurried to her.

"You sure look a lot better than the last time I saw you," he said.

"Thanks. So do you."

He laughed. "I *am* a lot better. Notice anything different about me?"

"A little better color, I think," Buck said. "And you might have gained a pound in the last day or two."

"Never shows on this frame," Ritz said.

"It has been a long time, Mr. Ritz," Tsion said.

Ritz shook the rabbi's hand. "Hey, we all look healthier than last time, don't we?"

"We really need to get going," Buck said.

"So nobody notices anything different about me, huh?" Ken said. "You can't see it in my face? It doesn't show?"

"What?" Chloe said. "Are you pregnant too?"

As the others laughed, Ken took off his hat and ran a hand through his hair. "First day I've been able to get a hat on this sore head."

"So that's what's different?" Buck said.

"That, and this." Ken ran his hand through his hair again, and this time left it atop his head with his hair pulled out of the way. "Maybe it shows on my forehead. I can see yours. Can you see mine?"

CHAPTER 16

RAYFORD MADE THE APPROACH for yet another landing in the Challenger 3. "They're getting tired of me hogging this runway. If I can't get it right, you may have to fly me to Illinois."

"Dallas Tower to Charlie Tango, over."

Rayford raised an eyebrow. "See what I mean?"

"I'll get it," Mac said. "This is Charlie Tango, over."

"Tango X-ray message for Condor 216 captain, over."

"Go ahead with TX message, tower, over."

"Subject is to call Supreme Commander at the following number. . . ."

Mac wrote it down.

"What now?" Rayford wondered aloud. He put the screaming jet down for his smoothest landing of the morning.

"Why don't you take her back up," Mac said, "then I'll take over while you call Captain Kangaroo."

"That's Supreme Commander Kangaroo to you, pal," Rayford said. He lined up the Challenger and hurtled down the runway at three hundred miles an hour. Once he was in the air and leveled off, Mac took the controls.

Rayford reached Fortunato at the ambassador's residence. "I expected an immediate call," Leon said.

"I'm in the middle of a training maneuver."

"I have an assignment for you."

"I have plans today, sir. Do I have a choice?"

"This is straight from the top."

"My question remains."

"No, you have no choice. If this delays our return, we will inform the respective ambassadors. His Excellency requests that you fly to Denver today."

Denver?

"I'm not ready to fly this thing solo yet," Rayford said. "Is this something my first officer can handle?"

"Intelligence sources have located the subject we asked you to communicate with. Follow?"

"I follow."

"His Excellency would appreciate his message being delivered as soon as possible, in person."

"What's the rush?"

"The subject is at a Global Community facility that can assist in determining the consequences of the response."

"She's at an abortion clinic?"

"Captain Steele! This is an unsecured transmission!"

"I may have to fly commercial."

"Just get there today. GC personnel are stalling the subject."

"Before you go, Cameron," Tsion said, "we must thank the Lord for our new brother."

Buck, Chloe, Tsion, and Ken huddled in the kitchen. Tsion put a hand on Ken's back and looked up. "Lord God Almighty, your Word tells us the angels rejoice with us over Ken Ritz. We believe the prophecy of a great soul harvest, and we thank you that Ken is merely one of the first of many millions who will be swept into your kingdom over the next few years. We know many will suffer and die at the hands of Antichrist, but their eternal fate is sealed. We pray especially that our new brother develops a hunger for your Word, that he possesses the boldness of Christ in the face of persecution, and that he be used to bring others into the family. And now may the God of peace himself sanctify us completely, and may our spirits, souls, and bodies be preserved blameless at the coming of our Lord Jesus Christ. We believe that he who called us is faithful, who will also do it. We pray in the matchless name of Jesus, the Messiah and our Redeemer."

Ken brushed tears from his cheeks, put his hat on, and pulled it down over his eyes. "Hoo boy! That's what I call some prayin'!"

Tsion trotted upstairs and returned with a dog-eared paperback book called *How to Begin the Christian Life.*

He handed it to Ken, who looked thrilled. "Will you sign it?"

"Oh, no," Tsion said. "I did not write it. It was smuggled to me from Pastor Bruce Barnes's library at the church. I know he would want you to have it. I must clarify that the Scriptures do not refer to us who become believers after the Rapture as Christians. We are referred to as tribulation saints. But the truths of this book still apply."

Ken held it in both hands as if it were a treasure.

Tsion, nearly a foot shorter than Ken, put an arm around his waist. "As the new elder of this little band, allow me to welcome you to the Tribulation Force. We now number six, and one-third of us are pilots."

Ritz went out to start the Suburban. Tsion wished Buck God's speed and headed back upstairs. Buck drew Chloe to him and enveloped her like a fragile china doll. "Did you ever get hold of Hattie? Do we know her alias?"

"No. I'll keep trying."

"Keep following Dr. Tsion's orders too, you hear?"

She nodded. "I know you're coming right back, Buck, but I don't like saying good-bye. Last time you left me I woke up in Minnesota."

"Next week we'll sneak Dr. Charles over here and get your stitches out."

"I'm waiting for the day I have no more stitches, cast, cane, or limp. I don't know how you can stand to look at me."

Buck cupped her face in his hands. Her right eye was still black and purple, her forehead crimson. Her right cheek was sunken where teeth were missing, and her cheekbone was broken.

"Chloe," he whispered, "when I look at you I see the love of my life." She started to protest and he shushed her. "When I thought I had lost you, I would have given anything to have you back for just one minute. I could look at you until Jesus comes and still want to share eternity with you."

He helped her to a chair. Buck bent and kissed her between her eyes. Then their mouths met. "I wish you were going with me," he whispered.

"When I get healthy, you're going to wish I'd stay home once in a while."

Rayford stalled as long as possible to get more comfortable with the Challenger 3 and also to make sure Buck and Ken Ritz got to Hattie before he did. He wanted to be able to tell Fortunato she was gone when he got there. Soon he would call Buck to warn him that the GC would try to keep her from bolting.

Rayford didn't like his instructions. Fortunato would not commit to a specific destination. He said local GC forces would give Rayford that information. Rayford didn't care where they wanted him to take Hattie. If this worked the way he hoped, she would be jetting back to the Chicago area with Buck and Ken, and his orders would be moot.

Buck would have to fly over a thousand miles to Denver, Rayford fewer than eight hundred. He throttled back, reaching nowhere near the potential of the powerful jet. An hour later, Rayford was on the phone with Buck. While they talked, a couple of calls came over his radio, but not hearing his call letters or name, he ignored them.

"Our ETA is noon at Stapleton," Buck said. "Ken tells me I was too ambitious, promising we'd see her that early. She still has to tell us how to get there, and we haven't been able to reach her. I don't even know her alias."

Rayford told him his own predicament.

"I don't like it," Buck said. "I don't trust any of them with her."

"The whole thing's squirrelly."

"Albie to Scuba, over," the radio crackled. Rayford ignored it.

"I'm way behind you, Buck. I'll make sure I don't get there until around two."

"Albie to Scuba, over," the radio repeated.

"That'll make it logical for Leon," Rayford continued. "He can't expect me to get there faster than that."

"Albie to Scuba, do you read me, over?"

It finally sank in. "Hold on a minute, Buck."

Rayford felt gooseflesh on his arms as he grabbed the mike. "This is Scuba. Go ahead, Albie."

"Need your ten-twenty, Scuba, over."

"Stand by."

"Buck, I'm gonna have to call you back. Something's up with Mac."

Rayford checked his instruments. "Wichita Falls, Albie, over."

"Put down at Liberal. Over and out."

"Albie, wait. I—"

"Stay put and I'll find you. Albie over and out."

Why had Mac had to use code names? He set a course for Liberal, Kansas, and radioed the tower there for landing coordinates. Surely Mac wasn't flying to Liberal on the Condor. But the chopper would take hours.

He got back on the radio. "Scuba to Albie, over."

"Standing by, Scuba."

"Just wondering if I could head back and meet you on your way, over."

"Negative, Scuba. Over and out."

Rayford phoned Buck and updated him.

"Strange," Buck said. "Keep me posted."

"Roger."

"Want some good news?"

"Gladly."

"Ken Ritz is the newest member of the Tribulation Force."

Just before noon, Mountain Time, Ritz landed the Learjet at Stapleton Airport, Denver. Buck had still not heard from Chloe. He called her.

"Nothing, Buck. Sorry. I'll keep trying. I called several reproductive centers there, but the ones I reached said they did only same-day surgery, no residents. I asked if they also delivered babies. They said no. I don't know where to go from here, Buck."

"You and me both. Keep trying her number."

Rayford pacified suspicious tower personnel at the tiny Liberal airport by topping off his fuel tank. The base operator was surprised how little he needed.

He set his laptop near the cockpit window and sat on the tarmac surfing the Internet. He found Tsion's bulletin board, which had become the talk of the globe. Hundreds of thousands of responses were added every day. Tsion continued to direct the attention of his growing flock to God himself. He added to his personal daily message a fairly deep Bible study aimed at the 144,000 witnesses. It warmed Rayford's heart to read it, and he was impressed that a scholar was so sensitive to his audience. Besides the witnesses, his readers were the curious, the scared, the seekers, and the new believers. Tsion had something for everyone, but most impressive was his ability, as Bruce Barnes used to say, to "put the cookies on the lower shelf."

Tsion's writing read the way he sounded to Rayford in person when the Tribulation Force sat with him and discussed what Tsion called "the unsearchable riches of Christ Jesus."

Tsion's ability with the Scriptures, Rayford knew, had to do with more than just his facility with the languages and texts. He was anointed of God, gifted to teach and evangelize. That morning he had put the following call-to-arms on the Internet:

Good day to you, my dear brother or sister in the Lord. I come to you with a heart both heavy with sorrow and yet full of joy. I sorrow personally over the loss of my precious wife and teenagers. I mourn for so many who have died since the coming of Christ to rapture his church. I mourn for mothers all over the globe who lost their children. And I weep for a world that has lost an entire generation.

How strange to not see the smiling faces or hear the laughter of children. As much as we enjoyed them, we could not have known how much they taught us and how much they added to our lives until they were gone.

I am also melancholy this morning because of the results of the wrath of the Lamb. It should be clear to any thinking person, even the nonbeliever, that prophecy was fulfilled. The great earthquake appears to have snuffed out 25 percent of the remaining population. For generations people have called natural disasters "acts of God." This has been a misnomer. Eons ago, God the Father conceded control of Earth's weather to Satan himself, the prince and power of the air. God allowed destruction and death by natural phenomena, yes, because of the fall of man. And no doubt God at times intervened against such actions by the evil one because of the fervent prayers of his people.

But this recent earthquake was indeed an act of God. It was sadly necessary, and I choose to discuss this today because of one thing that happened where I am hiding in exile. A most bizarre and impressive occurrence that can be credited to the incredible organizational, motivational, and industrial abilities of the Global Community. I have never hidden that I believe the very idea of a one-world government, or currency, or especially faith (or I should say nonfaith) is from the pit of hell. That is not to say that everything resulting from these unholy alliances will be obviously evil.

Today, in my secret part of the world, I learned via radio that the astounding Cellular-Solar network had made it possible already for television to be returned to certain areas. A friend and I, curious, turned on the television set. We were astounded. I expected an all-news network or perhaps also a local emergency station. But as I am sure you know by now, where television has returned, it is back full force.

Our television accesses hundreds of channels from all over the world, beamed to it by satellite. Every picture on every channel representing every station and network available is transmitted into our home in images so crisp and clear you feel you could reach inside the screen and touch them. What a marvel of technology!

But this does not thrill me. I admit I was never an avid TV watcher. I bored others with my insistence on watching educational or news programs and otherwise criticizing what was offered. I expressed fresh shock every month or so at how much worse television had become.

I shall no longer apologize for my horror at what has become of this entertainment medium. Today, as my friend and I sampled the hundreds of stations, I was unable to even pause at most offerings, they were so overtly evil. Stopping even to criticize them would have subjected my brain to poison. I concede that approximately 5 percent was something as inoffensive as the news. (Of course, even the news is owned and controlled by the Global Community and carries its unique spin. But at least I was not subjected to vile language or lascivious images.) On virtually every other channel, however, I saw—in that split second before the signal changed—final proof that society has reached rock bottom.

I am neither naive nor prudish. But I saw things today I never thought I would see. All restraint, all boundaries, all limits have been eradicated. It was a microcosm of the reason for the wrath of the Lamb. Sexuality and sensuality and nudity have been part of the industry for many years. But even those who used to justify these on the basis of freedom of expression or a stand against censorship at the very least made them available only to people who knew what they were choosing.

Perhaps it is the very loss of the children that has caused us not to forget God but to acknowledge him in the worst possible way, by sticking out our tongues, raising our fists, and spitting in his face. To see not just simulated perversion but actual portrayals of every deadly sin listed in the Scriptures left us feeling unclean.

My friend left the room. I wept. It is no surprise to me that many have turned against God. But to be exposed to the depths of the result of this abandonment of the Creator is a depressing and sorrowful thing. Real violence, actual tortures and murders, are proudly advertised as available twenty-four hours a day on some channels. Sorcery, black magic, clairvoyance, fortune-telling, witchcraft, séances, and spell casting are offered as simple alternatives to anything normal, let alone positive.

Is this balanced? Is there one station that carries stories, comedies, variety shows, musical entertainment, education, anything religious other than Enigma Babylon One World Faith? For all the trumpeting by the Global Community that freedom of expression has arrived, the same has been denied those of us who know and believe the truth of God.

Ask yourself if the message I write today would be allowed on even one of the hundreds of stations broadcast to every TV around the world? Of course not. I fear the day that technology will allow the Global Community to silence even this form of expression, which no doubt soon will be considered a crime against the state. Our message flies in the face of a one-world faith that denies belief in the one true God, a God of justice and judgment.

And so I am a dissenter, as are you if you count yourself part of this kingdom family. Belief in Jesus Christ as the only begotten Son of God the Father, Maker of heaven and earth, trust in the one who offered his life as a sacrifice for the sin of the world, is ultimately antithetical to everything taught by Enigma Babylon. Those who pride themselves on tolerance and call us exclusivists, judgmental, unloving, and shrill are illogical to the point of absurdity. Enigma Babylon welcomes every organized religion into its ranks, with the proviso that all are acceptable and none are discriminated against. And yet the very tenets of many of those same religions make this impossible. When everything is tolerated, nothing is limited.

There are those who ask, why not cooperate? Why not be loving and accepting? Loving we are. Accepting we cannot be. It is as if Enigma Babylon is an organization of "one-and-only true" religions. It may be that many of these belief systems eagerly gave up their claims of exclusivity because they never made sense.

Belief in Christ, however, is unique and, yes, exclusive on the face of it. Those who pride themselves on "accepting" Jesus Christ as a great man, perhaps a god, a great teacher, or one of the prophets, expose themselves as fools. I have been gratified to read many kind comments about my teaching. I thank God for the privilege and pray I will always seek his guidance and expound his truth with care. But imagine if I announced to you that not only am I a believer, but that I am also God himself. Would that not negate every positive thing I have ever taught? It may be true that we should love everyone and live in peace. Be kind to our neighbors. Do unto others as we would have them do unto us. The principles are sound, but is the teacher still admirable and acceptable if he also claims to be God?

Jesus was a man who was also God. Well, you say, that is where we differ. You consider him simply a man. If that is all he was, he was an egomaniac or he was deranged or he was a liar. Can you say aloud without hearing the vapidness of it that Jesus was a great teacher except for that business about claiming to be the Son of God, the only way to the Father?

One argument against a deep, sincere commitment to faith used to be that various religious beliefs were so similar that it did not seem to make much difference which somebody chose. Living a moral, spiritual life was assumed to entail doing the best you could, treating other people nicely, and hoping your good deeds outweighed your bad.

Indeed, those tenets are common to many of the religions that came together to form the One World Faith. As cooperating members they have cast aside all other distinctions and enjoy the harmony of tolerance.

Frankly, this clarifies the matter. I no longer must compare faith in Christ to every other belief system. They are all one now, and the difference between Enigma Babylon and the Way, the Truth, and the Life, is so clear that the choosing, if not the choice, has become easy.

Enigma Babylon, sanctioned by the Global

Community itself, does not believe in the one true God. It believes in any god, or no god, or god as a concept. There is no right or wrong; there is only relativism. The self is the center of this man-made religion, and devoting one's life to the glory of God stands in stark relief.

My challenge to you today is to choose up sides. Join a team. If one side is right, the other is wrong. We cannot both be right. Go to the page that walks you through those Scriptures that clarify man's condition. Discover that you are a sinner, separated from God, but that you can be reconciled to him by accepting the gift of salvation he offers. As I have pointed out before, the Bible foretells of an army of horsemen that numbers 200 million, but a crowd of tribulation saints—those who become believers during this period—that cannot be numbered.

Though that clearly indicates there will be hundreds of millions of us, I call you not to a life of ease. During the next five years before the glorious return of Christ to set up his kingdom on earth, three-fourths of the population that was left after the Rapture will die. In the meantime, we should invest our lives in the cause. A great missionary martyr of the twentieth century named Jim Elliot is credited with one of the most poignant summaries of commitment to Christ ever penned: "He is no fool who gives up what he cannot keep [this temporal life] to gain what he cannot lose [eternal life with Christ]."

And now a word to my fellow converted Jews from each of the twelve tribes: Plan on rallying in Jerusalem a month from today for fellowship and teaching and unction to evangelize with the fervor of the apostle Paul and reap the great soul harvest that is ours to gather.

And now unto him who is able to keep you from falling, to Christ, that great shepherd of the sheep, be power and dominion and glory now and forevermore, world without end, Amen. Your servant, Tsion Ben-Judah.

Rayford and Amanda had loved reading such missives from Bruce Barnes and then Tsion. Was it possible she was in hiding somewhere, able to access this very thing? Could it be they were reading it at the same time? Would a message from Amanda someday appear on Rayford's screen? Each day with no news made it harder for him to believe she was still alive, and yet he could not accept that she was gone. He would not stop looking. He couldn't wait to get back to the equipment that would allow him to dive and prove Amanda was not on that plane.

"Albie to Scuba, over."

"This is Scuba, go," Rayford said.

"ETA three minutes. Sit tight. Over and out."

Buck and Chloe agreed that he would keep trying Hattie's number while she continued to call medical facilities in Denver. Buck got a taste of Chloe's frustration when he began hitting the redial button for Hattie's phone every minute or so. Even a busy signal would have been encouraging. "I can't stand just sitting here," Buck said. "I feel like heading off on foot and searching for her."

"Got your laptop with you?" Ritz said.

"Always," Buck said. Ken had been riveted to his for some time.

"Tsion's online, rallying the troops. He's gotta be gettin' under Carpathia's skin. I know there's a lot more people who still love Carpathia than there are like us who finally saw the light, but look at this."

Ritz turned his computer so Buck could watch the numbers whiz by, indicating how many responses hit the bulletin board every minute. With a fresh message out there, the total was multiplying again.

Ritz was right, of course, Buck thought. Carpathia had to be enraged by the response to Tsion. No wonder he wanted credit for Tsion's escape and also for eventually bringing him back to the public. But how long would that satisfy Carpathia? How long before his jealousy got the best of him?

"If it's true, Buck, that the Global Community would like to sponsor Tsion's return to Israel, they ought to look at what he's saying about Enigma Babylon."

"Carpathia's got Mathews in charge of Enigma Babylon right now," Buck said, "and he regrets it. Mathews sees himself and the faith as bigger and more important than even the GC. Tsion says the Bible teaches that Mathews will only last so long."

The phone rang. It was Chloe.

"Buck, where are you?"

"Still sitting here on the runway."

"You and Ken head for a rental car. I'll talk as you walk."

"What's up?" Buck said, climbing out and signaling Ken to follow.

"I got through to a small, private hospital. A woman told me they were being shut down in three weeks because they're better off to sell to the Global Community than pay the ridiculous taxes."

Buck jogged toward the terminal but soon slowed when he realized Ken was lagging. "Is that where Hattie is?" he asked Chloe.

"No, but this woman told me there's a big GC testing laboratory in Littleton. It's housed in a huge church Enigma Babylon took over and then sold to Carpathia when attendance dwindled. A reproductive clinic in the old educational wing of that church takes in longer-term patients. She wasn't fond of it. The clinic and the lab work hand in hand, and apparently there's a lot of cloning and fetal tissue research going on."

"So you reached Hattie there?"

"I think I did. I described Hattie, and the receptionist

got suspicious when I didn't know what name she might be using. She told me that if someone was using a phony name, that meant they didn't want to be contacted. I told her it was important, but she didn't buy it. I asked if she would just tell every patient that one of them had a message to call CW, but I'm sure she ignored it. I called a little later and disguised my voice. I said my uncle was the janitor and could somebody get him to come to the phone. Pretty soon this guy came on and I told him I had a friend in there who forgot to give me her alias. I told him my husband was on the way there with a gift, but he would have to know whom to ask for to be able to get in. He wasn't sure he ought to help until I told him my husband would give him a hundred dollars. He was so excited he gave me his name before he gave me the names of the four women staying there right now."

Buck reached the rental car desk and Ken, knowing the drill, slapped his driver's license and credit card on the counter. "You're gonna owe me a ton," he said. "Let's hope they've got a decent-sized car."

"Give me the names, hon," Buck said, pulling out a pen.

"I'll give you all four just in case," Chloe said, "but you're gonna know right away which is hers."

"Don't tell me she called herself something like Derby Bull."

"Nothing so creative. It's just that with the makeup of the women represented, we got lucky. Conchita Fernandez, Suzie Ng, Mary Johnson, and Li Yamamoto."

"Give me the address, and have Uncle Janitor tell Mary we're on our way."

Mac set the chopper down close to the Challenger and jumped aboard with Rayford.

"I don't know what all's going down, Ray, but I wouldn't stall you like that without a reason. It gives me chills to think I almost missed this, but after you dropped me off, I taxied the Condor into that south hangar, like you said. I'm coming out of there and heading to the cab line when Fortunato pages me from the ambassador's house. He asks me will I let him back on the Condor because he's got a classified call he's gotta make and the only secure phone is on board. I tell him sure, but that I'm gonna have to unlock it for him and get some power on for his call and then lock up after him. He tells me that's OK as long as I stay in the pilot's quarters or in the cockpit and give him privacy. I told him I had stuff to do in the cockpit. Check this out, Ray."

Mac pulled a dictation machine from his pocket. "Do I think ahead, or what? I slipped in there, jammed on those headphones, and flipped the switch. I tucked the machine inside one of the phones and turned it on. Listen."

Rayford heard dialing, then Fortunato saying, "OK, Your Excellency, I'm on the Condor, so this is secure. . . . Yes, I'm alone. . . . Officer McCullum let me in. . . . In the cockpit. No problem. . . . On his way to Denver. . . . They're gonna do it right there? . . . It's as good a place as any. It's going to change our trip back, though. . . . One pilot simply can't physically do this whole trip. I wouldn't feel safe. . . . Yes, start telling the ambassadors we'll need more time to get back. Did you want me to try to hire a pilot from here in Dallas? . . . I see. I'll check in with you later."

"What do you make of that, Mac?"

"It's pretty clear, Ray. They want to take you both out at once. What got to me is when he rushed to the cockpit and knocked quickly. He looked flushed and shaken. He asked if I would come back and join him and to please sit down. He looks nervous, wiping his mouth and looking away, totally unlike him, you know. He says, 'I just heard from Captain Steele, and there's a chance he'll be delayed. I would like you to plot our return and work in enough rest time for yourself in case you have to do all the flying.'

"I say, '*All* the flying? The whole way back and all the stops en route?'

"He says I should make the schedule easy on myself and that with enough rest, they have full confidence I can do it. He adds, 'You will find His Excellency much in your debt.'"

Rayford was not amused. "So he recruited you to be the new captain."

"Just about."

"And I'm going to be delayed. Well, isn't that a nice way to say I'm going to be toast."

CHAPTER 17

By the time Buck and Ken got their car—with more room than they needed—and were informed of shortcuts around destruction, it took nearly forty-five minutes to get to Littleton. Finding a church that had been retrofitted into a testing laboratory and reproductive clinic was easy. It was on the only navigable street in a fifteen-mile radius. Every vehicle they saw was dusty and mud-caked.

Buck went in alone to see if he could sneak Hattie from the place. Ken waited out front with the engine idling and monitored Buck's phone.

Buck approached the receptionist. "Hi!" he said breezily. "I'm here to see Mary."

"Mary?"

"Johnson. She's expecting me."

"And who may I say is asking for her?"

"Just tell her it's B."

"Are you related?"

"We soon will be, I think. I hope."

"One moment."

Buck sat and found a magazine as if he had all the time in the world. The receptionist picked up the phone. "Ms. Johnson, were you expecting a visitor? . . . No? . . . A young man who calls himself B. . . . I'll check."

The receptionist motioned to Buck. "She would like to ask where you know her from."

Buck smiled as if exasperated. "Remind her we met on an airplane."

"He says you met on an airplane. . . . Very well."

The receptionist hung up. "I'm sorry, sir, but she believes you may have her confused with someone else."

"Can you tell me if she's alone?"

"Why?"

"That may be the reason she's not admitting she knows me. She may need some assistance and doesn't know how to tell me."

"Sir, she is recovering from a medical procedure. I'm quite sure she's alone and well taken care of. Without her permission, I am not at liberty to share anything more with you."

In his peripheral vision, Buck saw a small, dark figure shuffle past in a long robe. The tiny, long-haired, severe-looking Asian woman peered curiously at Buck, then quickly looked away and disappeared down the hallway.

The receptionist's phone rang. She whispered, "Yes, Mary? . . . You don't recognize him at all? Thank you."

* * *

"So, Mac, am I paranoid, or does it sound like they're using Hattie as bait to get the two of us together?"

"Sounds that way to me," Mac said. "And neither of you are going to walk away."

Rayford grabbed his phone. "I'd better let Buck know what he's getting into before I decide what to do about it."

* * *

It sounded to Buck as if the receptionist was calling security. It would do no good to be ushered out by security, or worse, detained by them. His first thought was to bolt. But still there was a chance to bluff his way past the receptionist. Maybe Ken could distract her. Or maybe Buck could convince her he didn't know what name his friend used and had been only guessing.

The receptionist stunned him, however, when she suddenly hung up and said, "You don't happen to work for the Global Community, do you?"

How she knew that was as puzzling as Hattie using an ethnic alias while an Asian girl was either named Mary Johnson or had selected that as *her* pseudonym. If Buck denied working for the Global Community, he might never find out why she asked. "Uh, yeah, as a matter of fact I do," he said.

The front door swung open behind him. Ken was on the run, Buck's phone in hand.

The receptionist said, "And does your name happen to be Rayford Steele?"

"Uh . . ."

Ken shouted, "Sir? Is that your car out there with the lights on?"

Buck could tell he should not hesitate. He spun, calling over his shoulder, "I'll be back."

"But, sir! Captain Steele!"

Buck and Ken bounded down the steps to the car. "They thought I was Rayford! I was almost in!"

"You don't want in there, Buck. Rayford's been set up. He's sure he would have walked into an ambush."

Ken tried to shift into Drive, but it wouldn't budge. "I thought I left this thing running." The keys were gone.

A uniformed GC security officer materialized at his window. "Here, sir," he said, handing Ken the keys. "Which of you is Captain Steele?"

Buck could tell Ken was tempted to race off. He leaned across Ken's lap and said, "That would be me. Were you expecting me?"

"Yes, we were. When your driver left the car, I thought I'd shut it off and bring him the keys. Captain Steele, we have your cargo inside, if you'll join us." Turning to Ken, he said, "Are you also with the GC?"

"Me? Nope. I work for the rental company. The captain here wasn't sure he'd be bringing the car back, so I drove him. He still pays for a round trip, of course."

"Of course. And if there's nothing you need from the car then, Captain, you may follow me." To Ken, "And we will provide transportation, so you may take the car."

"Let me settle up with him," Buck said. "And I'll be right with you."

Ken closed his window. "Say the word, Buck, and they'll never catch us. You go in there as Rayford Steele and neither you or Hattie will come out."

Buck made a show of taking out a few bills for Ken. "I have to go in," he said. "If they think I'm Rayford and that I smelled a rat and slipped away, Hattie's life is worthless. She's carrying a child, and she's not a believer yet. I'm not about to hand her over to the GC." Buck glanced at the guard on the sidewalk. "I gotta go."

"I'll stay close," Ritz said. "If you aren't out of there soon, I'm comin' in."

"I'm tempted to fly straight to Baghdad and prove to myself Amanda isn't buried in the Tigris. What's Carpathia going to do when I show up? Take credit for my resurrection?"

"You know where your daughter is, right? If they've found a place to hide, that's the place to go. By the time it gets back to Carpathia that you didn't show in Denver, you'll be hidden."

"It's not like me to hide, Mac. I knew this gig with

Carpathia was temporary, but it's strange to be a target. None of us are likely to make it to the Glorious Appearing, but that's been my goal since day one. What are the odds now?"

Mac shook his head.

Rayford's phone rang. Ritz told him what was going on.

"Oh, no!" Rayford said. "You shouldn't have let him go back in there. They may not figure out he's not me until after they've killed him. Get him out of there!"

"There was no stopping him, Rayford. He thinks if we do something suspicious, Hattie is history. Trust me, if he's not out in a few minutes, I'm going in."

"These people have unlimited weapons," Rayford said. "Are you armed?"

"Yes, but they're not going to risk shooting inside, are they?"

"Why not? They care for no one but themselves. What are you carrying?"

"Buck doesn't know, and I've never had to use it, but I carry a Beretta anytime I fly for him."

✺

Buck and the GC guard were met inside by an unhappy receptionist. "Had you simply told me who you were, Captain Steele, and used the proper name for the person you were seeking, I could have easily accommodated you."

Buck smiled and shrugged. A younger guard emerged. "She will see you now," he said. "Then we'll all fill out a little paperwork, and we'll run you both out to Stapleton."

"Oh," Buck said, "you know, we didn't put down at Stapleton after all."

The guards caught each other's eyes. "You didn't?"

"We were told the terrain between here and Stapleton was worse than between here and Denver International, so we—"

"I thought DIA was closed."

"Closed to commercial, yes," Buck said, scrambling. "If you can get us out there, we'll be heading back."

"Back where? We haven't given you your orders yet."

"Oh, yeah. I know. I just assumed New Babylon."

"Hey," the younger guard said. "If DIA is closed to commercial, where'd you get the car?"

"One outfit was still open," Buck said. "Guess they're serving the GC military."

The older guard glanced at the receptionist. "Tell her we're on our way."

As the receptionist reached for the phone, the guards asked Buck to follow them down the hall. They entered a room labeled "Yamamoto." Buck was afraid Hattie would say his name as soon as she saw him. She lay facing the wall. He couldn't tell whether she was awake.

"She's going to be surprised to see her old captain," Buck said. "She used to call me Buck for short. But in front of the crew and passengers, it was always Captain Steele. Yeah, she was my senior flight attendant at Pan-Con for many years. Always did a good job."

The older guard put a hand on her shoulder. "Time to go, dear."

Hattie rolled over, appearing puzzled, squinting against the light. "Where are we going?" she said.

"Captain Steele is here for you, ma'am. He'll take you to an intermediate site and then back to New Babylon."

"Oh, hi, Captain Steele," she said groggily. "I don't want to go to New Babylon."

"Just following orders, Ms. Durham," Buck said. "You know all about that."

"I just don't want to go that far," she said.

"We'll take it in stages. You'll make it."

"But I—"

"Let's get started, ma'am," the older guard said. "We're on a schedule."

Hattie sat up. Her pregnancy was beginning to show. "I would appreciate it if you gentlemen would excuse me while I dress."

Buck followed the guards into the hall. The younger said, "So, what did you fly up here?"

"Oh, one of the little jets that survived the quake."

The other asked, "How was the flight from Baghdad?"

Buck thought Rayford had told him Baghdad Airport was unusable. Relieved they hadn't asked more about the plane, he wondered if he was being tested. "We flew out of New Babylon," he said. "You wouldn't believe how fast the rebuilding is going."

"Long flight?"

"Very. But of course we stopped every so many hours to pick up another dignitary." Buck had no idea how many, when, or where, and he hoped they wouldn't ask.

"What's that like? All those muckety-mucks on the same plane?"

"Another day, another dollar," Buck said. "Pilots stay in the cockpit or in our quarters anyway. We don't get involved in the pageantry."

Buck knew he had already been inside long enough to worry Ken Ritz. No way these guys were taking him or Hattie to either airport, regardless of how he misled them. He was surprised they hadn't already offered them a poisoned drink. Apparently they had orders to make it neat and clean and quiet. There could be no witnesses.

When the older guard knocked on Hattie's door, Buck caught sight of Ken with a janitor down the hall, both carrying brooms. Buck engaged the guards in conversation, hoping Ken could get out of sight quickly. Though Ken was wearing a clinic cap like the janitor, there was no hiding his features.

"So what kind of a vehicle did you guys get issued?" Buck said. "Anything that'll get us through this terrain faster than a rented sedan?"

"Not really. A minivan. Rear-wheel drive, unfortunately. But we can get you to DIA with no trouble."

"Where are they sending us, anyway?" Buck said.

The younger guard pulled a sheet from his pocket. "I'll give you this in a few minutes in the other room, but it says Washington Dulles."

Buck eyed the man. He knew one thing for sure: There weren't even plans to rebuild Dulles. It had been obliterated in the war, and the earthquake had wiped out Reagan National. Reagan had an operable runway or two, Rayford had told him, but Dulles was a pile of debris.

"I'll be another second," Hattie called out. The guard sighed.

"What's in the other room?" Buck said.

"A debriefing. We give you your orders, make sure you've got everything you need; then we head to the airport."

Buck didn't like the idea of the other room. He wished he could talk to Ritz. Buck couldn't tell if the GC men were carrying sidearms, but they were purported to have Uzis in holsters strapped at their ribs in the back. He wondered if he was going to die trying to save Hattie Durham.

Rayford didn't want Fortunato to know he was not yet in Denver, in case GC forces there had already reported his arrival. If Denver was tipped off that the real Rayford was still in the air, Buck would be exposed, and neither he nor Hattie would have a chance. Rayford sat on the runway in Kansas as helpless as he had ever felt.

"You'd better get heading back, Mac. Fortunato thinks you were visiting friends, right?"

"I am, aren't I?"

"How does he contact you?"

"Has the tower call me, and then we switch to frequency 11 to talk privately."

Rayford nodded. "Safe trip."

"All right, ma'am," the guard said through Hattie's door. "Time's up. Now let's go."

Buck heard nothing from Hattie's room. The guards looked at each other. The older turned the doorknob. It was locked. He swore. Both yanked weapons from their jackets and banged loudly on the door, commanding Hattie to come out. Other women peeked from their rooms, including one from each end of the hall. The younger guard waved his Uzi at them and they ducked back in. The older burped four shots at Hattie's door, blowing the latch and lock housing to the floor and causing screams down the hall. The receptionist came running, but when she appeared in the corridor, the younger guard sprayed a fusillade that ripped from her waist to her face. She dropped loudly onto the marble floor.

The older guard rushed into Hattie's room as the younger spun to follow him. Buck was between them. He wished he'd had some defense or assault training. There must be some strategic response to a man in your face carrying an Uzi.

With nothing in his repertoire, he planted his right foot, stepped quickly with his left, and drove his fist square into the young guard's nose with all he could muster. He felt the crush of cartilage, the cracking of teeth, and the ripping of flesh. The guard must have been in midstride when Buck hit him, because the back of his head hit the floor first.

The Uzi rattled on the marble, but the strap wound up tucked under him. Buck turned and ran toward the last room to his left, where he'd seen a panicky face peek out a moment before. Swimming in his mind in slow motion were the curtains blowing from the open window in Hattie's room, the riddled body of the receptionist, and the whites of the eyes of the guard when Buck drove his nose so deep into his head that it was flush with his face.

Blood dripped from Buck's hand as he ran. He glanced back as he raced into the room at the end. No sign of the older guard yet. A pregnant Hispanic woman shrieked as he flashed into her room. He knew he looked awful, the sore on his cheek still fiery, his hand and shirt covered with the blood from the young guard's face. The woman covered her eyes and trembled.

"Lock that door and stay under the bed!" Buck said. She didn't move at first. "Now or you'll die!"

Buck opened the window and saw he would have to turn sideways to get out. The screen wouldn't budge. He backed up and lifted his leg, driving it through. The momentum carried him out and down into some bushes. As he regained his footing, bullets ripped through the door behind him, and he saw the woman cower under her bed. He raced along the side of the building past Hattie's open window. In the distance, Ken Ritz was helping her into the back of the car. The Global Community minivan sat between Buck and the sedan.

Buck felt as if he were in a dream, unable to move faster. He made the mistake of holding his breath as he ran and soon had to gasp for air, his heart cracking against his ribs. As he neared the van he shot a look back as the guard leaped from the window he had escaped through. Buck ducked around the other side of the van as bullets drilled the chassis. A block ahead, Ritz waited behind the wheel. Buck could stay put and be massacred or held hostage, or he could take his chances and run to the car.

He ran. With every step he feared the next sound would be a bullet crashing into his head. Hattie was out of sight on the seat or the floor, and Ken leaned right and disappeared as well. The passenger door flew open and beckoned like a spring in the desert. The more Buck ran, the more vulnerable he felt, but he dared not look back.

He heard a sound, but not gunfire. Duller. The van door. The guard had jumped into the van. Buck was within fifty yards of the car.

Rayford dialed Buck's phone. It rang several times, but Rayford did not want to hang up. If a GC man answered, Rayford would bluff him until he found out what he wanted to know. If Buck answered, Rayford would allow him to talk in code in case he was in front of people who shouldn't know who was on the other end. The phone kept ringing.

Rayford hated helplessness and immobility more than

anything. He was tired of games with Nicolae Carpathia and the Global Community. Their sanctimony and sympathy drove him wild. "God," he prayed silently, "let me be Carpathia's out-and-out enemy, please."

A petrified female voice answered the phone. "What!" she shouted.

"Hattie? Don't let on, but this is Rayford."

"Rayford! Buck's pilot scared me to death outside my window but then helped me get out! We're waiting for Buck! We're scared he's going to be killed!"

"Give me that phone!" Rayford heard. It was Ritz. "Ray, he looks fine, but he's got a guy shootin' at him. As soon as he gets to the car, I'm gone. I may have to hang up on you."

"Just take care of them!" Rayford said.

A few steps from the car, expecting to be leveled, Buck had heard nothing more. No shots, no van. He stole one last look as the GC man clambered out of the van. He dropped into a crouch and began firing. Buck heard a huge blast next to him as the right rear tire was blown. He dove for the open door, grabbing the handle and trying to get a foot inside. The back windshield blew through the car in pieces.

Buck tried to keep his balance. His left foot was on the floorboard, his right on the pavement. His left hand gripped the chassis and his right the door handle. Ken had leaned over onto the passenger's seat again to escape the bullets, and before Buck could pull himself in, Ken blindly floored the accelerator. The door swung open, and to keep from flying out Buck swiveled and sat on Ritz's head. Ken screamed as the car spun, flat tire flapping and good tires peeling rubber. Buck tried to keep out of the firing line too, but he had to get off Ken's painful head.

Ken let go of the wheel and used both hands to fight his way out from under Buck. He sat up to get his bearings and wrenched the wheel left, not in time to miss the corner of a building. The right corner panel tore and crumpled high. Ken straightened the car and tried to put some distance between them and the shooter.

The car was not cooperating. More bullets narrowly missed Ritz, and Buck saw his demeanor change. Ken went from scared to mad in a flash.

"That's it!" Ritz hollered. "I've been shot at for the last time!"

To Buck's horror, Ritz swung the car around and raced toward the guard. Buck peeked over the dashboard as Ritz pulled his 9mm automatic from an ankle holster, braced his left wrist between the outside mirror and the chassis, and fired.

The guard scrambled to the other side of the van. Buck hollered for Ken to head for the airport.

"No way!" Ken said. "This guy's mine!"

He skidded to a stop about fifty feet from the van and leaped from the car. He squatted, the Beretta in two hands, squeezing shots off just above ground level.

Buck screamed for Ritz to get back in the car as the GC

man turned and ran toward the building. Ritz fired off three more shots and one hit the guard in the foot, sending his leg shooting up in front of him and flipping him backwards. "I'll kill you, you—"

Buck ran from the car and grabbed Ritz, dragging him back. "No way he's alone!" Buck said. "We've got to go!"

They jumped into the car, and Ken spun the wheel with the accelerator on the floor. A huge cloud of dust boiled up behind them as they bounced and shimmied across the earthquake-ravaged terrain toward Stapleton.

"If we can get out of sight," Buck said, "they think we're headed toward DEN. Why couldn't he get that van started?"

Ritz reached under his seat and pulled out a distributor cap, wires dangling. "This might have somethin' to do with it," he said.

The car protested noisily. Buck put a hand on the ceiling to keep from hitting his head as they bounced along. With his other he reached across Ritz and buckled him in. Then he buckled himself in and saw his phone slide by his feet. He grabbed it and saw it was in use. "Hello?" he said.

"Buck! It's Ray! Are you safe?"

"We're on the way to the airport! We've got a blown rear tire, but all we can do is go till we stop."

"We've also got a gas leak!" Ritz said. "The gauge is dropping fast!"

"How's Hattie?" Rayford asked.

"Hanging on for dear life!" Buck said. He wanted to

buckle her in but knew it would be impossible in her condition, especially with the bouncing. She lay in the backseat, feet pressed against the door, one hand holding her stomach, the other pushing against the back of the seat. She was pale.

"Hold on!" Ritz hollered.

Buck looked up in time to see a tall dirt mound they would not be able to avoid. Ritz neither slowed nor tried to stop. He kept the pedal to the floor and steered for the center of the dirt. Buck braced himself with his feet and reached back to try to keep Hattie from flying forward upon impact. When the car dived into the dirt pile, Hattie slammed into the back of the front seat and nearly pushed Buck's shoulder from the socket. The phone flew from his hand, cracked into the windshield, and skidded to the floor.

"Call me when you can!" Rayford shouted, hanging up. He taxied the Challenger 3 to the end of the runway.

"Scuba to Albie," he said. "Albie, do you copy?"

"Go ahead, Scuba."

"Get back to base and find out what they know. The cargo is safe temporarily, but I'm going to need some kind of a story when I show up."

"Roger that, Scuba. Consider a Minot."

Rayford paused. "Good call, Albie. Will do. Need everything you can give me ASAP."

"Roger."

Brilliant, Rayford thought. He had long ago told Mac of an experience while he was stationed in Minot, North Dakota. His jet fighter malfunctioned, and he had to abort a training mission. He would tell Fortunato that's what had happened to the Challenger, and Leon wouldn't know the difference. Mac would vouch for whatever Rayford said. The biggest problem was that by the time he got back, Leon would know of the fiasco in Denver and would suspect Rayford's involvement.

What he needed was leverage to keep himself alive. Was Hattie important enough to Carpathia that he would keep Rayford around until he knew where she was? Rayford had to get back to Baghdad to know what had become of Amanda. There was no guarantee Carpathia wouldn't have him killed as an example to the rest of the Tribulation Force.

<hr />

"She's overheating!" Ritz said.

"I'm overheating too!" Hattie wailed. She sat up and braced herself with a hand on each of the front headrests. Her face was flushed, her forehead sweaty.

"We have no choice but to keep going," Buck said. He and Ken tried to brace themselves against the violent shuddering of the wounded vehicle. The temperature needle was buried in the red, steam billowed from under the hood, the gas gauge was perilously low, and Buck saw flames coming from the flat rear tire. "If you stop, the gas will hit those flames. Even if we get to the airport, make sure we're empty before we stop!"

Hattie shouted, "What if the tire burns up the car anyway?"

"Hope you're right with God!" Ritz shouted.

"You took the words right out of my mouth!" Buck said.

Rocketing toward Dallas at several hundred miles an hour, Rayford was afraid he would overtake Mac in the chopper. He had to time his arrival appropriately. Several minutes later he heard Fortunato contact Mac.

"Dallas tower to Golf Charlie Niner Niner, over."

"This is Golf Charlie. Go ahead, tower."

"Switch to alternate frequency for your superior, over."

"Roger that."

Rayford switched to frequency 11 to listen in.

"Mac, this is the Supreme Commander."

"Go ahead, sir."

"What's your location?"

"Two hours west of you, sir. Returning from a visit."

"Were you coming straight back?"

"No, sir. But I can."

"Please do. There was a major foul-up north of us, do you follow?"

"What happened?"

"We're not sure yet. We need to find our operative and then we need to get back on schedule as soon as possible."

"I'm on my way, sir."

Buck prayed the car would run out of gas soon, but he didn't know how they would get Hattie across the torn-up ground. The flames licked the back right side of the car, and only Ken's keeping the thing rolling kept them from exploding.

The fire was closest to Hattie, and even with the car jerking this way and that, she managed to crawl into the front seat, jamming between the men.

"The engine will blow before I run out of gas!" Ken shouted. "We may have to jump!"

"Easier said than done!" Hattie said.

Buck had an idea. He found his phone and punched in an emergency code. "Warn Stapleton tower!" he yelled. "Small craft approaching on fire!"

The dispatcher tried to ask something, but Buck hung up. The engine rattled and banged, the back of the car was a torch, and Ken nursed it over one last rise to the far end of the runway. A foam truck moved into position.

"Keep her rolling, Ken!" Buck said.

The engine finally quit. Ken shifted into neutral and both men grabbed their door handles. Hattie latched onto Buck's arm with both hands. The car was barely rolling when the foam truck reached it and unloaded, smothering the vehicle and snuffing the fire. Ken burst out one side and Buck the other, Hattie in tow. Lurching blindly through the foam, Buck lifted Hattie into his arms, stunned at her added weight. Weak from the ordeal, he fell in behind Ken and followed him to the Learjet. Ken lowered the steps, told Buck to hand Hattie to him and get aboard, then carried her to where Buck helped her into a seat. Ken had the door shut, the engines screaming, and the Learjet rolling within a minute.

As they jetted into the sky, the foam crew finished with the car and stared at the fleeing plane.

Buck spread his knees and let his hands dangle. His knuckles were raw. He couldn't wipe from his mind the images of the receptionist—dead before she hit the ground—the guard he rocked off his feet, and the woman trembling as she locked her door.

"Ken, if they find out who we are, you and I are fugitives."

"What happened to noon?" Hattie said, her voice thin.

"What happened to your phone?" Buck asked. "Chloe and I tried to reach you all morning."

"They took it," she said. "Said they had to run diagnostics on it or something."

"Are you healthy?" Buck said. "I mean, other than your condition?"

"I've felt better," she said. "I'm still pregnant, if you're curious."

"I gathered that while carrying you."

"Sorry."

"We're going to be in hiding," Buck said. "Are you up to it?"

"Who else is there?"

Buck told her.

"What about medical care?"

"I have an idea there, too," Buck said. "No promises, but we'll see what we can do."

Ken seemed to still be wired. "I couldn't believe my luck when I paid off that janitor and he took me outside where I could look right through the window."

"When you said you were with Buck," Hattie said, "I had to trust you."

"How in the world did you get out of there, Buck?" Ken said.

"I wonder that myself. That guard murdered the receptionist."

Hattie looked stricken. "Claire?" she said. "Claire Blackburn's dead?"

"I didn't know her name," Buck said, "but she's dead all right."

"That's what they wanted to do to me," Hattie said.

"You got that right," Ken said.

"I'll stay with you guys for as long as you'll have me," she said.

Buck got on his phone, updated Rayford and Chloe, then punched in the number of Dr. Floyd Charles in Kenosha.

Rayford concocted a story he believed would be convincing. The only problem, he knew, was that it might not be long before Buck was identified as his impostor.

CHAPTER 18

BEFORE RETURNING to Dallas, Rayford hoped to find out what Leon knew or believed had happened in Denver. But he was unable to reach Mac. Was it possible Buck had been recognized? No one would believe Rayford had not had a part in Hattie's escape if it was known his son-in-law was there. Rayford would accept the consequences of his actions in what he considered a holy war. He did, however, want to stay out of prison long enough to find Amanda and clear her name.

If Tsion was right, the 144,000 witnesses were sealed by God and protected from harm for a certain period. Though he was not one of the witnesses, Rayford was a believer; he had the mark of God on his forehead, and he trusted God to protect him. If God did not, then, as the apostle Paul put it, to die would be "gain."

Rayford had not heard from Mac and couldn't raise him. Either Mac could not get away from Leon long enough to get in touch with him, or something was wrong on the ground. Rayford had to do something. If he was to say he had aborted his mission, it only made sense to radio Leon before showing up again in Dallas.

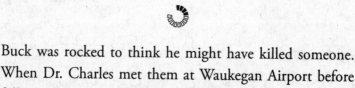

Buck was rocked to think he might have killed someone. When Dr. Charles met them at Waukegan Airport before following them to Mt. Prospect, Buck whispered his fear. "I have to know how bad I hurt that guard."

"I know a guy at the GC emergency facility outside Littleton," Dr. Charles said. "I can find out."

Dr. Charles stayed in his car on the phone after Ken wheeled the Suburban into the backyard. Chloe and Tsion demanded every detail. Chloe navigated the stairs with her cane, insisting that Hattie take the downstairs bed. Hattie looked exhausted. Ken and Tsion helped her up the stairs and urged her to call for them after her shower so they could help her back down.

Buck and Chloe spoke in private. "You could have been killed," she said.

"I'm surprised I wasn't. I just know I killed that guard. I can't believe it. But he had just murdered the receptionist, and I knew he would do the same to us. I reacted instinctively. If I'd thought about it, I might have frozen."

"There was nothing else you could do, Buck. But you can't kill a man with a punch, can you?"

"I hope not. But he had spun around and was moving right toward me when I hit him. I'm not exaggerating, hon. I don't think I could have hit him harder if I had been running at him. It felt as if my fist was inside his head. Everything crumbled beneath it, and he landed flush on the back of his head. It sounded like a bomb."

"It was self-defense, Buck."

"I don't know what I'll do if I find out he's dead."

"What will the Global Community do if they find out it was you?"

Buck wondered how long that might take. The young guard had gotten a good look at him, but he was likely dead. The other guard assumed he was Rayford Steele. Until someone showed him a picture of Rayford, he might still believe it. But could he describe Buck?

Buck moved to a mirror in the hallway. His face was grimy, his cheek red and purple almost to his nose. His hair was wild and dark with sweat. He needed a shower. But what had he looked like at that clinic? What might the surviving guard say about him?

"Charlie Tango to Dallas tower, over."

"Tower, go ahead, Charlie Tango."

"Relay urgent message to Global Community Supreme Commander. Mission aborted due to mechanical failure. Checking equipment before return to base. ETA two hours, over."

"Roger that, Charlie Tango."

Rayford put down at an unattended and seemingly abandoned airstrip east of Amarillo and waited for Leon Fortunato's call.

Buck worried when Dr. Charles finally came into the house and would not make eye contact. The doctor agreed to check Chloe, Ken, and Hattie before heading back to Kenosha. He appeared most concerned about Hattie and her baby. She was to remain at rest for other than nature calls. He told the others how to care for her and what symptoms to monitor.

The doctor removed Ken's stitches and advised him also to take it easy for several days.

"What, no more shoot-outs? Guess I can't work for Buck for a while."

The doctor told Chloe again that time was her ally. Her arm and foot casts were not ready to be removed, but he prescribed therapy that would help her snap back more quickly.

Buck waited, watching. If Dr. Charles ignored him altogether, that meant Buck had killed a man and the doctor didn't know how to tell him. "Could you check my cheek?" Buck asked.

Without a word, Dr. Charles approached. He held Buck's face in his hands and turned him this way and that in the light. "I need to clean that," he said. "You risk infection unless we get some alcohol in there."

The others left them while the doctor worked on Buck. "You'll feel better after a shower, too," he said.

"I'll feel better when you tell me what you found out. You were on that phone a long time."

"The man is dead," Dr. Charles said.

Buck stared.

"I don't see that you had any choice, Buck."

"They'll come looking for me. They had cameras throughout that place."

"If you looked like you look now, even people who know you might not have recognized you."

"I have to turn myself in."

Dr. Charles stepped back. "If you shot an enemy soldier during a battle, would you turn yourself in?"

"I didn't mean to kill him."

"But if you had not, he would have killed you. He killed someone right in front of you. You know his assignment was to take out both you and Hattie."

"How did a punch kill him?"

The doctor applied a butterfly bandage and sat on the table. "My colleague in Littleton tells me that either of the two blows—to the face or to the back of the head—could have done it. But the combination made it unavoidable. The guard suffered severe facial trauma, a shattering of cartilage and bone around the nose, some of it driven into his skull. Both optic nerves were destroyed. Several teeth were shattered, and the upper jaw cracked. That damage alone might have killed him."

"*Might* have?"

"My associate leans toward the posterior cranial damage as the cause of death. The back of his head hitting flush on the floor caused his skull to shatter like an eggshell. Several shards of cranial tissue were embedded in the brain. He died instantly."

Buck hung his head. What kind of a soldier was he? How could he be expected to fight in this cosmic battle of good versus evil if he couldn't handle killing the enemy?

The doctor began putting his things away. "I've never met anyone who caused another person's death and didn't feel awful for a while," he said. "I've talked with parents who killed someone while protecting their own child, but still they were haunted and sobered. Ask yourself where Hattie would be if not for what you did. Where would *you* be?"

"I'd be in heaven. Hattie would be in hell."

"Then you bought her some time."

✺

Rayford finally received a call from the Dallas tower, asking that he inform them when he was half an hour from touchdown. "The Supreme Commander awaits your arrival."

He told them he was about to get underway. Half an hour

out of Dallas, he radioed in, and forty minutes later he taxied to the hangar that also housed the Condor 216. He alighted to face a glowering Leon Fortunato, Mac McCullum behind him with a knowing look. Rayford couldn't wait to talk to Mac privately.

"What happened, Captain Steele?"

"It was sluggish, Commander, and only prudent to check it out. I was able to make an adjustment, but I was so far behind schedule I thought I'd better check in."

"You don't know what happened, then?"

"To the plane? Not entirely, but it was unstable and—"

"I mean what happened in Denver!"

Rayford glanced at Mac, who almost imperceptibly shook his head.

"In Denver?"

"I told you, Commander," Mac said, "I was unable to reach him."

"Follow me," Fortunato said. He led Rayford and Mac to an office, where he punched up on a computer a video and text e-mail from the Global Community office in Denver. The three bent over the monitor and watched as Fortunato narrated. "We knew Miss Durham was unwilling to return to New Babylon, but His Excellency believed it was in her best interest and in the best interest of global security. To protect his fiancée and their child, we assigned two security officers to meet with you and her and to give you your orders. Their top priority was the transfer of Miss Durham to you for her transport to the Middle East. They were to ensure she was still in Denver when you arrived.

"While the laboratory and clinic there were largely undamaged by the earthquake, we thought the surveillance system had been knocked out. However, the surviving security officer double-checked the system, just in case, and found a view of the impostor."

"The impostor?" Rayford said.

"The man claiming to be you."

Rayford raised his eyebrows.

"These were professionals, Captain Steele."

"These?"

"At least two. Maybe more. The cameras in front of the building and in the reception area were not operating. There are cameras at either end of the main corridor and one in the middle. The action you'll see here took place in the middle, but the only camera working was the one at the north end of the corridor. Nearly every view of the impostor is blocked by one of the security men, or the impostor has his back to the camera. The tape begins here with the security guards and the perpetrator stepping outside Miss Durham's door while she dressed for the trip."

It was clear Buck was the man between the two guards, but his face was indistinct. His hair was out of place, and he had an ugly cheek wound.

"Now watch, gentlemen. When the senior guard knocks on Miss Durham's door, the other also turns toward the door, but the perp glances down the hall. That's the clearest view we get of his face."

Again, Rayford was relieved that the image was not clear.

"The senior guard believes the perp was distracted by two janitors who appear earlier on the tape. He will interview them later today. Now here, a few moments later, he has lost patience with Miss Durham. He calls to her and both guards bang on the door. Here the junior guard orders curious patients back into their rooms. The perp backs up a couple of steps when the senior guard blows open the door. That brings the receptionist. While the junior guard is distracted, the perp somehow disarms him, and see? See the gunfire? He murders the receptionist where she stands. When the junior guard attempts to disarm him, he drives the butt end of the Uzi so hard into his face that the guard is dead before he hits the floor."

Mac and Rayford caught each other's eyes and leaned closer to study the video. Rayford wondered if Fortunato thought he had the power Carpathia possessed, to convince people they had seen something they had not. He couldn't let it pass.

"That's not what I see there, Leon."

Leon looked sharply at him. "What are you saying?"

"The junior guard did the firing." Fortunato backed up the tape. "See?" Rayford said. "There! He's firing. The perp is stepping back. The guard wheels back around, and the perp steps forward as the guard appears to slip on his own expelled shell casings. See? He has no footing, so the blow drives his head to the floor."

Fortunato looked angry. He reran the video a couple more times.

Mac said, "The perp didn't even attempt to grab the gun."

"Say what you will, gentlemen, but that impostor murdered the receptionist and the guard."

"The guard?" Rayford said. "He might have fallen on his head even if he hadn't been punched."

"Anyway," Fortunato continued, "the accomplice pulled Miss Durham through the window and sent her to the getaway car. As soon as the senior guard opened the door, the accomplice fired at him."

That was not, of course, the way Rayford had heard it. "How did he escape being killed?"

"He nearly *was*. He has a severe wound to his heel."

"I thought you said he was coming *into* the room when he was fired upon?"

"Correct."

"He was running *out* of the room if he got shot in the heel."

The computer beeped, and Fortunato asked an aide for help. "Another message is coming in," he said. "Bring it up for me."

The aide hit a few buttons, and a new message flashed from the senior guard. It read, "Foot being treated. Surgery required. Accomplice was second janitor in first scene on tape. Real janitor found with wad of cash. Says accomplice forced on him to appear like bribe. Says accomplice held knife to throat until he got information."

Fortunato's aide backed the video all the way to where the two janitors entered the hallway and walked toward the camera. Rayford, who had never met Ritz, guessed which one he was only by his incomplete janitorial outfit. The only thing resembling a uniform was the cap he had apparently borrowed from the janitor. He carried a broom, but his clothing was western.

"He could be from that area," Fortunato said.

"Good call," Rayford said.

"Well, it doesn't take a trained eye to identify regional clothing."

"Still, Commander, that's an insightful catch."

"I don't see a knife," Mac said, as the figures neared the camera. Ritz's cap was pulled low over his eyes. Rayford held his breath as he reached for the bill of his cap. He lifted it and reset it on his head, showing his face more clearly. Rayford and Mac looked at each other behind Fortunato.

"After they passed that camera," Fortunato said, "the accomplice got the information he needed and ran the janitor off. He absconded with Miss Durham and opened fire on our guard. And those guards were there only to protect Miss Durham."

The guard had conveniently left out details that would have made him appear an idiot. Until someone could thoroughly investigate the scene, the Global Community had not a shred of evidence implicating Rayford.

"She will contact you," Fortunato said. "She always does. You had better not have had anything to do with this. His

Excellency would consider that high treason and punishable by death."

"You suspect *me*?"

"I have come to no conclusions."

"Am I returning to New Babylon as a suspect or as a pilot?"

"A pilot, of course."

"You want me at the controls of the Condor 216?"

"Of course. You can't kill us without killing yourself, and I don't gauge you suicidal. Yet."

Buck spent more than three weeks working on the Internet version of *Global Community Weekly.* He was in touch with Carpathia nearly every day. Nothing was said about Hattie Durham, but Carpathia often reminded Buck that their mutual "friend," Rabbi Tsion Ben-Judah, would be protected by the Global Community anytime he chose to return to the Holy Land. Buck did not tell Tsion. He merely kept alive his promise that the rabbi could return to Israel within the month.

Donny Moore's duplex proved more ideal every day. Nothing else in the neighborhood had survived. Virtually no traffic came by.

Ken Ritz, now fully on the mend, moved out of the tiny sliver of the Quonset hut he had been allotted at Palwaukee and commuted between Wheeling and Waukegan from his new digs in the basement of the safe house. Dr. Charles visited every few days, and every chance they got, the Tribulation Force met together and sat under Tsion's teaching.

It was no accident that they met around the kitchen table with Hattie not eight feet away on her sickbed. Often she rolled onto her side with her back to them, pretending to sleep, but Buck was convinced she heard every word.

They were careful not to say anything that might incriminate them with Carpathia, having no idea what the future held for Nicolae and Hattie. But they cried together, prayed together, laughed, sang, studied, and shared their stories. Dr. Charles was often present.

Tsion rehearsed the entire plan of salvation in nearly every meeting. It might come in the form of one of their stories or his simply expositing a Scripture passage. Hattie had lots of questions, but she asked them only of Chloe later.

The Tribulation Force wanted Dr. Charles to become a full-fledged member, but he declined, fearful that more frequent daily trips to the house might lead the wrong people there. Ritz spent many days tinkering in the underground shelter, getting it into shape in case any or all of them needed complete seclusion. They hoped it would not come to that.

The flight from Dallas to New Babylon, with several stops to pick up Carpathia's regional ambassadors, had been a harrowing one for Rayford. He and Mac both worried that Fortunato might enlist Mac to eliminate him. Rayford felt vulnerable, assuming Fortunato believed he was involved in the rescue of Hattie Durham.

The device that allowed Rayford to hear what was going on in the main cabin yielded fascinating listening throughout the trip. One of the strategically placed transmitters was near the seat usually occupied by Nicolae Carpathia himself. Of course, Leon had appropriated that one, which was propitious for Rayford. He found Leon an incredible master of deceit, second only to Nicolae.

Each ambassador came aboard with attendant fanfare, and Fortunato immediately ingratiated himself. He ordered the cabin crew to wait on them, whispered to them, flattered them, took them into his confidence. Each heard Fortunato's tale of having been raised from the dead by Carpathia. It sounded to Rayford as if each was either truly impressed or put on a good front. "I assume you know that you're among His Excellency's favorite two regional potentates," Fortunato privately told each king.

Their responses were variations of "I didn't know for sure, but I can't say it surprises me. I am most supportive of His Excellency's regime."

"That has not gone unnoticed," Fortunato would say. "He appreciates very much your suggesting the ocean harvesting operation. His Excellency believes this will result in huge profits to the entire world. He's asking that your region split the income equally with his Global Community administration, and he will then redistribute the GC share to the less fortunate regions."

If that made a king blanch, Fortunato went into overdrive. "Of course, His Excellency realizes the burden this puts on you. But, you know the old saying: 'To whom much is given, much is required.' The potentate believes you have governed with such brilliance and vigor that you can be counted on as one of the globe's great benefactors. In exchange, he has given me the liberty to show you this list and these plans for your personal encouragement and comfort." As Fortunato would unroll papers—which Rayford assumed were elaborate architectural drawings and lists of perquisites—he would say, "His Excellency himself pleaded with me to assure you that he does not in any way believe this is anything but appropriate for a person of your stature and station. While it may appear opulent to the point of ostentation, he asked that I personally convey that he believes you are worthy of such accommodations. While your new domicile, which will be constructed and equipped within the next six months, may appear to elevate you even beyond where he is, he insists that you not reject his plans."

Whatever Fortunato showed them seemed to impress. "Well," they would say, "I would never ask this for myself, but if His Excellency insists . . ."

Fortunato saved his slimiest approach. Just before his official conversation with each king was finished, he added: "Now, sir, His Excellency asked that I broach with you a delicate matter that must remain confidential. May I count on you?"

"Certainly!"

"Thank you. He is gathering sensitive data on the workings of the Enigma Babylon One World Faith. Being careful not to prejudice you, but also not wanting to act without your insight, he is curious. How do you feel about Pontifex Maximus Peter Mathews's self-serving—no, that is pejorative—let me state it another way. Again, being careful not to sway you, do you share His Excellency's, shall we say, hesitation over the pontiff's independence from the rest of the Global Community administration?"

To a man, every king expressed outrage over Mathews's machinations. Each considered him a threat. One said, "We do our share. We pay the taxes. We are loyal to His Excellency. With Mathews, it's just take, take, take. It's never enough. I, for one, and you may express this to His Excellency, would love to see Mathews out of office."

"Then let me broach a yet more sensitive issue, if I may."

"Absolutely."

"If it came to taking an extreme course of action against the very person of the pontiff, would you be one upon whom His Excellency could depend?"

"You mean . . . ?"

"You understand."

"You may count on me."

The day before the Condor 216 was to deliver the dignitaries to New Babylon, Mac received word from Albie. "Your delivery is early and ready for pickup."

Rayford spent nearly an hour scheduling his and Mac's

time in the cockpit and in the sleeping quarters so both would feel as fresh as possible at the end of the trip. Rayford penciled himself in for the last block of piloting. Mac would sleep and then be available to make the chopper run to make the pickup and pay off Albie. Meanwhile, Rayford would sleep in his quarters at the shelter. Come nightfall, Rayford and Mac would slip away and helicopter to the Tigris.

It worked almost as planned. Rayford had not anticipated David Hassid's eagerness to debrief him on everything that had happened in his absence. "Carpathia actually has missiles pointing into outer space, anticipating judgmental meteors."

Rayford flinched. "He believes the prophecies that God will pour out more judgments?"

"He would never admit that," David said. "But it sure sounds like he's afraid of it."

Rayford thanked David and finally told him he needed rest. On his way out, Hassid shared one more bit of news, and it was all Rayford could do to stay off the Internet. "Carpathia has been manic the last several days," David said. "He discovered that Web site where you can tap into a live camera shot of the Wailing Wall. He spent days carrying his laptop everywhere he went, watching and listening to the two preachers at the wall. He's convinced they're speaking directly to him, and of course they are. Oh, he's mad. Twice I heard him scream, 'I want them dead! And soon!'"

"That won't happen before the due time," Rayford said.

"You don't have to tell me," David said. "I'm reading Tsion Ben-Judah's messages every chance I get."

Rayford posted coded notes on bulletin boards all over the Net, trying to locate Amanda. He may have been too obscure, but he didn't dare make it more obvious. He believed she was alive, and so unless it was proven otherwise, to him she was. All he knew was that if she could communicate with him, she would. As for the charges that she was working for Carpathia, there were moments he actually wished that were true. That would mean she was alive for sure. But if she had been a traitor—no, he would not allow himself to run with that logic. He believed the only reason he had not heard from her was that she did not have the means to contact him.

Rayford was so eager to prove Amanda was not entombed in the Tigris that he wasn't sure he could sleep. He was fitful, peeking at the clock every half hour or so. Finally, about twenty minutes before Mac was due, Rayford showered and dressed and accessed the Internet.

The camera at the Wailing Wall carried live audio as well. The preachers Rayford knew to be the two witnesses prophesied in Revelation were holding forth. He could almost smell their smoky burlap robes. Their dark, bony bare feet and knuckled hands made them appear thousands of years old. They had long, coarse beards, dark, piercing eyes, and long, wild hair. Eli and Moishe they called each other, and they preached with power and authority. And volume. The video identified the one on the left as Eli, and subtitles carried his message in English. He was saying, "Beware, men of Jerusalem! You have now been without the waters of heaven since the signing of the evil pact. Continue to blaspheme the name of Jesus Christ, the Lord and Savior, and you will continue to see your land parched and your throats dry. To reject Jesus as Messiah is to spit in the face of almighty God. He will not be mocked.

"Woe unto him who sits on the throne of this earth. Should he dare stand in the way of God's sealed and anointed witnesses, twelve thousand from each of the twelve tribes making a pilgrimage here for the purpose of preparation, he shall surely suffer for it."

Here Moishe took over. "Yea, any attempt to impede the moving of God among the sealed will cause your plants to wither and die, rain to remain in the clouds, and your water—all of it—to turn to blood! The Lord of hosts hath sworn, saying, 'Surely, as I have thought, so it shall come to pass, and as I have purposed, so it shall stand!'"

Rayford wanted to shout. He hoped Buck and Tsion were watching this. The two witnesses warned Carpathia to stay away from those among the 144,000 coming to Israel for inspiration. No wonder Nicolae had been seething. Surely he saw himself as the one who sits on the throne of the earth.

Rayford appreciated that Mac did not try to dissuade him from his mission. He had never been more determined to finish a task. He and Mac latched their gear to the struts for the short hop from New Babylon to the Tigris. Rayford strapped himself in and pointed toward Baghdad. By the time they landed, the sky was dark.

"You don't have to do this with me, you know," Rayford

said. "No hard feelings if you just want to keep an eye out for me."

"Not a chance, brother. I'll be right there with you."

They unloaded at a steep bank. Rayford stripped down, pulled on his wet suit and booties, and stretched the rubber cap over his head. Had the suit been any smaller, it would not have worked. "Did I get yours?" he asked.

"Albie says one size fits all."

"Terrific."

When they were completely outfitted with eighty-cubic-foot tanks, buoyancy control devices (BCDs), weight belts, and fins, they fog-proofed their masks with spit and pulled them on.

"I believe in my heart she's not down there," Rayford said.

"I know," Mac said.

They inspected each other's gear, inflated their BCDs, stuffed in their mouthpieces, then slid down the sandy bank into the cold, rushing water, and slipped beneath the surface.

Rayford had only guessed where the 747 dropped into the river. While he agreed with Pan-Con officials who told Carpathia the plane was too heavy to have been affected much by the current, he believed it could have gone dozens of feet downstream before embedding itself in the bottom. Because no vestige of the plane had ever surfaced, Rayford was convinced the fuselage had holes front and back. That would have resulted in the plane hitting the bottom rather than being held aloft by air pockets.

The water was murky. Rayford was a good diver, but he was still claustrophobic when unable to see more than a few feet, even with the powerful light strapped to his wrist. It seemed to shine no more than ten feet in front of him. Mac's was even dimmer and suddenly disappeared.

Did Mac have bad equipment, or had he turned his off for some reason? It made no sense. The last thing Rayford wanted was to lose sight of his partner. They could spend too much time searching for the wreckage and have little time to investigate it.

Rayford watched clouds of sand shoot past and realized what had happened. Mac had been pulled downstream. He was far enough ahead that neither could see the other's light.

Rayford tried to steer himself. It only made sense that the lower he went, the less the current would pull him. He let more air out of his BCD and kicked harder to dive, peeling his eyes to see past the end of his beam. Ahead a dim, blinking light appeared stationary. How could Mac have stopped?

As the blinking beam grew larger and stronger, Rayford kicked hard, laboring to align himself with Mac's light. He was coming fast when the top of his head smacked violently into Mac's tank. Mac hooked Rayford's elbow in the crook of his own arm and held firm. Mac had snagged a tree root. His mask was half off and his regulator mouthpiece was out. With one arm holding Rayford and the other gripping the root, he wasn't free to help himself.

Rayford grabbed the root, allowing Mac to let go of him.

Mac reinserted his regulator and cleared his mask. Dangling in the current, each with a hand on the root, they were unable to communicate. Rayford felt the spot on his head where he had banged into Mac's tank. A flap of rubber rose from his cap; a matching patch of skin and hair had been gouged from his scalp.

Mac pointed his light toward Rayford's head and motioned him to lean over. Rayford didn't know what Mac saw, but Mac signaled to the surface. Rayford shook his head, which made his wound throb.

Mac pushed away from the root, inflated his BCD, and rose to the top. Rayford reluctantly followed. In that current, he could do nothing without Mac. Rayford popped out of the water in time to see Mac reach an outcropping on the bank. Rayford labored to join him. When they had raised their masks and snorkels, Mac spoke quickly.

"I'm not trying to talk you out of your mission, Ray. But I am telling you we have to work together. See how far we've come from the chopper already?" Rayford was stunned to see the dim outline of the helicopter way upriver.

"If we don't find the plane soon, that means we're probably already past it. The lights don't help much. We're going to have to be lucky."

"We're going to have to pray," Rayford said.

"And you're gonna have to get that head treated. You're bleeding."

Rayford felt his head again and shined the light on his fingers. "It's not serious, Mac. Now let's get back to it."

"We've got one shot. We need to stay close to the bank until we're ready to search in the middle. Once we get out there, we'll be going fast. If the plane is there, we could run right into it. If it's not, we've got to get back to the bank. I'm going to wait for your lead, Ray. You follow me while I'm navigating the edge of the river. I'll follow you when you signal me it's time to venture out."

"How will *I* know?"

"You're the one doing the praying."

CHAPTER 19

IT WAS JUST BEFORE one o'clock in the afternoon in Mt. Prospect. Tsion had spent the morning logging another long message to the faithful and to the seekers on the Internet. The number of messages back to him continued to spiral. He called out to Buck, who trotted upstairs and looked over his shoulder at the quantity meter.

"So," Buck said, "it's finally slowed?"

"I knew you would say that, Cameron," Tsion said, smiling. "A message came across at four this morning explaining that the server would now flash a new number not for every response but for every thousand."

Buck shook his head and stared as the number changed every one to two seconds. "Tsion, this is astounding."

"It is a miracle, Cameron. I am humbled and yet energized. God fills me with love for every person who stands with us, and especially for all who have questions. I remind them that almost anywhere you click on our bulletin board, you find the plan of salvation. The only problem is, because it is not our own Web site, all this has to be posted new every week."

Buck put a hand on the rabbi's shoulder. "It won't be long before the mass meetings in Israel. I pray God's protection for you."

"I feel such boldness—not based on my own strength, but on the promises of God—that I believe I could walk alone to the Temple Mount without being harmed."

"I'm not going to let you try that, Tsion, but you're probably right."

"Here, look, Cameron." Tsion clicked onto the icon allowing him to see the two witnesses at the Wailing Wall. "I long to talk with them again in person. I feel a kinship even though they are supernatural beings, come from heaven. We will spend eternity with them, hearing the stories of God's miracles from people who were there."

Buck was fascinated. The two preached when they wanted to and fell silent when they chose. Crowds knew to keep their distance. Anyone trying to harm them had dropped dead or had been incinerated by fire from the witnesses' mouths. And yet Buck and Tsion had stood within a few feet of them, only a fence separating them. It seemed they spoke in riddles, yet God always gave Buck understanding. As he watched now,

Eli sat in Jerusalem's gathering darkness with his back to an abandoned room made of stone. It looked as if guards may have once used it. Two heavy iron doors were sealed, and a small barred opening served as a window. Moishe stood, facing the fence that separated him from spectators. None was within thirty feet. His feet were spread, his arms straight at his sides. He did not move. It appeared Moishe was not blinking. He looked like something carved from stone, save for the occasional wisp of hair ruffling in the breeze.

Eli shifted his weight occasionally. He massaged his forehead, making him appear to be thinking or praying.

Tsion glanced at Buck. "You are doing what I do. When I need a break, I go to this site and watch my brothers. I love to catch them preaching. They are so bold, so forthright. They do not use Antichrist's name, but they warn enemies of the Messiah of what is to come. They will be so inspiring to those of the 144,000 who can make it to Israel. We will join hands. We will sing. We will pray. We will study. We will be motivated to go forth with boldness to preach the gospel of Christ around the world. The fields are ripe and white unto harvest. We missed the opportunity to join Christ in the air, but what an unspeakable privilege to be alive during this time! Many of us will give our lives for our Savior, but what higher calling could a man have?"

"You should say that to your cyberspace congregation."

"As a matter of fact, I was reciting the conclusion of today's message. Now you do not have to read it."

"I never miss."

"Today I am warning believers and nonbelievers alike to stay away from trees and grass until the first Trumpet Judgment is passed."

Buck looked at him quizzically. "And how will we know it has passed?"

"It will be the biggest news since the earthquake. We need to ask Ken and Floyd to help us clear several feet of grass from around the house and maybe trim some trees."

"You take the predictions literally then?" Buck said.

"My dear brother, when the Bible is figurative, it sounds figurative. When it says all the grass and one-third of all trees will be scorched, I cannot imagine what that might be symbolic for. In the event our trees are part of the one-third, I want to be out of the way. Do you not?"

"Where are Donny's garden tools?"

The Tigris was not frigid, but it was uncomfortable. Rayford used muscles he hadn't used in years. His wet suit was too tight, his head throbbed, and keeping from being dragged downriver made navigating a chore. His pulse was higher than it should have been, and he worked hard to regulate his breathing. He worried about running out of air.

He disagreed with Mac. They may have only one shot, but if they didn't find the plane that night, Rayford would come back again and again. He wouldn't ask Mac to do the same, though he knew Mac would never abandon him.

Rayford prayed as he felt his way along behind Mac. Mac eased himself lower by releasing air from his BCD, and Rayford followed. When either Rayford or Mac went more than ten feet without something to grip on the side, the current threatened to pull them away from the bank.

Rayford worked hard to stay with Mac. "Please, God, help me finish this. Show me she isn't there, and then direct me to her. If she's in danger, let me save her." Rayford fought to keep from his mind the possibility that Carpathia had been telling the truth about Amanda's true loyalties. He didn't want to believe it, not for a second, but the thought nagged him nonetheless.

While the souls of bodies in the Tigris were either in heaven or in hell, Rayford sensed he was to leave every one in the plane. *If* he found any. Was that feeling a signal from God that they were near the wreck? Rayford considered tapping Mac's trailing fin, but he waited.

The plane had to have hit with enough force to immediately kill everyone on board. Otherwise, passengers would have been able to unstrap and get out through holes in the fuselage or doors and windows that had burst open. But no corpses had surfaced.

Rayford knew the wings would have been sheared off, and perhaps the tail. These planes were marvels of aerodynamics, but they were not indestructible. He dreaded seeing the result of such an impact.

Rayford was surprised to see Mac two or three feet from the bank now, not holding onto anything. Apparently they were low enough that the powerful current was diminished. Mac stopped and checked his pressure gauge. Rayford did the same and gave a thumbs-up. Mac pointed to his head. Rayford gave the OK sign, though his head was only so-so. He moved ahead, leading the way. They were within six feet of the bottom now. Rayford sensed he would soon find what he was looking for. He prayed he would not find what he did not wish to find.

Away from the sidewall of the river, less muck was stirred with their movements, and their lights had more range. Rayford's picked up something, and he put up a hand to stop Mac. Despite the relative calm, they angled toward the side to keep from drifting. Both shined lights where Rayford indicated. There, bigger than life, was the huge, wholly intact right wing of a 747. Rayford fought for composure.

Rayford scanned the area. Not far ahead they found the left wing, also intact except for a huge tear from the flaps to where it had connected to the plane. Rayford guessed they'd find the tail section next. Witnesses said the plane went in nose first, which would have brought the back of the plane down with such force that the tail should have been ripped apart or broken off.

Rayford stayed low and moved approximately midway between where they had found the wings. Mac grabbed Rayford's ankle just before Rayford collided with the gigantic tail of the plane. It had been severed. The plane itself had to be dead ahead. Rayford moved twenty feet ahead of the tail and turned upright so he was almost standing on the bottom.

When one of his fins touched he realized how mushy it was and how dangerous it would be to get stuck.

It was Buck's turn to feed Hattie, who had become so weak she could barely move. Dr. Charles was on his way.

Buck spoke softly as he spooned soup to her lips. "Hattie, we all love you and your baby. We want only the best for you. You've heard Dr. Ben-Judah's teaching. You know what's been foretold and what's already happened. There's no way you can deny that the prophecies of the Word of God have been fulfilled from the day of the disappearances until now. What will it take to convince you? How much more proof do you need? Bad as these times are, God is making clear that there is only one choice. You're either on his side or you're on the side of evil. Don't let it get to where you or your baby are killed in one of the judgments to come."

Hattie pressed her lips together and refused the next offering of soup. "I don't need any more convincing, Buck," she whispered.

Chloe hobbled over. "Should I get Tsion?"

Buck shook his head, keeping his eyes on Hattie. He leaned close to hear her. "I know this all has to be true," she managed. "If I needed more convincing, I'd have to be the biggest skeptic in history."

Chloe brushed Hattie's hair away from her forehead and tucked the bangs up. "She's really hot, Buck."

"Crumble some Tylenol in this soup."

Hattie seemed to be sleeping, but Buck was worried. What a waste if they somehow lost her when she was this close to a decision for Christ. "Hattie, if you know it's true, if you believe, all you have to do is receive God's gift. Just agree with him that you're a sinner like everyone else and that you need his forgiveness. Do it, Hattie. Make sure of it."

She appeared to be struggling to open her eyes. Her lips parted and then closed. She held a breath, as if to speak, but she did not. Finally, she whispered again. "I want that, Buck. I really do. But you don't know what I've done."

"It doesn't make any difference, Hattie. Even people who were raptured with Christ were just sinners saved by grace. No one is perfect. We've all done awful things."

"Not like me," she said.

"God wants to forgive you."

Chloe returned with a spoonful of crushed Tylenol and stirred it into the soup. Buck waited, praying silently. "Hattie," he said gently, "you need more of this soup. We put medicine in it for you."

Tears slid down Hattie's cheeks, and her eyes closed. "Just let me die," she said.

"No!" Chloe said. "You promised to be my baby's godmother."

"You don't want somebody like me for that," Hattie said.

"You're not going to die," Chloe said. "You're my friend, and I want you for a sister."

"I'm too old to be your sister," she said.

"Too late. You can't back out now."

Buck got some soup down her. "You want Jesus, don't you?" he whispered, his lips near her ear.

He waited a long time for her response. "I want him, but he couldn't want me."

"He does," Chloe said. "Hattie, please. You know we're telling you the truth. The same God that fulfills prophecies centuries old loves you and wants you. Don't say no to him."

"I'm not saying no to him. He's saying no to me."

Chloe tugged at Hattie's wrist. Buck looked at her in surprise. "Help me sit her up, Buck."

"Chloe! She can't."

"She has to be able to think and listen, Buck. We can't let her go."

Buck took Hattie's other wrist, and they pulled until she sat up. She pressed her fingers against her temples and sat moaning.

"Listen to me," Chloe said. "The Bible says God is not willing that *any* should perish. Are you the one person in history who did something so bad that not even the God of the universe can forgive you? If God forgives only minor sins, there's no hope for any of us. Whatever you've done, God is like the father of the Prodigal Son, scanning the horizon. He stands with his arms wide open, waiting for you."

Hattie rocked and shook her head. "I've done bad things," she said.

Buck looked at Chloe, helpless, wondering.

It was worse than Rayford could have imagined. He came upon the colossal fuselage, its nose and a quarter of its length buried in the muck of the Tigris at a forty-five-degree angle. The wheel housings were gone. Rayford could only dread what he and Mac were about to see. Everything in that plane, from equipment to carry-on luggage, seats and seat backs, tray tables, phones, and even passengers, would be in one massive heap at the front. An impact violent enough to snap landing gear from a plane would immediately break the neck of any passenger. The seats would have ripped from the floor and accordioned atop each other, passengers stacked upon each other like cord-wood. Everything attached would have broken loose and been forced to the front.

Rayford wished he at least knew what seat Amanda was supposed to have been in, so he could save the time of digging through the entire wreckage to rule her out as a victim. Where to start? Rayford pointed up to the protruding tail end, and Mac followed him as they ascended.

Rayford grabbed the edge of an open window to keep from being pulled by the current. He shined his light into the cabin, and his worst fears were confirmed. All Rayford could make out in that back section was bare floor, walls, and ceiling. Everything had been driven to the other end.

He and Mac used the windows as grips to pull themselves down at least fifty feet to the top of the debris. The rear lavatories, storage compartments, walls, and overhead bins lay atop everything else.

Hattie hung her head. Buck worried they were pushing her too far. Yet he would have a hard time forgiving himself if he didn't give her every opportunity and something happened to her.

"Do I have to tell him everything I've done?" Hattie breathed.

"He already knows," Chloe said. "If it makes you feel better to tell him, then tell him."

"I don't want to say it out loud," Hattie said. "It's more than affairs with men. It's even more than wanting an abortion!"

"But you didn't go through with it," Chloe said.

"Nothing is beyond God's power to forgive," Buck said. "Believe me, I know."

Hattie sat shaking her head. Buck was relieved to hear the doctor drive in. Floyd examined Hattie quickly and helped her lie down. He asked about medication, and they told him of the Tylenol. "She needs more," he said. "Her temperature is higher than you reported just a few hours ago. She'll be delirious soon. I need to find whatever is causing the fever."

"How bad is it?"

"I'm not optimistic."

Hattie was moaning, trying to talk. Dr. Charles held up a

finger to keep Buck and Chloe away. "You and Tsion might want to pray for her right now," the doctor said.

Rayford wondered about the wisdom of swimming through hundreds of corpses, especially with an open wound. Well, he figured, whatever might contaminate him had already done so. He worked feverishly with Mac to start removing the debris. They kicked wider a gash in the hull between two windows, through which they painstakingly pushed chunks of the interior.

When they reached an unusually heavy panel, Rayford got beneath it and pushed. He quickly realized what added the weight. It had been the rear seat for the flight attendant. She was still strapped in, hands balled into fists, eyes open, long hair floating free. The men gently set the panel aside. Rayford noticed Mac's light was dimmer.

That panel had protected the bodies from fish. Rayford wondered what they were subjecting these corpses to now. He shined his light through the mass of tangled seats and trash. Everyone had been strapped in. Every seat appeared occupied. No one could have suffered long.

Mac smacked his light and the beam grew brighter. He shined it into the carnage, touched Rayford's shoulder, and shook his head as if to say they should not go farther. Rayford couldn't blame him, but he couldn't quit. He knew beyond doubt that the search would put him at ease about

Amanda. He had to go through this grisly ordeal for his own peace of mind.

Rayford pointed to Mac and then to the surface. Then he pointed to the bodies and smacked himself on the chest as if to say, you go and I'll stay.

Mac shook his head slowly as if disgusted. But he didn't go anywhere. They began lifting bodies, belted into seats.

Buck helped Chloe up the stairs, where they met with Tsion to pray for Hattie. When they finished, Tsion showed them that Carpathia had become his computer competition. "He must be jealous of the response," Tsion said sadly. "Look at this."

Carpathia communicated to the masses in a series of short messages. Each sang the praises of the rebuilding forces. They encouraged people to show their devotion to the Enigma Babylon faith. Some reiterated the Global Community's pledge to protect Rabbi Ben-Judah from zealots, should he choose to return to his homeland.

"Look what I put in response to that," Ben-Judah said.

Buck peered at the screen. Tsion had written, "Potentate Carpathia: I gratefully accept your offer of personal protection and congratulate you that this makes you an instrument of the one true, living God. He has promised to seal and protect his own during this season when we are commissioned to preach his gospel to the world. We are grateful that he has apparently chosen you as our protector and wonder how you feel about it. In the name of Jesus Christ, the Messiah and our Lord and Savior, Rabbi Tsion Ben-Judah, in exile."

"It won't be long now, Tsion," Buck said.

"I just hope I can go," Chloe said.

"I didn't think there was an option," Buck said.

"I'm thinking of Hattie," she said. "I can't leave her unless she's healthy."

They made their way back downstairs. Hattie was asleep, but her breathing was labored, her face flushed, her forehead damp. Chloe dabbed at her face with a cool washcloth. Dr. Charles stood at the back door, gazing through the screen.

"Can you stay with us tonight?" Buck asked.

"I wish I could. Actually, I wish I could take Hattie for care. But she's so recognizable, we wouldn't get far. After that caper in Minneapolis, I'm being looked upon with suspicion myself. I'm being watched more and more."

"If you have to go, you have to go."

"Take a look at the sky," the doctor said.

Buck stepped closer and looked out. The sun still rode high, but dark clouds formed on the horizon.

"Great," Buck said. "What will rain do to the ruts we call roads?"

"I'd better check on Hattie and get going."

"How did you get her to sleep?"

"That fever knocked her out. I gave her enough Tylenol to dent it, but watch for dehydration."

Buck didn't respond. He was studying the sky.

"Buck?"

He turned. "Yeah."

"She was moaning and mumbling about something she feels guilty about."

"I know."

"You do?"

"We were urging her to receive Christ, and she said she wasn't worthy. She's done some things, she says, and she can't accept that God would still love her."

"Did she tell you what those things were?"

"No."

"Then I shouldn't say."

"If it's something you think I should know, let's have it."

"It's crazy."

"Nothing would surprise me anymore."

"She's carrying a tremendous load of guilt about Amanda and Bruce Barnes. Amanda is Chloe's father's wife?"

"Yeah, and I told you all about Bruce. What about them?"

"She cried, telling me that she and Amanda were going to fly together from Boston to Baghdad. When Hattie told Amanda she was changing plans and flying to Denver, Amanda insisted on going with her. Hattie kept telling me, 'Amanda knew I had no relatives in Denver. She thought she knew what I was up to. And she was right.' She told me Amanda actually canceled her reservation for Baghdad and was on her way to the counter to buy a ticket to Denver on Hattie's plane. Hattie pleaded with her not to do this. The only way she could keep Amanda from going was to swear that she herself would not go if Amanda tried to accompany her. Amanda made her promise she would not do anything stupid in Denver. Hattie knew she meant not having an abortion. She promised Amanda she would not."

"What's she feeling so bad about?"

"She says Amanda went back to get on the original flight to Baghdad but that it was now sold out. She told Hattie she wasn't interested in waiting on a standby list and that she would still be more than happy to accompany her on her flight west. Hattie refused, and she believes Amanda boarded that plane to Baghdad. She said over and over that she should have been on it too, and she wishes she had been. I told her she shouldn't say things like that and she said, 'Then why couldn't I have let Amanda come with me? She'd still be alive.'"

"You haven't met my father-in-law or Amanda yet, Floyd, but Rayford doesn't believe Amanda got on that plane. We don't know that she did."

"But if she wasn't on that plane and didn't go with Hattie, where is she? Hundreds of thousands died in the earthquake. Realistically, don't you think you would have heard from her by now if she had survived?"

Buck watched the gathering clouds. "I don't know," he said. "It's likely that if she's not dead, she's hurt. Maybe, like Chloe, she can't contact us."

"Maybe. Uh, Buck, there were a couple of other issues."

"Don't hold back."

"Hattie said something about what she knew about Amanda."

Buck froze. Was it possible? He tried to maintain composure. "What was it she supposedly knew?"

"Some secret she should have told but now can't tell."

Buck was afraid he knew what it was. "You said there was something else?"

Now the doctor appeared nervous. "I'd like to attribute this to delirium," he said.

"Shoot."

"I took a blood sample. I'm going to check it for food poisoning. I'm worried that my colleagues in Denver might have poisoned her in advance of the projected hit. I asked her what she had eaten out there, and she caught on to what I suspected. She shuddered and appeared petrified. I helped her lie down. She grabbed my shirt and pulled me close. She said, 'If Nicolae had me poisoned, I'll be his second victim.' I asked what she meant. She said, 'Bruce Barnes. Nicolae had him poisoned overseas. He made it all the way back to the States before he was hospitalized. Everyone thinks he died in the bombing, and maybe he did. But if he wasn't dead already, he would have died even if the hospital had never been bombed. And I knew all about it. I've never told anyone.'"

Buck was shaken. "I only wish you could have met Bruce," he mumbled.

"It would have been an honor. You can know for sure about his death, you know. It's not too late for an autopsy."

"It wouldn't bring him back," Buck said. "But just knowing gives me a reason. . . ."

"A reason?"

"An excuse, anyway. To murder Nicolae Carpathia."

CHAPTER 20

THOUGH WATER PROVIDED nearly the same weightlessness as outer space, pushing debris up and out and displacing rows of seats with bodies attached was grueling. Rayford's light was dim and his air supply low. His scalp wound throbbed, and he felt light-headed. He assumed Mac was in the same shape, but neither signaled any intention of quitting.

Rayford expected to feel awful searching corpses, but deep foreboding overwhelmed him. What a macabre business! Victims were bloated, horribly disfigured, hands in fists, arms floating. Their hair waved with the motion of the water. Most eyes and mouths were open, faces black, red, or purple.

Rayford felt a sense of urgency. Mac tapped him, pointed to his gauge, and held up ten fingers. Rayford tried to work faster, but having checked only sixty or seventy bodies, there was no way he could finish without another air tank. He could work only five more minutes.

Directly below was an intact middle section row. It faced the front of the plane, as did all the others, but had rotated a little farther. All he saw in his fading light were the backs of five heads and the heels of ten feet. Seven shoes had come loose. He had never understood the phenomenon of the contraction of human feet in the face of violent collision. He estimated this row had been driven forward as many as twenty-five feet. He motioned to Mac to grab the armrest at one end while he took the other. Mac held up one finger, as if this needed to be the last effort before they surfaced. Rayford nodded.

As they tried to pull the row upright, it caught something and they had to reposition it and yank again. Mac's end came up slightly ahead of Rayford's, but when Rayford jostled his it finally rotated. The five bodies now rested on their backs. Rayford shined his flickering light into the panic-stricken face of an elderly man in a three-piece suit. The man's bloated hands floated before Rayford's face. He gently nudged them aside and directed his beam to the next passenger. She was salt-and-pepper-haired. Her eyes were open, her expression blank. The neck and face were discolored and swollen, but her arms did not rise as the others. She had apparently grabbed her laptop computer case and hooked its strap in the crook of her arm. Entwining her fingers, she had died with her hands pressed between her knees, the computer bag secure at her side.

Rayford recognized the earrings, the necklace, the jacket. He wanted to die. He could not take his eyes from hers. The irises had lost all color, and her image was one he would fight to forget. Mac hurried to him and gripped a bicep in each hand. Rayford felt his gentle tug. Dazed, he turned to Mac.

Mac tapped urgently on Rayford's tank. Rayford was drifting, having lost sense of what he was doing. He didn't want to move. He suddenly became aware his heart was thudding and he would soon be out of oxygen. He didn't want Mac to know. He was tempted to suck in enough water to flood his lungs and reunite him with his beloved.

It was too much to hope for. He should have known Mac would not have used up his own air supply as quickly. Mac pried apart Amanda's fingers and pulled the case strap over his head so the laptop hung behind his tanks.

Rayford felt Mac behind him, his forearms under his armpits. Rayford wanted to fight him off, but Mac had apparently thought ahead. At Rayford's first hint of resistance, Mac yanked both hands out and pinned Rayford's arms back. Mac kicked mightily and steered them out of the carcass of the 747 and into the rushing current. He made a controlled ascent.

Rayford had lost the will to live. When they broke the surface, he spit out his regulator and with it the sobs gushed out. He cried a fierce, primal wail that pierced the night and reflected the agonizing loneliness of his soul. Mac talked to him, but Rayford was not listening. Mac manhandled him, kicking, staying afloat, dragging him toward the bank. While Rayford's system greedily took in the life-giving air, the rest of him was numb. He wondered if he could swim if he wanted to. But he didn't want to. He felt sorry for Mac, working so hard to push a bigger man up the muddy slope onto the sand.

Rayford continued to bawl, the sound of his despair frightening even himself. But he could not stop. Mac yanked off his own mask and popped out his mouthpiece, then reached for Rayford's. He unstrapped Rayford's tanks and set them aside. Rayford rolled over and lay motionless on his back.

Mac peeled back Rayford's torn headliner to reveal blood inside his suit. With his head and face bare, Rayford's cries turned to moans. Mac sat on his haunches and breathed deeply. Rayford watched like a cat, waiting for him to relax, to step back, to believe this was over.

But it was not over. Rayford had truly believed, truly felt Amanda had survived and that he would be reunited with her. He had been through so much in the last two years, but there had always been grace in just enough measure to keep him sane. Not now. He didn't even want it. Ask God to carry him through? He could not face five more years without Amanda.

Mac stood and began unzipping his own wet suit. Rayford slowly lifted his knees and dug his heels deep into the sand. He pushed so hard he felt the strain deep in both hamstrings as the thrust carried him over the edge. As if in slow motion, Rayford felt cool air on his face as he dropped headfirst into the water. He heard Mac swear and shout, "Oh, no you don't!"

Mac would have to slip off his own tanks before jumping in. Rayford only hoped he could elude him in the dark or be lucky enough to have Mac land on him and knock him unconscious. His body plummeted through the water, then turned and began to rise. He moved not a finger, hoping the Tigris would envelop him forever. But somehow he could not will himself to gulp in the water that would kill him.

He felt the shock and heard Mac splash past him. Mac's hands brushed him as he slid past feet first. Rayford couldn't muster the energy to resist. From deep in his heart came sympathy for Mac, who didn't deserve this. It wasn't fair to make him work so hard. Rayford carried his own weight enough on the way back to the bank to show Mac he was finally cooperating. As he hauled himself up onto the sand again, he fell to his knees and pressed his cheek to the ground.

"I have no answers for you right now, Ray. Just hear me. To die in this river tonight, you're going to have to take me with you. You got that?"

Rayford nodded miserably.

Without another word, Mac pulled Rayford to his feet. He examined Rayford's wound with his fingers in the darkness. He removed Rayford's fins, stacked them with the mask on top of his tanks, and handed the set to Rayford. Mac picked up his own gear and led the way back to the chopper.

There he stored the gear, helped Rayford out of his wet suit like a little boy getting ready for bed, and tossed him a huge towel. They changed into dry clothes.

Without warning, Rayford's punctured scalp felt as if it were being pelted by rocks. He covered his head and bent at the waist but now felt the same sharp stings on his arms, his neck, his back. Had he pushed too far? Had he been foolish to continue a dive with an open wound? He peeked as Mac lurched toward the chopper.

"Get in, Ray! It's hailing!"

Buck had always enjoyed storms. At least before he lived through the wrath of the Lamb. As a boy he had sat before the picture window in his Tucson home and watched the rare thunderstorm. Something about the weather since the Rapture, however, spooked him.

Dr. Charles left instructions on how to care for Hattie, then departed for Kenosha. As the afternoon steadily grew darker, Chloe found extra blankets for the dozing Hattie while Tsion and Buck closed windows.

"I am taking only half a risk," Tsion said. "I am going to run my computer on batteries until the storm passes, but I will remain connected somehow."

Buck laughed. "For once I am able to correct the brilliant scholar," he said. "You forget we are running the electricity on a gas-powered generator, unlikely to be affected by the storm.

Your phone line is connected to the dish on the roof, the highest point here. If you are worried about lightning, you'd be better to disconnect the phone and connect the power."

"I will never be mistaken for an electrician," Tsion said, shaking his head. "The truth is, I need not be connected to the Internet for a few hours either." He went upstairs.

Buck and Chloe sat next to each other at the foot of Hattie's bed. "She sleeps too much," Chloe said. "And she's so pale."

Buck was lost in his thoughts of the dark secrets that burdened Hattie. What would Rayford think of the possibility that Bruce had been poisoned? Rayford always said it was strange how peaceful Bruce looked compared to the other victims of the bombing. Doctors had come to no conclusions about the illness he had brought back from the Third World. Who would have dreamed Carpathia might be behind that?

Buck also still struggled with his killing of the Global Community guard. The video had been shown over and over on television news channels. He couldn't bear to see it again, though Chloe insisted it was clear from the tape he had had no choice. "More people would have died, Buck," she said. "And one of them would have been you."

It was true. He could come to no other conclusion. Why couldn't he feel a sense of satisfaction or even accomplishment from it? He was not a battle-minded man. And yet here he was on the front lines.

Buck took Chloe's hand and pulled her close. She laid her cheek on his chest, and he brushed the hair from her wounded face. Her eye, still swollen shut and morbidly discolored, seemed to be improving. He touched her forehead with his lips and whispered, "I love you with my whole heart."

Buck glanced at Hattie. She had not moved for an hour. And the hail came.

Buck and Chloe stood and watched out the window as the tiny balls of ice bounced in the yard. Tsion hurried downstairs. "Oh, my! Look at this!"

The sky grew black, and the hailstones got bigger. Only slightly smaller than golf balls now, they rattled against the roof, clanged off the downspouts, thundered on the Range Rover, and the power failed. A chirp of protest burst from Tsion, but Buck assured him, "The hail has just knocked the cord out, that's all. Easily fixed."

But as they watched, the sky lit up. But it wasn't lightning. The hailstones, at least half of them, were in flames!

"Oh, dear ones!" Tsion said. "You know what this is, do you not? Let us pull Hattie's bed away from the window just in case! The angel of the first Trumpet Judgment is throwing hail and fire to the earth."

Rayford and Mac had left their scuba equipment on the ground near the chopper. Now protected by the Plexiglas bubble of the tiny cockpit, Rayford felt as if he were inside a popcorn popper. As the hailstones grew, they pinged off the oxygen tanks and drilled the helicopter. Mac started the engine and set the blades turning, but he was going nowhere. He would not leave the scuba equipment, and helicopters and hailstorms did not mix.

"I know you don't want to hear this, Ray," he shouted over the din, "but you need to leave that wreckage and your wife's body right where they lie. I don't like it or understand it any more than you do, but I believe God is going to get you through this. Don't shake your head. I know she was everything to you. But God left you here for a purpose. I need you. Your daughter and son-in-law need you. The rabbi you've told me so much about, he needs you too. All I'm saying is, don't make any decisions when your emotions are raw. We'll get through this together."

Rayford was disgusted with himself, but everything Mac—the brand-new believer—said sounded like so many hollow platitudes. True or not, it wasn't what he wanted to hear. "Tell me the truth, Mac. Did you check her forehead for the sign?"

Mac pursed his lips and did not respond.

"You did, didn't you?" Rayford pressed.

"Yes, I did."

"And it wasn't there, was it?"

"No, it was not."

"What am I supposed to think of that?"

"How should I know, Ray? I wasn't a believer before the earthquake. I don't know that you had a mark on your forehead before that either."

"I probably did!"

"Maybe you did, but didn't Dr. Ben-Judah write later about how believers were starting to notice the sign on each other? That came after the earthquake. If they had died in the quake, they wouldn't have had the mark either. And even if they had it before, how do we know it's still there when we die?"

"If Amanda wasn't a believer, she probably *was* working for Carpathia," Rayford spat. "Mac, I don't think I could handle that."

"Think of David," Mac said. "He'll be looking to us for leadership and guidance, and I'm newer at this than *he* is."

When plummeting tongues of fire joined the hailstones, Rayford just stared. Mac said, "Wow!" over and over. "This is like the ultimate fireworks!"

Huge hailstones plopped into the river and floated downstream. They accumulated on the bank and turned the sand white like snow. Snow in the desert. Flaming darts sizzled and hissed as they hit the water. They made the same sound when they settled atop the hailstones on shore, and they did not burn out right away.

The chopper lights illuminated an area of twenty feet in front of the craft. Mac suddenly unclipped his belt and leaned forward. "What is that, Ray? It's raining, but it's red! Look at that! All over the snow!"

"It's blood," Rayford said, a peace flooding his soul. It did not assuage his grief or take away his dread over the truth about Amanda. But this show, this shower of fire and ice and blood, reminded him yet again that God is faithful. He keeps his promises. While our ways are not his ways and we can never understand him this side of heaven, Rayford was assured again that he was on the side of the army that had already won this war.

Tsion hurried to the back of the house and watched the flames melt the hail and set the grass afire. It burned a few moments, and then more hail put the fire out. The entire yard was black. Balls of fire dropped into the trees that bordered the backyard. They burst into flames as one, their branches sending a giant orange mushroom into the air. The trees cooled as quickly as they had ignited.

"Here comes the blood," Tsion said, and suddenly Hattie sat straight up. She stared out the window as blood poured from the skies. She struggled to kneel on the bed so she could see farther. The parched yard was wet with melted hail and now red with blood.

Lightning cracked and thunder rolled. Softball-size hailstones drummed the roof, rolling and filling the yard. Tsion shouted, "Praise the Lord God Almighty, maker of heaven and earth! What you see before you is a picture of Isaiah 1:18: 'Though your sins are like scarlet, they shall be as white as snow; though they are red like crimson, they shall be as wool.'"

"Did you see it, Hattie?" Chloe asked.

Hattie turned and Buck saw her tears. She nodded but

looked woozy. Buck helped her lie back down, and she was soon asleep.

As the clouds faded and the sun returned, the results of the light show became obvious. The bark on the trees had been blackened, the foliage all burned off. As the hail melted and blood seeped into the ground, the charred grass showed through.

"The Scriptures told us that one-third of the trees and all of the green grass in the world would be burned," Tsion said. "I cannot wait until we have power so we can see what Carpathia's newsmen make of this."

Yet another clear movement of God's hand had moved Buck. He longed for Hattie to stay healthy so she could pursue the truth. Whether Bruce Barnes had been poisoned by Nicolae Carpathia or had lost his life in the first volley of bombs in World War III made little difference in the larger scheme of things. But if Hattie Durham had information about Amanda that could confirm or deny what Tsion had stumbled onto in Bruce's computer files, Buck wanted to hear it.

Mac left the chopper running, but Rayford was cold. With nothing green to scorch in that part of the world, the fire and blood had been overcome by the hail. The result was the chilliest night in the history of the Iraqi desert.

"Stay put," Mac said. "I'll get the stuff."

Rayford reached for the door handle. "That's all right, I'll do my share."

"No! Now I mean it. Just let me do this."

Rayford wouldn't admit it, but he was grateful. He stayed inside as Mac sloshed in the melting hail. He stored the scuba equipment behind the seats. When he reboarded he had Amanda's waterlogged laptop computer.

"What's the point, Mac? Those things aren't waterproof."

"True," Mac said. "Your screen is shot, your solar panels are ruined, your keyboard won't function, the motherboard is gone. You name it, that much water had to kill it. Except for the hard drive. It is encased and waterproof. Experts can run a diagnostic and copy any files you want."

"I don't expect any surprises."

"I'm sorry to be blunt, Rayford," Mac said, "but you didn't expect to see her in the Tigris. If I were you, I'd look for evidence to prove Amanda was everything you thought she was."

Rayford wasn't sure. "I'd have to use someone I know, like David Hassid or someone else I can trust."

"That narrows it to David and me, yes."

"If it's bad news, I couldn't let a stranger discover it before I do. Why don't you handle it, Mac? In the meantime, I don't even want to think about it. If I do, I'm going to break your confidence and go straight to Carpathia and demand he clear Amanda's name with anybody he ever talked to about her."

"You can't do that, Ray."

"I might not be able to help myself if I have exclusive access to that computer. Just do it for me and give me the results."

"I'm not an expert, Ray. How about if I supervise David, or let him run me through it? We won't look at one file. We'll just find whatever is available."

⌇

Nicolae Carpathia announced a postponement of travel due to "the strange natural phenomenon" and its effect on airport reconstruction. Over the next few weeks, as the expanded Chicago contingent of the Tribulation Force grew closer to their departure date for Israel, Buck was dumbfounded at the improvement in Chloe. Floyd Charles took her casts off, and within a few days, atrophied muscles began to come back. It appeared she might always have a limp, residual pain, and a slightly cockeyed face and frame. But to Buck, she had never looked better. All she talked about was going to Israel to see the incredible mass rally of the witnesses.

The first twenty-five thousand to arrive would meet with Tsion in Teddy Kollek Stadium. The rest would gather at sites all over the Holy Land, watching on closed-circuit television. Tsion told Buck he planned to invite Moishe and Eli to join him in the stadium.

Following God's shower of hail, fire, and blood, remaining skeptics were few. There was no longer any ambiguity about the war. The world was taking sides.

Rayford's head healed quickly, but he still had an aching heart. He spent his days mourning, praying, studying, following Tsion's teaching carefully on the Internet, and e-mailing Buck and Chloe every day.

He also kept his mind occupied with route plans, mentoring David Hassid, and discipling Mac. For the first few days, of course, their roles had been reversed as Mac helped Rayford through the worst period of grief. Rayford had to admit God gave him just enough strength for each day. No extra, none to invest for the future, but sufficient for each day.

Nearly a month from the night Rayford had discovered Amanda's body, David Hassid presented him with a high-tech disk with all of Amanda's computer files listed. "They're all encrypted and therefore inaccessible without decoding," David told him.

Rayford was so quiet around Carpathia and Fortunato, even when pressed into flying them here and there, that he believed they had become bored with him. Perfect. Until God released him from this assignment, he would simply endure it.

He was astonished at the progress of rebuilding around the world. Carpathia had troops humming, opening roads, airstrips, cities, trade routes, everything. The balance of travel, commerce, and government had shifted to the Middle East, Iraq, New Babylon, the capital of the world.

People around the world begged to know God. Their requests flooded the Internet, and Tsion, Chloe, and Buck worked day and night corresponding with new converts and planning the huge Holy Land event.

Hattie did not improve. Dr. Charles looked into a secret medical facility but finally told Buck he would take care of her where she was while Buck and the others were in Israel. It would be risky for them both, and she might have to occasionally be alone longer than he was comfortable with, but it was the best he could come up with.

Buck and Chloe prayed for Hattie every day. Chloe confided in Buck, "The only thing that will keep me from going is if Hattie has not received Christ first. I can't leave her in that state."

Buck had his own reasons for wishing she would revive. Her salvation was paramount, of course, but he needed to know things only she could tell him.

Through his own observation and the input of David Hassid, Rayford saw how enraged Carpathia was with Tsion Ben-Judah, the two witnesses, the upcoming conference, and especially the massive groundswell of interest in Christ.

Carpathia had always been motivated and disciplined, but now it was clear he was on a mission. His eyes were wild, his face taut. He rose early every day and worked late every night. Rayford hoped he would work himself into a frenzy. *Your day is coming,* Rayford thought, *and I hope God lets me pull the trigger.*

Two days before their scheduled departure for the Holy Land, the beeping of his computer awakened Buck. A message from Rayford said, "It's happening! Turn on the TV. This is going to be some ride!"

Buck tiptoed downstairs and flipped on the television, finding an all-news station. As soon as he saw what was going on, he woke up everyone in the house except Hattie. He told Chloe, Tsion, and Ken, "It's almost noon in New Babylon, and I've just heard from Rayford. Follow me."

Newscasters told the story of what astronomers had discovered just two hours before—a brand-new comet on a collision course with Earth. Global Community scientists analyzed data transmitted from hastily launched probes that circled the object. They said *meteor* was the wrong term for the hurtling rock formation, which was the consistency of chalk or perhaps sandstone.

Pictures from the probes showed an irregularly shaped projectile, light in color. The anchorman reported, "Ladies and gentlemen, I urge you to put this in perspective. This object is about to enter Earth's atmosphere. Scientists have not determined its makeup, but if—as it appears—it *is* less dense than granite, the friction resulting from entry will make it burst into flames.

"Once subject to Earth's gravitational pull, it will accelerate at thirty-two feet per second squared. As you can see from these pictures, it is immense. But until you realize its size, you cannot fathom the potential destruction on the way. GC astronomers estimate it at no less than the mass of the entire Appalachian Mountain range. It has the potential to split the earth or to knock it from its orbit.

"The Global Community Aeronautics and Space Administration projects the collision at approximately 9:00 a.m., Central Standard Time. They anticipate the best possible scenario, that it will take place in the middle of the Atlantic Ocean.

"Tidal waves are expected to engulf coasts on both sides of the Atlantic for up to fifty miles inland. Coastal areas are being evacuated as we speak. Crews of oceangoing vessels are being plucked from their ships by helicopters, though it is unknown how many can be moved to safety in time. Experts agree the impact on marine life will be inestimable.

"His Excellency Potentate Nicolae Carpathia has issued a statement verifying that his personnel could not have known earlier about this phenomenon. While Potentate Carpathia says he is confident he has the firepower to destroy the object, he has been advised that the unpredictability of fragments is too great a risk, especially considering that the falling mountain is on course to land in the ocean."

The Tribulation Force went to their computers to spread the word that this was the second Trumpet Judgment foretold in Revelation 8:8-9. "Will we look like expert prognosticators when the results are in?" Tsion wrote. "Will it shock the powers that be to discover that, just as the Bible says, one-third of the fish will die and one-third of the ships at sea will sink, and tidal waves will wreak havoc on the entire world? Or will officials reinterpret the event to make it appear the Bible was wrong? Do not be fooled! Do not delay! Now is the accepted time. Now is the day of salvation. Come to Christ before it is too late. Things will only get worse. We were all left behind the first time. Do not be left wanting when you breathe your last."

The Global Community military positioned camera-toting aircraft strategically to film the most spectacular splash in history. The more than thousand-mile-square mountain, finally determined to consist largely of sulfur, burst into flames upon entry to the atmosphere. It eclipsed the sun, blew clouds out of its path, and created hurricane-force winds between itself and the surface of the sea for the last hour it dropped from the heavens. When it finally resounded on the surface of the deep, geysers, waterspouts, and typhoons miles high were displaced, rocketing from the ocean and downing several of the GC planes. Those able to film the result produced such incredible images that they would air around the clock on TV for weeks.

Damage inland was so extensive that nearly all modes of travel were interrupted. The Israel rally of the Jewish witnesses was postponed ten weeks.

The two witnesses at the Wailing Wall went on the offensive, threatening to continue the Holy Land drought they had maintained since the day of the signing of the covenant between the Antichrist and Israel. They promised rivers of blood in retaliation for any threat to God's sealed evangelists. Then, in a comical display of power, they called upon God to let it rain only on the Temple Mount for seven minutes. From a cloudless sky came a warm downpour that turned the dust to mud and brought Israelis running from their homes. They lifted hands and faces and stuck out their tongues. They laughed and sang and danced over what this miracle would mean to their crops. But seven minutes later it stopped and evaporated, and the mud turned to dust and blew away.

"Woe unto you, mockers of the one true God!" Eli and Moishe shouted. "Until the due time, when God allows us to be felled and later returns us to his side, you shall have no power over us or over those God has called to proclaim his name throughout the earth!"

Rayford had at first been warmed by the commiseration of Chloe and Buck and Tsion in his grief over Amanda. But as he extolled her virtues in e-mailed memories, their responses were tepid. Was it possible they had been exposed to Carpathia's innuendoes? Surely they knew and loved Amanda enough to believe she was innocent.

The day finally came when Rayford received from Buck a long, tentative message. It concluded, "Our patient has rallied enough to be able to share troubling secrets of the past that have kept said patient from taking a vital step with the Creator. This information is most alarming and revealing. Only face-to-face can we discuss it, and so we urge you to coordinate a personal meeting as soon as feasible."

Rayford felt as low as he had in ages. What could that message mean other than that Hattie had shed light on the charges about Amanda? Unless Hattie could prove those charges bogus, Rayford was in no hurry to meet face-to-face.

Just days before the rescheduled departure of the Tribulation Force for Israel, the GCASA again detected a threat in the heavens. This object was similar in size to the previous burning mountain but had the consistency of rotting wood. Carpathia, eager to turn the attention from Christ and Tsion Ben-Judah to himself again, pledged to blast it from the skies.

With great fanfare, the press showed the launch of a colossal ground-to-air nuclear missile designed to vaporize the new threat. As the whole world watched, the flaming meteor the Bible called Wormwood split itself into billions of pieces before the missile arrived. The residue wafted down for hours and landed in one-third of the fountains, springs, and rivers of the earth, turning the water a bitter poison. Thousands would die from drinking it.

Carpathia once again announced his decision to delay the Israel conference. But Tsion Ben-Judah would not hear of it. He posted on the Internet bulletin board his response and urged as many of the 144,000 witnesses as possible to converge on Israel the following week.

"Mr. Carpathia," he wrote, purposely not using any other titles, "we will be in Jerusalem as scheduled, with or without your approval, permission, or promised protection. The glory of the Lord will be our rear guard."

The list of encrypted files from Amanda's hard drive evidenced extensive correspondence between her and Nicolae Carpathia. Much as Rayford dreaded it, his desire grew to decode those files. Tsion had told him of Donny's program that unveiled material from Bruce's files. If Rayford could get to Israel when the rest of the Tribulation Force was there, he might finally get to the bottom of the ugly mystery.

Wouldn't his own daughter and son-in-law put his mind at ease? Every day he felt worse, convinced that regardless of the truth or anything he could say to dissuade them, his own loved ones had been swayed. He had not come right out and asked their opinions. He didn't have to. If they were still standing with him—and with the memory of his wife—he would know.

Rayford believed the only way to exonerate Amanda was to decode her files, but he also knew the risk. He would have to face whatever they revealed. Did he want the truth, regardless? The more he prayed about that, the more convinced he became that he must not fear the truth.

What he learned would affect how he functioned for the rest of the Tribulation. If the woman who had shared his life had fooled him, whom could he trust? If he was that bad a judge of character, what good was he to the cause? Maddening doubts filled him, but he became obsessed with knowing. Either way, lover or liar, wife or witch, he had to know.

The morning before the start of the most talked-about mass meeting in the world, Rayford approached Carpathia in his office.

"Your Excellency," he began, swallowing any vestige of pride, "I'm assuming you'll need Mac and me to get you to Israel tomorrow."

"Talk to me about this, Captain Steele. They are meeting against my wishes, so I had planned not to sanction it with my presence."

"But your promise of protection—"

"Ah, that resonated with you, did it not?"

"You know well where I stand."

"And you also know that I tell you where to fly, not vice versa. Do you not think that if I wanted to be in Israel tomorrow I would have told you before this?"

"So, those who wonder if you are afraid of the scholar who—"

"Afraid!"

"—showed you up on the Internet and called your bluff before an international audience—"

"You are trying to bait me, Captain Steele," Carpathia said, smiling.

"Frankly, I believe you know you will be upstaged in Israel by the two witnesses and by Dr. Ben-Judah."

"The two witnesses? If they do not stop their black magic, the drought, and the blood, they will answer to me."

"They say you can't harm them until the due time."

"I will decide the due time."

"And yet Israel was protected from the earthquake and the meteors—"

"You believe the witnesses are responsible for that?"

"I believe God is."

"Tell me, Captain Steele. Do you still believe that a man who has been known to raise the dead could actually be the Antichrist?"

Rayford hesitated, wishing Tsion was in the room. "The enemy has been known to imitate miracles," he said. "Imagine the audience in Israel if you were to do something like that. Here are people of faith coming together for inspiration. If you are God, if you could be the Messiah, wouldn't they be thrilled to meet you?"

Carpathia stared at Rayford, seeming to study his eyes. Rayford believed God. He had faith that regardless of his power, regardless of his intentions, Nicolae would be impotent in the face of any of the 144,000 witnesses who carried the seal of almighty God on their foreheads.

"If you are suggesting," Carpathia said carefully, "that it only makes sense that the Global Community Potentate bestow upon those guests a regal welcome second to none, you may have a point."

Rayford had said nothing of the sort, but Carpathia heard what he wanted to hear. "Thank you," Rayford said.

"Captain Steele, schedule that flight."

EPILOGUE

Then I saw another angel ascending from the east, having the seal of the living God.

And he cried with a loud voice to the four angels to whom it was granted to harm the earth and the sea, saying, "Do not harm the earth, the sea, or the trees till we have sealed the servants of our God on their foreheads."

And I heard the number of those who were sealed. One hundred and forty-four thousand of all the tribes of the children of Israel were sealed.

REVELATION 7:2-4

ABOUT THE AUTHORS

JERRY B. JENKINS, former vice president for publishing at Moody Bible Institute of Chicago and currently chairman of the board of trustees, is the author of more than 175 books, including the best-selling Left Behind series. Twenty of his books have reached the *New York Times* Best Sellers List (seven in the number-one spot) and have also appeared on the *USA Today*, *Publishers Weekly*, and *Wall Street Journal* bestseller lists. *Desecration*, book nine in the Left Behind series, was the best-selling book in the world in 2001. His books have sold nearly 70 million copies.

Also the former editor of *Moody* magazine, his writing has appeared in *Time*, *Reader's Digest*, *Parade*, *Guideposts*, *Christianity Today*, and dozens of other periodicals. He was featured on the cover of *Newsweek* magazine in 2004.

His nonfiction books include as-told-to biographies with Hank Aaron, Bill Gaither, Orel Hershiser, Luis Palau, Joe Gibbs, Walter Payton, and Nolan Ryan among many others. The Hershiser and Ryan books reached the *New York Times* Best Sellers List.

Jenkins assisted Dr. Billy Graham with his autobiography, *Just As I Am*, also a *New York Times* best seller. Jerry spent 13 months working with Dr. Graham, which he considers the privilege of a lifetime.

Jerry owns Jenkins Entertainment, a filmmaking company in Los Angeles, which produced the critically acclaimed movie *Midnight Clear*, based on his book of the same name. See www.Jenkins-Entertainment.com.

Jerry Jenkins also owns the Christian Writers Guild, which aims to train tomorrow's professional Christian writers. Under Jerry's leadership, the guild has expanded to include college-credit courses, a critique service, literary registration services, and writing contests, as well as an annual conference. See www.ChristianWritersGuild.com.

As a marriage-and-family author, Jerry has been a frequent guest on Dr. James Dobson's *Focus on the Family* radio program and is a sought-after speaker and humorist. See www.AmbassadorSpeakers.com.

Jerry has been awarded four honorary doctorates.

He and his wife, Dianna, have three grown sons and six grandchildren.

Check out Jerry's blog at http://jerryjenkins.blogspot.com.

DR. TIM LAHAYE (www.timlahaye.com), who conceived and created the idea of fictionalizing an account of the Rapture and the Tribulation, is a noted author, minister, and nationally recognized speaker on Bible prophecy. He is the founder of both Tim LaHaye Ministries and The PreTrib Research Center.

Dr. LaHaye speaks at many of the major Bible prophecy conferences in the U.S. and Canada, where his prophecy books are very popular.

Dr. LaHaye earned a doctor of ministry degree from Western Theological Seminary and received an honorary doctor of literature degree from Liberty University. For 25 years he pastored one of the nation's outstanding churches in San Diego, which grew to three locations. During that time he founded two accredited Christian high schools, a Christian school system of ten schools, and San Diego Christian College (formerly known as Christian Heritage College).

There are over 59 million copies of Dr. LaHaye's 50 nonfiction books, some of which have been published in over 37 languages. He has written books on a wide variety of subjects, such as family life, temperaments, and Bible prophecy. His fiction works include the Left Behind series and the Jesus Chronicles, written with Jerry B. Jenkins. LaHaye's other fiction series of prophetic novels consist of the Babylon Rising series and The End series. Dr. LaHaye is the father of four grown children, grandfather of nine, and great-grandfather of eleven.

THE TRUTH
BEHIND THE FICTION

THE PROPHECY BEHIND THE SCENES

In their book *The Truth Behind Left Behind* (Multnomah, 2004) , prophecy experts Mark Hitchcock and Thomas Ice talk about people questioning the possibility of salvation after the Rapture. In their chapter on *Soul Harvest*, they talk about those who believe the Left Behind series spreads false hope:

> One preacher recently said that it was foolish to
> think that someone like Bruce Barnes (a character
> in Left Behind) could be an unsaved pastor before
> the Rapture and then find salvation *after* the

TEST YOUR PROPHECY IQ

+ What is the fifth Trumpet Judgment and why is it significant?
See answer at the end of this section.

Rapture. This pastor believes that Barnes, who would have heard the gospel many times prior to the Rapture, would become hardened to the message of salvation—and would no longer be capable of responding during the Tribulation days that follow. The preacher went on to warn of the danger of the Left Behind series because of this supposed error. (pp. 76-77)

Here is how Tim LaHaye and Jerry B. Jenkins address the issue in chapters 24 and 25 of their nonfiction book *Are We Living in the End Times?*

Evangelists by the Thousands

One of our Lord's well-known promises about the end of the age is found in Matthew 24:14: "And this gospel of the kingdom will be preached in all the world as a witness to all the nations, and then the end will come."

Most prophecy scholars assume this feat will be accomplished during the Tribulation through the ministry of the 144,000 witnesses described in Revelation 7, who reach a "multitude which no one could number, of all nations, tribes, peoples, and tongues" (verse 9).

Revelation 7 suggests that before the world is plunged into the plagues and disasters ushered in by the sixth seal judgment at the end of the first quarter of the Tribulation, God will raise up an army of 144,000 Jewish evangelists to spread across the globe and bring in a soul harvest of unimaginable proportions. Each of these "servants" of God will receive a "seal" on his forehead. In *Soul Harvest*, the believer's mark is visible to other believers but not to its owner or to unbelievers.

Whatever the seal is, it affords these 144,000 Jewish witnesses supernatural protection, at least until the great soul harvest can be accomplished:

> After these things I looked, and behold, a great
> multitude which no one could number, of all
> nations, tribes, peoples, and tongues, standing before
> the throne and before the Lamb, clothed with white
> robes, with palm branches in their hands, and crying
> out with a loud voice, saying, "Salvation belongs to
> our God who sits on the throne, and to the Lamb!"
>
> REVELATION 7:9-10

Some interpreters have a hard time believing that the Tribulation could usher in such an enormous soul harvest, but we are convinced this text shows that more men and women will be won to Christ in this period than at any time in history.

Believers in the Time of Wrath

The Scriptures do not tell us much about believers in Christ during the time of the Tribulation, but what they do say both thrills and chills us. We thrill to the prophecies about millions of men and women coming to the Savior during this period of wrath—but a cold wind chills our souls when we read of the shocking persecution and martyrdom that will fill those years. Read Daniel 7 and Revelation 6:9-11; 13:7; 14:13-14; 17:6.

Several important points should be emphasized from these texts to help us understand God's program for his people during the Tribulation.

1. **The Tribulation will see a great soul harvest.** The Holy Spirit will be alive and well on planet Earth during the Tribulation, convicting all who are open to the gospel. The key then will be exactly what it is today and always has been—repentance and faith.

2. **God is still in control.** Despite the horrific numbers of saints who will lose their lives in the Tribulation, God is still very much in control throughout the whole period. Note the careful language both Daniel and John use to describe the Antichrist's power over the people of God: "The saints shall be *given into his hand*" (Daniel 7:25, emphasis added); "*It was granted to him* to make war with the saints" (Revelation 13:7, emphasis added). Both of these texts stress that the Antichrist does nothing without the permission of God. The Beast does not tear the saints from God's grasp, nor does he somehow outmaneuver the Lord.

3. **The death of a believer is blessed.** "Blessed are the dead who die in the Lord," declares Revelation 14:13. The world will believe these martyrs are

ignorant, foolish, idiotic. They will be thankful
(if that word fits) that they are not among the ones
marked for death. Some of the more tenderhearted
(if there will be any) may even pity these saints who
would rather die than deny their Lord.

4. **God will avenge the death of his children.** When the
slain saints cry out in heaven, "How long, O Lord,
holy and true, until You judge and avenge our blood
on those who dwell on the earth?" (Revelation 6:10),
the Lord does not rebuke them. Instead he tells them
to wait a little while longer. In many ways throughout
Scripture God says, "It is mine to avenge; I will
repay" (see Deuteronomy 32:35; Romans 12:19;
Hebrews 10:30; among others).

Victory Is Theirs

We should thank God that his Word does not leave the story
of the Tribulation saints with their earthly demise, but loudly
proclaims their ultimate victory through the blood of the
Lamb. (See Revelation 12:11.)

Hitchcock and Ice agree, ending their chapter with this
statement:

We believe that millions of unbelievers will be saved
during the terrible time of the Tribulation. For that
we can all be thankful. Many of those saved will
include some who had heard the gospel many times
before the Rapture. In the meantime, we believers

should make every effort to preach the gospel of God's grace *before* the Rapture so that as many as possible will believe and escape the horrors of the Tribulation. (p. 87)

IN THE MEANTIME . . .
since the Left Behind series was first published.

Since the publication of *Soul Harvest* in 1998, God has been on the move around the world—even in the Muslim-dominated "10-40 Window," where information is difficult to get and converting to Christianity can be extremely dangerous. Author Joel C. Rosenberg has become an expert on the region around Israel that he calls the Epicenter. On April 10, 2009, he wrote an entry on his blog (joelrosenberg.com) titled "More ex-Muslims will celebrate Easter this year than any other time in history." Following are highlights:

Jesus said in Matthew 16:18, "I will build My Church, and the gates of Hell shall not prevail against it" (KJV). Guess what? He wasn't kidding. You rarely hear about it on the news. You rarely even hear about it in churches in the West, in the East, or even in the Middle East. But the big, untold story is that more Muslims are coming to faith in Jesus Christ today than at any other time in history.

After crisscrossing the Islamic world over the last several years and interviewing more than 150 pastors and ministry leaders operating deep inside the

most difficult countries for *Inside The Revolution*
[Tyndale, 2009], I can report that in Iran, more
than 1 million Shia Muslims have turned to Christ
since 1979. In Pakistan, there are now more than 2.5
million followers of Jesus Christ. In Sudan, there are
now more than 5 million followers of Christ. Not
every country has seen millions leave Islam to become
adherents of the New Testament teachings of Jesus.
In Syria, there are between 4,000 and 5,000 believers,
but this is up from almost none in 1967. In Saudi
Arabia, there are about 100,000 followers of Jesus
now, up from almost none in 1967. But overall, the
trend has been dramatic and largely unreported.

For many Muslims, despair and despondency
at what they see as the utter failure of Islamic
governments and societies to improve their lives
and give them peace, security, and a sense of purpose
and meaning in life are causing them to leave Islam
in search of truth. Some have lost their way entirely
and become agnostics and atheists. Others, as we
have seen, have sadly turned to alcohol and drug
abuse. But millions are finding that only Jesus Christ
heals the ache in their hearts and the deep wounds in
their souls.

For other Muslims, it is not depression but rage
that is driving them away from the Qur'an and the
mosque. They are seeing far too many Muslim leaders
and governments and preachers both advocating and

acting out cruelty toward women and children and violence even against fellow Muslims.

You can keep posted using online resources, but be aware that reliable information is often difficult to get and individual converts may already be in extreme danger, made worse by telling their stories to outsiders. Pray for your brothers and sisters in Christ who face persecution every day.

TEST YOUR PROPEHCY IQ—ANSWER

The fifth of the seven Trumpet Judgments is also the first of three woes pronounced by the angel of Revelation 8:13, which take the judgments to an even greater level of ferocity. When this trumpet sounds, an angel unlocks the "bottomless pit," which belches smoke and "locusts" with scorpion-like power to sting and torment unbelievers for five months. They are led by Apollyon, the chief demon of the abyss. Read more about the roles of angels and demons in the next book, *Apollyon*.